MATT BROLLY

Following his law degree, where he developed an interest in criminal law, Matt Brolly completed his Masters in Creative Writing at Glasgow University. He is the bestselling author of the DCI Lambert crime novels *Dead Eyed* and *Dead Lucky*. Matt lives in London with his wife and their two young children. You can find out more about Matt at his website www.mattbrolly.co.uk or by following him on twitter: @MattBrollyUK

**Also by
Matt Brolly**

Dead Lucky

Dead Eyed

Matt Brolly

ONE PLACE. MANY STORIES

HQ
An imprint of HarperCollins*Publishers* Ltd
1 London Bridge Street
London SE1 9GF

www.harpercollins.co.uk

HarperCollins*Publishers*
Macken House, 39/40 Mayor Street Upper,
Dublin 1, D01 C9W8, Ireland

This paperback edition 2019

First published in Great Britain by
HQ, an imprint of HarperCollins*Publishers* Ltd 2019

Copyright © Matt Brolly 2019

Matt Brolly asserts the moral right to be
identified as the author of this work.
A catalogue record for this book is
available from the British Library.

ISBN: 978-1-84845-799-7

Printed and bound in the UK using 100% Renewable
Electricity at CPI Group (UK) Ltd

For Alison

Prologue

The man hovered on the edge of the dance floor. His elongated limbs and thinning hair made him stand out from the young lithe bodies. Sam Burnham watched him from the bar, nursing the same brandy he'd ordered an hour ago.

The track ended and the man shuffled his feet. He scanned the mirrored dance area before heading towards the bar.

Burnham ordered a second drink. He sensed the man in his periphery, and turned to face him. He placed his hand on the younger man's arm, and looked him directly in the eyes.

'Can I buy you a drink?' he asked.

The man nodded, staring at Burnham. Twenty minutes later they left the club together.

'What now?' asked Burnham, pulling his jacket tight against his body. It was a late September evening in Bristol, and the temperature had dropped since he'd set out earlier that day.

'Where are you staying?' asked the man. His eyes darted in random directions, not once focusing on Burnham.

'Hotel. You wouldn't like it. Do you live near?' Burnham knew exactly where he lived.

'I'm not sure,' said the man. 'I don't know you.'

Burnham touched the man's arm again. It was the simplest of techniques, but highly effective.

The man relented. 'It's not far away. We can walk.'

The man lived in Southville, a small suburb of Bristol less than a mile from the centre. They walked in an awkward silence, peppered with the occasional question from the man.

The man stopped outside a block of flats. 'I don't mean to sound weird, but do I know you from somewhere?'

'I don't think so. I guess I must have one of those faces,' said Burnham, following him inside.

The flat was hospital clean, the air fragranced artificially. The living area was an array of various gleaming surfaces: glass, chrome, marble. Burnham accepted a glass of brandy. The man's hands trembled as he handed it over.

They moved to the living room sofa and the man made life easy for him. 'I'll be back in a minute,' he said, his voice faltering.

As soon as Burnham heard the bathroom door click shut, he removed the phial from his inside jacket pocket. He broke the seal and spilled the clear liquid into the man's drink, stirring it with his left index finger.

It took five minutes for the man to take a drink. A further five minutes for the drug to take effect. Burnham dragged him to the bedroom, the man's skeletal body insubstantial in his thick arms. He placed the man on the bed and made a phone call.

Burnham's boss arrived at the flat two minutes later carrying a small leather case. Burnham watched in silence as he removed a surgical outfit, a set of scalpels, and a second phial filled with a different substance. 'Wait in the car,' he ordered.

It was three hours before his boss left the building. Burnham hurried from his seat and opened the back passenger door for him.

'Do you need me to clean up?' he asked.

'No, not this time.'

Chapter 1

Michael Lambert waited at the back of the coffee shop. To his right, a group of new mothers congregated around three wooden tables. Some held their tiny offspring; the others allowed their babies to sleep in the oversized prams which crowded the area. Two tables down, a pair of men dressed in identical suits stared at their iPads. Next to them, a young woman with braided hair read a paperback novel. All of them looked up as Simon Klatzky walked through the shop entrance and shouted over at him.

Lambert ignored the glances. He'd arrived thirty minutes earlier, out of habit checking and rechecking the clientele. He hadn't noticed anything out of the ordinary. He stood and beckoned Klatzky over. He'd last seen him two years ago at the funeral. 'Good to see you again, Simon,' he said.

'Mikey,' said Klatzky. Like Lambert, Klatzky was thirty-eight. He'd lost weight since the last time they'd met. His face was gaunt, his eyeballs laced with thin shards of red. When he spoke, Lambert noticed a number of missing teeth. The rest were discoloured and black with cheap fillings. His face cracked into a smile. He stood grinning at Lambert. In his left hand he clutched an A4 manila envelope.

'Sit down then. What do you want to drink?' said Lambert.

Klatzky shrugged. 'Coffee?'

Lambert ordered two black Americanos and returned to the table.

'Sorry I'm late,' said Klatzky.

Klatzky had called earlier that morning desperate to meet. He'd refused to tell Lambert the details over the phone but had insisted that it was urgent. From the smell of him, it hadn't been important enough to stop him visiting a bar first.

Klatzky's hands shook as he sipped the coffee. 'I thought it best you see for yourself,' he said, looking at the envelope still clutched tight in his hand.

Lambert sat straight in his chair, scratching a day's growth of stubble on his face. It was genuinely good to see his old friend. He'd only agreed to meet him as he'd sounded so scared on the phone. Now he was here, Lambert regretted not seeing more of him in the last two years.

'How have you been, Si?'

'So-so. I'm sorry I haven't called before.' He hesitated. 'And now, contacting you in these circumstances.' He still had a strong grip on the envelope, his knuckles turning white with the effort.

'I'm not working at the moment, Simon.'

'I didn't know who else to talk to.' Klatzky produced a bottle of clear liquid from his grainy-black rain jacket and poured half the contents into his coffee cup.

Some things didn't change. 'Are you going to show me then?' Lambert didn't want to rush him, but he didn't like surprises. He needed to know what Klatzky wanted.

Klatzky drank heavily from the alcohol-fused drink, momentarily confused.

'The envelope, Si.'

Klatzky stared at the envelope as if it had just appeared in his hand. He handed it to Lambert, his body trembling.

Klatzky's name and address were printed on the front. There was no stamp. 'You received this today?'

'It was there when I got back.'

'Back from where?'

'I was out last night. Got in early this morning.' He looked at Lambert as if expecting a reprimand.

Lambert opened the envelope and pulled out a file of A4 papers. Each page had a colour photo of the same subject taken from a different angle. Lambert tapped the table with the knuckles of his left hand as he read through the file.

'It's him, Mike,' said Klatzky.

The subject was the deceased figure of an emaciated man. The skin of the corpse was a dull yellow. Wisps of frazzled hair clung to the man's cheek bones, matted together with a green-brown substance. The corpse's mouth was wide open, caught forever in a look of rictus surprise. Where the man's eyes should have been were two hollow sockets. Tendrils of skin and matter dripped down onto the man's face. Lambert recognised the Latin insignia carved intricately into the man's chest. He placed the file back in the envelope, wiping a bead of sweat from his brow.

'Well?' asked Klatzky.

'Where did you get this from?'

Klatzky poured more of the clear liquid into his cup. 'I told you. It was there this morning when I got back. Why the hell has this been sent to me, Mike?' he asked, loud enough to receive some disapproving looks from the young mothers.

Lambert rubbed his face. If he'd known what was in the envelope, then he would never have suggested meeting in such a public place. 'I'll talk to some people. See what I can find out. I'll need to keep this,' he said.

'But why was it sent to me, Mikey?'

'I don't know.' Lambert checked the address on the envelope. 'You're still in the same flat, over in East Ham?'

'Afraid so.'

'Have you seen anyone else recently?'

'You mean from Uni? No. You're the first one I've seen since the…' he hesitated. 'Since, the funeral.'

Lambert replayed the images in his head, trying to ignore the expectation etched onto Klatzky's face. The inscription on the victim's chest read:

In oculis animus habitat.

The lettering, smudged by leaking blood, had dried into thick maroon welts on the pale skin of the man's body. Lambert didn't need to see the man's eyeless sockets to work out the translation:

The soul dwells in the eyes.

They left the coffee house together. 'Do you have somewhere else you can go?' asked Lambert.

'Why? Do you think I'm next?' asked Klatzky.

Lambert wasn't sure what Klatzky had put in his coffee but the man was swaying from side to side. He placed his hand on the man's shoulder. 'Let's not panic. These might not have come from the murderer. But until we do find out where they came from, and why they were sent to you, it would be sensible to stay away from the flat.'

'Should we tell Billy's parents or something? Christ, what are they are going to think?'

Billy Nolan had been the ninth and, until now, last victim of the so called Souljacker killer. A close friend of Lambert and Klatzky, Nolan was murdered in his final year at Bristol University where they had all studied. The killer had never been caught and everything Lambert had seen in the file suggested that he had started working again.

'Look, you need to get somewhere and rest up. Let me worry about the details.'

'I want to help, Mikey.'

'You can stay out of trouble. That will help the most. I'll contact you when I know something.' He grabbed Klatzky's hand and shook it. 'It'll be okay, Si.'

Klatzky's handshake was weak, his palm wet with sweat. He swayed for a second before stumbling across the road to a bar called The Blue Boar.

Lambert stood outside the coffee shop, his hand clutched tight to the envelope. Years ago Lambert would have jumped straight into the investigation. The responsible thing would be to locate the Senior Investigating Officer on the case, inform them that Klatzky had received the material. But he needed time to process the information, to decipher why Klatzky had received the photos.

He walked to Clockhouse station and caught a train to Charing Cross, his mind racing. Making sure no one could see him, he opened the envelope. He scanned each page in turn, studied every detail. The photographs were direct copies from a crime report. The photographer had captured the corpse from all angles. The camera zoomed in on the victim's wounds. The ragged skin around the eye sockets, the incision marks magnified in gruesome detail, the intricate detail of the Latin inscription, each letter meticulously carved into the victim's skin. It was definitely a professional job.

Reaching London, Lambert took the short walk to Covent Garden. His wife, Sophie, was waiting for him in a small bistro off the old market building. She sat near the entrance, head buried in a leather folio. 'Oh, hi,' she said, on seeing him.

'Hi, yourself.'

She shut the document she'd been reading. 'Shall we order?' she asked, business-like as usual.

They'd been married for twelve years. Sophie was half-French on her mother's side. A petite woman, she had short black hair, and a soft round face which made her look ten years younger than her actual age of thirty-nine.

They both ordered the fish of the day. 'So how was Simon?' she asked.

'Not great,' said Lambert.

'Well, don't keep me in suspense. What did he want?'

Absentmindedly, Lambert touched the document in his inside jacket pocket. 'Oh, nothing dramatic. He was thinking of putting together some sort of reunion.'

He could tell she knew he was lying. They ordered water to go with the fish and sat through the meal in companionable silence. Each avoiding discussing the reason they were there.

'Everything's booked,' she said, finally. 'The same church as last year. We can use the church hall afterwards. All the catering is organised.'

Lambert drank the water, cracking a fragment of ice which had dropped into his mouth. A shiver ran through his body as the cold water dripped down his throat. 'Okay,' he said, realising how useless the words sounded. Now he was, even after all this time, still unable to deal with the enormity of the situation.

'We need to finalise the music,' said Sophie.

Lambert gripped his glass of water, tried to focus on something more positive. 'Do you remember that track she loved in the summer before she started school? She used to go crazy. Blondie, wasn't it? She used to pick up her tennis racket and play along. I can't remember for the life of me what it was called.'

Sophie beamed, reliving the memory. Then, in an instant, her eyes darkened. It had been two years since their daughter, Chloe, had died. They'd decided to hold a memorial service each year on Chloe's birthday. Sophie's mother had suggested they postpone it this year. She'd argued that rekindling the same memories every twelve months denied a necessary part of the grieving process. In principle Lambert agreed, but it was not a subject he could broach with Sophie. He blamed himself for Chloe's death, and though she insisted otherwise, he was sure Sophie did too.

Eventually they agreed on a small song list.

'I need to go,' said Sophie. She stood and kissed him on the cheek, a perfunctory habit devoid of emotion. At home, they slept in separate rooms rarely spending more than five minutes together. This was the first meal they'd shared in almost a year.

Lambert hadn't worked since Chloe's death. He'd been hospitalised, and received substantial compensation. The last time Sophie had raised the subject of him returning to work they'd argued. Now the matter was never discussed.

'I'll be home early this evening,' she said. 'Then I'm out for dinner.'

She loitered by the table and regarded him in the way only she could. Lambert saw love in the gesture, tinged with compassion and empathy. But what he saw most of all was pity.

After she left, he paid the bill and walked outside. He found a secluded spot and took out the manila envelope once more. The easiest thing would be to send the file to the authorities and forget Klatzky had ever given it to him. And if he hadn't just had lunch with Sophie, and seen that look of pity, that would have been his course.

Instead, he put the envelope back in his jacket and walked along the Strand. On a side street, he entered a small establishment he'd used in the past.

Inside, he purchased a pre-charged Pay As You Go mobile phone in cash.

From memory, he dialled a number he hadn't called in two years.

Chapter 2

As expected, the man didn't answer. Lambert left a message asking for a meeting. Ten minutes later he received a text message with an address and time.

Lambert caught the tube to Angel in Islington and located a set of rented offices. He showed his identification to the male receptionist but didn't mention the name of the man he was supposed to meet. The receptionist led him to a small office area. He entered a four-digit code on a side panel and ushered Lambert into the room. The room had the feel of a prison cell. It had no window, only four brick walls and a steel-framed door. Lambert sat on one of the three faux-leather office chairs situated around a rectangular glass table and studied the photos once more.

Glenn Tillman exploded into the room five minutes later. A bulldog of a man, almost as wide as he was tall, Tillman had a pouty, baby-like face which looked out of place on top of his heaving muscle-strewn body.

'I don't like to be summoned,' he said, as way of greeting.

'Good to see you too,' said Lambert. The last time he'd seen Tillman had been shortly after Chloe's funeral. Both men had agreed that Lambert should take some extended time away from work. Lambert hadn't heard from him since.

Lambert dropped the envelope onto the glass table. Tillman

moved towards him and picked it up, his expression passive as he scanned the photos.

'And?' he said.

'I hoped I would have been informed if anything came in on this,' said Lambert.

Tillman sat, his breathing heavy. A blue striped tie bulged rhythmically against his thick neck. 'You don't work for us at the moment, Michael.'

'This relates directly to me, sir. It would have been a courtesy.'

Tillman studied the photos again. 'This goes back to your University days, doesn't it? I remember it from your file. What did the press call him, the Souljacker or something?' He put the file down. 'Look, this is the first I've heard of it. It must be with the local CID. It's not something that would come our way, you know that.'

'I want access,' said Lambert.

Tillman smirked. 'There's no access, Michael. If you're not working for us then no way.'

'Employ me then. Private contract.'

'We don't do that any more. We're part of the NCA now. Sort of,' he said, as an afterthought. The National Crime Agency had replaced SOCA, the Serious Organised Crime Agency, the previous year.

'Right,' said Lambert. Lambert had been working for SOCA when Tillman had recruited him. They'd previously worked together when Lambert had first joined CID. Tillman had been his first DI.

Tillman now headed a department known simply as The Group. It was a cross alliance with military intelligence. There had been five others in Lambert's team. Aside from Tillman, The Group comprised one DI and one DS from the MET, and two operatives from MI5. For the first time in his career, Lambert had signed the Official Secrets Act for work and received a security clearance level. Lambert had long suspected that there were a number of similar groups working independent from Tillman's collective.

'Look, sir. I don't want to push this but I need access.' He was taking a calculated risk speaking to his superior this way. It was not beyond Tillman to tell him where to go, to leave him in the room for twenty-four hours to dwell on his insolence.

Tillman lifted his hand to his face. 'You're calling it in?'

Tillman didn't really owe him anything, but his superior didn't see it that way. Lambert had protected him once and still held potentially incriminating evidence on the man. He would never betray Tillman, but Tillman was honour bound to repay the favour. 'I don't want it to be like that, but if it has to be that way.'

Tillman rubbed his left temple, a familiar gesture Lambert had seen countless times before. 'I will say you stole the access codes if it ever comes to light.'

'I realise that.'

'Then we're done, Michael. Unless you come back to us, it will be the last time you have access to The System.'

'Thank you, sir,' said Lambert, getting to his feet.

'I will email you the access codes within the next two hours. Any work you do on this Souljacker business is yours alone. Make no records. Understand?'

'Sir.'

Tillman left the room without acknowledging him.

Lambert thanked the receptionist as he left the building. He doubted the man had any idea who he was, or who Tillman was for that matter. Lambert savoured the fresh air once outside, buoyed by the meeting. He'd thought he'd have to argue his case for access to The System but Tillman had given in almost immediately. He'd even given a suggestion of Lambert returning to work for him in the future.

The access codes arrived two hours later. Lambert was back at his desk in his home office, a three-storey Edwardian house in Beckenham, Kent, which bordered south-east London. Before him, information scrolled across six computer monitors. It had been a long time since he'd last activated them.

The System had been the reason Lambert had signed the OSA. As far as he was aware, only a handful of people outside The Group knew of its existence. The System was an amalgamation of existing computer systems and databases, as well as something else entirely. The System had direct access to a number of worldwide criminal databases including HOLMES and the PNC in the UK, and limited access to databases used by Interpol and European forces. In addition, The System could access the back end of nearly all social media sites.

Lambert experienced a rush of adrenalin as he logged into The System with codes sent to him by Tillman. He spent a few minutes acclimatising to the new layout, and exhaled sharply as he accessed details of the new Souljacker murder. The case appeared on HOLMES, the system used by the police to record details on major crimes.

A neighbour had discovered the body of Terrence Vernon five days ago, in a two-bedroom top floor flat in an area called Southville, a mile from the city centre of Bristol. The smell of the corpse had alerted the neighbour who had duly informed the police. The Senior Investigating Officer was Detective Superintendent Rush, though it was apparent that the chief investigator was Detective Inspector Sarah May.

The pathologist's initial report suggested that the deceased had endured every part of the attack, including the removal of his eyes, the man's eventual death resulting from a cut to his carotid artery. It had been no real leap to link the killing to the notorious Souljacker murders, the last of which had taken place eighteen years ago.

Lambert opened the window in the office. He could still picture Billy Nolan. In their last year at University together, his small group of friends had all managed to secure a place at the halls of residence. Nolan had lived six doors down from Lambert on the fifth floor.

It was Lambert who had broken down Nolan's door that night. Nolan sprawled on his bed, giant bloody holes where his eyes should have been. Lambert had recognised it was Latin carved into his friend's body but couldn't translate it. He'd stared, dumbfounded, at the lifeless form, hoping it was some twisted joke being played on him. Then the smell had over-whelmed him and he'd struggled into the corridor and vomited.

Lambert shuddered. Similar scenes played on the computer screens now. Photos of Terrence Vernon's corpse scrolled across each screen, lying askew on his bedroom floor, the two gaping holes in his skull looking too wide to have ever held human eyes. Next, the close-up pictures of the Latin, In oculis animus habitat. Like on all the previous victims, each letter was carved into Vernon's chest in faultless detail, suggesting the killer had spent hours on the inscription.

Lambert recalled the fallout from Billy's Nolan's death, the number of lives forever affected by the senseless murder. He remembered the desolate look on the faces of Nolan's parents as they arrived at the University. The students who had witnessed the sight of Billy's disfigured corpse, who would never be quite the same again, who would always equate University with that one defining moment. He counted himself amongst their number.

Sophie knocked on the office door and Lambert closed the screens with a single punch of the keypad.

'Hungry?'

'I had something earlier, thanks.'

'Working?' asked Sophie, unable to hide the hope in her voice.

'Sort of.'

She hesitated by the door. 'That's good.' She was holding back, wanted to find out more but was probably afraid of how he might respond.

Lambert stared ahead at the blank computer screens, desperate to get on with work, ashamed that he didn't know how to talk to his estranged wife any longer.

'Okay, just popping out for dinner.'

'See you in the morning,' said Lambert.

Sophie shut the office door and Lambert returned to the computer screens. He had to blank out what was happening in his marriage for the time being. He returned to the screens and read through the case details uploaded onto the HOLMES system.

In oculis animus habitat. The soul dwells in the eyes.

During the weeks following Nolan's murder there had been much discussion as to the meaning of those words. The SIO at the time, DCI Julian Hastings, had questioned Lambert about his understanding of the words. Lambert had studied Latin in school but couldn't translate the words exactly without looking it up.

Billy Nolan had been the ninth and, supposedly, final Souljacker victim. Now, from nowhere, the killer was back.

From her notes, Lambert read that DI May had begun researching the older cases. The first victim, Clive Hale, had been murdered over twenty two years ago, the next eight victims falling foul of the Souljacker over a period of four years. May had assigned a number of junior officers the duty of trawling through witness reports and suspect interviews. During the Nolan investigation, a local surgeon, Peter Randall, had been the chief suspect, but the case had never gone anywhere near the courts. There had been no forensic evidence and Randall had a clear alibi for the time of the murder. It had been the only significant arrest there had ever been on the case.

Lambert had kept in contact with DCI Hastings after the murder. Hastings had offered him advice on joining the force. Now a retired Chief Superintendent, Hastings had stayed obsessed with the Souljacker cases even into retirement. If May had any sense, Hastings would be the first person she contacted.

Lambert clicked a button on his keyboard and sat back in his office chair. DI Sarah May's file on the latest killing played through his six computer screens in a reel of information. Lambert sat transfixed and absorbed the material. He often worked this way, viewing the details from an abstract position searching for a key word, sentence, or picture that would change everything.

The same age as Lambert, Vernon had worked as a retail manager for a large supermarket in the Cribbs Causeway area of Bristol. Described by family, friends, and colleagues as a shy, awkward sort of person, his hard work ethic had helped him reach a reasonable level in his career. Vernon was single. He had divorced parents and no siblings. He had strong links with a local evangelical church, Gracelife Bristol, the minister of which, Neil Landsdale, had described Vernon as a hard-working and selfless member of his congregation who 'would be sorely missed'.

Lambert watched unblinking as the pages scrolled across the screens. He read and reread the information until something made him pause. It was a picture of Vernon, taken with his work colleagues at the supermarket. Vernon towered over everyone else. Thin and ungainly in an ill-fitting shiny polyester suit, he was clean shaven with short cropped hair, a well-defined face with high cheekbones, and strong jaw.

Lambert couldn't make out the colour of his eyes. He stared hard at the image of Vernon, a memory returning to him. He clicked onto another screen and accessed details on Vernon's personal file. He scanned down the file and stopped at Terrence's mother, Sandra Vernon. He clicked on her name.

It took him less than sixty seconds to find out what he was looking for.

Sandra Vernon's married name was Sandra Haydon. She had officially divorced Terrence's father, Roger Haydon fifteen years ago, though they had separated when Terrence was a child.

Lambert reloaded the photo of the victim, Terrence Vernon. Lambert cursed under his breath. Terrence must have changed his surname to his mother's maiden name.

At University, Lambert had known him as Terrence Haydon.

24

Chapter 3

Lambert emailed DI May requesting a meeting for the following day. He didn't share any information on the photos he'd received from Klatzky. He wanted to meet the woman face to face. After which he would decide if he wanted to take his personal investigation any further.

The fact that Klatzky had been sent the photos was obviously hugely significant but Lambert needed to know why he'd been sent them before he shared the details with anyone. His first thought was that the photos were a warning but the more he thought about it the less likely that seemed.

It came down to the sender. Lambert's gut told him the killer had sent the photos and there was no logical reason for him to send a warning. It was possible the killer was playing a game with Klatzky. Like Lambert, Klatzky had been there the day Billy Nolan's body had been found. Klatzky had been closer to Billy than anyone, and his life had spiralled out of control ever since Nolan's death. Why the killer wanted to involve Klatzky now after all these years was anyone's guess at the moment but at least it was a starting point for Lambert to pin his investigation on. A second starting point was the possibility that the killer was using Klatzky to lure Lambert into action. A more worrying thought had also occurred to him: that somehow the killer was attempting to set them up.

A nervous energy ran through him as he printed up relevant parts of the file. It was good to be back working, even on something so close to him. He took the files to the small bedroom at the top of the house. It was sparsely decorated with a single bed, desk, and chair, the flat screen television which hung on the wall taking up most of the space in the room. He flicked through the channels, unable to find anything of interest. He checked his email on his phone noticing that Klatzky had emailed him five times since their meeting, becoming more incoherent with each email. By the final email his words made little sense.

Lambert switched off the television and closed his eyes. His body hummed with tension, his chest tight as if an invisible weight pushed down on him. Eventually, the first flicker occurred. A fiery orange glow appeared to his left and blossomed into a collage of bright colour taking over his entire visual field. Infinite shades of red, yellow, and orange began to fade as his breathing slowed and he fell asleep.

He slept for three hours and reached Paddington station by six a.m. The station already teemed with commuters. Lambert booked his ticket and ordered a large black coffee from one of the shops in the large open-spaced concourse. He stretched his legs, alert and awake despite the meagre hours of sleep.

Lambert had survived most of his adult life on three to four hours a night and hadn't suffered any detrimental side effects until four years ago when the hallucinations started. They occurred when he was overly tired or stressed. He had self-diagnosed his condition as a rare form of narcolepsy. It was something he'd never had checked out, fearing that an official diagnosis would affect his work. He had learned that the hallucinations were a signal that he was ready for sleep.

He could control them now, to an extent. Unfortunately, that had not always been the case.

Lambert drank the bitter coffee, impatient for the train to arrive. May had yet to respond to his request for a meeting. He would give her until nine a.m. to reply to his email or his first destination would be her police station. Lambert watched the commuters and wondered if his own face mirrored the dull and sullen faces which hurried by him, everyone impatient and tired.

A different type of figure emerged from the set of escalators which rose from the underground. The unsteady figure of a man dressed in faded jeans and tattered leather jacket staggered towards him.

'Great,' whispered Lambert to himself. He considered hiding from the figure but Klatzky had already spotted him.

'Mikey,' he said, a little too loud. 'I knew you would be here.' Klatzky embraced him.

Competing odours overwhelmed Lambert. Sweat, cheap aftershave and stale nicotine were all linked by the reek of alcohol. Lambert kept his hands by his sides, tried to breathe through his mouth. 'What the hell are you doing here, Simon?' Despite the revulsion at Klatzky's state, Lambert could not help but admire the man for finding him.

'I knew Bristol would be the logical place for you to start,' said Klatzky, slurring half of his words. 'You never sleep, so it would have to be the first train. I'm coming with you.'

Lambert took a couple of steps back. 'You're not going anywhere, except home. Do you have any idea what you look like? What you smell like for that matter? I wouldn't even sit in the same carriage as you let alone share a train journey.'

'I need to come with you, Mikey. Look, I'm not afraid to admit it but I'm scared. He's back. I want to know what's happening, why he sent me the pictures. You told me not to go home, so I didn't.' Klatzky eyes darted around the station, as if he was surprised by his location.

Lambert shook his head. 'You've been out all night?'

Klatzky shrugged his shoulders, a grin spreading across his face.

This was the last thing he needed. 'Jesus. Listen, I'll keep you informed. Where are you staying? Go and sleep it off. It'll do you no good coming with me to Bristol.'

'I need to know, Mikey,' insisted Klatzky. He placed a shaking hand on Lambert's shoulder, the leathery skin laced with wrinkles and a fine layer of black hair, the hand of a much older man. Lambert tried not to recoil from the touch.

The train was about to depart. Lambert took another step back and Klatzky's shaking hand fell away. If the killer had sent Klatzky the file to get Lambert involved then the fear he saw in his friend's eyes was at least partly his responsibility. 'Okay, Simon. You can come with me but you can't interfere. Is that understood?'

'You're a saint, Mikey,' said Klatzky.

'Shall we go then?'

'I need a ticket,' said Klatzky.

'Oh I see. I'll get you one on the train.'

Mercifully, Klatzky fell asleep before the train pulled out of Paddington station. He collapsed in a heap, his frail body lying at an awkward angle in the seats opposite Lambert.

Lambert opened his holdall and searched its contents. He pulled out a newspaper, and the file he had compiled on the

Souljacker murders. There was still nothing from May on his phone. The conductor approached and Lambert purchased a return ticket for Klatzky with his credit card.

Klatzky snored himself awake as the train pulled into Swindon. His body spasmed, his head cracking against the underside of the table with a thud. Lambert tried not to laugh as the man composed himself.

'How long have I been asleep?' said Klatzky, rubbing his head.

'Fifty minutes or so.'

Klatzky dusted himself down, his aged leather jacket creaking at each movement. He shuffled himself into position, sitting opposite Lambert. A waft of pungent air drifted across the table.

'Your ticket,' said Lambert.

'Thanks, I'll pay you back.'

Lambert stopped the woman pushing a drinks trolley down the aisle of the carriage.

'Coffee,' groaned Klatzky.

'Make that two,' said Lambert. They sat for a while in silence. Klatzky wincing as he took the occasional sip of coffee.

'What happened to us eh, Mikey?' said Klatzky a few minutes later.

Lambert was reading one of the three books he'd brought with him, a mostly useless textbook on lucid sleeping. 'What do you mean?'

'Don't you remember those train journeys we used to take to Bristol on our way to University? We'd be half cut by now.'

'You are half cut.'

'Maybe,' said Klatzky. 'What happened to you, anyway?

You were so happy go lucky then. You didn't take anything seriously, not even your degree. Now look at you.'

'That was twenty years ago, Simon.' Lambert linked his hands together and rested his chin on them, staring at Klatzky.

In response, Klatzky leant towards him. Pointing his finger, he said, 'We all grow up, Michael, but you changed. You've changed intrinsically as a person.'

Lambert laughed, but felt his facial muscles tighten as his face reddened. 'Intrinsically? What are you talking about, Simon?

Klatzky slumped back in his seat. 'If you don't know what I'm talking about then there's no point in explaining,' he said. He drank the last of his coffee, screwing his eyes shut as he downed the dregs.

Lambert thought about continuing the bizarre argument, realising it was pointless arguing with Klatzky when he was in this mood. He opened his newspaper and spent the rest of the journey skimming through the despairing stories, his thoughts constantly returning to the file in his jacket pocket and what it all meant. At face value, it didn't make much sense. Serial killers like the Souljacker didn't just take eighteen years off between killings. If it was the same killer then there must have been a reason for the killer to have stopped in the first place, and more importantly a catalyst which had propelled him back to work.

Once in Bristol, they ordered breakfast at a small greasy spoon café outside Temple Meads station. Klatzky's head drooped as they waited for their orders, his hangover clearly reaching its peak.

A teenage girl in a pink apron placed their breakfasts on

the table. She grinned, the white of her teeth obscured by a thick metal brace. Piling his fork with a mixture of sausage, bacon and egg, Klatzky perked up. With his mouth half full he mumbled, 'So what are our plans for today?'

'Well, I plan to go to the University and have a look at our old halls of residence. And if I haven't heard back from her I'm going to call the lead investigator on the case.'

'Are we going to get a hotel?' asked Klatzky, slicing through an egg yolk smothered in ketchup.

'No, I want to be out of this place by the end of the day.'

'Oh come on, Mikey, we could visit some old haunts. For old times' sake.'

Lambert turned his face to the side, stretching his neck muscles. 'It's not a jolly, Simon. You asked me to help. This is work for me.' He already regretted allowing Klatzky to accompany him on the journey, and sensed things were only going to get worse.

Klatzky returned to his breakfast, sulking like a scolded child. 'I was thinking of calling the others,' he said, a couple of minutes later. He finished his breakfast, wiping his plate clean with a thin slice of white bread. He looked Lambert in the eyes for the first time since they'd left the train.

'That's not a good idea,' said Lambert.

'Why not? We haven't all been together for years,' said Klatzky.

There had been six of them in their group. They'd spent their three years at University together as the tightest of cliques, all deciding to reapply for halls in the third year. 'There's a reason for that, Simon.' Lambert placed some money on the table and left the café before Klatzky could argue further.

Over the years, Klatzky had been the only one who had tried to keep the group together. There had been the occasional impromptu reunion every few months after they'd graduated but the get-togethers had never been successful. They would initially start off well but after a few drinks it always became apparent that everyone was avoiding talking about Billy Nolan; it would reach the point where someone would mention his name just to break the tension.

Then the bad memories would return and the drinking would intensify until everyone reached a state of maudlin drunkenness which would occasionally descend into bouts of violence.

The others had all managed to put the Nolan incident behind them to one extent or another. Lambert knew getting the group together again would only reignite bad memories.

They caught a taxi from the long line of black cabs outside the station. 'You're a bit young to be students,' said the rotund taxi driver, after being told their destination.

'We're alumni,' said Lambert, his tone suggesting that all forms of communication between the driver and his two passengers should now cease. Lambert had only returned to Bristol occasionally over the last eighteen years, mainly for work. The city had transformed in that time but the changes had been gradual. Lambert couldn't date any of the buildings. It was only when the taxi pulled up outside their destination that he felt a stab of nostalgia. Klatzky was almost tearful as they left the car.

'Can't you feel it in your bones, Mikey?' he said, stretching his arms out as if he wanted to embrace the building.

Memories came to Lambert. Glimpsed images of the

numerous nights out he'd enjoyed with his friends, of the girls he'd kissed, each memory tainted with the image of Billy Nolan, dead in his room.

Inside, Lambert had to produce his old warrant card before the grey-haired man behind the security desk would allow them entry into their old hall of residence. They took the unsteady lift to the fifth floor, Lambert enduring the odour which resulted from Klatzky's lack of personal hygiene. 'When did you last shower?'

'I was out all night before I met you at Paddington.'

'Of course you were,' said Lambert. Lambert had yet to tell Klatzky about Terrence Haydon. Klatzky was in too fragile a state at the moment to take in the news that he'd once known the latest victim.

None of them had known Haydon well. He'd been an odd character who, like the report suggested, kept himself to himself. The other students had considered Haydon as somewhat of an eccentric. He'd studied Religious Studies and always carried a Bible with him, though Lambert could never recall him trying to push his views on anyone. He wasn't even sure Haydon had been that religious. He couldn't remember him being a member of the Christian Union.

Although the halls had been refurbished they looked essentially the same to Lambert. More memories came to him, mostly childish recollections of late-night drinking, water fights in the corridor, desperate early mornings of coffee-fuelled revision and the occasional romantic encounter. Klatzky was once again close to tears. Lambert knew the man's hangover was intensifying his emotional response but it didn't make it any easier to endure.

'Why are we here, Mikey?'

'I thought it would do good to reacquaint myself,' said Lambert. He didn't want to explain to Klatzky that he wanted to revisit the beginning from a professional viewpoint. He had been in his early twenties when Nolan's life had been taken. Lambert had been just another dazed student at the time. Although it was nearly twenty years later, Lambert thought there might be the opportunity to see something afresh. Something he may have missed, or had not been looking for all those years before.

A middle-aged woman in a blue checked apron stopped them both. 'Can I help you?' she asked, in a deep West Country accent.

Lambert flashed his old warrant card. 'I wanted to see Room 516,' he said. When the cleaner showed him to a room halfway down the corridor Lambert realised the room numbers had been rearranged. The fifth floor had a rectangular corridor and Nolan's room had been on the left-hand side corner with the window facing east onto the main road. Lambert followed his memory to where Nolan's room should have been. On the door where Nolan had once lived hung a sign marked Storage Cupboard.

'How long has this room been a cupboard?' asked Lambert.

'It's always been a cupboard,' said the woman.

'Don't be ridiculous,' said Klatzky indignantly.

'Listen, I've only been working here six years, love,' said the woman.

'It's fine, it's fine,' said Lambert. 'Could we possibly look inside?'

'Suit yourself,' said the woman, producing a key. 'I haven't all day, mind you.'

Shelves full of cleaning material and crisp folded sheets filled out the room. It bore no resemblance to the untidy and poster-ridden room which had once been Billy Nolan's. The change of use had destroyed the room's potency. Lambert had feared he would be overcome with more memories of that day. Now it was hard to believe the incident had ever occurred in such a space.

'Let's go,' said Klatzky. 'This place is giving me the creeps.' His eyes sagged towards his cheeks, his lips trembling beneath the random spikes of black and grey hair which sprung from his sallow face.

'Simon, go and get a coffee or something down in the cafeteria. I'm going to have a look around. I'll meet you in ten minutes.'

Klatzky slumped off towards the lift. Lambert thanked the cleaner who locked the store cupboard giving him a confused and pitiful look. Once Klatzky was inside the lift, Lambert walked up the stairs to the sixth floor. He made a full circuit of the floor but couldn't summon the memory of where Haydon had resided. A nagging sense told him that Haydon had lived almost directly above Billy Nolan but he couldn't be sure. It felt too much of a coincidence. Before joining Klatzky for coffee, Lambert called Bristol CID and asked to be put through to DI May.

'Can I ask what it's regarding?' enquired a female voice on the other end of the line.

'Tell her it's about the Terrence Vernon case,' said Lambert. Thirty seconds later a strong deep female voice said, 'DI May, how can I help?'

Lambert explained his position, telling May he was a former

police officer who had important information about the Vernon case. Lambert presumed May had already discovered that Terrence Vernon was originally called Terrence Haydon, but wasn't about to discuss the matter over the phone.

'Where are you now?' asked May.

'In Clifton.'

'Okay, there's a little café on The Triangle called Liberties. Could you meet me there at midday?'

'Done,' said Lambert.

Chapter 4

Klatzky sat alone in the student cafeteria, woefully out of place. Facedown, he nursed a small coffee occasionally giving the students a suspicious look. He was at once vulnerable and unsettling, and the café's patrons subconsciously sat as far away from him as possible.

After Klatzky declined his offer of a second coffee, Lambert ordered a large black Americano from a young man behind the counter. Klatzky looked up at him with sullen eyes when he returned. 'I thought I'd enjoy being here, Mikey, but there are way too many memories. Being here makes it feel like it happened yesterday. I can remember everything, what that sicko did to his body.' Klatzky sipped at his coffee. 'Christ, and the smell, Mikey. I can taste it now more than ever. Do you ever feel like that? It's part of me now. The blood and the smell...what was that stuff called?'

'The incense?'

'Yeah.' He took another longer sip of his coffee as if trying to drown out the memory. 'One good thing came out of it though,' he quipped, 'I never went back to church again. Too much incense in Catholic churches. I don't even feel the need to go to confession.'

'Small mercies, I guess,' said Lambert. Pontifical incense had been found on the body of each Souljacker victim, and Billy

Nolan had been no exception. Traces of the incense, which contained frankincense, matched that used by a number of Catholic churches in the country. However, the substance was freely available so it had proved impossible for any trace to be made.

'Listen, Si, I have a meeting later with the officer in charge of the case. I have some information that she may or may not know.'

'Okay,' said Klatzky.

'The body they found last week, the body in the pictures you showed me, were of somebody called Terrence Vernon.' Lambert tensed waiting for Klatzky's response.

'Terrence?'

'Yes, Terrence. I found out last night that Terrence Vernon was using his mother's maiden name as a surname. He used to be called Terrence Haydon. Do you remember Terrence Haydon, Si?'

'Mad Terry?' Klatzky's face fell, his eyes wide in recognition. 'He killed Mad Terry? Fucking hell, Mikey. What does this mean? What the hell's going on?' His words came out in short, rapid bursts, oblivious to the other people in the room.

'Keep it down, Si,' said Lambert, through gritted teeth. A few of the students looked in their direction. Mad Terry had been the uninspired nickname given to Terrence Haydon whilst at University. The nickname resulted from a few eccentric behaviours, such as walking with long, exaggerated steps as he made his way around. 'I don't know. It's partly why I need to see DI May. There are so many possibilities at this juncture it's not worth hypothesising.'

Klatzky gripped Lambert's wrists, his hands sweaty. 'But Billy hardly knew Mad Terry, what's this to do with anything?'

Lambert unpeeled Klatzky's fingers, and, grimacing, wiped the sweat off onto the plastic table covering. 'It could mean anything or nothing,' he said, softening his voice. 'Maybe the killer thought Haydon knew something about him.'

'After all this time?'

'It's a possibility. Perhaps Haydon contacted the authorities. There's no way for me to know until I look into it in more detail.'

'What if the killer's coming after everyone involved in Billy's killing? Everyone who knew him?'

'Don't be dramatic, you need to snap out of this. If he's going to kill someone once every eighteen years there's a good chance that we're all going to be safe. Listen, I need to go. I'm not sure how long I'll be but I'll call you when I'm finished. Try to get some rest somewhere.'

'Where do you suggest?' asked Klatzky.

'I don't know. Find a sofa. But stay away from the bars.'

'Any other orders?'

'No.'

Lambert reached the coffee shop thirty minutes early. Like London, Bristol basked in the heat of the Indian summer. A number of people sat outside the glass-fronted café. One of the crowd, a woman with shoulder-length black hair, stood up as Lambert walked towards the entrance. 'Mr Lambert?' she said.

Lambert turned to face the woman. 'Yes?'

'I'm DI May. Sarah.'

'How did you know who I was?'

'Forgive me,' said May, not once taking her gaze away from him. 'Can I get you a coffee and perhaps we can go inside and talk.'

'Decaf, thanks,' said Lambert.

A blast of cold air hit Lambert as he entered the high-ceilinged coffee shop, at first refreshing then uncomfortable. DI May directed him to a small booth with high wooden benches. She returned with two drinks and smiled as she sat down opposite him. Her large brown eyes shone bright, full of confidence and intelligence. She wasn't wearing make-up and Lambert wondered if her looks were a benefit or hindrance in her professional life. From his experience, he imagined it was probably a bit of both.

'So tell me DI May...'

'Sarah, please,' said the woman with a soft, yet firm voice.

'Sarah. Tell me what you found out about me?'

DI May leant forward in her chair, her gaze remained steady, never once leaving Lambert's eyes. Most people would have found her glare unnerving, would have felt obliged to look away, but Lambert matched her look. She spoke with a sly amusement. 'Well, first of all, possibly most importantly, I know you're a friend of the last Souljacker victim, Billy Nolan. In fact, Mr Lambert ...'

'Please, Michael.'

May squinted her eyes. 'Michael. You were initially a suspect.'

Lambert crossed his arms, deciding not to answer.

'Of course, you were one of many potential suspects and were cleared very early on in the case.'

Lambert's eyes widened, prompting the DI to continue.

'After graduation you were accepted into the accelerated programme, where you excelled.' She nodded in admiration, and let out a small laugh. 'You moved up the ranks and reached DCI.'

Impressed by her research, Lambert didn't interrupt.

'And then the mystery.'

'The mystery?'

'Yes, six years ago your work becomes classified. I received a phone call from a Chief Super this morning for trying to access the details.'

'Which one?'

'Tillman.'

'Right.'

'So can you fill in those blanks for me, Michael?'

'Afraid not. As the file says, classified.' Lambert hadn't given much thought to his personnel file before though it was obvious that his work with Tillman was classified. The blanks coincided from when he'd joined The Group. He made a mental note to access it later on The System. Although government sanctioned, in many ways the organisation were a law unto themselves. Their remit had been to investigate politically sensitive cases, and as such the need to avoid public scrutiny. It had been a tough transition for Lambert moving from normal CID to The Group. He'd found out early on that it was a balancing act. They'd worked out of the same offices as other task forces, and were supposedly subject to the same governing rules, but at times Lambert had been given leeway he'd never experienced before. The small team had been issued firearms and had received military intelligence-level training. Lambert had known it was somewhat of an experiment, and from his meeting yesterday Tillman wasn't about to tell him if things had changed.

'But apart from that, you've done very well, Sarah.'

She shot him a glance, but he could tell she knew he was teasing her. 'So what can you tell me, Michael?'

Lambert didn't want to be too pushy at the outset. 'I've been doing a little reading on the case,' he said.

'Naturally,' said May.

'I was particularly interested in the victim, Terrence Vernon.' He studied May for a response. If she was surprised she didn't show it.

'What about him?'

'I was wondering how much you knew about him.'

'How much information do you have on the case?'

'As I said, I've read some notes.'

'I understood you are not active at the moment. I read something on your file about an absence of leave?' said May. The words were matter of fact, contained no hostility.

'Something like that. I take it you've made the same connection I'd had about Mr Vernon.'

'You're talking about Mr Vernon's other name?'

'Yes.'

'It was his mother who let it slip. I spent some time with her. She told me about her divorce and how Terrence had changed his name back from Haydon to Vernon after leaving University. From there, we made the link with Billy Nolan. They were at University together. He lived one floor above Billy Nolan.' She paused. 'One floor above you.'

Lambert paused, assessing the underlying words. 'I needn't have bothered you, then,' he said.

'You're not bothering me. So tell me what else you know.'

'Not much more than that,' replied Lambert.

May's face contorted into a half smile, half frown. 'Oh come on, we're not going to play those games are we?'

Lambert shrugged. 'From what I can see it's highly probably

that it's the same killer,' he said, checking no one was eavesdropping.

'Of course, you saw the original body. Your friend Nolan.'

Lambert thought back to the day when they'd kicked down Billy Nolan's door. Nolan's corpse with its bloodied sockets, lying naked on the bed. The smell, a terrifying mixture of death and decay, not fully masked by the overpowering perfume of the incense. Klatzky had been right. That smell was part of Lambert too. He could taste it now at the back of his throat. He took a large swig of his coffee mirroring Klatzky's earlier actions. Once he'd composed himself he said, 'The carving is the same. Identical. And the eyes. He was alive when they were removed?' he asked, knowing the answer.

May pursed her lips. 'They haven't been recovered. Like the others. Were Nolan and Haydon friends at University?'

'No. We all knew Terrence but he wasn't what we'd call a friend.'

'And what was he like as a person?' May raised her eyebrows and tilted her head. A practised gesture which had no doubt obtained many a confession from helpless suspects.

'I'm sure you know all this but he was bit of a strange one.'

'Mad Terry,' said May, surprising him once more.

'Mad Terry. He was a nice enough guy, though. Intelligent. I assume he was hardworking because he was always at lectures. Never slept in. Hardly went out.'

'Any enemies?'

'No. People talked about him behind his back obviously, me included I'm afraid. He wasn't a threat to anyone and no one had any grievance with him.'

'No altercations with Nolan?'

43

'Not as far as I'm aware. I would say it is highly unlikely.'

May ordered another coffee from the counter. Lambert asked for a glass of water, his bloodstream thick with caffeine. When she returned he tried to take the initiative. 'So what are you working on at the moment?' he asked.

'Normal procedures. We're looking into Haydon's church. As before, there was incense at the crime scene so we've contacted local churches to see if any amounts have gone missing. But the problem with these guys is that they just don't have strong stock control.' She raised her eyebrows again, a completely different look to before. The gesture softened her face and made Lambert feel like she was being companionable.

'We're crosschecking the other murders too but the connection between this murder and Billy Nolan's is our main focus at present. In fact if you hadn't found me there was a good chance that I'd have had to find you.'

'How can I help now?' asked Lambert.

'Maybe you could stick around for a bit. I could do with some insight on the Nolan murders, if that wouldn't affect you too much? Obviously I would prefer it if you didn't conduct your own investigation.' Her eyes narrowed, Lambert understanding the warning. She hesitated for a beat, the first sign of indecisiveness he'd seen. 'Perhaps we could meet for dinner this evening?' she said.

'Sure,' said Lambert, a little quicker than he would have liked.

DI May stood up to leave. 'It was a pleasure meeting you,' she said, shaking his hand.

'I'll see you this evening,' said Lambert. He relaxed as he watched May cross the floor of the coffee shop. The encounter

44

had surprised him. May was more open than he'd expected, and he imagined how easy it would be to work with her.

As he was about to look away, May stopped and turned. 'Oh, Michael. Please feel free to bring along Mr Klatzky this evening as well if you wish.'

Chapter 5

Light blazed through the office windows on the third floor of the Bristol Central Police Station. DI Sarah May pulled down the blinds in her temporary office, blocking the piercing September sun and opened the window an inch to allow fresh air into the musty-smelling room. After switching on her computer, for the second time that day she turned her attention to Michael Lambert's file. She'd enjoyed meeting Lambert. So much so that she'd suggested they meet that evening. It had been an impulsive request which she'd convinced herself she'd made for professional reasons.

His file made for interesting reading. He'd joined the force a year after leaving University, joining the same accelerated programme she was on at the moment. After two years' probation, he'd moved straight to CID. His training officer, Glenn Tillman, was now a Chief Superintendent working for the NCA.

Lambert worked in major crimes and had reached the level of Detective Chief Inspector by the time Tillman recruited him again for a division in SOCA. The trail went cold after that. Lambert's last three years of service had been almost blanked from the records. Even her Super didn't have the clearance required to access details on Lambert's term in SOCA.

She dropped the file on the desk and stared at the photo

supplied with the file. If it had been taken some time ago, it didn't show. Lambert was six foot one with the kind of slim, wiry body she associated with athletes. The photo captured his sad, doleful hazel eyes but missed the lopsided grin she'd encountered during their meeting at the coffee shop.

It had been convenient he'd emailed last evening. It hadn't taken her long to link him to Terrence Haydon. Lambert had been friends with the last Souljacker victim, Billy Nolan, eighteen years ago. May had subsequently discovered that Haydon had lived in the same halls of residence as Nolan and Lambert.

May placed her hands on her cheeks and stared at Lambert's photo. He'd made a good lunchtime companion. Funny and intelligent, self-depreciating, he was the sort of man she'd always been attracted to. Still, he was definitely holding back on something. They had tiptoed around the case, each only sharing the minimum of information. She'd asked him not to start his own investigation. His response had been non-committal at best.

A shadow lurked behind the glass panelled door of her office. She recognised the shape.

'Yes,' she shouted.

DS Jack Bradbury opened the door. 'Christ, bit fresh in here isn't it?'

May had been so wrapped up in Lambert's file that she hadn't noticed the cold air leaking through the window. 'Jack, what have you got for me?'

'The file you wanted. Simon Klatzky. Bit thin, I'm afraid.'

'Thanks.'

Bradbury dropped the file and exited the office without a word. They had dated, if it could be called that, for two months prior to May becoming an Inspector. It had been an impulsive thing, and like all her impulsive actions it was something she'd had to learn to live with. Two years later, and still he moped after her. They'd managed to keep the affair a secret back then. Now she wished they had been more open about it. That way they would never have ended up working together, and she wouldn't have to see his wounded look every time she refused to pay him attention.

The file on Klatzky was indeed thin. Like Lambert, and fifty other students, Klatzky had been interviewed following the death of Billy Nolan. In his statement, Klatzky had declared that out of the small group of Nolan's friends, he was probably the closest. His life following his friend's death suggested that he had not taken the incident very well.

Klatzky had been a promising engineering student, and had left Bristol University with a first. Yet, he had never held down a significant job since graduating. Now there was an arrest warrant out on him for failure to appear at court following a bout of shoplifting. One of Lambert's former colleagues had spotted Lambert and Klatzky arriving at Temple Meads station that morning. Knowing that May was working on the Souljacker case, and Lambert's tenuous link, he had called May with the information. It had been worth it to see the look on Lambert's face when she'd asked him to bring Klatzky along for dinner that night.

May stretched her legs, tensing her calf muscles. She hadn't been for a run since Haydon's body had been discovered. The lack of exercise filled her body with tension. She'd been struggling to sleep recently, her legs twitching her awake at night. She promised herself she would make time for a quick run that evening, before her meeting with Lambert. It would be negligent not to do so. Healthy body, healthy mind, as her father would say.

Talking of healthy body, she hadn't had a coffee in nearly an hour. She walked to the small kitchen office and dropped some instant coffee into a mug. It wasn't ideal but was the best available. Two DCs, Tony Chambers, and Lyle Coombes, stopped talking as she entered.

'Not interrupting anything, am I?' she asked.

'No, ma'am.'

Both men worked on the Souljacker case. Clearly, they felt awkward with her presence in the kitchen but they were waiting for the kettle to boil so couldn't leave the close confines of the room. She didn't make it easy for them. She leant back on the sideboard and folded her arms, both men doing everything to avoid her gaze. Strange how a simple change of title could affect the way people interacted with you. How you interacted with them. 'Any news for me?'

'Um, no, ma'am,' said Chambers. 'We've interviewed some more of his work colleagues, and they all spouted the same stuff.'

'Nice enough guy, kept himself to himself,' said Coombes, gaining courage from his partner.

The kettle boiled. 'Don't mind if I jump the queue?'

The men shook the heads, desperate for her to leave.

Back at her desk, she examined the old case files. Ten Souljacker victims in a twenty-one year period, but an eighteen year gap since the last murder. She may have considered Haydon's death a copycat had there not been the link between him and the last victim, Nolan.

Absurd as it sounded, they had called in a handwriting expert to compare the indentations ripped into the torso of Terrence Haydon, with that of the previous victims. Going on photographic evidence, the expert had suggested there was a high probability that the Latin carved onto the victims, In oculis animus habitat, was made by the same person.

'How probable?' May had asked.

'Hard to say for sure. I could be more precise if I was judging perhaps his handwriting on a piece of paper, but I would say ninety to ninety-five percent chance. If the latest, um, inscription, was made by a copycat, for instance, then I would say they are an expert forger.'

Not only an expert forger, but an expert killer. It would take skill, along with an exceptional coldness to keep someone alive whilst you extracted their eyeballs. The inscription on the body would have taken hours. Each letter was always carved with extreme precision.

One anomaly had sprung up from the handwriting expert. He'd said that the writing on the first victim's torso, Clive Hale, from twenty-two years ago, didn't match the others. It was possible that it had been his first kill, and he'd been nervous, but the expert was adamant the writing was not the same as the others.

May opened the office door and called for Bradbury. He appeared two minutes later, the hound dog look replaced with a look of professional attention, as if he'd given himself a pep talk in the intervening minutes. She realised she shouldn't be so hard on him. In retrospect, he'd always wanted more from their time together than she did. She could have, and should have handled it better. She made a mental note to speak to him about it.

'Jack, do you know anything about the SIO on the Nolan case all those years ago? Julian Hastings?'

Bradbury stood by the desk. 'Not much more than I've read in the file. He was working here until the late nineties. I heard he was a bit of an old school copper. Bit strict. Not hugely talkative. From what I've heard the Nolan case fucked him up a bit.'

May looked up from her file for the first time since Bradbury had entered.

'Sit down, Jack, for Christ's sake.'

Hastings had retired six years earlier with the rank of Chief Superintendent, having spent his last eight years in Kent. 'How was he fucked up, as you so eloquently put it?'

'He became a bit obsessed with it, you know how it is. Rumour has it that was why he left the city. You know he's a writer now?' said Bradbury.

'Yes, I picked up one of his titles today. Blood Kill.' May picked up the book from her desk. A crude paperback, the words BLOOD KILL taking up half of the cover in a thick maroon font.

'Catchy title. Wonder what it's about?'

May offered him smile. 'Read any?'

'One. His first one. Can't even remember the name now.'

'Memorable then?'

'I'm no expert. You could tell he was a copper though. Had all the procedures down to a tee. And the violence, though there wasn't enough of that.'

The review didn't bode well. Hastings had published three books since retiring. All police procedurals. Blood Kill was his latest according to the young woman who had sold May the book but according to the inlay page it was published three years ago.

'Could you try and contact him for me?' said May. 'I'd like to get his take on the Nolan case. See if we're missing anything.'

'Sure. Anything else?'

'No. Thanks, Jack.'

It would be good to get Hastings' input. As things stood there was very little to work with. The killer was still an expert at hiding his traces, though forensics had managed to extract another man's DNA from Haydon's hair.

May withdrew the photos of Lambert and Klatzky from their files and entered the open-plan office where the incident room was situated. She walked to the incident board and pinned up the two photos, and drew three lines.

One line connected Klatzky and Lambert.

The other two lines connected the two men with the photos of the last two Souljacker victims.

Chapter 6

May stared at the photos on the whiteboard. Lambert and Klatzky, best friends of the ninth Souljacker victim, and acquaintances of the tenth. It was too much of a coincidence. 'Jack, get everyone together in five. I want to go through everything again from scratch.'

Five minutes later, the team filtered into the conference room and May silenced them by standing. 'Okay, let's go from the beginning. Presuming we are looking at the Souljacker killer, and everything points that way at the moment, let's start with the first victim and work from there.'

Bradbury cleared his throat. 'Clive Hale. Twenty-two years ago. Body found in a bedsit in Clevedon. Same MO as the subsequent killings.'

May wrote Hale's name onto the whiteboard, the marker making a squeaking noise on the vinyl covering. 'Same MO but not as tidy as the others. The incision marks around the eyes were less precise. Bits of the eyeballs were actually found at the scene, which never happened again. Also, the carving on the body not as intricate or smooth.'

'He was less experienced then, probably fuelled by adrenalin and rushed the job,' said Bradbury.

May agreed. It was normally the pattern with the serials. The first kill rushed, as if the killer had to get it out of their system, the subsequent killings becoming more sophisticated as the killer became more practised. There was also the opinion of the handwriting expert to consider. 'Lana, what do we know about Clive Hale?'

As DC Lana Williams stood, May noticed Bradbury roll his eyes. 'Hale was nineteen, and unemployed. He'd been in the care system most of his life. No immediate family, no convictions. He attended a local Presbyterian church in Clevedon on occasions but the investigating team at the time discovered that he hadn't been going there for months.' Lana's delivery was succinct and confident.

'What can we glean from this?' May asked the team in general, nodding at Lana to sit down.

'Looking at the subsequent victims, and the latest victim, a common theme is the lonely male and a certain religious affiliation,' said Bradbury.

'That is a very tentative link,' said DC Stuart Welling. Welling was the oldest member of the team. Forever doomed to remain a DC, Welling carried a permanent chip on his shoulder. His role within the team seemed to be to question everyone else's decision making. It was because of this that May had included him on her task force.

'Why's that, Stuart?' she asked.

Welling frowned, and remained sitting. 'For one, I wouldn't agree that Terrence Haydon was a loner exactly. He lived alone but had a good job, and flat, and had some social interaction with his colleagues. The previous victim...' May caught the slight reddening of Welling's cheeks as he checked his notes. 'Billy Nolan. Very socially active and a student at University. As for the religious aspect, that's a lazy generalisation. Some of the victims went to church, many of different denominations, and the killer carves Latin onto them. That in itself doesn't prove a religious aspect to the killings.'

Bradbury turned his head so he could see his colleague. His elbows were held out wide, his chest thrust forward. 'It was only an observation,' he said.

Welling's eyes widened. He scratched his jaw as if in contemplation. 'A poor one.'

Bradbury sighed and returned his focus to May.

'Victim two,' said May.

'Proves the point,' said Welling.

May stood with her arms by her sides and shifted her stance as she waited for Welling to speak.

Welling finally took the hint. 'Graham Jackett. Local vet.'

'Unmarried,' said Bradbury.

'Yes, but socially active. Killed three months after Hale. Like Hale, he was found in his home. This time a semi-detached property in Nailsea.'

'Religious affiliation?' asked May.

Welling sighed. 'He attended the local Anglican church but I can't see the relevance. The work on the body is much smoother this time. It almost becomes a template for the subsequent murders. The removal of the eyes is pristine.'

'Pristine?' said Bradbury.

Welling shifted in his seat. 'No trace of jelly was left at the scene,' said Welling, to general amusement. 'The carving on the body was much neater. He took his time on this one.'

They went through each victim one by one until they reached

David Welsh, the victim prior to Billy Nolan. 'Twenty-eight year old welder,' said Welling.

'Lived alone, went to church,' added Bradbury.

'Means nothing. Then we reach the popular student, Billy Nolan,' said Welling.

'And then, eighteen years later, Terrence Haydon,' said May. They had decided to stick to his original surname for the investigation. She began writing on the whiteboard. 'So what we know? Prior to the thirty-eight year old Haydon, each former victim was a white male aged twenty to thirty. They all lived alone except the ninth victim, Billy Nolan.'

'Technically, he did live alone. He had his own room in halls,' said Bradbury.

'Okay. White, male, twenty to thirty, lived alone. Anything else?'

'I still think the religious aspect is important. Of the nine victims, we know six attended church,' said Bradbury. 'With Haydon, that makes seven out of ten.'

Everyone in the room turned to look at Welling. 'I'm not saying it isn't relevant but at the moment it isn't a definite link.'

May agreed with both of them. 'We need to look closer at the victims. There has to be something more than gender and age which links them. Lana, start looking at those victims who didn't have a religious background. See if there was any oversight here. Maybe it was an area not considered by the investigative teams. Everyone else, I want to know everything about each of the victims. Go back to the start, go through the case notes and search for anything which links the victims. Bradbury, we've enough resources here for this. Assign a team to each victim starting with Hale. Let's see what we have by nine a.m. tomorrow.'

May returned to her office and shut the door. She paced the room, recounting the details of the team meeting. She played with the files on her desk, opened then shut the blinds. She needed to calm down. They were close to something. There was already a tentative link between the victims, and it would only take one thing, one small link she was confident she would be able to connect everything. Despite Welling's protestations, she thought the religious aspect was relevant and hoped the investigative teams would find something of value in their research.

She sat and tried to banish the negative thought that the one small link would never be discovered, that they would always remain just out of reach.

Bradbury called through on the internal phone line. 'I've managed to track down the SIO on the former cases, Julian Hastings. He wants to meet at seven a.m. tomorrow.'

'Good,' said May, hanging up. The retired Chief Super-intendent had taken over as SIO from the Jackett case onwards. She could only imagine his frustration as he'd investigated victim after victim with no result. She bounced up and down on her chair, trying to control the adrenalin leaking into her system. From her office drawer, she took out her Kindle and downloaded a copy of Hastings' last novel, Blood Kill, and began reading.

Chapter 7

Klatzky had already started drinking. Lambert found him sitting with a giggling group of students, swigging from a pint of lager. The students were all girls. In their late teens, early twenties, they were strikingly beautiful, particularly in comparison to the rough and jaded figure of Klatzky. Unbelievably, they were enjoying his company. One of their number, a tall slender girl, laughed every time Klatzky opened his mouth, stroking her dark hair absentmindedly with her left hand. Klatzky had always been successful with women at University but Lambert was surprised that these women would have anything to do with him now.

'Mikey, come and join us,' shouted Klatzky, on seeing Lambert.

The young women stared at Lambert as he approached. A small blonde girl with an obvious fake tan and a face lined with over-enthusiastic make-up echoed Klatzky's words. 'Yes, Mikey, come and join us,' she said, provoking good-natured laughter from the others. It was clear the whole group had been drinking for some time.

'Simon, can I have a word?' said Lambert, ignoring the young woman's request.

'Sure, sure,' said Klatzky getting to his feet. 'Here, girls, get another round in.' Klatzky placed a twenty pound note on the table which was snapped up by the dark-haired girl.

Lambert led Klatzky outside. He decided not to reprimand him about the drinking. 'I'm thinking of staying for a couple of nights,' he said.

'Fantastic,' said Klatzky. 'Where do you have in mind?'

'Listen, Si, I don't think this is going to work, you being here.'

'Don't mind me, Mikey. I'll keep out of your way. One city is much the same as another.'

It was pointless arguing. 'Fine, there's a Marriott at the bottom of the hill. I'll book us in separate rooms for the night. Then we can discuss the situation tomorrow. I'll ring you later with the room number.'

'Great. Listen, Mikey,' Klatzky hesitated.

Lambert sighed and took his wallet from his trouser pocket and handed Klatzky eighty pounds. 'Don't let those girls screw you over, Simon. And for God's sake get something to eat.'

'Yes, mum,' said Klatzky, returning inside.

Following his meeting with May, Lambert decided he would continue with his own investigation for the time being. He didn't want to impede her in any way, but there were questions he was impatient to have answered. It was too coincidental that Billy Nolan and Terrence Haydon had lived one floor apart at University. There was a connection to be discovered between the two, however unlikely that sounded at the moment. Since joining the force, he'd always resisted the temptation to revisit the Souljacker case. He'd understood that he'd been too emotionally involved. Now it was unavoidable. Klatzky had forced his hand. Lambert decided to start where he would normally start: the victim's closest relation.

He hailed an approaching taxi and ordered the driver to

take him to a small suburb of Bristol called Whitchurch where Terrence Haydon's mother, Sandra Vernon, lived.

Twenty minutes later, he reached his destination. Whitchurch was a grey area, populated by uninspired near-identical houses with ashen facades and dull brown-red tiled roofs. Sandra Vernon lived opposite a crumbling supermarket in a small terraced house. The front of the house was well maintained with UPVC windows. A stone pathway led through a neatly mowed front garden to the front door. Lambert waited for a beat and rang the doorbell.

A small plump woman with large circular rimmed spectacles answered. The smell of cinnamon and burnt toast drifted from behind her. 'Yes, what do you want?' she inquired, in a high-pitched Welsh accent.

Lambert told the woman that he was a friend of Terrence who had recently heard the terrible news and had come to pay his condolences. The rotund woman looked him up and down for an uncomfortable amount of time before inviting him in.

Lambert surveyed the living room whilst Sandra Vernon made tea in the kitchen. The room was sparsely decorated with white walls and a couple of mass market reproduction paintings in cheap frames on the wall. A small flat screen television sat beneath one of the rectangular PVC windows. A simple wooden crucifix hung above the fireplace. Beneath it, taking pride of place on the mantelpiece, was a picture of Sandra Vernon and her son on his graduation day.

'He was a good boy,' said Sandra Vernon, returning with a tray.

Lambert couldn't detect any emotion in the woman, her face blank. 'He was, here let me take that for you.' Lambert took the tray from the woman's unsteady hands.

'What did you say your name was again?' she said, the lilt of her accent deeper now.

'Michael Lambert. I lived on the floor below Terrence in his final year at University. We were not the best of friends but I knew him.'

Sandra Vernon poured him a cup of tea.

'How are you coping, Mrs Vernon?' asked Lambert, sipping the weak tea.

'Day by day, Mr Lambert, but it is Miss Vernon. The church is a great help to me as you can imagine.'

'Of course. Terrence was always very religious at University,' said Lambert, unsure if he was saying the right thing.

'He had a strong relationship with God. For that he will be rewarded.'

'I didn't realise his home was in Bristol whilst he was at University. My parents lived in London. To be fair, I couldn't wait to get away from them,' said Lambert. He ignored the comment about God. Tension was always high when religion was involved. Experience told him it was best to steer clear unless the conversation was necessary. Like Klatzky, he was a lapsed Catholic. Apart from the odd occasion, wedding, baptism, or funeral, he hadn't attended church since he was a teenager.

Vernon drank her tea, studying him, her eyes lifeless behind the covering of her spectacles. 'I always was close to Terrence. I decided to stay near to him when he moved to University. We lived in Wales before then.'

Lambert had never heard of a parent moving with their child to University. Though not inconceivable, it suggested an over-familiar relationship between parent and child. 'It's been a while since I've seen Terrence. Did he ever marry?'

Vernon laughed. 'No, no.'

'Was he seeing anyone?'

'As I said, Mr Lambert, he had a strong relationship with God. He had no time for such nonsense. God was all he needed.' Sandra Vernon looked away as she said the last words, as if threatened by Lambert's suggestion.

'What was that church he was with? It was one of those really evangelical ones wasn't it?'

'It's called Gracelife. It is a proper church, with true believers and proper morals. It's one of the reasons I moved here in the first place.'

'Of course, sorry I don't know much about these things.' With the conversation failing, Lambert knew he had a decision to make. Either leave things as they were, or push the woman further. She had recently suffered a great loss, and for that he was sympathetic, but he wasn't blind to the tone she was using. She had taken a clear disliking to him, speaking down to him as if he was a child.

'One thing that did confuse me, Miss Vernon. I see that Terrence had changed his name to Vernon. We'd known him as Terrence Haydon at University.'

'That was his father's name.' Sandra Vernon sat on the edge of her seat. Her face had reddened and she glared at Lambert, her small eyes magnified by her oversized spectacles.

Lambert didn't mind the woman's discomfort. He pushed further. 'Ah yes, I remember Terrence mentioning him. Is his father not around any more?'

The woman's eyes narrowed. 'He was no father,' she said, lowering her voice.

'Did Terrence ever see him?'

'He ceased being his father many years ago,' said Vernon. Her voice came out as a screech as the colour in her cheeks deepened, her eyes narrowing once more.

Lambert poured himself some more tea. He tipped the clear brown liquid into Sandra Vernon's cup. 'Oh. I hadn't realised. I'm sure I remember Terrence mentioning him. I'm sorry, I didn't mean to upset you. I just wanted to understand.' Lambert kept his voice low and steady, focusing all his attention onto the flustered woman.

Vernon leant back in her chair. 'His daddy was an evil man, Godless. Left us when Terrence was a child. Terrence never forgave him. It was his decision. He waited until he left University, but he didn't want that man's name sullying him any more.'

Vernon was over-protesting. 'Despicable. Is he aware that Terrence has gone to a better place? I hope you'll forgive my forwardness, but I could inform him if you had an address.'

The woman let out a small sound which sounded like a wounded animal. Her facial muscles tensed and Lambert watched, bemused, as her upper lip rose revealing the redness of her gums. 'I don't have his address. Who cares if he knows? He was nothing to Terrence, to us.' she snarled.

Lambert stood. 'No, you're completely right. I'm really sorry to bother you. I should go. I was hoping to visit his church before I left for London. Thank you for the tea.' He had what he'd wanted. Any sympathy he'd had for the woman had faded. He sensed the hatred in the woman, knew it wasn't simply a reaction to her son's death. It resonated within her, and he sighed with relief when he was out of the claustrophobic confines of her house. He had to speak to Terrence's father, but first he had to see his church.

A white painted building, the result of two terraced houses knocked together, the church had a small sign nailed to the side wall announcing the occupants as Gracelife, Bristol. Minister, Neil Landsdale.

An elderly woman wrapped in a pink-check clothed apron opened the front door. 'Yes?'

'I'm here to see the minister,' said Lambert.

The woman glared at him as if he'd said something incomprehensible. 'Minister?'

'Neil Landsdale.'

'I'm just the cleaner,' said the woman. 'You can come in and check the offices if you want. There are some people moving about up there.' She walked back inside, leaving the door open.

Apart from a giant wooden crucifix hanging from the far wall, little else suggested the interior was that of a church. It was more like a small dance studio. Stacks of plastic chairs and folded tables surrounded a polished wooden floor. Dull brown walls propped up the low ceiling.

'Up there,' said the cleaner, pointing to a panelled door which led to a flight of stairs.

Lambert heard talking as he moved up the dark staircase. One male, one female voice. He reached the office door and knocked. The voices stopped and the door was opened by a smiling woman, wearing a long-sleeved dress, patterned with large garish flowers, 'Mr Lambert by any chance?' she said, her face twitching.

Sandra Vernon had obviously called ahead. He kept his tone light. 'Yes, you have me at a disadvantage, Miss…'

The woman kept the painted smile on her face but didn't invite him to enter.

'May I speak to Neil Landsdale?' asked Lambert, when she didn't answer.

'I'm afraid he's awfully busy at the moment,' said the woman, her light voice lined with the trace of a West Country accent. 'Would it be possible to come back later?'

Lambert stiffened. 'Not really, I'm afraid. I'm only in Bristol for the day. It will only take a few minutes of his time.' Lambert pictured the minister sitting at a desk behind the door. He had no idea why the man was avoiding him, but one thing was clear, he would not be leaving without first speaking to the minister.

'Please wait here,' said the woman, shutting the door behind her.

Lambert placed his ear to the door, but couldn't hear the muffled conversation. He stepped back as the door opened.

'Mr Landsdale will see you now,' said the woman.

Two chrome-framed desks sat side by side in the office, each with an old box-style computer monitor on them. A grey-haired man stood in front of one of the desks. His hair fell to his shoulder, a week's growth of stubble protruding from his face. His smile was as prominent and false as his colleague's. 'Mr Lambert, pleased to meet you. I am the minister of our humble little church. You can call me Neil.'

Lambert accepted the weak handshake. 'Thank you, Neil.'

'Please sit, how may I help?'

'As I am sure Miss Vernon has informed you, I was Terrence's friend at University. I'd come to pay my respect to Miss Vernon. Whilst here, I thought I'd see the church Terrence was so fond of.'

'That he was, Mr Lambert. Terrence was an active parishioner, ever since he joined our congregation when he was at University. He will be sorely missed.'

'You've been minister all that time?'

'Yes,' said Landsdale, holding his hands in front of him, his fingers interlocked. 'It is my church.'

'So you know Terrence's father?'

'I'm afraid not. Sandra and Terrence's father had divorced some time before they moved here.'

'Did Terrence ever speak of him?'

'With all due respect, what business is it of yours? I thought you came to pay your respects.' The smile was still there, but the humour had disappeared from the minister's eyes.

'I have, and I wanted to pay my respects to both parents,' said Lambert, his voice rising, his patience fading.

Landsdale understood. He unlinked his fingers and sat back in his chair, as if trying to escape Lambert's gaze. 'Look, there's not much I can tell you. Terrence's parents were parishioners of our sister church in Neath, when Terrence was a child. The church had a different approach then. From what I heard, there was a bit of a nasty business when they separated. Terrence never mentioned him.'

'Do you know where Mr Haydon is now?' It would only take a minute to find the father's address on The System, but Lambert wanted to hear the address from Landsdale. He tapped his knuckles on the minister's desk, and waited.

'Now how would I know that, Mr Lambert? Perhaps you should ask the police.'

Lambert continued tapping the desk, despite the threat. He inched closer to Landsdale who shifted in his chair, looking everywhere but back at him. 'Okay. Thank you for your time.' Lambert stepped back from the desk, Landsdale letting out a sigh. 'Before I go, do you ever use incense during your services?'

Landsdale was on his feet, mirroring Lambert. A smile still stuck on his face. 'Bit Old Testament for us. Let me show you out, Mr Lambert.'

Lambert ordered a taxi back to the city centre and waited outside the church for it to arrive. On the journey back, he replayed the meeting with Terrence's mother. He hadn't appreciated it at the time, but what he recalled most now was the coldness of her house. The sparse religious decorations, the hostility from the small bespectacled woman. Lambert hadn't sensed much love for her son from Sandra Vernon, only the bitterness and hatred she felt towards her ex-husband. Lambert tried to picture what it must have been like for Terrence to be raised by such a woman and found himself feeling a bit sorry for Terrence's father even though he had never met the man.

Landsdale was less straight forward. He gave the outward impression of being approachable and helpful, but he had a touch of steel about him. He'd refused to be budged on Haydon's father, even though Lambert was certain Landsdale knew where the man was. Something was going on with Sandra Vernon and Landsdale. They were hiding something whether it was relevant to Terrence Haydon's death or not. Lambert was lifted by the thought. In his eyes, secrets were a sign of progress.

Back in the town centre, he checked into the hotel at the bottom of Park Street, ordering a room for Klatzky. He sent Klatzky a text instructing him to pick up the room card from reception. He logged onto The System and checked HOLMES for updates. He was mildly surprised to see his name mentioned. May had reported meeting him for lunch, and that she had warned him not to start his own investigation. She had posted a picture of him as well as one of Klatzky. No mention of their meeting tonight had been entered.

He read through the details of the previous Souljacker victims, starting way back with Clive Hale. May's team had noted the transition in style of the killer from the first hurried job on Hale. How from Graham Jackett onwards, the killer had been much more meticulous from the eye removal to immaculate inscriptions carved onto his victim's torsos. May had ordered a closer look at all the previous victims which made sense to Lambert. He was particularly interested in the connection between six of the victims who had all been members of a church of various denominations. Billy Nolan hadn't attended church at any time during University but maybe there was some link from the past which had escaped the initial investigative team. Reading further, he realised that May would likely find out. She was due to meet the SIO on eight of the last ten Souljacker killings, Chief Superintendent Julian Hastings, tomorrow morning.

It didn't take long to find an address for Terrence's estranged father. Roger Haydon lived in Weston-super-Mare, a small seaside town twenty miles from Bristol. Roger Haydon had been on housing and unemployment benefit for most of his life. One of May's team, DS Jack Bradbury, had questioned the man. Haydon had claimed not to have seen Terrence since he was a child.

Lambert ordered a late lunch from room service and called Tillman.

'You're not working for me, so you don't need to call in and report,' said Tillman.

'I had an interesting chat with the DI on this case, Sarah May,' said Lambert, ignoring him.

'And I should be interested because?'

'What's my official classification, sir?'

'You know that, Michael. Leave of absentia or some shit.'

'She managed to obtain my personnel file. Well, parts of it. She thinks I'm a man of mystery.'

'We all think that, Michael. Now if there is nothing else? We shouldn't even be discussing this on the phone.'

'It made me think,' said Lambert.

'A new one, but go on.'

'About coming back.'

Tillman didn't respond. Lambert's leave had been out of necessity. The accident had left him in an induced coma, followed by months of physical and mental rehabilitation. Tillman had never visited him during that time, but Lambert still received a small salary despite the accident occurring out of work.

'Sir?' said Lambert.

'You want to come back?' said Tillman.

'I want to know where I would stand.'

'We'll meet once you've finished playing detectives,' said Tillman, hanging up.

Lambert placed the phone on the bedside table and collapsed into the softness of the bed. Talking to Tillman had deflated his new enthusiasm. He'd never blamed anyone else for what had happened to Chloe. He'd revelled in his guilt, replaying the incident time after time, day after day. He'd refused all offers of help, from his wife and extended family, from his work colleagues. He carried his child's death around with him like a millstone, and it impacted on everything. His wife wanted nothing more to do with him, and Tillman knew he wouldn't be ready for work until he had dealt with it.

A tightness filled his chest, and he sat upright fighting the sensation. He stumbled to the bathroom and drank heavily from the sink tap. Forgetting his guilt would be a betrayal of Chloe's memory but maybe there was another way to honour her. It could never bring her back, and he could never be redeemed, but he needed to move forward with the case.

Chapter 8

Lance Crosby left the small bookshop opposite the University building. He'd been waiting for three hours, ever since Lambert had caught the taxi. He watched Lambert enter the building and called it in.

'Sit tight,' said the man on the other end of the line.

Lance did as instructed. It was his third day on the job. The last two days had been spent in London following Lambert's friend, Simon Klatzky. Keeping track of Klatzky had meant visiting an unending array of public houses, until yesterday when he'd contacted Lambert.

Lance had photographed the second man and forwarded the photos onto Campbell, who had taken great pleasure in the news.

In an instant, the focus changed. Lance had been following Lambert ever since. Following Lambert was more complicated. Campbell had warned him that Lambert was a professional and so it had proved. Lance hoped the other two would arrive soon. Sooner or later his luck would run out and Lambert would spot him. He'd kept his distance this morning on the tube and latterly on the train but Lambert was police. He'd told Campbell as much but the words went unheeded.

Before he had time to react, Lambert left the University building. Lance followed at a distance as Lambert walked down Park Street, heading for the Marriott hotel at the bottom of the hill.

Lance updated his boss.

'Go back to the University and watch Klatzky,' instructed Campbell.

Back at the building, following a gruelling trek back up Park Street, Lance showed the security guard a fake ID and went in search of the union bar. It was no surprise to find the second man there. Simon Klatzky sat at a table drowning his sorrows. Somehow he'd convinced a number of female students, attractive ones at that, to join him.

Lance ordered a Diet Coke from the bar and took a seat, imagining he was in for a long day.

Chapter 9

Like Bradbury had suggested, Blood Kill was full of authentic procedural detail but May found herself drawn to the story as well which was about the murder of teenage girl, a girl blind from birth. The main detective was a methodical and morally superior Superintendent. From what Bradbury had told her, Hastings had become obsessed with the Souljacker case during his time on the force. It had proved to be the major case he never solved, and there was an obvious parallel to the girl in his novel. She wondered if writing the book was cathartic for Hastings, if the success of his fictional hero in finding the killer alleviated his own perceived failings. She closed the book halfway through, surprised how engrossed she had become with the case.

Jack Bradbury stopped her as she left the office.

'I thought you'd want to know. Sandra Vernon called. Apparently your friend Michael Lambert paid her a visit earlier on today.'

'How long ago?' asked May.

'A few minutes. She called as soon as he'd left. She wasn't very happy. He claimed he was a friend of Terrence Haydon and had called around to pay his respects.'

'True in a way, I suppose. Did she have anything else to add?'

'That he was asking some odd questions. In particular about Terrence's father.'

'What did he want exactly?'

'She sounded a bit pissed,' said Bradbury. 'Lambert wanted to know the man's address. Vernon didn't pass on the details.'

Although she didn't consider him a serious suspect, May had placed Lambert's picture on the incident board next to Klatzky's. She'd warned him not to start his own investigation but knew he would still get involved. Procedurally it would be difficult to officially get him working on the case, though it would definitely be beneficial. 'You saw Terrence's father yesterday?' she asked Bradbury.

Bradbury nodded. She remembered his report. The man lived alone in a council estate in Weston-super-Mare. Sad figure by all accounts. He hadn't seen his son in over twenty years. 'Okay, I'll have another word with him today.'

'What, Lambert?'

May crossed her arms. 'Yes, Lambert. Is there anything else?'

'No, ma'am,' replied Bradbury. With a brief flash of the puppy dog eyes, he turned away.

The hospital was less than a mile from the Central Police Station so she decided to walk. As she left the building, she thought she saw a figure from her past. She rubbed her eyes, as the figure disappeared around a corner, and retrieved a pair of sunglasses from her bag.

May had arranged to meet Siobhan Callahan at the hospital. Callahan worked as an Occupational Therapist. She'd been one of the students on the fifth floor of the halls of residence during the period when Billy Nolan's body was discovered eighteen years ago.

She'd also been Michael Lambert's girlfriend.

May uncovered her following a thorough reading of the student statements. She couldn't believe her luck when she'd discovered the woman worked less than a mile from her office.

The extended heatwave still gripped the city, the late September sky a cloudless blue. May trekked up the hill which led to the hospital and searched for Callaghan's department on the noticeboard in the main foyer. She followed the green line which led to the occupational therapy department. She recalled her own time at University, and the boyfriends she'd had there. She didn't know how she would have reacted if someone wanted to talk to her about any of them. She rarely dwelled on the past, couldn't relate to the wide-eyed girl she'd been in her early twenties. She viewed her past like a voyeur, her memories akin to a reader imagining a character from a book.

Siobhan Callaghan was not what she'd expected. May had pictured a stereotypical Irish girl, buxom and red-haired. The woman in front of her had short, spikey black hair, and a thin wiry body. Her face had a boyish quality to it.

'Oh yes, Inspector. Sorry, I've been rushed off my feet today. Please come on through.' She led her through to a small white cubicle, with a desk, two plastic chairs and an elevated bed. Like the rest of the hospital, the small area had a clean anti-septic smell. 'Please take a seat. Sorry, I didn't quite get the gist of your call earlier. You mentioned something about that incident at the University all those years ago.'

'Yes, thank you for seeing me at such short notice,' said May. 'You've read about the recent murder in Southville?'

'Yes. Ghastly. I thought about poor Billy when I read it. You think it's the same person? It's what the papers think, isn't it?'

May studied the woman. She sounded genuine, and nothing

about her body language suggested otherwise. 'I can't comment on that. We're speaking to everyone who was in halls on the night Billy Nolan's body was discovered. I read your statement from that time.'

Callaghan struggled to keep eye contact with May. Her eyes darted upwards, as if replaying that night in her head. 'I was asleep when all the commotion happened, thank God. I never saw him. Christ, am I thankful for that. I can imagine it really fucked most people up. Oh, sorry, excuse my language.'

May waved her hand dismissing the apology.

'This one girl, Laura, she could barely speak. Her whole body was shaking. I remember putting my arm around her. She buzzed. It's the only word I can use to describe it. It was like touching someone who'd had an electric shock. Her parents collected her the day after. I never saw her again. I'd known her for three years at University and that was that.'

'It says on your file you had a boyfriend at the time?'

Callahan shifted in her chair. 'Michael,' she said, a slight lilt to her voice.

'Yes, Michael...Lambert,' said May, pretending to glance at her notes.

'Poor guy,' said Siobhan. 'He was the one who found Billy. Broke down his door. Have you spoken to him about it?'

May nodded.

Siobhan's eyes widened. 'Oh.' She took a deep breath. 'He was a bit like Laura to begin with, and then he went silent. He was close to Billy, you know.'

'Yes, what was he like?'

'Billy or Michael?'

'Michael.'

A brightness overcame Siobhan's face, the memory clearly a fond one. 'He was a sweet guy. What can I say, we were young. It was quite intense.'

'Were you going out with him for long?'

'Six, seven months.'

'Was it a monogamous relationship?'

'As far as I'm aware. Why all these questions about Michael?'

'The most recent victim, he was also at University with you.'

'What?' said Siobhan, the colour vanishing from her face. 'Michael wasn't the victim, was he?'

'No, no. Sorry, Siobhan. I didn't mean to confuse you. The latest victim was called Terrence Haydon. He was at University at the same time as you.'

Siobhan caught her breath. 'He was in halls with us? What floor was he on?'

'Floor six. Some people called him Mad Terry?'

'Don't remember him. What's this to do with Michael?'

'Oh, nothing directly.'

Siobhan placed her hands in her lap. 'You can't think he has anything to do with it? That would be ridiculous.'

May leant forward, catching a waft of antiseptic from the corridor. 'No, of course not. We're examining all the connections in the two cases. And obviously Michael knew Billy very well. Did you know Michael's other friends?'

Siobhan relaxed, her shoulders dropping. 'Yeah, there was a gang of them.'

'What were they like as a group?'

'They were nice enough guys. They basically liked to drink and go with girls, like all boys that age.'

'Remember Simon Klatzky?'

Siobhan pursed her lips. 'He was hot,' she said, giggling. 'God, listen to me. Yeah, he was good friends with Michael. We'd all go out as a gang sometimes. I think he was really close with Billy. From what I heard it hit him really hard as well.'

May thought about the photo of Klatzky she'd posted on the whiteboard, the hard life he'd had since leaving University. 'Was there any trouble amongst them as a group? Any fights, things like that?'

'There were the odd fallings out but nothing significant. They all got on really well.'

'Well, thanks for your time, Siobhan. It's been much appreciated. As I said it's a routine thing.'

Siobhan had grown in confidence during the meeting. Her eyes were more focused. As they both stood, she asked, 'So when did you see Michael?'

May noted the keen interest in the question, was surprised that the inquiry made her bristle. 'He's in Bristol at the moment. I met him today.'

'What's he like now?'

'Yeah, he seems really nice. What happened to you guys after University?'

Siobhan walked her to the hospital elevator. 'We met up once. He came to stay with me at my parents' house for a week. He decided to go travelling for a year.'

'And you didn't want to go with him?'

'We talked about it. I had another year at University as I was studying for my Masters. We said we'd stay in touch,' said Siobhan. 'But we never did.'

Back at the station, May changed into her running gear, skin-tight running trousers and a fluorescent yellow jacket.

She thought about the touch of melancholy in Siobhan's voice as she recalled not staying in touch with Lambert, and briefly regretted that no one from her past could provoke the same reaction in her. She tied up her running shoes, pulling the laces tight until it squeezed her feet and left the locker room.

As she left the changing room one of the uniforms, a constable by the name of Bickley, laughed. 'Shit, I'm deaf,' he said, pretending to shield his ears from the loudness of May's jacket.

'Very amusing. Better safe than sorry, don't you think, Constable?' she said, playing along.

'No one's going to miss you, that's for sure, ma'am.'

May tried to run at least three times a week. It was five miles from the station to the house she shared with her father. He had moved in with her three years ago following the death of her mother. She couldn't face him living alone, and they'd managed to make the living arrangements work.

Approaching rush hour, the roads next to the station were gridlocked with traffic. She started at a steady pace, her breathing increasing as she upped her pace. She noticed admiring glances as she ran but kept her eyes straight on the road ahead. Running gave her time to think. She never wore earphones like some of the other runners. She liked the sound of the world moving by, the rush of the air as she pounded the pavement.

It had been five days now since she'd been put in charge of the Souljacker case. Superintendent Rush had yet to apply any firm pressure. If it was the same killer, then it was the tenth victim in twenty-three years and although no one had come close to catching the killer, something about the way things were unfolding told her things were different this time. The link between Haydon and Nolan was crucial and in addition it was conceivable that lack of practice had made the killer sloppy. Seven different strands of unidentified DNA had been found at Haydon's flat, but only one strain on the corpse. It had been found in Haydon's hair but nowhere else in the house.

Now all they needed was a suspect to match the DNA on Haydon's body. The thought drove her on, her pace increasing as additional adrenalin pumped into her bloodstream.

She started to tire four miles into the journey. Her legs filled with lactic acid as she tried to maintain her pace. It was unusual for her but not unexpected. She'd hardly slept since she'd been assigned to the case and her diet had been awful, cheap takeaways for breakfast, lunch and dinner. She needed an early night, a chance to clear her head but she'd suggested meeting Lambert later that evening. It had sounded like a good idea at the time but she was beginning to regret her decision. It had been impulsive, and if any of her previous staff appraisals were anything to go by, impulsiveness was her one major character flaw. It had led her into trouble more than once, both personally and professionally.

She pushed through the pain in her legs and increased her pace for the last mile. She liked to sprint the last few hundred metres home. She enjoyed the sensation of her body working at full throttle, everything pulling together, driving her forward. She reached the gates to her house and clicked her stopwatch. With her hands behind her head, she leant forward, her open mouth sucking air into her lungs.

'Good time?' asked her father as she opened the front door. He held a glass of red wine in one hand, the crossword section of the newspaper in the other.

'It wasn't a personal best,' said May, her breathing returning to normal.

Her father went to reply. She could tell by the way he looked at her jacket that he was about to unleash some quip about the brightness of the material. He thought better of it, knowing her humour wasn't at its highest at the end of a long run.

She read a few more chapters of Blood Kill before showering, and found herself relating more and more with the protagonist of the story. She sensed the man's anguish as he searched for the killer of the blind girl and wondered if the real life Hastings would be similar to his fictional counterpart. Hastings had stipulated a meeting time of seven a.m. for tomorrow which had destroyed her plan of a good night's sleep.

It was too late to cancel Lambert now. Anyway, she wanted to talk to him. He'd visited Sandra Vernon, and subsequently the minister of their small church, despite agreeing not to pursue his own investigation. She had to show him she should be taken seriously. What better way to do so than by going out for dinner with him, she thought ruefully.

She tried on a number of dresses before finding the perfect balance, a standard long-sleeve black dress which stretched below her knees. She scrubbed up well in the mirror but didn't want Lambert to get the wrong idea.

She checked her email before leaving and was surprised to see an email titled:

Why did you ignore me?

At first she thought it was a joke but then she read the name of the sender, Sean Laws. She'd thought she'd imagined it, but it must have been him she'd seen on the way to the hospital. He hadn't waved, so she hadn't ignored him. She opened the email.

Hi Sarah, Only joking. I don't know if you saw me but I spotted you out and about today. I'm in Bristol for a few days on work. I didn't want to disrupt you. You looked so beautiful, walking along. It was really good to see you again. Maybe if you've time we could meet up for a chat?

He signed the email Sean with a solitary kiss and his phone number.

May slammed her laptop shut, her hands shaking. She had an absurd impulse to run down the stairs and tell her dad. Despite his age, she knew he would grab his coat and start scouring the city until he found Sean.

Sean Laws, the ex-boyfriend she'd once threatened to take to court.

Chapter 10

Lambert spotted the car two minutes after leaving the hotel. A silver Mercedes, this year's plates, too grandiose to be police. Through the blacked out windows, he made out the vague silhouetted figure of the driver. He made a mental note of the number plate and took the short walk up Park Street to the restaurant, stopping occasionally to see if the car had followed him.

Twenty minutes early, he took a seat and ordered a cold bottle of lager as he waited for Sarah May to arrive. He'd left Klatzky at the hotel bar holding court with the four students from this morning, his concerns about the photos temporarily washed away.

Sarah May arrived at exactly eight o'clock. Dressed in a figure-hugging black dress, she carried a small handbag. Her hair hung loose on her shoulders, and Lambert wished he'd made more of an effort with his own appearance. He rose from his seat and offered his hand. She shook it, ignoring his awkwardness, her manner half-professional, half-cordial.

After ordering drinks, Lambert questioned May about her career. She described a meteoritic rise through the ranks that, to some extent, mirrored Lambert's progress. She talked about her colleagues and some of the issues she faced as a woman in the force.

It began to feel like a date until May dashed that notion during the main course.

'Now, Michael,' she said, her tone snapping from casual to business-like. 'I believe I told you not to follow your own investigation.'

Lambert straightened up in his chair. 'You're talking about my meeting with Sandra Vernon?'

'Yes.'

His eyes widened in mock surprise. 'You're not having me followed are you, DI May?'

May blinked, her mouth curling into the slightest of smiles. 'I'm afraid we don't have resources for such frivolous behaviour. But I thought if you were the interfering type, and I thought that perhaps you were, your first port of call would be with Miss Vernon.'

He couldn't tell if she was playing with him or if her annoyance was genuine. 'You spoke to her today?' asked Lambert.

'After you visited her house.'

Lambert drank long from his glass of red wine, enjoying May's scrutiny. Clearly he was being tested. 'I was paying my condolences.'

'That's right. And the questions about Haydon's father?'

Lambert laughed. 'I wanted to pay my condolences to him as well.'

May leant in. 'We've spoken to Mr Haydon. There's nothing much to be gained from him. From the report I was given, he's just a sad, washed up alcoholic.'

'It was only condolences,' said Lambert.

May lowered her voice. 'Because you and Haydon were so close? Look, I understand the experience you can bring to

84

the case. I'd be happy to share information with you but you must understand the complications that arise from you being involved. You've really pissed off Miss Vernon. It could damage our investigations.'

Lambert lifted his glass again and placed it back down without taking a drink. He'd been waiting for May to speak her mind. How the next few minutes went could possibly define their relationship. 'I do appreciate that,' he said. There was little the DI could do about his involvement and she probably understood that as well as he did, but he didn't want to upset her at this stage. 'I'll keep a low profile for the time being,' he conceded.

'Thank you,' said May.

They sat in silence for a time, Lambert sneaking the odd glance at his companion. He thought about his former colleagues, how rarely he had enjoyed a strong professional relationship with someone. He held onto his wine glass, went to speak and stopped.

'What did you think of Miss Vernon?' asked May, choosing to rescue him from his inaction.

Lambert sat back, decided he would trust May for the time being. 'I would say eccentric if I was being polite.'

'And if you weren't being polite?'

Lambert thought about the coldness he'd sense from the woman, the hatred she'd vocalised about her ex-husband. 'I couldn't possibly say. Did you speak to her about her Terrence's father?'

'Not in great detail.'

'Her reaction was over the top to say the least. I think you need to dig deeper, there's something she's holding back.'

'Okay. I'll question her again. You think the father is involved?'

'Not directly.' As this was a serial case it was unlikely the killer was a family member. 'But there is definitely something she is not sharing. How about you, where are you on the case?'

'You'll know about the DNA found at the scene? No match on the databases, unfortunately. Our main area of investigation is the link between Haydon and Nolan.'

'Makes sense. And the older cases?' he asked, remembering what he'd read on HOLMES.

May tilted her head back. She didn't answer immediately. Lambert sensed she was debating whether or not to share the information with him. 'We're looking at the older cases one by one. As you know, it's nearly twenty years since the last murder. It's possible something was overlooked in the past, or that there is a link we can tie in with Terrence Haydon.'

'Anything significant so far?'

'Not for me. There is a vague theory about churches at the moment. A high proportion of the victims were affiliated one way or another to a church. It might be significant but I can't see how at the moment.'

'Billy wasn't religious,' said Lambert, pleased that May was sharing the information even though he already knew it.

'There you go. I was going to ask, have you ever done any cold case work on this over the years? I'm sure it must have been tempting.'

Lambert shifted in his seat. 'I've tried to put it behind me. You can let these things define you if you're not careful,' he said, thinking that Billy's death would always be a part of him even if he ever caught whoever was responsible.

After dinner, May walked him back to his hotel. She quizzed him again about the blank entries in his work record, the inquiry light-hearted.

'There's no great mystery.' He'd drunk too much wine, her company relaxing him.

'Who said anything about a mystery? Don't hype yourself up.' She gently shoulder-charged him, forcing him to stumble.

'You're quite impressive, DI May. I can never tell for sure if I'm being interrogated or not. Such confusion is not normal for me.'

'I'm off the clock now,' she said, as they reached the hotel entrance. She turned to him, her left cheek curling slightly into a smile: a beautiful and stark contrast to the snarl he'd seen earlier that day on Sandra Vernon's face. He wondered what would happen if he leant in to kiss her, and took a step backwards realising he'd drunk even more than he'd imagined.

'Thank you for a lovely evening,' said May, saving him the embarrassment. She offered her hand which he shook savouring the warm softness of her flesh.

He said goodbye and retreated to the hotel, a sudden sense of fatigue spreading through him. He spotted Klatzky in the hotel bar, his arms wrapped around the black-haired student from the morning. They were alone, two wine bottles on the table before them. Lambert tried not to think about how much it would be costing. He retreated upstairs before either of them saw him.

Back in his hotel room, he checked his email and phone messages. Sophie had left a voicemail asking when he would be home. She would be asleep now so he sent her a text. Restless, he logged into The System. As he was using the hotel's Wi-Fi, he had to pass through a number of extra security measures before gaining access.

He checked Sarah May's file first, verifying what he'd been told over dinner. He checked for updates on HOLMES, and saw the name of his ex-girlfriend, Siobhan Callahan. May had met her earlier that day, not long after speaking to him. DI May moved fast and hadn't shared as much with him as he'd thought. He tried to picture what Siobhan would look like now. She'd been such a slight thing, wild, spikey hair, a tattoo on her shoulder. He couldn't imagine her now, wasn't sure he wanted to know how time had changed her.

He studied the rest of the Haydon file. He knew most of the document by heart now, but began reading from the start again. He always worked this way. The repetition helped him process the information, his mind working on the finer details he may have initially missed. Instead of merely scanning, he studied each page of the file, analysing the structure and each individual word of the report until it stopped making sense.

He switched off the light and lay on the bed listening to the hum of the air conditioning circling the room. His head was overrun with images. Sleep was elusive, the wine he'd drunk keeping him awake. Alone in the darkness, his thoughts always returned to his daughter, Chloe. During the day he tried to keep busy, distracting himself with the mundane activities of life. But she never totally left him. She lingered in the faces of strangers, her voice whispered in their conversations. At night he had no way of deflecting her. He tried to turn his thoughts to the case, but however hard he concentrated they spiralled back to Chloe. His throat constricted as he fought back tears. He snapped the light back on and left the room, in time to see Simon Klatzky, his arm draped across his young student friend, trying to open the door to his hotel room. Lambert stepped back and took the opposite route around the floor towards the lift.

It was eleven-thirty. Most of the city's bars had kicked out. The day's heat, retained by the tall city buildings, hung in the air. Lambert walked down the hill to the waterfront. He passed a group of leering men, and jaded women unsteady in their high heels. The river smelt dank and sulphurous. He crossed the road towards a large water feature which spewed jets of regurgitated water into the air. Youngsters sat on concrete walls and wooden benches smoking and nursing cans of energy drink.

As he headed out of the centre, he spotted the same silver Mercedes from earlier that evening, parked on a side street. He walked up Gloucester Road, trying to draw the car out. The area had improved since he'd been a student. Coffee shops, trendy bars and a multitude of restaurants lined the street. Yet, it still retained that air of darkness he'd always associated with the place, as if the bulbs in the street lamps were a few watts dimmer.

A group of six men in their early to mid-twenties passed him as he rounded a corner. One of their number barged into him, his shoulder forcibly jarring Lambert's left arm. Lambert slowed down but the group didn't stop. The man had probably been too drunk to even realise he'd made contact.

The car reappeared, two hundred yards in the distance. Lambert took a side street, and upped his pace along streets he didn't recognise. He found himself in the St Pauls area. Most of his previous fear about the region had been the result of ignorance. At University, the talk at the student bar had been about gangs of locals who would attack any passing student, legends of smashed bottles and knife wounds. The St Pauls riots had occurred years before Lambert joined the University. It was decades ago now. In comparison to the streets and the estates he had worked on as a beat cop in London, this place was a wonderland populated by reasonably well-maintained Victorian houses, and the occasional new build.

The car still followed. Lambert knew he'd taken a risk leaving the main road. He continued walking until he came to a dimly lit subway which led to the drab grey buildings of the Frenton estate. Three youths guarded the entrance to the subway, all three were dressed in black hoodies and sat atop BMX bikes. Lambert put their ages somewhere between fourteen and sixteen. The youths glared at Lambert but said nothing as he walked past them, his eyes focused ahead. The subway tunnel smelt of stale urine and something akin to fungus. Damaged light bulbs flickered on the ceiling, highlighting images of crudely sprayed graffiti. At the other end of the tunnel were three almost identical youths. One of them stopped him.

'All right?' said the youth, in a thick West Country drawl.

Lambert lowered his head a touch. The boy hesitated and let him pass. Three high-rise buildings, grey and featureless, were the centrepiece of the estate. Light shone out from the buildings, the occasional blank face looking down on him.

He moved through the complex, the stench of rubbish bins billowing out from building one. Bin bags were piled high next to the entry for the stairwell. From one of the lower levels came the powerful thump of some form of dance music. To Lambert's ears the bass was out of sync. The noise vibrated, shaking the windows. As he walked into the courtyard area, the stench of the dustbins was replaced by the aroma of something more exotic. Two men followed him into the poorly lit area.

They were both over six foot tall. The shorter of the two was black, dressed in dirty jeans and a navy blue hoody. The taller man was Mediterranean, possible Italian. He had thick broad shoulders and a fake diamond stud in his ear.

'What the fuck do you want?' said the black man.

Lambert stared them down. He tried not to move his head as he calculated the different exit points. He glanced up to see if anyone was watching from the towers. His chosen exit was at two o'clock on the north-east corner. It ran between building one and two. A lane led back onto the street where he could disappear amongst the shadows.

'I said, what the fuck do you want?' repeated the man.

Lambert's attention was focused on the second man who was silent. Up close, he towered above him at least six foot four.

The black man pulled down his hood revealing a large dome of a skull and moved towards Lambert, his movements large and exaggerated. Lambert knew the display all too well.

'Are you fucking deaf?' said the man, swiping his right arm up in a short, sharp, diagonal movement.

The other man stood calculating Lambert, sizing him up. Finally he moved over and joined his companion.

'Are you five-O?' he said.

Lambert smirked as he tried to control the slight tremble in his limbs from the adrenalin. 'They still use that term?' he replied.

'Fuck me,' said the black man, who was moving from foot to foot as if the ground beneath him was alight.

Neither man had a Bristolian accent. Their aggressiveness sounded forced but he couldn't dismiss their potential threat. He could tell by the position of their hands that both carried weapons. 'Why are you following me?' he asked.

The three of them stood in silence before the Mediterranean attacked. 'Fuck this,' he said, aiming a loose punch at Lambert's head.

Lambert swerved and counteracted the move with a sharp elbow to the man's kidneys. The man fell to his knees. Lambert should have finished the man off with a blow to the head and possibly the back of the neck. But he left him there to recover as the second man ran towards him. The second man had a short flick-knife in his right hand which he lunged at Lambert. Lambert had practised defending such a move thousands of times. He grasped the man's wrist and used his aggressive force against him. The snap of the bone echoed around the courtyard. Lambert kicked the man's kneecap and a second cracking noise rang out in the courtyard, sending the man into a heap before him, next to his groaning friend.

'Who sent you?' said Lambert.

'Fuck you,' said the Mediterranean man.

Lambert was about to drag the men to their feet when flashing blue lights filled the shadows of the courtyard. Lambert waited for a few seconds, then sped through his chosen exit.

He reached the main road in ten minutes and was back at his hotel room by one-thirty.

Chapter 11

Lambert showered and disinfected the minor grazes on his hands. He hadn't looked back once the police arrived. He'd broken the leg of one of his attackers. The man would not have escaped the police. Lambert would have to contend with the possibility that the man would be able to identify him if shown his picture.

He paced the room, replaying the scene in his head until it stopped making sense. It was clear it had been a specific attack, and that he was the intended target, but everything about it had been poorly orchestrated. If the police hadn't arrived then he would have found out why he was being singled out. His only thought at this stage was that he was being warned off the Souljacker case and the two injured men would have easily given up whoever had sent them. If it was a warning then it had backfired. He was more motivated than ever. He wished it was the morning already so he could start working, but he had to try and get some sleep.

He lay in bed and switched off the lights but his body still hummed with adrenalin. Although he could survive on three to four hours a night, too little sleep was dangerous for him especially when not in a controlled environment.

His thoughts returned to the attack. Whoever the assailants were, their work was amateurish. It would have made more sense for them to surprise him, not follow him and announce their presence before attacking. Again, it suggested that they had meant simply to leave him a message and that it had got out of hand, due to their incompetence.

But what was the message and who wanted to send it?

He tried to divert his attention from the scene, his mind replaying it over and over again, the crunch of the man's leg echoing around his head as if the scene was being replayed in his hotel room. His mind drifted, his thoughts turning to Chloe. She'd been nine at the time of the accident. Mature for her age, a child full of curiosity and wonder. A different scene started to play in his head and he heard himself scream before he'd realised he must have briefly slipped into sleep. He sat up and wiped the drool from the side of his mouth, wishing as he did every morning that he could close his eyes and swap places with his daughter.

He switched on the lamp by the side of his bed. Returning to his laptop, he searched through the old case files on the Souljacker murders, reluctantly going over the details of Billy Nolan's murder once more. His own name appeared more than once, as witness, and potential suspect. He started a sub-routine, crosschecking details from the older cases, and the Haydon case.

He scanned through case notes and autopsy reports going back to Clive Hale. The horrific crime scene photographs followed the same pattern. Each of the victim's eyes removed, and the same Latin phrase carved into their skin. On each occasion, the victim had lived through the ordeal of the blinding and carving, the fatal cut of the artery taking place afterwards. Although each victim had a form of anaesthetic in their blood stream, the pathologist could never be sure if the victims had been conscious or not during their attacks.

Lambert arranged the file reports onto a slide show on his laptop. As random images from the murders played out on the screen, Lambert took a bottle of sparkling water from the minibar and paced the room. He considered the murder of Terrence Haydon once more. He made a mental note of potential suspects, and lines of investigations. It was a simple enough job. Terrence's family and friends, his work colleagues, the people he knew from his local church. Nothing the police were not already investigating.

Lambert understood that he was a potential suspect. May had yet to ask him for an alibi for the date of Haydon's murders. He'd enjoyed having dinner with her but knew that, at least in part, she was investigating him.

He sat on his bed and scanned the random pieces of information. At times, it was like looking at an old photo album. Photos of Billy Nolan, Klatzky, and his other friends from his time at University filtered into view, as did an unnerving version of his youthful self.

A photo from the Haydon crime scene cut short his reminiscing. He stopped the slide show and studied the ruptured skin on Haydon's corpse.

In oculis animus habitat. The soul dwells in the eyes.

One of the early theories proposed that the Souljacker was under the illusion he was stealing his victim's soul, as well as their life. It was not a theory which had helped the lead investigator of the original murders, DI Hastings. Lambert had read the case reports enough times to know that Hastings' investigation had failed at every step. He knew from his many conversations with the man since how much this had professionally hurt him. Hastings considered it his one true failure. His investigations failed to uncover any links between the victims, other than their age and sex. No identifiable DNA had ever been found at the scenes. Hastings eventually concluded that the victims were random and Lambert had subsequently agreed with him. But with Terrence's death, Lambert was no longer sure. It was too hard to believe that the connection between Billy and Terrence was coincidental.

The Latin inscription ripped through Haydon's skin, the same exact style as the inscription which had adorned Billy Nolan's body. Lambert retrieved the file Klatzky had given him at the coffee shop from his bag. The picture on the screen of Haydon's corpse was an exact copy of one of the pictures in the file.

Lambert returned to the start of the document on his laptop. He clicked on Simon Klatzky's name and a separate file opened up in a second window with a flattering picture of his friend, twenty years out of date. Next to it, in red capital letters were details of an existing arrest warrant for shoplifting. Klatzky had apparently helped himself to some wine from a supermarket in Plaistow, East London. He'd been caught by a security guard and had been duly charged. He'd failed to turn up to his agreed magistrate's date, and as such, was technically on the run. Something he had failed to tell Lambert.

A combination of that night's events, and Klatzky's behaviour that day, proved too much for Lambert. He picked up his room card and went into the hall. It was four a.m. He knocked on Klatzky's door but there was no answer so he went to the hotel's reception. The desk was deserted. He rang an electric buzzer and waited for five minutes until one of the hotel's staff, a tired-looking woman painted in cheap make-up, appeared.

'I seem to have locked myself out of my room,' said Lambert. The woman smiled, the gesture perfunctory. After checking Lambert's details, she gave him a pass card to Klatzky's room.

Lambert returned to their floor and knocked again on Klatzky's door, as loud as he felt able considering the time of the morning. When there was no answer, he placed the card into the chrome slot in the door. Klatzky's lies helped assuage his guilt for invading his friend's privacy.

It was not a pretty sight. Klatzky lay naked on the bed, next to the black-haired student. Both of them were comatose, not even stirring as Lambert crossed the room.

'Simon, it's Michael,' he whispered into Klatzky's ear.

Klatzky didn't stir. The room stank of alcohol, cigarettes and something else Lambert didn't want to consider at that moment. He lifted Klatzky's head from the pillow. A line of dried vomit trickled from the right-hand corner of his mouth, down his chin and onto the pimpled flesh of his body.

'Wake up, Simon,' said Lambert, slapping the man gently on his cheeks. He didn't want to wake the sleeping student, fearing that she would scream on seeing him there. 'Simon, wake up,' he said, through gritted teeth.

No response.

He considered pulling Klatzky from the bed and kicking him into wakefulness but knew it would be pointless. Instead he scribbled a note on the hotel stationery, instructing Klatzky to contact him as soon as he woke.

Back in his room he chided himself for allowing Klatzky to accompany him on the journey to Bristol. On the laptop, he noticed an entry from one of May's junior officers he'd not spotted before. A robbery had occurred at a local church three weeks before the murder. Part of the missing inventory included a package of incense. May had not shared this information with him. The church was located in Weston-super-Mare, the same town where Haydon's father lived, the same place May had instructed him not to visit.

Giving up on sleep, he showered again and changed. Downstairs, he arranged for a hire car to be delivered to the hotel. He ordered a light breakfast of scrambled eggs and wholemeal toast and ate alone in the hotel's restaurant. He told the tired-looking receptionist that Klatzky would be checking out that day and gave her the pass key to Klatzky's room. 'You may need a few reminder calls to get my friend out of bed,' he told her.

The hire car arrived at six-thirty a.m. Five minutes into the journey his phone rang.

'Inspector May,' he said, turning on the phone's hands-free system. 'You have incredible timing. You're not watching me, are you?'

Chapter 12

Lance didn't know the injured man's name and didn't want to know. He just wanted him to be quiet. The man lay in the back of the van, his friend motionless next to him. They were two strangers Lance had first met the day before, hired to do one job which they had royally fucked up earlier that night, a job Lance had been supervising.

The roads surrounding Frenchay hospital were quiet in the early morning, and they managed to make quick time away from the place. The injured man howled in pain. On removing him from the hospital, they'd had to rip out the morphine drip which had been pumping painkiller into his system at intermittent intervals. The injured man's black skin had turned a shade of blue. He writhed in convulsions as if Lambert had shattered his leg that very second. He'd been due for an operation that morning. The consultant had mentioned pins, and metal plates. Lance kept stealing glances at the damaged limb in his rear-view mirror. Alien in size and colour, the leg was bent at an odd inverted angle. No wonder the guy was in agony.

'Can you shut him up?' demanded Lance.

'What do you want me to do? Put a pillow over his head?'

Lance could barely hear the second man over the din of the howling. The comment may have been sarcastic, but everything considered it would probably be the best thing for him.

Five minutes from their destination, a safe house in Bedminster, Lance called the number he'd been given. He told the person who answered, a third man whose name he didn't know, their ETA. 'You better have something ready for him, or the noise is going to attract attention.'

Lance manoeuvred the van down a side street, and up the gravel drive of what appeared to be a deserted house. The garage doors had been left open and he parked inside. The doors slid shut as he switched off the engine, flooding the interior in darkness. The injured man began screaming again.

A side door opened, and two men entered the garage. Lance left the van. Together they opened the back door and, with the help of Lance's colleague, hoisted the injured man out of the van. The screams reverberated around the hollow confines of the garage.

'Don't worry, mate, we've something for you inside. Hold on for a couple more minutes,' said one of the men.

Lance left the key in the ignition and followed the men into the interior of the house. They carried the injured man into a large open space, the partitions to all the downstairs rooms having been knocked out to create the area. They placed the body on the uncarpeted floor. One of the men produced a syringe from a cloth bag, and filled it with a clear liquid. 'This will see you good,' he said, spearing the injured man's upper thigh.

The man stooped struggling. For a second Lance thought he was dead. Then he saw his chest move, taking in shallow breaths.

Four conscious men, one unconscious. No one knew anyone's name. It was the way Campbell wanted it. The less you knew, the less you could talk.

'You're the driver,' said the man Lance had spoken to on the phone.

Lance nodded.

'New instructions. Leave the van here.' He gave Lance a set of keys, and a piece of paper with an address on it. 'It's on the main road. You can go through the front door.'

Lance left the building alone.

Chapter 13

Although the remark had been flippant, it was conceivable that one of May's colleagues had monitored him leaving the hotel and relayed the information to their superior.

'How can you ask me that, Michael, after last night?' replied May, a mischievous lilt to her voice. 'Actually, I was wondering if you could pop into the office when you are free. We have someone here you might wish to speak to.' She refused to divulge any more details.

Lambert pulled over and checked his rear-view mirror. It didn't seem as if anyone was following him. Deciding to postpone his visit to Haydon's father until later, he drove the short distance to Sarah May's police station. He parked the car and walked into the station. They had moved the incident room from the newer police headquarters in Portishead, to the central station on Bridewell Street.

'Michael Lambert to see DI May,' he said, to the duty sergeant.

The duty sergeant studied him as if verifying he was actually there. 'You're Michael Lambert?' he said, as if something about his appearance made this unlikely.

'I'm here at her request,' he said, his tone dropping an octave as he locked onto the sergeant's gaze.

The sergeant scratched a line of hair which fell from his

chin. 'Inspector May's expecting you?' he asked, as if Lambert had yet to speak.

Lambert pinched his nose, blinked his eyes. 'Do you need to see some identification, Sergeant? Pick up the phone and speak to her. She called me ten minutes ago.' Up close, he could smell the fetid breath of the man who had probably been at the desk all night. He could excuse the coldness in the man's tone, it was his station and Lambert was an outsider, but drew a line at disrespect.

The sergeant scratched his chin again, his eyes not leaving Lambert's, as if he was too tired to turn his face away. Lambert was about to reach over and strike the man into action when a door to Lambert's left buzzed open. 'Second floor.'

May stood at the top of the stairs, waiting. 'Michael, how are you?' she asked, immaculate in a sharp grey suit.

'So what's the great mystery?' he asked, though he had a good idea why she'd asked to see him.

'Come on through.'

The open-plan office was alive with sleep-starved officers already busy on their phones, punching keys on their computers. 'What's going on in here?'

May rubbed her eyes. 'There was a bit of fun last night on the Frenton Estate. Three men were involved in a fight.'

'And that's unusual?'

'Obviously not. We arrested one of the men, had to take him to hospital with a broken leg and wrist.'

The sound of the man's leg snapping echoed again in Lambert's head. He couldn't feel any remorse for what he'd done. He'd been under attack, and in many ways the two men had escaped lightly. After joining The Group, Tillman had insisted that Lambert undergo extensive special operations training. He'd spent three months in the UK, followed by a ten-week course in the States. He'd been trained to use extreme force when under attack and in many ways he'd held back last night. Lambert shrugged. 'And?'

'Only he escaped from the hospital this morning.'

'I see,' said Lambert. The incident explained the frantic scenes in the office, and the tired looks on May's colleagues. Lambert imagined there hadn't been much security at the hospital. It suggested that there were more than two of them involved, as it was unlikely that the Mediterranean-looking man had helped the injured man escape alone. 'Was he under arrest at the time?'

'We were waiting to question him.'

'Could be worse,' said Lambert.

'It's the last thing I need at the moment, though,' said May.

A sea of faces watched Lambert as he followed May into the open-plan office. He recognised the unwelcoming glare of police officers when a stranger entered their home turf all too well. The eyes analysed him, reached conclusions. Lambert had been a suspect on the original Souljacker case and here he was again. Most of the office would know about his past and possibly considered him a suspect now. He would have thought that being one of them, albeit on a leave of absence, would give him some dispensation. At the moment, he couldn't tell.

A straight-backed man, in his early sixties stood and greeted him. 'Michael Lambert,' he said, his face not betraying any sense of emotion.

'I thought it might be you, sir,' said Lambert, shaking hands with the retired Chief Superintendent, Julian Hastings. Lambert hadn't seen the man in over ten years. Time had softened him a bit. His stomach carried more weight and his face was rounder than before, but his eyes had retained their sharp quality.

'Inspector May here wanted a quick chat with me about this new incident. She mentioned you were back in town.'

'Yes, visiting old haunts.'

'Take a seat,' said May. Three other officers sat around the table with Hastings but no further introductions were made.

May stood at the head of the table. An incident board hung on the wall behind her decorated with pictures of the ten Souljacker victims, before and after their attacks. Various lines had been added onto the board linking the photos with other images at the periphery of the board: former victims, family members, friends, colleagues, and potential suspects. Lambert had studied an almost replica version of the board on The System back at his hotel. He'd analysed each link and knew the past histories of everyone involved.

'Chief Superintendent Hastings has been helping us fill in some missing gaps on the previous Souljacker murders,' said May.

Lambert noted the predominantly male workforce. 'What have you learnt?' asked Lambert.

'Not much I'm afraid, Michael,' said Hastings. His voice was an octave lower than the last time they'd met, now a gravelly tenor. 'These guys are pretty thorough.'

'You're being modest there, sir,' said May. 'But we thought you may be able to add to what Chief Superintendent Hastings has told us, Mr Lambert.' The sociable, even flirtatious May he'd dined with the previous evening had disappeared.

'How can I help?'

'As you can imagine, we're trying to find a link between the old victims and Terrence Haydon. Chief Superintendent Hastings can find no mention of Haydon in his previous notes, apart from a brief statement from him. Did Haydon and Billy Nolan know each other?'

'They knew each other,' said Lambert, 'though not very well as far as I'm aware. Haydon lived one floor above Billy at University and he wasn't really in Billy's social circle. My social circle. I thought that would have been in your notes, sir.' It should also have been in May's notes, as he had told her as much the previous day.

Hastings turned towards him, the slightest nod of his head.

'Is there any way they could have known each other outside your social circle?' said May.

'Such as?'

'Any groups they may have gone to, classes they may have shared?'

Lambert thought about the church angle May had mentioned last night. 'Terrence studied theology, Billy studied English. Their paths wouldn't have crossed in lectures. 'I don't know if Terrence was a member of any club or association. From what I know of Billy, and from what I remember about Haydon, their interests were not very similar. I do remember one thing though.'

May tilted her head, signalling him to continue.

'I remember Haydon commenting on the smell of incense once we'd broken down Billy's door. He said it was like the incense they used in church.'

The police officers exchanged glances. Lambert waited for

them to share their information about the stolen incense which had appeared on The System earlier that morning.

'So Haydon saw the crime scene?' asked May.

'Yes. A lot of the students had a peek before the police arrived, those who could stomach it. I imagine most wished they hadn't afterwards.'

'And you remember him specifically commenting on the incense?' said May.

'It was a long time ago, but I seem to remember it was him that noticed it. Most of us didn't go to church. We thought it was standard student stuff, the embers of a joss stick. I think it was frankincense or something?'

'Pontifical Incense,' said one of the detectives sitting to May's right, a surly-looking man in a cheap linen suit.

'DS Bradbury,' said May.

Lambert nodded at the detective who didn't acknowledge the gesture.

May sat down, the lightness returning to her eyes. 'Whilst you're here, Mr Lambert, maybe we could take advantage of your experience.' She acted like they hadn't met the previous evening, hadn't already discussed the case in full. It was possible she hadn't told Bradbury about their meeting, or that it was a show for Hastings.

'I'm here to help,' said Lambert.

'Before you arrived, we were discussing the possible motivation for the killer starting again eighteen years on.'

'My initial thought would be unfinished business. It's possible that Haydon was his original target, not Nolan,' said Lambert. Though not entirely convinced by this theory, he wanted to gauge the reaction in the room.

Hastings' face remained impassive.

'And he waited eighteen years to correct his mistake?' sneered DS Bradbury.

'Who knows what he's been up to during that time? Maybe he was close to being discovered after Nolan's murder. Perhaps he was spooked, was waiting for the Chief Super here to retire.'

Hastings didn't respond.

'Perhaps we should move on to your friend, Mr Lambert,' said Bradbury, rubbing a loose strand of black hair from his forehead. The DS lacked subtlety. The mood in the room had changed in an instant from a friendly, professional consultation, to something of an interrogation. Lambert allowed it to continue, kept his body language neutral.

'Which friend?'

'Simon Klatzky.'

Lambert crossed his arms and waited for the DS to elaborate.

May sent Bradbury a warning look but the DC composed himself and continued. 'Were you aware that Mr Klatzky has an outstanding arrest warrant?'

'I wasn't, no. What for?'

'He failed to turn up at a Magistrate's hearing.'

May raised her shoulders apologetically. 'Oh, what charge?' asked Lambert.

'Shoplifting.'

'Did you not think to pick him up yesterday? I thought you knew he was with me,' said Lambert. Although unfazed by the questioning, the inconsistency of it all was beginning to annoy him.

'We couldn't care less about his arrest warrant,' said Bradbury. 'We're keen to know what he's doing with you, what you're both doing here.'

'Thank you, Jack,' said May, trying to ease the growing tension. 'What DS Bradbury is really asking is, is there anything we should know about Klatzky? Did he have a relationship with Nolan in any way?'

'Well, they were best friends, Inspector. I think that is common knowledge.'

'And Haydon?'

'Again, we were a close-knit group. There were six of us, and Haydon had no part in that group. We would only ever see him in the halls. Klatzky would be better able to answer that for himself.'

'You have no reason to believe that Klatzky would want to hurt Terrence Haydon in any way?' asked Bradbury. 'Maybe settle some old score from University?'

'You will need to be more specific. What old score could they have?'

'A girl or something?'

Lambert sighed. 'Have you seen the photos of Klatzky at University? Or now? This is not someone who has ever had trouble with girls, or anyone for that matter. Read your reports more carefully.' He stood up, tired of the interrogation, the rudeness of Bradbury's approach, the general ineptitude. 'Well, thanks for the meeting.'

'Sit down, Mr Lambert,' said Bradbury, placing his hand on Lambert's arm.

Lambert tensed. 'Remove your hand,' he said.

'Or what?' said Bradbury.

'Sit down, DS Bradbury,' said May. 'Thanks for your help, Mr Lambert. We'll invite Mr Klatzky in for questioning shortly.'

Lambert exchanged a quick look with the chastened DS,

then, 'Good to see you again, sir,' he said, turning towards Hastings, who stood to shake his hand.

'Michael.'

As Lambert walked towards the exit, an officer rushed through the door, shoulder-charging him out of the way. 'Inspector, you have to see this,' he said, handing a piece of folded paper to May.

Lambert waited by the door as May read the note.

Bradbury walked over and with a mocking smile slammed the door shut in his face.

Chapter 14

Lambert started the car and sped away from the station. His pulse raced and he opened the car's window, the early morning breeze cooling his skin. He clenched the steering wheel as he pictured DS Bradbury slamming the door in his face, and laughed as he realised he was overacting. Bradbury was nothing more than a little jumpstart and would get what was coming to him. He would call May later and sort everything out. They should never have discussed Klatzky like that in front of him.

The escape from the hospital was more of a concern to him. Everything pointed to some type of team being involved. It had to relate to the Souljacker case, and that possibility opened up so many new avenues it made his head swim. New questions sprung to his mind as he drove. Did the Souljacker have a team working for him? Or was there more than one killer? Neither explanation explained why Klatzky had been sent the photos, or why the two men had followed and attacked Lambert last night.

Thirty minutes later he arrived in Weston-super-Mare. He drove along the seafront, stealing glances at an expanse of dull sand blurred into thick, brown mud. If there was any sea it was out close to the horizon. He'd visited the town occasionally whilst at University, and couldn't remember a time when the tide had been in. He drove out of the centre until he reached the estate where Terrence Haydon's father resided. Roger Haydon lived in a red brick house identical to a line of other buildings, all of which had been purpose-built sometime in the eighties. Weeds poked through the concrete path leading to Haydon's front door, the smell of blocked drains in the air.

Lambert knocked on the door but there was no answer, the faded patterned curtains behind the front window drawn shut. Lambert knocked again, harder this time. As he did so he heard the sound of footsteps behind him.

'What do you want?'

Lambert turned. Before him stood a young man, possibly in his late teens. He had the bulk of a rugby player and the eyes of someone very much older. He held a clear plastic bag which contained two large bottles of White Lightning Cider. His body swayed as he stood staring at Lambert. 'What do you want?' he repeated, his voice slurred.

'I'm here to see Mr Haydon.'

'He's not in,' said the man, who stood poised, his knees bent as if about to pounce.

'And you are?' asked Lambert.

'Who am I? Who the fuck are you?'

'I'm a friend of Terrence, Mr Haydon's son.'

The boy relaxed his posture. 'Terrence is dead,' he said, seemingly confused by the exchange.

'I know. I've come to pay my condolences.'

'Wait there,' said the boy. He opened the door and went inside. Lambert waited as, for the second time that day, someone slammed a door shut in his face.

Lambert waited five minutes before knocking again. The boy had been so out of it that it was possible he'd forgotten their exchange by the time he'd slammed the door shut. Lambert's patience was running out. He knocked for the last time and began counting to sixty.

He reached fifty-nine and was about to force the door when it was opened. The boy stood in the doorway, a glass of clear cider in one hand, the other jammed across the door frame as a barrier. 'What did you say your name was again?' he slurred.

'Michael Lambert. I was a friend of Terrence at University.'

The boy looked him up and down then moved aside to let him through. The house was ripe with body odour. A dimly lit hallway led to the cramped interior of what Lambert presumed was the living room. The room could have come straight out of the 1970s. Everything was tinged with brown. The curtains were pulled shut, with only a small lamp on the corner table giving the room any illumination. On a tattered cloth sofa sat an elderly man wearing boxer shorts and a stained vest. Like the boy, he drank cider from a pint glass.

'Mr Haydon?' asked Lambert.

'Depends who's asking.' The man's voice surprised Lambert; a booming Welsh accent, lyrical and powerful, coming from the small-framed man.

Lambert explained his connection to Terrence Haydon once more.

'Okay, I'll bite for now. Take a seat. Would you like a drink?'

The teenager stood in the hallway staring at Lambert. His relationship to the elderly man was not clear.

'I'm okay,' said Lambert, 'thank you.'

'Take a seat then. You don't look like someone who'd be a friend of Terrence. How did you know him?' began the father, gulping at the cider.

'We weren't that close. He lived on the floor above me at University. One of my friends told me the terrible news, and I wanted to pay my respects.'

'Really, is that so?' said Haydon, glancing over at the boy.

As Lambert's eyes grew accustomed to the dark, he took in the sparsely decorated room. To his right stood a mahogany sideboard decorated with ashtrays brimming with half-finished cigarettes. Opposite him a bookshelf doubled up as a makeshift drinks cabinet. Whiskey the drink of choice.

Roger Haydon leant forward and refilled his glass from the plastic bottle. His baggy skin hung from his frail frame. His left arm was decorated with a tattoo of a faded blue rose. A long, pronounced vein dissected his meagre bicep muscle. From his seated position, Lambert couldn't see any sign of drug abuse. The man and boy were chronic alcoholics but nothing more. DS Bradbury had interviewed Roger Haydon and had ruled him out as a suspect. Lambert agreed with the assessment but sensed Bradbury had missed something. He remembered Sandra Vernon's visceral reaction when he'd mentioned her ex-husband's name and wanted to know more.

'You say you've come to pay your respects? Surely if you knew Terrence you knew that he wasn't my number one fan.'

'Well, sort of, sir, but I'm a father. I know it is something I would appreciate.'

'You've visited his mum?'

'Yes, I saw her yesterday.'

The boy refilled Haydon's drink and sat next to the man, his red eyes never leaving Lambert's. 'Then you would have seen what she's like?' he said.

'She mentioned that you didn't get to see Terrence much, Mr Haydon.'

'That would be right,' said the boy.

Haydon put his hand on the boy's knee.

'She poisoned him against Roger,' the boy said.

'Poisoned him how?'

Haydon drank his glass in two large gulps. 'Her and her bloody church.'

'Religion was important to Terrence? I know he studied theology at University,' said Lambert.

'There's nothing theological about what her group did. All they preached was hatred.'

'Preached?' asked Lambert.

'I'm not talking about whatever church she is with now. I'm talking about the church she used to go to when Terrence was a child. We lived in South Wales. Sandra followed the boy to Bristol when he moved to University.'

Lambert kept quiet. His experience in such situations was to remain silent, and allow the information to come out.

'You don't have to say anything, Roger,' said the teenager.

'Aw, come on,' said Haydon. 'This man's come all the way to pay his condolences. He should know the full story.'

He refilled his glass, and leant forward. 'We should never have married, but in those days, and I don't want to sound like some stupid old man, but in those days it was the done thing. I knew she went to church, which wasn't so unusual then. Are you a religious man, Mr Lambert?' asked Haydon, changing tack, as if concerned he was insulting Lambert in some way.

'No, no,' said Lambert.

'Well, I don't know about all of them,' continued Haydon, 'but her group, nutcases one and all.'

The boy laughed, and Lambert joined in.

'Of course we should never have done it, but then Terrence came along, which was a wonderful thing. But then I was stuck, Mr Lambert. It's a cliché, but I was stuck in a lie.' The man drank again, his hand shaking.

'He's gay,' said the boy, as if Lambert needed clarification.

Haydon laughed this time. 'I think Mr Lambert's understands that, Thomas, but thank you anyway.'

The boy's acne-pitted skin glowed red with embarrassment. Haydon placed his hand on the boy's arm. 'I would have lived with the lie, as well, for Terrence's sake, but she found out. I could have been a mass murderer and been treated with more compassion. As far as she was concerned, I was evil incarnate.'

'And she made Terrence feel the same way?' asked Lambert.

The young man held Haydon's hand as he began to cry. Lambert wished he hadn't been there under false pretences but knew what was being said could be relevant.

'There was one more thing,' said Haydon, dragging the back of his nicotine-stained hand across his eyes.

'Don't,' urged the boy.

Lambert waited. The teenager, Thomas, was almost as agitated as Haydon. The two of them were an odd pair, sitting together on the sofa, drinking their morning cider, at least forty years between them.

'You don't have to tell him anything,' urged Thomas.

Haydon drained his glass, the younger man dutifully refilling it.

'When Terrence was seven, and Sandra had heard the truth

about me, she wanted me to leave the house. At first I refused to go. It was not for my sake. We were both young and had no experience but even then I knew she was a horrible mother. She was bringing Terrence up in the way of her church and there was nothing I could do about it. When I refused to leave, she threatened me.'

'What with?'

'She said that she would tell the authorities I had…' He moved his head from side to side, the words seemingly hard to say. 'She said she would tell the authorities that I touched Terrence.' The last words came out as a tortured squeak.

Haydon's arm trembled, the tattoo of the blue rose dancing on his skin. Thomas leant over and placed his hand on the man's wrist. 'That's enough,' he urged.

'It was a simple ultimatum, Mr Lambert. She had the backing of her church. She made me doubt myself, and to my eternal shame, I fell for it.'

'You agreed to leave?'

'Not only to leave, but never to see them again. You don't understand, I was a labourer at the time. It was a very small community. Only her and that damn church knew about me. That alone would have been an end to me. With the evil accusations she was suggesting, I would have feared for my life. And ultimately, although it was a very selfish act, I thought it would be better for Terrence.'

'You see, there is no depth to that woman's darkness,' said Thomas, patting Haydon's arm.

'Can I use your bathroom?' asked Lambert.

The younger man nodded not looking in Lambert's direction.

The rest of the house was in a state of decay. Strips of yellowing wallpaper fell from the walls. The carpets were threadbare, decorated with numerous stains. Lambert crept upstairs and peered into the rooms. The upper floor was low-ceilinged. It contained two bedrooms, each with a double bed, and a small unkempt bathroom. Random items of junk cluttered the place. The second bedroom looked as if it belonged to the teenage boy. A couple of posters hung on the drab walls, and a small weights bench sat in one corner. On the sideboard Lambert riffled through a number of old tabloid newspapers, and came across a plastic wallet. He found a driver's licence. The boy's name was Thomas Langtree. According to the licence he was twenty-one years of age. Lambert replaced a couple of bank cards in the wallet and a crumpled five pound note. Nothing else in the room suggested Thomas was a permanent fixture. Lambert placed the wallet back where he'd found it.

He turned to leave but the figure of Thomas Langtree covered the exit.

'What the hell are you doing in here?' asked Langtree, rigid with tension.

'I got lost.'

'You got lost? There are only three rooms up here.'

Lambert held out his hands in mock surrender. 'What's the deal here?' he asked.

'What's it to you?' replied Langtree, not moving from the doorway.

'Curious, that's all.'

'It's none of your business. We look after each other, that's all.'

'What about your parents?'

The question triggered a response. The boy's lips trembled. He assessed Lambert, deciding what his chances would be in a confrontation. 'I think you should leave,' he slurred.

Lambert brushed past him as he left the room, the boy's skin rank with body odour and alcohol. Lambert walked downstairs and returned to the living room, Langtree close behind.

'Before I go, Mr Haydon. Could you tell me when you last saw Terrence?'

'You're not really his friend, are you?' growled the older man. 'What are you? Police?'

'I haven't lied to you, Mr Haydon. I did know your son at University. We weren't exactly the closest of friends. He was an acquaintance and I want to find out what happened to him.'

The two-litre bottle of cider was nearly empty. The old man drank what was left in his glass. 'Tell him, Thomas,' he instructed.

'Oh come on. He's snooping.'

'Just tell him.'

The boy hesitated. 'I saw him on the night he went missing,' he said, eventually.

'Where?' asked Lambert

'I saw him going into a club in Bristol. I hadn't seen him in there before. I didn't realise it was his scene.'

'Have you told the police this?'

'The police don't know Thomas lives here. I decided not to tell them,' said Haydon. 'Now I think I may have made a mistake.'

'It was a gay club,' said Thomas.

'How well did you know Terrence?' Lambert asked Langtree.

'I didn't know him to speak to, but Roger has photos.

I recognised him from them. I've seen him out and about now and then.'

'Was he alone?'

'I didn't go in once I saw him enter. I think he was on his own.' Langtree gave Lambert the name and address of the club.

'Why didn't you tell the police?' Lambert asked before leaving.

Haydon closed his eyes as if disgusted with himself. 'I didn't want his mother finding out.'

Chapter 15

Lambert was back in Bristol within thirty minutes. It was hard to completely accept Roger Haydon's story. He checked through the HOLMES entry once more. Bradbury's report didn't mention Thomas Langtree, or Terrence entering the nightclub on the night of his disappearance. The anger he'd felt at Bradbury's action towards him at the station intensified. His ineptness could have cost dearly.

Lambert parked the hire car. The club was situated off the centre beneath a footbridge. Lambert walked down a darkened lane and stood outside the club. A small gold-plated sign stated that the club opened at ten p.m. Thursday to Sunday. It was only midday and the front doors leading to the club were locked. He knew he should really inform May about his discovery but she could wait. He was disappointed with her for the crude line of questioning at the station that morning.

Lambert found a second door to the side of the building. He turned the handle, and was surprised when it opened. He walked past a shabby glass-fronted booth, and down a winding staircase which led to the cavernous space of the club. Whatever magic the place held when filled with people, music, and lights, was missing now. In the dimness all Lambert could see was a vacant space, and mirrored walls. He tried to picture

Terrence Haydon in such a place but it was impossible to do in the quiet surroundings.

He called out, his voice echoing in the space. He moved across the dance floor, and opened the hatch at the end of one of the bars. A small archway led to a low-ceilinged hallway. Lambert rounded the corner and to his right saw a glass-panel door with the word 'Office' stencilled on it. He was about to turn the door handle when something hard was struck against the back of his head.

His body tensed. Thankfully, the blow was poorly aimed. Lambert staggered but managed to keep his feet. He saw the second blow arrive through the mirrored doorframe and managed to dodge the full force of the impact, his left shoulder taking the brunt. He grabbed the assailant's arm, pushing his elbow into his body. A miniature silver baseball fell from the man's hand. Lambert swung around and pushed the assailant against the office door, his right arm thrust under the man's chin.

'What the hell are you doing?' said Lambert, through gritted teeth, a dull ache spreading across his head.

'You're hurting me,' said the man, taking short, quick intakes of breath.

'I'm hurting you?' Lambert eased the pressure from the man's neck and let him free. 'What was that about?' He rubbed the back of his head thankful not to see any blood on his hand.

The man adjusted his collar and patted down his clothes. 'You're asking me? You're the one who broke in.'

'I'm police,' said Lambert.

The man squinted his eyes. 'Can I see some ID?'

'I'm not that type of police.'

The man glanced down at the dropped baseball bat. 'Bullshit. Get the fuck out of here,' he said, with little conviction.

Lambert picked up the bat to stop it being a distraction. 'Look, I only wanted to ask some questions and the door was open.'

The man backed away. 'I was expecting a delivery. Not someone wandering through my club. We've had some break-ins before.'

'Perhaps you should review your security procedures then. I'll level with you. I'm ex-police. A friend of mine has been murdered. He was last seen here on the night he went missing.'

'Oh come on,' said the man.

'Why would I make up such a story?'

'Maybe I should wait for the real police to arrive.'

'Maybe you should. Or maybe you could help me out,' he said, glancing down at the baseball bat in his hand. 'The man's name was Terrence Haydon. You may have read about him in the newspapers.'

The man's face paled. 'What, that Souljacker murder?'

'That's the one.'

'He was here on the night he disappeared?'

'Correct.'

'Why haven't the real police come here then?'

'They don't know yet.' Lambert told the man what Roger Haydon had told him.

'I don't know many of their names. I don't know anyone called Langtree or Haydon.' The man was still on edge, stealing nervous glances at the baseball bat.

'Do you have any CCTV here?' asked Lambert.

'We've two cameras. I can access the details on my PC. Not the greatest system I'm afraid.'

'Show me.' Lambert followed the man into his office, close enough to persuade him not to risk anything stupid.

The man turned on his PC. 'The first camera is outside the club. The other takes a sweeping view of inside. It's a rudimentary system. We only have it for insurance purposes.'

The pictures were fuzzy. Lambert had seen better pictures on mobile phone cameras.

'Could you download a copy of the files for that evening?' asked Lambert.

'I'm not giving you anything,' said the man.

'I'm not asking you to delete anything. Just download those two files.' Lambert placed his left hand on the man's shoulder and squeezed it tight, his fingers reaching the man's neck.

The man began to squirm. 'Fine,' he said, trying to shrug Lambert off. He took a data key from inside a desk drawer. 'When are you going to tell the police?' asked the man once he'd downloaded the files.

'Once I've looked through these. It will give you a chance to clean up anything you don't want them to see. Don't try to follow me,' said Lambert, leaving the office.

'Hey, what was your name again?' said the man, as he left.

Lambert waved the data key at the man and threw him the baseball bat.

He found a coffee shop not far from the club. Whilst waiting for his laptop to load, he called Sophie's mobile which went straight to answerphone. They hadn't talked in over forty-eight hours. Since Chloe's death, this wasn't unusual but he wanted to hear her voice. He considered calling her office but she hated receiving personal calls there. He placed the phone back in his pocket. He ordered a black Americano with an extra shot of espresso and accessed The System through his secured Wi-Fi dongle. He studied the Haydon file on HOLMES once more, confirming that there was no mention of the club, and very little on Roger Haydon save for the brief interview conducted by DS Bradbury.

He loaded the files from the club onto the laptop and found a blurry image of a particularly tall man resembling Terrence Haydon entering at eleven-thirty p.m., and exiting some hours later. He couldn't see anyone with him, but a second man followed him out of the club seconds later. Both videos were next to useless, the images only illuminated by the glare of neon from the club's sign and the internal lights from the surrounding buildings. The second man kept his back to the camera at all times. It was probably coincidental, but Lambert played it over and over and began to wonder if the man was avoiding the camera on purpose. It was conceivable that the blurred image was the killer. He saved the image and emailed it to May with a brief explanation of how he'd obtained it.

His phone rang, an unidentified number. Possibly his wife calling from work.

'Lambert.'

'Michael, it's Julian Hastings. I wanted to call to apologise for this morning's débâcle. That DS was a jumped-up shit. I told young DI May that you shouldn't have been treated that way. Very amateurish.'

Lambert took another sip of coffee before replying. 'Not your fault, sir,' he said.

'That may well be, but I really should have said something when you were there. Anyway, let me make it up to you.'

Hastings' tone never changed during their interaction, always the same, matter-of-fact monotone.

'No need, sir.'

'I am going to give up on stopping you calling me sir, but I would like to share some information with you. I am sure you're desperate to know what the commotion was about when you left?'

Lambert had been too busy since to have given it much thought.

'Another body has been found. Exact same MO as Terrence Haydon.'

Lambert hid his surprise. 'What details can you give me, sir?'

'Not much at the moment, but I would get to London if I was you.'

'The body was found in London?'

'Yes, and this time the victim was a woman.'

Chapter 16

After leaving the safe house, Lance had driven to the hotel in time to see the man they had attacked the previous night, Lambert, leave the car park.

He immediately called in his sighting of Lambert only to be told to sit tight and focus his attention on the other man, Klatzky.

That had been six hours ago. Plenty of time to sit and think about the previous evening's fuck-up. The two men from last night had been incompetent. That worried him. If he didn't know better, if it wasn't impossible, then he would say Campbell was getting sloppy. The two men had not been fit for purpose. He'd sensed it immediately.

Campbell's reaction was impossible to read. If he'd been upset with Lance then it hadn't been evident.

Lance had watched the second man, Klatzky, arrive at the hotel late the previous evening, hand in hand with the young student he'd encountered earlier that day. The woman had been too young, and in Lance's opinion, too pretty for her companion. Both of them had staggered into the hotel foyer.

It had been amusing watching them amble across the street, holding each other up. It was not amusing now, sitting in the car waiting.

The woman had already left. Fifty-eight minutes ago. Her

coat pulled high around the back of her head, she'd snuck out of the hotel as if she knew she was being watched. She'd walked directly past the car, her face deathly white. Lance had felt sorry for her then. He recognised the look of remorse and wondered how willing a partner she'd been to the older man, how much drink he'd had to buy for her to stay the night.

Lance had a daughter and an ex-wife, and shuddered to think of either being in such a situation. It was his reason for being here now. He owed Campbell and Campbell knew of their existence. That was enough.

An hour later, Klatzky stumbled onto the street. Dressed in last night's clothes, he was in an even worse state than the woman. He looked about him like a lost tourist.

Lance left the car and practised his lines as he approached.

'Mr Klatzky?' he said, breathing through his mouth to escape the alcoholic fumes emanating from the man.

'Who are you?' replied Klatzky. The man was on edge. His whole body shaking, his eyes darting in random directions.

'Mr Lambert sent me.'

'Michael? But he's just had me kicked out of the hotel.'

Lance improvised. 'That's why he sent me. To take you back to London.'

Klatzky blinked, absorbing the information.

If he went for his phone, then Lance would have to take action. 'The car is over there,' he said, pointing.

Klatzky shrugged and followed him across the road.

'Please take a seat in the back.'

'Where's Michael?'

Lance locked the doors. 'Care for a drink?' he asked, producing a hip flask from the glove compartment.

Klatzky snatched the drink away and took a heavy gulp.

'Keep it,' said Lance.

He waited for the man to fall asleep before calling it in.

'Change of plan,' said Campbell. 'You need to take him back on your own.'

Lance didn't protest. 'Where shall I meet you?'

'I have made other travel arrangements. Make sure he is secure, and silent,' said Campbell, hanging up.

Twenty minutes later, Lance pulled the car over and climbed into the back seat. 'Sorry, buddy,' he said, cuffing Klatzky's hands behind him and switching off the man's mobile phone. He sealed his mouth shut with perforated tape, and laid the sleeping figure into the recovery position.

Chapter 17

Thirty minutes into the journey May realised she'd made another mistake.

The first mistake had been inviting Lambert to the station that morning. She'd called him on a whim after meeting with Hastings who'd appeared at the station an hour earlier than planned. She'd wanted to see if Lambert could get anything out of the retired policeman who was proving at best elusive. Instead the conversation had unravelled as they discussed Klatzky. She could understand Lambert's reaction and would have reprimanded Bradbury had it not been for the latest development.

Her second mistake had been asking Hastings to accompany her on the journey to London. The news had come through that there had been another Souljacker victim. An incident team had been set up in London, and the SIO, DCI Nielson, had naturally contacted her once the similarities had been discovered. May had instructed Bradbury to stay and head the case during her absence.

Hastings had hardly said a word since they'd set off, following a pattern he'd set earlier that morning. She'd heard more from him in the brief time Lambert had appeared at the station than the rest of the morning combined.

Worse still, she hadn't learnt anything more from him about

the previous Souljacker murders she couldn't have read in the file. His answers to her questions were monosyllabic, bordering on avoidant. She'd invited him to London because she thought he may have had some interesting thoughts on the new victim, and DCI Nielson had made the suggestion.

The body of Sandra Hopkins had been found earlier that morning in a ground-floor flat in Sydenham, southeast London. The address was displayed on May's satnav system.

'Is that near to where you live, sir?' she asked Hastings.

'Right sort of area. Fifteen, twenty miles away.'

'What do you know about the place?'

'Sydenham ? Nothing much. Mixed, like most of London. It's had its problems. Good transport links with Central London.'

May sighed inwardly. 'What do you think about this change of victim?'

Hastings sat stiff-backed, his body pushed back against his seat. 'I've been running it through my mind since we left Bristol. It doesn't make any sense to me. All the previous Souljacker victims were male, aged twenty to thirty, and all the bodies had been found in south west England. This latest victim was a forty-two year old woman and her body is in London. Doesn't ring true to me. I'll be interested to see the victim.'

'From the preliminary reports I received from London the MO was identical,' said May.

Hastings grunted. 'If it's him, why a woman? Why now?'

May sensed the man's frustration, knowing he'd been tracking the Souljacker since the first killings all those years ago. 'I think it could possibly be a good thing,' she said.

Hastings sneered.

'I think he wants to get caught. There's a link between two of the victims, and now days later he kills a woman.'

Hastings didn't respond. He sat motionless, staring ahead through the windscreen.

May continued, undeterred, thinking aloud. 'My guess is this killing is personal. If so, we may find a motive. I would be surprised if there is not something that links this woman, Sandra Hopkins, with either one or both of Haydon and Nolan, and if not them one of the older victims.'

'Quite a leap, Inspector. Let's hope you're right.'

The drive continued in silence, broken only by Hastings' laboured breathing.

'I hope we didn't cause you any embarrassment this morning,' said May, for something to say.

'How would I be embarrassed?'

'With what happened with Michael Lambert. In retrospect I don't think it was handled very well. Particularly not by DS Bradbury.'

'I agree. You need to take more control of your officers.'

May ignored the slight. 'You seemed to get on well with Lambert?'

Hastings turned to look at her, his face a mask devoid of emotion. What would he think if he knew she'd been out for dinner last night with Lambert? Her own feelings about it were jumbled. The evening had been a continuation of their lunchtime meeting. She'd enjoyed Lambert's company, and only a small percentage of the time had been spent discussing the case.

'I've known Michael on and off since that first time during the Nolan case.'

'What was he like back then?' asked May.

'You could tell he was sharp straight off the bat. He was shaken up. They all were. But even then I recognised he had an eye for detail. Meticulous. He recalled things none of the others did. The exact detail of what Nolan had been wearing the last night they'd seen him. Little things about the room. Even what he'd seen of the corpse when he'd broken the door down. I don't know if you'd call it a photographic memory, but he remembered the Latin inscription. The exact position of the body on the floor.'

'What did that lead you to think?' said May.

'I never considered him a suspect if that's what you're getting at.'

'Of course not.'

'I noticed his picture was on the board before he arrived this morning. You don't seriously consider him a suspect do you?'

May ignored the question. 'He told me you put him up to joining the force.'

'I wouldn't go that far,' said Hastings, turning his gaze back to the road. 'He asked me about it and I gave him an insight into what life is like.'

'And he foolishly went ahead anyway,' said May. She turned to look at Hastings. His upper lip rose a touch, the gesture something like a smile. 'I don't know when you last read his file but the last five or six years of it is pretty much blanked out.'

'I can't help you with that. I knew he was transferred to SOCA. Perhaps he was doing some undercover work for them.'

'And the last two years?'

Hastings bristled. 'You don't know?'

'I'd heard some rumours but I didn't want to ask him about it.'

Hastings didn't reply straight away, possibly debating what he should share with her. 'I'll tell you what's public knowledge. There was an accident two years ago. Lambert was driving. His daughter was killed outright and he was hospitalised. He had to endure an enforced coma. Last time I saw him was at his daughter's funeral. He was barely lucid then, still in a wheelchair. I don't know the ins and outs of it but I believe a position in his old team is still open to him. I'd imagine he'd have to pass a psych evaluation, but as far as I'm aware the link has yet to be severed.'

So it was true. His file had not stated why he was currently on leave and she'd only heard rumours. It was not the sort of thing she'd felt comfortable bringing up in conversation the previous night. She didn't question Hastings further.

They came off the M25 and took the A3 to the crime scene in Sydenham. The SIO, DCI Nielson, greeted them. Superintendent Rush had been at pains to point out to her that Nielson was in charge of the Sandra Hopkins case before she'd left Bristol.

'What are you suggesting?' she'd asked.

'I'm not suggesting anything. I simply want you to remember that he will be the SIO. It's his case, and he is a senior officer.'

'You think I'm going to stroll into London and take over?'

'No.' He'd hesitated then. 'Not exactly. But cooperation is the way forward on this. Assistant Chief Constable Regan will be overseeing the joint investigations. So don't go causing a shit storm.'

Motivating parting words were one of Rush's specialties.

May introduced Hastings to Nielson. The men shook hands. 'Good to see you again, Charles,' said Hastings.

Ten years her senior, Nielson had the haircut of a Marine,

and the body of a nightclub bouncer. Albeit, one who was slightly out of shape. His accent was East End London, almost comically so. 'The SOCOs have cleared the crime scene. I have some pictures of the scene here,' he said, handing her a computer tablet. 'Let's go through to the room where the incident took place. You can match the pictures to the location.'

'Thank you,' said May, following.

'You'll be used to the smell,' said Nielson, once inside.

The smell. The sight. Used to it was perhaps not the best way to describe it. Remarkable as it seemed, considering the scene before her, and the pictures she held in her hand, she'd seen worse. She'd worked in the docks in Bristol for a period and had seen her share of mutilation, and decomposing bodies.

One in particular had always stayed with her. Emily Sutton. A retired man found Sutton's body on the banks of the River Avon, close to the Clifton Suspension Bridge. The man who'd been walking a dog, it was always someone walking a dog, had said he'd found the corpse and called it straight in. He apologised to May for the pool of vomit to the side of the body.

The body lay in a puddle of mud, wrapped in a blanket sodden with filth. May remembered the texture of the blanket, the damp material, the stench of urine, as she removed it to uncover the body. The face would haunt her to her dying day. She'd been unable to tell the sex of the victim at the time. The face was hardly a face. It had two misshapen eyes, at misplaced angles to one other. Both cheek bones were smashed, as was the jaw. It was as if someone had taken a sledgehammer to the face, more than once. Reluctantly, May had reached towards the corpse's neck, only to find the faintest of pulses.

Somehow, unlike the figure in the images on the screen

before her now, Emily Sutton survived. She'd undergone extensive facial reconstruction surgery and currently resided in an institute in North Bristol.

Such miracles would not occur with Sandra Hopkins. The first picture showed her lifeless body lying on what was once a beige carpet at the foot of her bed. May looked away from the screen to the patch of maroon on the floor, a number of markers highlighting where Hopkins' corpse had lain before it was discovered. May accustomed herself to the smell. She had learnt early on not to fight it, though she was trying as hard as possible to breathe through her mouth.

She recognised the sickly smell of incense after a few seconds. It didn't mask the gasses of the rotting body, it only highlighted them.

'Sandra Hopkins,' said Nielson. 'Forty-two. Commercial solicitor. Worked out of Liverpool Street. The smell was reported after midnight last night by one of the tenants. A second tenant called early this morning.'

The picture of what once was Sandra Hopkins lay at an awkward angle. A squat black woman, a little over five foot five, her naked body sprawled on the carpet. The Latin phrase, consistent with all the other victims, carved intricately into her bloated stomach. In oculis animus habitat. The soul dwells in the eyes.

May could close her eyes and see the photos of every other Souljacker victim. They'd all been remarkably the same, the removal of the eyes creating an alien visage. The gaping holes made their other features indistinguishable. May looked again at the photos of Hopkins, a mop of black hair matted to her mangled face. If she'd been looking only at her face, May was not sure she would have realised Hopkins was female.

'No sign of sexual molestation, or even signs of a struggle. From what I've read, it follows the pattern of the previous murders. There are two separate puncture wounds where the victim was injected. We believe she was alive, hopefully not conscious, until the carotid artery was slit. We'll know more after the AR.'

Hastings viewed the scene dispassionately. May handed him the tablet, and he flicked through the pictures, occasionally looking up at the crime scene. May wondered if he was thinking about Billy Nolan and the others. It was hard not to take it personally. It was possible he blamed himself for the death of Sandra Hopkins, saw her death as a result of him not catching the killer earlier.

Hastings zoomed in on one of the pictures.

'What is it?' asked Nielson.

'The carving on the body. It looks a bit off to me. Best check it with the others,' said Hastings.

May studied the image. The writing was harder to read on the black skin. The lettering was smaller but she thought it was the same as on the other victims. The Souljacker had carved the Latin onto the male victims' chests. With Hopkins, he'd been forced to improvise, using the soft flesh of her stomach.

'I guess the killer had a couple of objects he needed to work around this time,' said Nielson, prompting a nervous giggle from one of the uniformed officers. Nielson cut it short with a glare. 'We'll get it checked immediately,' he said to Hastings.

May's breathing returned to normal outside. Being in the small confines of Sandra Hopkins' bedroom had been like entering a dislocated world. It was difficult to equate with the bright open space where May now stood. Nielson and Hastings hovered on either side of her, neither speaking.

'We have a sighting of her entering the building yesterday evening,' said Nielson, breaking the silence.

May noticed the two uniformed officers had followed them outside, and stood a few metres behind Nielson like bodyguards.

'A woman from across the street, Gail Lane. She was shutting her bedroom curtains last night, and happened to notice the victim entering the communal front door with a man.'

'Did she know Hopkins?' asked May.

'Not to speak to but she'd seen her on occasions. They sometimes shared the same tube to work but had never talked to one another.'

The dislocation of city life, thought May. Two people who saw each other most days, and couldn't bring themselves to say hello. 'What time did she see them?'

'Approximately nine to nine-thirty p.m. Description of the man is vague at best. Tall, dark hair. Wearing a rain jacket. She only saw the back of him and it was dark.'

'Anyone else in the flat see him come or go?' asked Hastings.

'Not that we are currently aware of. Most of the neighbours are still at work, so we'll catch them this evening.'

'Lovely scene to come home to,' said May.

'Looks like one of them is back early,' said Nielson.

Over to their left, a man was arguing with a young policeman who was guarding the police cordon tape.

May looked over at the figure, and then at Hastings who raised his eyebrows in surprise. The most emotive he'd been all day.

Chapter 18

Three hours earlier, Lambert had left for London without Klatzky, who was not returning any of his calls.

He'd spent twenty minutes negotiating the Bristol traffic and trying to contact Tillman. 'Tell him it's Lambert, for pity's sake,' he informed the third operative he'd spoken to, his hands gripping the steering wheel as if holding it in place.

He was an hour along the motorway by the time Tillman returned his call. 'This is not a secure line, is it?' said Tillman.

'No, but I have nothing secure to tell you.'

'What do you want?'

'I need an update on the latest Souljacker murder.'

'That's not secure?' asked Tillman.

'It's public knowledge, you have a professional interest.'

'That's where you're wrong, Lambert, I couldn't give two shits.'

'I'm driving towards London. I need some detail.' Over the years, Lambert had come to realise it was often best to ignore his superior. Tillman liked to reaffirm his authority but could be counted on to help out when necessary.

'What is it exactly you need to know?'

'He's killed a woman.'

'So I've heard.'

'Do you have a name?'

'I'm beginning to regret giving you access to The System, Lambert. I'm trying to decide if you're too close to this.'

'Of course I'm fucking close to it, Glenn. You knew that before you gave me access.' Lambert's pulse quickened, a familiar rage threatening to reach the surface.

'I've already heard some chatter from Bristol.'

'Chatter? Fuck that, Glenn. Just tell me what you know.'

Tillman didn't normally accept such insolence. Lambert imagined him on the other end of the line, debating if it was time to cut him off. Thinking about the favour he owed.

'The victim is Sandra Hopkins. A solicitor. Her firm has offices in Bristol and London but she works out of the London office. Liverpool Street. She was found this morning by the caretaker at her block of flats.'

'Where?'

'Sydenham.'

Lambert relaxed his grip on the steering wheel, his heart rate returning to normal. The car entered an average speed zone which he ignored, snaking in and out of the slowing traffic. The other drivers flashed their headlights, or made obscene hand gestures as if his speeding was the most important thing in their life. The car limped onwards, a reel of mundane green scenery playing out in Lambert's peripheral vision.

'Thank you, sir.'

'I'll send you through the exact coordinates,' said Tillman, hanging up.

He agreed with Tillman that he was too close to the case and realised he had to detach himself emotionally. Lambert had spent his whole professional life looking at the small details. That was his expertise, why Tillman had recruited him for The

Group. And the small details were not making much sense to him at the moment. There were too many discrepancies. It was not impossible that the killer had started again after so many years. It was also plausible that the long period of silence had caused the changes which had led to a female victim. Nevertheless, Lambert had a sense that things were a little too orchestrated. He'd been followed and attacked the previous evening, had possibly been under surveillance by the police in Bristol, and then there were the photos which had been sent to Klatzky. Someone wanted him involved in this case, for whatever reason, and he wasn't sure at the moment who he could trust.

It took him a further hour to reach south-east London. May was already at the crime scene. She was standing beyond the police tape, talking with Julian Hastings, and a second man.

Hasting stood expressionless listening to the other man speak. In contrast, May's body language was more open. She nodded as the man spoke, glanced at Hastings who remained passive.

'Can you tell DI May that Michael Lambert is here to see her,' Lambert said to the uniformed policeman guarding the tape.

'Is she expecting you?'

Lambert glared at the officer who decided not to take the questioning any further, beckoning over a colleague to guard the tape.

The constable whispered his message in May's ear and she broke conversation and looked over. She exchanged words with the man next to Hastings and signalled to Lambert.

'Shall I even ask how you found us?' asked May, as Lambert approached.

'I have a little of my own investigative ability,' replied Lambert, nodding in Hasting's direction.

'Michael, this is DCI Nielson. Michael Lambert, sir,' said May.

Nielson scowled and didn't offer his hand. 'Mr Lambert. DI May has informed me of your interest in this case.'

Lambert nodded, taking an instant dislike to the man. Lambert was still technically a DCI himself, despite his leave of absence. He knew what the man would say next.

Nielson rocked on his heels. He had the upper body of a nightclub bouncer who had not visited the gym in a few months, his cheap navy suit a size too small for him. 'Whilst I appreciate your experience, and…' he struggled for the word, 'expertise, I need to state now that we will not tolerate any interference from you.'

Lambert mirrored Hastings' non-committal body language.

'That extends to questioning anyone involved in this case. Do we have an understanding?'

'What can you tell me about the victim?' asked Lambert, as if he hadn't heard.

Nielson rubbed his hand through his close-shave haircut and looked at May, expecting support.

'Sandra Hopkins,' said May. 'Forty-two-year-old solicitor. She was on annual leave. No one at her work has heard from her in the last three days.'

'Time of death?'

Nielson grimaced. 'The last twelve to eighteen hours. This is not public information, Mr Lambert. You are not involved in this case.'

'I understand that but I could find out all the details with one phone call. It would be easier if you could share the basic details. I won't interfere. If I come up with anything potentially useful I will share it with you.'

Nielson sighed and pulled his jacket tight against his huge frame.

'Could I see the crime scene?' added Lambert.

'I can vouch for him,' interjected Hastings.

'Whilst I appreciate that, sir, it's not the point.'

'Let me accompany Mr Lambert,' said May. 'The scene has been released now so he can't do any damage.'

'Ten minutes,' said Nielson, walking away.

'Hopkins' landlord, Geoffrey Moon, found the body,' said May, leading Lambert inside.

Although the SOCOs had removed the mutilated corpse some time ago, the air was still heavy with the scent of incense. It prompted two emotional memories from Lambert. One from his childhood, alone at mass on a Sunday morning, the other from the time he'd discovered Billy Nolan's body. Neither were positive associations. The scene had been photographed and videoed, small markers placed on the floor where Hopkins had endured her last minutes.

'No sign of a break-in,' said May.

'You think Hopkins knew the killer?'

'At least well enough to invite him into her house.' She told him about a neighbour seeing Hopkins entering the building with a man. 'Thank you for the information you received from Haydon's father, by the way. I've sent a team over to the club.'

Lambert knew the admission was embarrassing for May.

'Try not to piss Nielson off, though,' she continued, handing him a computer tablet. 'Here, these are the photos from today.'

Lambert grimaced, trying to detach himself from what he was seeing. Like Haydon, Sandra Hopkins had been found with her eyes removed and the usual inscription carved into her stomach. 'Was she alive throughout the attack?'

'We believe so. Do you really think the killer believes he takes their souls when he kills them?' asked May.

'No,' replied Lambert. 'The papers invented that part of the story.'

'Didn't Hasting investigate the religious aspect?'

'Yes, but that had a lot to do with the Latin and the incense.'

'We think we know where the incense at Haydon's crime scene came from. A small church in Weston-super-Mare. We're going to check the incense on Hopkins' body. See if it comes from the same source.'

'It's amazing what they can do with incense processing nowadays,' said Lambert.

'Staggering how we've developed in the last few years,' replied May, playing along with the joke.

'Anyway, I've had to reassess my working theory. In the past, I thought it was some religious nut-job making a point about immorality. Though I still don't know why Billy Nolan was victimised,' said Lambert.

'Wasn't he immoral?'

'Aren't we all?'

'We know that at least four of the victims were homosexual. From what we've discovered, thanks primarily to you, it's possible Haydon was gay.'

'Looks that way. You should speak to Hastings. They looked at the hate crime angle.'

'Was Billy Nolan gay?'

'He did a good job concealing it if he was. What about Hopkins?' asked Lambert.

'From what Nielson has ascertained, she was known to date men and women.'

They walked outside. The sky had darkened. A scattering of officers still manned the street outside Hopkins' flat. 'So you'll be working the two cases in tandem with Nielson?'

'For the time being.'

'Are you staying in London?'

May smirked. 'For the time being.'

Lambert went to say something but stopped. His mouth was dry and he realised he hadn't had anything to drink since leaving Bristol. May was staring at him, that slight tilt of her mouth suggesting that she wanted him to ask her something.

In the end she broke the silence. 'Care to show me around?'

Lambert hesitated, and May interrupted him before he had time to speak. 'No, don't worry. I'm sure you have other things to do.'

Lambert went to argue but the moment had been lost. 'I've a few things to catch up on,' he said, hoping the heat he sensed spreading on his face wasn't visible.

'That's fine,' said May, walking away. Twenty metres down the road, she stopped. The breath caught in Lambert's throat as she returned, handing him a card with her hotel details on it. 'I'm staying here, if you change your mind,' she said.

Lambert took the card without replying, hoped he didn't look too dumbstruck.

Lambert called Sophie's office on the drive home. Sydenham was only a couple of miles away from his house, and he couldn't help but dwell on the possible coincidence. 'I'm afraid she's going straight to answerphone,' said one of the firm's reception-ists. 'Would you like to leave a message?'

'No, that's fine. I'll try her mobile again.' The mobile went straight to answerphone.

The house was empty. It felt like he'd been away for longer than a day. He didn't call out. Sophie would still be at work, or dining out with a client, or one of the firm's partners. Lambert placed a ready meal in the microwave and moped around the house, restless.

He stopped at Sophie's bedroom door. Cursing himself, he opened it. Light blue sheets were pulled tight across the mattress. He checked her bathroom. There were no signs that she'd showered there that morning. The towels were dry as were the bristles on her toothbrush. 'Idiot,' he mouthed to himself, wondering when he would resort to reading her emails, or intercepting her text messages.

He walked along the corridor to Chloe's room. She would have been eleven this year. He hadn't been in her room since the accident, couldn't face the potential memories it would evoke, but could picture it with total clarity. His hand went to the door handle, when a shrill ring from the oven's timer diverted his attention.

Lambert laboured over his ready meal and retreated to his office. A note on The System signalled a private message from Tillman. It was an update on the Souljacker case. The detail was as thin as he'd expected. He'd learnt more from attending the crime scene.

He searched The System for details on Sandra Hopkins. Information came in from various sources. Nielson's team had entered the case on HOLMES. Lambert read details of the preliminary investigations, statements from Hopkins' neighbours, colleagues, friends and family. Lambert composed a file on the woman from records he accessed from her firm's database, her social media and email accounts. He didn't see anything salacious. She was a forty-two-year-old professional woman, single, no children. From her emails it looked as if she was dating two women she'd met on a dating site. He crosschecked with HOLMES, discovering that the police had already interviewed both women.

DCI Nielson had already made a tenuous link between Hopkins and the other victims. Hopkins had studied at Bristol University and had been completing her training contract with a local firm of solicitors during the period when Billy Nolan was murdered. She was still with the same firm but had been working out of one of their London offices for the last ten years specialising in contract law.

For the sake of completion, Lambert ran a sub-routine cross referencing Sandra Hopkins with the other victims, and narrowed the search to her, Billy Nolan, and Terrence Haydon but again came up blank.

He shut down The System and called Sophie's mobile for a final time. He needed to hear her voice. He felt absurdly alone in the house, still reeled from having almost entered Chloe's room. He hung up on the answerphone message, regretful that his wife would see so many missed calls. The tension of the case was getting to him. He checked in with Klatzky who was also avoiding him.

He'd only know her for twenty-four hours but his thoughts kept returning to Sarah May, and the brief time they'd spent together alone. He took her card from his wallet and turned it over in his hands. It was a dangerous game, and the wrong time to play it. He paced the lower floor of his house debating it. 'Fuck it,' he mouthed, and called her.

They met at a poorly lit pub in Bromley. The gloom hid the faded carpet and scratch marks on the wooden furniture. Lambert ordered a bottle of red wine, grimacing on his first sip.

'I can taste hints of copper, and rust,' he said.

May leant forward and winced as she drank from her glass. Her skin looked fresh, a gleam in her eyes. The tiredness he'd noticed in her before evaporated. She twisted her hair with her left hand and held his gaze. 'What do you expect for £8 a bottle?'

'Fair point. So how are you finding the big smoke?'

'You kidding? This is my home town.'

'You're a cockney?' Lambert already knew she had studied in London from her file. He was surprised again at how relaxed he felt in her company.

'Something like that. North of the river, though.'

'Snob,' replied Lambert. 'I'm sarf London.'

'Well, I did venture south for University. Goldsmiths.'

Lambert took a second sip of wine, the taste mellowing. 'How come you're in Bristol?'

May shrugged. 'Just worked out that way. I followed the openings.'

'Would you like to return one day?'

'It's only ninety minutes on the train,' she said.

Lambert tried not to read anything into the sentence. He took a longer drink of the wine, glad he'd decided to call her. Although she put him at ease, there was something intriguing about her. She gave conflicting signals and he found himself enjoying the challenge of being in her company.

'Sorry again about this morning. DS Bradbury is a strong copper but can be a tad aggressive with strangers. It was clumsy,' said May.

'No need to explain. How's the investigation at the nightclub going?'

'We received a warrant to close the place down for the night. Not expecting much but you never know. Apparently the owner, a Mr Collins, is a little bit shaken.'

'Really?' said Lambert, rubbing the back of his head where the nightclub owner had attacked him. 'And Roger Haydon?'

'We went to speak to him but he wasn't at his house. We have a car waiting for his return. We plan to speak to Mr Langtree as well.'

May agreed to a second bottle of wine. 'I'll leave the majority of the drinking to you, though,' she said. 'I don't want to turn up to my first full day in London with a hangover now, do I?'

'Hastings has a lot of good things to say about you,' said May, when Lambert returned from the bar with the most expensive bottle of wine he could order.

'Oh yes? Don't tell me that old bastard showed some emotion? Maybe he'll include me in his next book. Fifteen pounds,' he said pouring her a glass.

'I wouldn't go that far, but he was praising your analytical skills. He mentioned that even during the Billy Nolan case, you remembered details no one else recalled.'

The new wine tasted no better than the last bottle. 'Oil and vinegar,' he said, turning up his nose. 'You ever read any of his books?'

'Hastings? Yeah, they're quite good actually. I'm reading his latest, where the victim is blind,' said May.

Lambert recalled the details of Hastings' book. 'Blood Kill?'

'Yep, great title.'

'You think Hastings' time on the Souljacker case has filtered into his writing?'

'It's certainly interesting. I keep searching for clues in his writing, in case he's slipped some details about the Souljacker into the work.'

Lambert leant forwards, May only inches away from his face. Beneath the smell of wine, he caught a hint of vanilla from her skin. 'What's the name of the protagonist again?' he asked, leaning back, not wanting to invade her space.

'Trent.'

'Yes, Trent. A tall, sullen Superintendent?'

'Write what you know, I guess,' said May. 'What do you think about Hastings?'

Lambert pictured the first time he'd seen Hastings, standing outside Billy Nolan's room. He remembered the sense of calm which exuded from the man, as if the scene was nothing new to him. 'He helped me get into the force, and I've been in contact with him on and off over the years, but I don't really know him that well.'

'Is he always so forthcoming?' said May.

'Not the most talkative is he? I think that's his way. What did he tell you about his previous work on the Souljacker cases?'

'Nothing I haven't read about in his files.'

'He can be stubborn. It might be that he's waiting for the right questions.'

'And what are those?' asked May, the side of her lip snaking upwards as she grinned, the gesture already a familiar one.

'There's the rub. Any news on your missing hospital patient?'

May looked momentarily surprised. 'I'd managed to put that to the back of my mind,' she said.

Lambert played with his glass. If the events were linked, then he should divulge the information to her. It may be more important than she realised to find the missing patient.

'Something you need to tell me?' she said, picking up on his hesitation.

He poured her another glass of wine. 'Enough shop talk,' he said. The time wasn't right. Confessing to breaking the man's leg would only draw attention to him. He needed to find out for himself why he was being targeted and couldn't afford any obstacles for the time being.

They spent the next hour avoiding talk about the case, the second bottle improving as the first had done. May told him about an ex-boyfriend who'd recently returned to Bristol and had begun bothering her. When he jokingly vowed vengeance, Lambert realised he'd drunk too much.

The landlord practically threw them out of the bar. May interlinked her arm with his and he accompanied her back to her hotel.

'Here we are then,' she said. Her body was inches away, her blouse lifting in rhythm with her increased heartbeat, the smell of vanilla from her skin in the air. 'There may be some more cheap wine in my minibar,' she suggested.

Lambert wanted nothing more than to join her inside but he hesitated. It was the wrong moment. 'Sorry,' he said, reluctantly turning away.

Chapter 19

The man hadn't stirred since falling asleep two hours ago. Lance had kept an even pace, first through the city then on the motorway. He didn't know, and didn't want to know, what was in store for the man.

On the radio, a jovial DJ played an unending line of eighties classics. Lance sang along to the tunes, for a time imagining that he wasn't transporting a prisoner to his death.

He'd first met Campbell five years ago. A friend of a friend had put them in touch. The man was almost impossible to get hold of. It had taken Lance six appointments with various underlings before Campbell had granted him an audience. The first thing Campbell did on meeting him was place a folder in front of Lance. The folder contained pictures of his wife and children in various locations.

'They will be monitored, on and off, during our time together,' said Campbell. 'A number of pre-determined check-in times are already established. If anything happens to me, preventing me meeting you at these check-in times, for whatever reason, including me being under arrest and not excluding death, then a series of consequences will ensue. Do we have an understanding?'

Lance remembered the smile on Campbell's face at his distress. The line of his upper lip, as devoid of humour as the man was devoid of a conscience.

'Yes,' agreed Lance.

'Good. You will know me as Campbell. How may I be of service?'

Money. Always money.

Lance's gambling had once again grown out of control and he was in debt, and his creditors were not the sort of people who accepted payment plans. He explained the situation to Campbell who insisted on hearing every detail. He quizzed Lance over his addiction. When had it started? Why did he feel out of control? Had he never thought about his wife and family? He was half-therapist, half -disappointed parent discovering his son was not the perfect boy he'd dreamt he would be.

'If I give you the money, then our agreement is permanent. Do you understand?'

'I think so.'

'You understand or you don't.'

'Yes, I understand.'

'I will give you the money, and you will work for me.'

'Okay,' said Lance. 'What sort of work will I be doing?'

Campbell grinned, the humour momentarily spreading to his eyes. 'I don't normally provide a detailed job description. You will be given minor and major duties, some of which may not be pleasant. You will stop working for me when you have repaid the debt. The terms are non-negotiable.'

Five years later, and he'd nearly repaid the debt. In that time, he'd acted as a go-between for people who wanted to use Campbell's services, filtering out the time-wasters and the investigators. Of the so-called major jobs, the worse had been the removal of a body following one of Campbell's lengthy interrogations, the easiest his present journey with the drugged man in the back of his car.

He'd seen the occasional person cross Campbell. The response was always the same: swift and savage. What had kept him going during the last five years were those people who had been permitted to leave Campbell's orbit. The workers who'd paid off their debt left unhurt. They could never truly feel completely free, but the possibility of leaving was a real one.

Lance's instructions were to head off the M4 at junction four and head for one of the safe houses in Uxbridge. He was approaching the junction when a call came through.

'Change of plan.' Campbell's voice boomed through the car's Bluetooth system.

'Sir?'

It was unusual for Campbell to call him directly, and Lance sat upright in the car as if under surveillance.

'It's Mr Klatzky's lucky day. Dump him somewhere in London. Alive.'

'But he's seen me, sir.'

There was a pause on the other end. Lance sensed the man's impatience and regretted having spoken out of turn.

'Let him see,' said Campbell, hanging up.

Chapter 20

He'd immediately regretted not following May inside. If she'd been upset, she'd hid it well. She'd kissed him on the cheek and walked inside the hotel, leaving him abandoned at the hotel entrance. He'd almost followed her through the hotel doors. It had been years since he'd had such an instant attraction to someone, and the attraction seemed to be reciprocated, but it would have been a mistake. They were going to be working together and the last thing they needed was a further complication.

The scent of vanilla lingered on his skin from where she'd kissed him goodnight. He thought of nothing else as he walked home. He stopped at least three times, and considered returning to the hotel. He pictured her waiting for him in her room. Then his thoughts became clouded with thoughts of Sophie. Although effectively separated, he couldn't help but feel guilty for what had nearly happened with May.

It was after midnight. The main road which led from Bromley to Beckenham was empty, only the hum of the street lamps and the occasional passing vehicle keeping Lambert company. His training always kicked in at such times. With nothing else to do, he began memorising each car which drove past noting the digits on the number plates. Eventually, he reached Beckenham high street. A couple of bars were still open. He noticed the faces of the late-night revellers, took in their features as they stumbled along the street. He walked along Croydon Road, still checking each car on the route. As he turned into the side street where he lived a Jaguar XK8 with this year's plates drove by. Lambert watched the car drive down the road admiring the shape of the vehicle. He paused as it stopped outside his house.

He was three hundred yards away from the vehicle. He saw two figures in the car. Crossing the road, he edged along the path until he was close enough to see the silhouetted figure of his wife in the passenger seat. A pang of jealousy overcame him as he watched her talking to the car's driver. He had no right to feel possessive. Their marriage was little more than a perfunctory agreement. They were simply flatmates sharing a mortgage and the bills, both trying to ignore the shared pain of loss.

Acknowledging his hypocrisy after his evening with May, he walked past the car. He stopped fifty yards on and pretended to tie up his shoe laces, stealing glances at the two people in the car who were oblivious to his presence. His wife was in deep conversation with Jeremy Taylor, one of the partners at her law firm. The same partner she had dined with the evening Lambert had been in Bristol.

Sophie laughed, tilting her head back to the left, a gesture he'd seen her doing thousands of times before, though previously only in response to him. Lambert knew he should stop watching. He was acting like a lovesick teenager, or worse still, a jealous, voyeuristic husband.

They had stopped laughing and were both leaning slightly in towards each other. Lambert imagined the atmosphere within the confines of the car. His fingers involuntarily clenched as Taylor leant closer to his wife. For one horrendous second he thought he was going to witness his wife's first kiss with her new lover. Despite his restricted viewpoint and the gloom of the poorly lit street, he saw Sophie hesitate. At the last second she darted her head to the right leaving Taylor nothing more than the soft flesh of her cheek.

Lambert scurried away, as his wife opened the passenger door of the car. He walked the streets for another hour before returning home.

He closed the front door as gently as possible, and climbed the stairs to the first floor. Sophie's door was shut. What would happen if he knocked on the door, undressed and climbed into bed with her as he'd done for so many years before? Would she scream and demand that he leave, or would she edge close to him and allow him to stay for one more night? His left eye twitched, the lights appearing in the corners of his vision. He couldn't remember the last time he'd slept. He tiptoed upstairs to his own room before the hallucinations began. He collapsed on the bed. Fire-coloured specks danced before his eyes, a haze of colours merging into a violet blur. His breathing became heavy, his heart pulsating in his chest until his body eventually let go and he fell asleep.

He was awake two hours later, the short period of sleep enough to have refreshed him. He switched on The System and began a number of sub-routines. He began with a search on DCI Nielson. The man had worked for the MIT out of Lewisham for the last four years and had been SIO on a number of high profile cases.

Lambert grinned, noting that Nielson had instructed one of his DSs to check out Lambert's background, and to assess his link with the latest Souljacker victims. It was a logical move. Lambert was linked to Billy Nolan and Terrence Haydon, and the latest victim was killed less than two miles from his house. It would have made sense for Nielson to have discussed the issue with DI May, as her officers were running a similar investigation at that time. He was less amused to see Simon Klatzky's name again, the red line for the outstanding arrest warrant prominent on the screen.

Lambert opened Klatzky's file. He searched through a list of misdemeanours his friend had committed over the last ten years. Each one was the result of excessive drinking.

What Nielson didn't know was that someone had sent Klatzky the crime scene photos of Haydon's murder. He needed to speak to Klatzky. The last time he'd seen the man had been in the hotel room in Bristol where he'd been comatose, vomit bubbling from his mouth and trickling down his chin. It was too early in the morning to call again. He was probably lost in some bar nursing a drink with the money Lambert had given him.

Lambert was about to look through the Haydon case once more when the sound of a soft thud diverted his attention. He shut off the computer screens and listened. He heard it again, the sound growing in volume and intensity. Somebody was pounding on his front door. A wild, uncontrolled banging as if they were smacking their knuckles against the wood. It was four-thirty a.m.

Lambert took a set of keys from his coat pocket and unlocked the bottom left drawer of his desk. He removed the Mark 3 knife he'd been issued when working for The Group, and began running down the stairs.

A high-pitched scream stopped him before he'd reached the bottom of the first stairwell.

Chapter 21

'Jesus Christ, Michael.' Sophie stood outside her bedroom door wrapped in a silk kimono dressing gown. 'I didn't know you were coming back today,' she said, regaining her composure.

'Obviously not,' said Lambert. 'Sorry, I did try calling you.' They stared at each other, stuck in a stand-off as the banging from the front door grew in intensity. 'You going to answer that?' she said, her eyes glued on the knife by his side.

'Maybe you should go back inside,' said Lambert, gesturing to her room. He turned off the hallway light and walked downstairs. 'Who is it?' he shouted.

The banging stopped. From outside he heard a familiar voice. 'Mikey?' it questioned, half pleading, half accusing.

Lambert opened the door and Klatzky fell through the threshold. Lambert held out his arm to stop the man smashing his face on the wooden floorboards. He hoisted Klatzky onto his feet and held him against the wall as he slammed the door shut. Klatzky was drenched, his hair matted across his forehead. Lambert turned away from the stench and wiped his hand on his trouser leg.

'What the hell, Mikey?' slurred Klatzky.

Lambert stood with his legs planted wide, every muscle in his body tensed. The pressure of the last two days swelled up and he punched Klatzky full force in the stomach, the soft flesh yielding under the pressure of the blow.

Klatzky collapsed to the floor with a groan. Lambert considered following it with a kick but noticed Sophie glaring down at him from the top of the stairs, hand on hips. 'What's going on, Mike?' She didn't look scared, only annoyed.

'Nothing. It's Simon. He's pissed out of his head. Go to bed and I'll sort it.'

She remained for a second, silent.

'I'll sort it,' he said, softer this time.

She sighed and left him to it.

Klatzky began coughing. Yellow dribble fell from his mouth and congealed on his stubble. 'How could you do that, Mikey?' he mouthed in short gasps, wiping his face with the back of his hand.

'Its four-thirty, Simon, and you're banging on my door like an idiot. What did you expect, a warm embrace?'

Klatzky adjusted his position, pushing himself off the floor until he sat at a lopsided angle, his back slouched against the hallway wall. 'I'm not talking about that. I mean the little deal with your psychotic limo driver.'

Lambert rubbed his eyes. 'Jesus, Simon, what have you being taking?'

'The driver you sent to collect me from the hotel in Bristol.'

'You think I have my own driver?'

'Someone picked me up. Silver Mercedes CLK. He told me you'd arranged for him to drive me back from Bristol.' Klatzky tried to get to his feet but collapsed back to the floor, groaning as he fell.

'Come on, Si. Is this a joke?'

Klatzky waved his right index finger in front of his face. 'I shit you not,' he said, the faintest smile forming on his face.

The humour was short-lived. Lambert dragged him into the living room and switched on a table lamp. The light illuminated the ordered room. Two antique sofas faced each other. Klatzky collapsed onto one, his face darting to the numerous bookcases which served as the room's decorations. 'Right. What happened?' said Lambert.

Klatzky explained how he was approached by a man outside the hotel. 'It sounded plausible. I thought you may have felt guilty about having had me kicked out of the hotel. Either that or you wanted to be totally sure I'd leave.'

'Could you describe this driver?'

'Maybe. No. I don't know, Mikey. Didn't you send him?'

'No, I didn't. Did you get the car's number plate?' asked Lambert, thinking about the Mercedes which had followed him through the streets of Bristol the night before.

'No. I didn't look. I just took the lift.'

'What happened once he had picked you up?'

Klatzky squirmed in his seat, curling into himself. 'He gave me a drink.'

'And you took it?'

'I thought you'd sent him,' said Klatzky, his voice rising. His eyes were continuously moving, darting around the room, snatching the occasional glance at Lambert.

'Then what?'

'I fell asleep. Next thing I know, I'm lying on the ground surrounded by dumpsters. I think he stuck something over my mouth. My lips hurt like hell.'

The story was implausible but Lambert could see no reason why Klatzky would make it up. 'Where exactly?'

'It took me hours to find out I was in Uxbridge of all places. I had to hitch a ride here which believe me was not easy. What's happening, Mikey? First the photos and now this. What do they want from me?'

It was a good question. 'Is there something you're not telling me? Something about Billy or Terrence?'

Klatzky shrugged.

'Look, Si, I want to help you but if you're holding something back then what can I do?'

'Michael.' Sophie was shouting from upstairs.

'Think on,' said Lambert, leaving the room.

'He can't stay here,' said Sophie. She stood outside her room, her arms holding the slight kimono around her body. Despite the circumstances, Lambert felt the first rush of desire for his wife he'd had in months.

'He's in trouble, Soph, I need to help him.'

'He's a useless drunk.'

'I know, but he wasn't always that way. He's not a bad guy. I'll make sure he's gone by tomorrow.'

Sophie sighed, and leant towards him. Lambert's pulse raced, his body stuck in position. 'Okay,' she whispered. 'But both of you please get to bed, I need to be up for work in a couple of hours.'

Klatzky was asleep on the sofa by the time he came down again. His putrid smell overwhelmed the room. Lambert opened a window and adjusted Klatzky's position on the sofa so he looked almost comfortable.

Upstairs, he tried to reconcile what Klatzky had told him.

First the photographs and now the mysterious lift. Someone was interested in Klatzky, or possibly Lambert himself. He flicked through The System, hoping for inspiration. He searched through recent incidents handled by Major Incident Teams. Text and visuals scrolled across the six screens in his office. A number of gang-related drug busts, two with fatalities. An armed robbery at a small local bank. A missing nine-year-old boy, last seen walking home alone from his school.

He locked the screen as a particularly nasty image appeared: a father brutally murdered in his house by his wife and teenage daughter. The wife had poured a pot of boiling fat over the man's head, and the girl had proceeded to stab the man repeatedly in the back with a kitchen knife. Lambert read the case notes, sickened by the instances of abuse seemingly ignored by social services. He'd seen it happen countless times before. The abuse eventually became too much. From the notes, it was unlikely that the mother and daughter would face prosecution.

Lambert was about to switch The System off when another case caught his eye. He stopped the screen, amazed at what he was reading. With a click of his mouse, he printed off a set of case notes. He knew the SIO, DCI Josh Bardsley. He read the printed notes, examined the crime scene photos in detail.

A corpse, captured from many angles.

It was the face which held Lambert's interest.

More specifically the eyes, which had both been sealed shut.

Chapter 22

Lambert read the details on HOLMES. The victim, Samuel Burnham, had died two days ago. His eyes had been sealed shut with a thin line of thread. As in the Souljacker murders, the evidence suggested that the victim was alive during the procedure. In addition to sealing Burnham's eyes, the killer had carved off the man's lips.

Lambert searched through the HOLMES entry once more. A connection on The System had already been made with the murders of Terrence Haydon, and Sandra Hopkins. Nielson had made contact with Bardsley, but nothing in the report linked the killings, other than the obvious.

Sophie's door creaked open downstairs. Lambert sprung off his chair and headed down to meet her.

'Still up?' she asked.

'Couldn't sleep.'

'There's a surprise.' She'd changed into her work clothes. Water from her hair, still wet from showering, dripped onto her cream blouse.

'I wanted to apologise about last night.'

'Specifically?'

'Scaring you. Simon. I'll get rid of him, I promise.'

She shrugged and turned away. Halfway down the stairs she

stopped, and with some kindness asked, 'You know it is only two weeks away now, don't you?'

Lambert rubbed his cheeks, his palms massaging the prickly growth of his stubble. 'I know,' he said. He hadn't forgotten about Chloe's memorial service. It was not something he had to actively engage with. His daughter was constantly in his thoughts.

'Whatever this is all about, don't forget.' She fixed him with the coldest of stares. He went to argue but she'd already turned away.

He checked up on Klatzky and decided to let him sleep. He caught a taxi to May's hotel, hoping he'd catch her before she went into the office. He wanted to discuss the killing he'd discovered on The System.

She was in the hotel's dining room, sharing a continental breakfast with Julian Hastings. Lambert wasn't sure if the retired officer was tagging along to get material for one of his books, or was still hoping he could salvage some professional pride by helping to solve the case.

'Good morning, Michael,' said Hastings, as he approached. He stood to shake hands with Lambert.

May glanced his way, betraying nothing about the previous evening.

'I'm glad you're here,' continued Hastings. 'I was explaining to DI May here that I have some connection with the latest victim, Sandra Hopkins. Can I get you something to drink?'

Lambert took a seat next to May, as Hastings ordered coffee from a waitress. 'Oh, really?'

'Twenty years ago, would you believe? I had to check my records, but I knew the name rang a bell. It was a criminal negligence case. Hopkins' firm represented the accused. She was a trainee solicitor. Nothing more than a paper holder, but I spoke to her on a number of occasions.'

'When exactly?' asked Lambert.

Hastings gave him the date. It coincided with the investigation into the sixth Souljacker victim, William Perryman.

'Hopkins was still in Bristol at that time. She'd completed her training contract and was working in the firm's commercial section,' said May.

'Does Nielson know?' asked Lambert.

'Yes,' said May. 'But there's something more. The case was an NHS negligence case involving an eye surgeon.'

Lambert stared at her. 'You're joking?'

'No. The surgeon was cleared and still practices, now in Gloucester. We have him under surveillance. DS Bradbury and the team are working through the old cases, seeing if they can find something substantial so we can get him in for questioning. I'm going back shortly to assist.'

'Sounds a bit convenient,' said Lambert.

May didn't respond.

'What do you think, sir?' asked Lambert.

'Obviously it's worth pursuing, but I agree, it all sounds too convenient. I would be surprised if the killer would be so sloppy, after so long,' said Hastings.

'Unless he wants to get caught,' said May.

Hastings shrugged. Lambert ran through everything in his head. Now would be the time to tell May about the photos Klatzky received, and his mysterious lift home from Bristol. First he wanted some answers. 'Have you read the Samuel Burnham case?' he asked.

'DCI Nielson and I have been liaising with the team in Hertfordshire. At the moment, we're ruling out any direct link.'

Hastings slanted his head, and May updated him on details about the killing. 'The eyes have it,' he said.

Two uniformed officers entered the hotel. 'My chariot awaits,' said May. 'Thank you for the coffee,' she said to Hastings.

Hastings dropped his head half a centimetre, his face blank.

Lambert followed May out of the hotel. 'I presume Nielson wouldn't approve of my accompanying you?'

'No, but there is something you could do for me. Your friend, Simon Klatzky. Have you seen him recently?'

'Why?'

'It would be a good idea if he attended a local police station. There was somewhat of a fracas at the University student union the other evening. Mr Klatzky caused a bit of damage.'

'Jesus Christ.'

'And Nielson is on the warpath for him, especially with that arrest warrant still outstanding.'

'Okay. I'll advise him when I see him.' He couldn't bring himself to tell her about Klatzky. Klatzky was his only link to the Souljacker, and he wasn't willing to give him over to May or anyone else at that moment. 'Is Nielson going with you to see the surgeon?'

'No, not yet at least. Listen, about last night,' she began.

'No, no. You've more important things to be getting on with,' he said.

May swept a piece of hair from her eyes, offering him a brief smile. 'See you soon,' she said, lowering herself into the back of the waiting police car. Lambert didn't know if it was a question or a statement.

'I'm going to get going, Michael,' said Hastings, surprising him with a light tap on the back. 'I've settled up inside. I'm heading home on the train. Like the old days this. Can't say I miss all the drama. Be seeing you.'

'Sir.'

Lambert called Bardsley. He hadn't spoken to the man in five or six years. Bardsley had started in CID on the same day as Lambert. Glenn Tillman, then a mere DI, had been their divisional leader. They'd worked together for three years before Bardsley moved stations.

He was now a DCI out of Watford Central Station. They agreed to meet later that morning. Lambert caught the overground out of Bromley and was surprised to reach Watford in less than an hour.

Lambert spotted Bardsley as soon as he entered the greasy spoon called Terry's. He sat alone, nursing a mug of tea. He beckoned Lambert over as he entered the café.

'You look older,' said Lambert, sitting on the yellow plastic chair.

Bardsley smirked. He was the same age as Lambert with a drawn, thin face which made him look about ten years older.

'What's this about, Mike?' Bardsley's voice still had a lilt of the Black Country to it. The combination of his face and slow voice often made people underestimate the man. Something Bardsley always used to his advantage.

'As I mentioned on the phone, I have some questions about the Burnham case.'

'You're not working at the moment.'

'Not officially. I'm helping out with a case.'

'The Souljacker murders,' said Bardsley, taking a sip from his tea and smirking again.

'Glad you're up to speed on that. What do I need to get a coffee around here?'

Bardsley shouted over to the proprietor. 'Coffee, John. I've exchanged words with the fragrant DI May on the subject, if that's what you're after.'

An obese red-haired man stumbled over and handed Lambert a chipped mug of milky coffee. 'You have me at a disadvantage then, Josh. So what do you know?'

'About the case or about you?'

'Enlighten me.'

'Well, she is one good-looking woman that's for sure.' Bardsley leant forward and smiled, conspiratorially.

'I wouldn't know anything about that.'

'Bullshit. Anyway, we've been in contact since that Haydon boy was slaughtered. Nasty business. As you know it happened within two days of the Burnham kid dying. It was May who contacted me about the potential link.'

Lambert hadn't seen any notes to that effect on The System. May had never mentioned Burnham or Bardsley in their time together, apart from that morning when he had questioned her. 'So what can you tell me?'

Bardsley scratched his head, playing the dumb officer role. 'If the situation was reversed, would you share anything with me?'

Lambert considered everything he'd read on The System. With a little time, he believed he'd know more than Bardsley about Burnham's murder. If there was any link, then he would find it. 'I don't really know, Josh. You know this is personally relevant to me?'

'Of course I do, and that's why I agreed to meet you.'

Over Bardsley's shoulder, the red-haired proprietor hacked

away at some onions and dropped them onto a grime-covered hot plate. Within seconds, a cloud of stale fat hovered over the café.

'Okay, I'll give,' said Bardsley. 'What do you want to know?'

'Thanks, Josh. You've answered one of my questions already.'

'Whether we've examined the link between the Burnham and Haydon killings?'

'Yes.'

'Apart from the eyes, there doesn't seem to be anything in it.'

'And Burnham's the first?'

'Yes. As far as we are aware. Badly beaten, eyes sealed shut.'

'Before or after death?' asked Lambert.

'During would be more apt. From what I've discussed with May, the Souljacker victims were all drugged first.'

'So I believe.'

'Well, this guy didn't anaesthetise.'

'So was there a struggle?'

'Not exactly. There was a heavy blow, signs of restraint. Burnham never had the chance to fight back. The fucker sliced his lips off.'

'The lips? Was he a grass?'

'Could be. We know him as a petty criminal. Two prison terms both for burglary.'

'Some sort of vigilante killing?' asked Lambert.

'Perhaps. But Burnham was small fry, at least from what we know of him.'

'And you're sure there's no link with the Souljacker killings? Seems bloody coincidental to me.'

'No one's ruling it out. It's plausible considering the times and locations of the two recent Souljacker murders. But from what I understand I don't think they're linked. The Burnham scene was a mess. It was a frenzied attack, a lot of damage to the body. From what I've seen of the Souljacker, he seems more restrained.'

'Yeah, he's a fucking delight,' said Lambert.

Bardsley ordered some more drinks. 'Listen, Mike. I never told you how sorry I was to hear about Chloe,' he said.

Bardsley had been at funeral but Lambert had been on such heavy medication at the time, the memory of that day was fuzzy at best. He'd never told anyone but he'd felt cheated afterwards. The grief he'd felt during the funeral had been abstract, as if he was viewing himself grieving from afar. The full impact of his loss didn't hit him until months later, when Chloe's absence overtook him. He'd holed himself up in his room, and had barely left for weeks. He'd never had the chance to properly say goodbye, and wished now he'd gone to the funeral drug-free, whatever physical agony that would have caused him.

'You've heard about this eye surgeon in Bristol?'

Bardsley frowned. 'No.'

Lambert told him about Hastings' link to Sandra Hopkins, the eye surgeon's negligence case. Lambert was once again struck by how orchestrated things felt. He was convinced the eye surgeon was a dead end, thought it possible that the Souljacker was deflecting their attention.

'Fingers crossed there. How's Hastings keeping? Haven't seen him in years.'

'Same old. You worked much with Nielson?'

Bardsley ground his teeth, his eyes widening a touch.

'I see,' said Lambert. 'Anyway, thanks for your time, Josh.'

'Pleasure. You've my number if that brain of yours comes

up with anything we may have missed.' He didn't get up as Lambert left the café.

Lambert assessed the faces on the train and tube as he returned home. He made a plausible case for each one's involvement in some form of criminal activity. From London Bridge, he caught the train back to Beckenham. Walking back to his house, he went to call Sophie twice but each time hung up before the phone started ringing.

Whatever Nielson, May and Bardsley were telling him, Lambert was convinced the cases were linked. It had to be the same killer, out of retirement and making up for lost time. Furthermore, he was positive the killer was using accomplices. It was possible this would be his undoing.

He heard the noise as he turned onto his street. A distant ringing sound which crescendoed into a full-blast concert by the time he reached his house.

Somehow, he'd forgotten about Klatzky. A wave of cigarette smoke rushed his eyes as he opened his front door. In the living room, a half-dressed Klatzky drank vodka from a cut glass goblet. 'Mikey,' he said, one shaking hand holding a cigarette over Lambert's record player, the other holding a vintage piece of vinyl as if it was a scrap piece of paper.

In the corner sat another man.

Someone Lambert hadn't seen in fifteen years.

Chapter 23

By the time May reached Bristol, the investigation into the Surgeon, Peter Randall was already over. By late afternoon, she'd been called to face Superintendent Rush. Rush loved reading the riot act. It was so familiar that May had already tuned out. She would have rather been out working than sitting in Rush's cramped office, listening to him rant. Rush wiped a bead of sweat off his forehead. Freckles and random tufts of red hair spotted his balding scalp.

Rush slammed a file of papers onto his desk. His face blazed with colour as he loosened his tie. Although initially excited by the possible link between the surgeon, Randall, and Sandra Hopkins, the evidence linking Randall to the latest killing had proved flimsy at best. During questioning he'd provided an air-tight alibi.

'So where are we now?' asked Rush.

'DCI Nielson's team is following up a number of leads in London, sir. Our attention is on Sandra Vernon and the church.'

'And the gay club?'

May suppressed a snigger. Rush had almost spat out the word gay. 'We are sending officers there every night, questioning the patrons.'

'Right.' Rush shuffled the papers on his desk, a signal for her to leave.

May remained standing. 'Sir, what do you know about Julian Hastings?'

Rush looked up at her, the colour draining from his face. 'I never worked with him, why?'

'I'm not sure, we've been looking through the old Souljacker cases in some detail, and...'

Rush propped his elbows on the table. 'I'm not sure I want to hear this.'

'No, it's nothing major, though it's possible some avenues of investigation could have been explored a bit better.'

A sigh escaped from Rush as he tilted his head. 'It was a different time then, quite often less of a team effort. Someone with Hastings' previous experience would have been given the case and would have had pretty much a free rein.'

'Even if he was unsuccessful?'

'If you look at his case history, his record is exemplary. If you count the unsolved Souljacker murders as a whole it's his only major failing.' Rush strained his neck. 'Sit down, May.'

May flattened her skirt, and sat back down. Rush was experiencing some internal debate. She understood the pressure he would be receiving from higher up. It was possibly proving too much for him. Patches of sweat lined his forehead, and his shirt was damp from perspiration. She was going to suggest opening a window when he spoke. 'Do you understand the man-hours which would be needed if we reopened each case in detail?'

May knew all too well. It would be like running nine murder cases simultaneously, albeit with the added difficulty of all the evidence and those involved being twenty years older, if not dead. 'It may not come down to that. I wanted to look at the first two cases to begin with, Clive Hale and Graham Jackett. Hastings wasn't SIO on the first case. The Jackett case was the first one he worked. There might we something in those two which were overlooked, something which could relate to the others.'

Rush loosened his tie and unbuttoned his shirt, a wisp of red hair springing out over the cotton. 'What do you have in mind, specifically?'

'I wanted to speak to some of Hastings' colleagues at the time. Find out more about how the investigation was conducted.'

'And?'

May thought about the religious aspect highlighted by Bradbury, the tentative way it had been investigated. Motive was the key aspect to this case. She'd hoped Hastings would have offered some more insight, but his suggestions had been vague at best. 'Let me start there. Talk to those involved and we can see where we go next.'

'I take it you've already made appointments.'

May didn't answer.

'Go,' said Rush. 'I want a full report by tomorrow.'

Back at her desk, May confirmed the appointment she'd made before speaking to Rush. Before leaving, she logged onto her private email and saw another email from Sean.

Dear Sarah, I only have a few days left in Bristol. I would really love to see you before I return. Love, Sean x

Her pulse increased as a jet of adrenalin shot through her body. It was ridiculous. He was basically harmless, and she knew how to defend herself, but still she always reacted. It would have been easier to block his email and forget he'd ever existed. Her father would call it Catholic guilt. She guessed that dealing with such occasional missives was a small penance to pay for what she'd done.

Prior to leaving for London, she'd managed to track down a Latin expert, Dr Alison Atwal. She'd agreed to meet the woman in the same coffee shop where she'd first met Lambert. She still had an hour so she checked through the working file on Haydon, and ensured that her team were all busy.

She stood outside her office and summoned Bradbury. She leant against the doorway as he approached. He walked towards her with his head high, not wishing to look weak in front of his colleagues.

'Sit,' she said, closing the door behind her.

Bradbury sat, back straight on one the office chairs. 'I want you to pay a visit to Haydon's old church again. They have a service this lunchtime. Some saint's day. Try to mingle. Find out some more about them. The minister in particular.'

'They'll know me,' said Bradbury.

'That will make it easier then. But don't do anything stupid. Be discreet and diplomatic. Charm not coercion.'

'What about Klatzky and Lambert?'

'They're both in London. Nielson has people on it. Not our concern for the time being. Now, if there is nothing else?' She decided not to tell him about her talk with Rush. She'd made an appointment with the original SIO on the Clive Hale case, Iain Hill. Hill had taken early retirement after the Hale case. He lived in a village called Backwell which was only a short journey from the centre. She wanted to speak to Hill before she told the rest of the team in case it was a dead end.

She left the station, and walked through the centre along

Park Street. She was about to cross at the traffic lights when she felt a hand on her shoulder. Two taps, the hand strong, the gesture familiar. It can't be, she thought, turning to see the grinning face of her ex-boyfriend.

She didn't betray any emotions. She was a professional now, and acted as such. 'Sean, what do you think you're doing?' She didn't raise her voice, her tone cool and neutral.

The smile faded for a second then reappeared. He'd always been good-looking, and he'd aged well. His skin was less smooth, the odd wrinkle on his forehead and beneath his eyes, but he still had those almost feminine features. The ridiculously pronounced cheekbones, full lips, and bright eyes, which had attracted him to her all those years ago.

'I tried to email you but you didn't reply,' he said, his smile not faltering once.

'Sean, I thought this was all settled. I told you I would take a restraining order out on you if you came near me again.'

'Oh, Sarah. That was years ago. We were kids.'

'That's not the point, Sean, and you know it.' She looked about her, embarrassed that she'd raised her voice.

'Have a coffee with me.'

'No,' she said, through gritted teeth.

'I've grown up, Sarah. That was all years ago. I admit I was foolish, and I guess reckless. But you had... Well, that's not important. I wanted to see you. To make amends. To move forward. To start again.'

She shook her head in disbelief. She turned away from him, and began walking up the hill. Sean followed close behind. May kept her gaze straight ahead, hoping he would stop following. Approaching the coffee shop on The Triangle, she stopped and rounded on him. She took a deep breath. 'Listen to me, Sean. I don't need you to make amends. I understand that you were hurt.' She tried to placate him, to sound sympathetic. 'But you know it didn't give you the right to do what you did. Yes you were young, we both were.' She lowered her voice. 'But you need to take this on board. It is the last time I am going to tell you. There will never be a time when we start again. Is that clear?'

'Please, just five minutes,' he said.

'If you are ever within five hundred metres of me again, I will arrest you, understand?'

For the first time his smile faltered, a coldness spreading to the man's eyes, like an actor coming out of character. 'You'd do that, and let all your colleagues know what you did?'

'There we go, the real Sean at last. You're good. You almost had even me convinced.' He flinched as she moved towards him. 'I've told you what will happen.'

'I would tell them everything,' he said, stepping back.

'Everything? There's nothing to tell. I had an abortion and you went crazy. Do you think they would care?'

'They'll hold it against you.'

'They won't care. If anything they'll think you're unbalanced and would arrest you. Stalking is a criminal offence. Stop bothering me. If I see you again, I promise you'll be arrested.' She walked across the road to the coffee shop.

This time he didn't follow.

Chapter 24

May composed herself, waited for her breathing to return to normal and entered the coffee shop. She ordered a latte and waited for the academic to arrive. Sean was the last thing she needed now. Maybe she should have given him the time to talk, to get it over with, but she was in no mood to allow anyone to dictate to her, especially him. She focused on the case, banished Sean to the back of her thoughts.

Dr Atwal arrived twenty minutes later. In her early thirties, she had light brown skin and large, green eyes. 'Thank you for seeing me on such short notice,' said May.

'My pleasure. I hope I can help. It's not often I'm called in by the police for my expertise,' a lilt of excitement in her broad Bristolian accent.

'The Latin phrase I sent you. I imagine you understand our interest.'

'Yes, that poor man who was killed the other week. Horrible. My colleagues and I thought there may have been another University victim years ago. Is that right?'

'That's correct. I can't go into specifics with you, but can talk about anything that is public record.' May gave the academic a file with pictures of the Latin inscription. 'So what can you tell me?'

Atwal produced a small pair of reading glasses and studied

the papers. Her face changed as she began to read. Her brow furrowed in concentration, and she winced on more than one occasion. 'I'm sure you don't need me to tell you that In oculis animus habitat translates as The Soul Dwells in the Eyes. I believe the killer derived his nickname from the translation. I did a little research for you. The first recorded instance of the phrase occurs in a book called Naturalis Historia, an encyclopaedia of ancient knowledge written around the first century AD. It was a common belief at the time that the eyes revealed the inner soul. There are echoes of the belief in modern parlance as well. I'm sure you've heard phrases such as the eyes see into the soul and evil eye?'

May nodded. She wasn't hearing anything new.

'You might be interested to know that the modern word envy comes from the Latin invidia, which literally means to see into.'

The possibility that the killer was envious of his victims was not an avenue they had yet explored. 'Is there something more specific about the phrase? Something which would give us an indication of why the killer would use it and not some other phrase or saying? Something religious perhaps?'

'Not that I can ascertain. The author of Naturalis Historia, Pliny the Elder, was a noted natural history philosopher. I can't see any further significance. Certainly nothing religious.'

'I see. Where would someone pick up the phrase?'

'How do you mean?'

'It seems quite an obscure saying. Would someone who uses it have a strong knowledge of Latin?'

Atwal pursed her lips as she considered the question, pushing her glasses up the bridge of her nose. 'Not really. On the internet you'll see hundreds of sites dedicated to Latin. Although it's rarely studied in school any more, there's still a lot of interest out there. You could do a search for Latin phrases matching the soul and eyes, and I'm sure this phrase would appear.'

'It does,' said May. 'How about twenty-three years ago?'

'It might well have been different then. I don't believe the phrase appears in any religious texts. However, it would take only a little research to unearth a list of Latin phrases. Anyone could have accessed the information from the Central Library for instance.'

May had already done that, the day after Terrence Haydon's body was discovered.

'You look disappointed,' said Atwal.

'Sorry, no, you've been very helpful.'

Atwal hesitated. Her expressive eyes lent credence to the phrase they had come to discuss. 'Is it true about what they say? That he keeps them alive when he does...'

'It's not worth thinking about, Dr Atwal.'

The afternoon sky had clouded over. May thanked Dr Atwal and walked back to the station, scanning occasionally for Sean as she went. At the station she met with the senior members of the team and told them about her conversation with Atwal.

'Obviously, if envy was a motive then the killer would have known each of the victims,' said Welling.

'Not necessarily. You can envy from afar,' said May.

'Thou should not covet thy neighbour's wife,' said Lana.

'You haven't seen my neighbour's wife,' said Welling.

'I thought it was Ox,' said Bradbury.

'As I said, you haven't seen my neighbour's wife,' said Welling.

'If we can focus,' said May.

'What was there to be envious of? Most of the victims had little of material value, apart from Haydon and now this solicitor, Hopkins,' said Bradbury.

'It doesn't have to be something material. He could envy their soul for example. We're not dealing with someone playing with a full deck of cards here, Bradbury,' said Welling. 'It could explain why he's active again. Something could have triggered his envy. Something different to before.'

May sighed. She didn't like this idea. It threw up too many variables and different lines of investigation. 'Let's keep it as a background thought. I want more research on the former victims. We need a link between them and Haydon. Bradbury is going back to Haydon's church. Welling, I want some more research on that place. How does it link with the churches of the other victims? How much influence did it have over Haydon's life?'

May took one of the pool cars and made the journey to Backwell.

Iain Hill lived in a detached house surrounded by a large of area of land. May sat out on the patio waiting for the retired policeman who was in the kitchen with his wife, making tea. Before her was a large expanse of lawn, freshly mowed, the smell of cut grass still in the air. She was wearing sunglasses and closed her eyes for a time, enjoying the relative silence of the place, the gentle hum of insects and bird calls. She listened harder, the distance sound of traffic ruining the illusion.

Hill returned with a tray. 'I was wondering if someone would contact me,' he said, placing the tray on the table. 'All this nasty business again. I'd hoped that had all ended with the last one, the poor lad at the University.'

Hill poured tea for her. In his early seventies, he was in good shape, his figure lean. He had an air of authority about him, similar to Hastings. He'd made the rank of DCI before retiring.

'Thank you for your time. You were SIO on the first Souljacker case, Clive Hale.'

Hill nodded, the loose skin on his neck dancing at the movement. 'My last case, unfortunately. I was down for early retirement due to a dodgy ticker.' He placed his hand on his heart. 'I told them it was nothing but they wouldn't listen. Anyway, you don't want to hear about that. Clive Hale. Horrible scene. Bits of eye and God knows what.'

'I've been reading the case files.'

Hill drank his tea. 'I wasn't that much involved to tell you the truth,' he said.

'Really, I thought…'

'I signed everything off, naturally, but my mind was elsewhere by that point. It was a transitional time. I gave free rein to my junior.'

'Julian Hastings?'

A look of suspicion crossed Hill's face. 'Do you have anything specific you wanted to discuss with me, Inspector?'

Out of nowhere, a cat jumped on her. The tabby curled up on her lap, May holding her hands in the air.

Hill laughed at her surprise. 'Don't mind Holmes,' he said.

May relaxed and stroked the cat who'd started purring. 'He's friendly. Named after the detective, or the computer system?'

'My wife calls him a tart. You'll have to ask his brother, Sherlock, about the origin of the name. So, Julian Hastings…'

The cat shifted in her lap to find a more comfortable position.

'I'll come clean. I'm looking at a few lines of investigations that Hastings may have overlooked.'

'Overlooked? On the Hale case, or the others?'

'It's a general thing, probably nothing. It's just that I would have thought there would have been research conducted on the victims. The reports go into their background but...'

'It could have gone further,' interrupted Hill.

'Possibly.'

'You'll have to speak to Julian about that. We all had our own way of doing things back then. I know it's different now, more structured and reliance on teams and what have you. Is that what you're really asking me, Inspector?'

May sensed Hill studying her. She could imagine him in his prime, a keen and intelligent interrogator. 'Ticking the boxes, that's all,' said May.

Hill's eyes widened but he didn't question further.

'Were you satisfied with Hastings' work at the time?'

Hill paused, the sun highlighting the crisscross pattern of wrinkles on his face. 'There it is,' he said, nodding.

It was May's turn to wait. She removed her sunglasses, noticed the slight tremor in Hill's hands. It was possible it was a sign of age, but May thought she had struck a nerve.

The nodding increased in tempo as Hill considered the words. 'I have to admit, I left him to it. I signed off the work without question. He was a very able policeman. He'd headed up a number of cases on his own, and had a very high success rate.'

'What was he like?'

'Like? What a strange question.' Hill poured some more tea, his hand steadier. 'What was he like? I've already told you he was a strong officer. Very methodical, quite relentless in his pursuit.'

'And as a person?' asked May, thinking about her torturous journey to London with Hastings as her companion. The monosyllabic answers to her questions about the case.

'He wasn't the easiest to be around, that I would concede. Not the most charismatic man, but he did install a sense of respect in the team. He was a good leader. Very good, actually. His, how shall I put it, sense of detachment probably made him more suitable for a place higher up the ranks. He was less strong being part of a team. I guess it would be different now but it worked for him.'

May could see Hastings in a position of authority. Like in any other profession, she'd seen different types of management styles in the force. Each came with its own set of pros and cons. 'Could you see him missing anything?'

Hill shielded his eyes from the glare of the sun. 'You know how the job is. As I said, things were different then. We didn't have all those checks and controls in place. Things could go awry, but I would say in Hastings' case it would be highly unlikely. He was very strong on these things. What's this really about, Inspector?'

'As I said, just some background. You've been very helpful.'

Back at the station, she was pleased to see the team still busy in the incident room. She called DCI Nielson in London, leaving a message when he didn't answer. She ran home, pushing herself through the steep inclines. She remembered what Hill had told her about Hastings. What a great leader he was, and how methodical. Why, then, had he not focused more on the links between the victims?

Her heart raged as she sprinted the last three hundred metres to the front door. Her father looked shocked as he opened the door for her. 'You'll do yourself some mischief. You can barely breathe.'

'I'm fine, Dad,' she said.

It took a few minutes for her heart rate to return to its normal rhythm. She peeled off her running clothes and switched on her computer. She checked her email, a part of her daring Sean to have sent an email. He hadn't. Neither had Michael Lambert. She considered calling him. It had been an awkward way to leave things. With Hastings there, she'd been unable to properly apologise for effectively making a pass at him the night before. Not that she fully regretted that. She liked him but it was unprofessional. She already knew the complications which arose from having a relationship with someone she worked with.

She stayed under the shower for ten minutes until her skin reddened from the heat. She thought about what Dr Atwal had asked her, about the victims being alive when the Souljacker performed on them. It was something she'd learnt to ignore early on in her career. It was impossible to fully empathise with the victims she came across without going mad. If she thought about the pain and fear the Souljacker victims endured as he removed their eyes, and carved the words viciously into their bodies, then she would never be able to function.

The smell of fried meat and spices drifted up from the kitchen. Her father cooked every evening. It was his way of contributing.

'Tea's up, Sarah,' he called, for some reason in a northern accent.

She pulled on a dressing gown and went downstairs, grateful for his presence. He had set out two places on the dining table. 'For your delectation,' he said, pointing to plate of lamb chops and couscous. 'Wine?'

'Yes, please.'

He poured her a glass, emptying the bottle he'd obviously started earlier. 'So tell me about it,' he said.

'What.'

'Whatever's bothering you. Why you went to London.'

'You know I can't talk about the case, Dad.'

'No, but you can talk about how you feel.'

Her father had become more open in the last few years, as if he felt obliged to compensate for her mother's absence. 'I'm tired, Dad. This is the first major case I've headed, and it doesn't seem to be progressing the way I'd envisaged.'

She took a bite of the lamb, the meat flaking off the bone. She wanted to tell him about her encounter with Sean but didn't want to upset him. She remembered the day she'd told both her parents that she was pregnant. She'd put off telling them for as long as possible. She'd recently turned seventeen and had only been sleeping with Sean for a month. Compared to everyone else in the school, she was practically a nun. She told them during a meal such as this. She would remember the silence following her announcement until the day she died, the pause as the words filtered into her parents' reality. She would remember their response more. The way they both left their seats and moved towards her, how they wrapped their arms around her, without words; without judgment.

They let her decide. As a family they'd been active parishioners of the local Catholic church and May attended the adjoining

Catholic school. News of her planned abortion reached the parish priest who visited their house one night. The priest sat down with them as a family, and warned her against having an abortion.

May had never seen her Dad angrier, before or since. He practically manhandled the priest out of the house. None of them ever went to church again.

As her father went to open a second bottle of wine, the doorbell rang. 'I'll get it,' he said. 'You're not decent.'

May pulled the belt on her dressing gown.

Her father returned a few seconds later, DS Bradbury in tow. 'Sorry, ma'am,' said Bradbury, noticing May's horrified look. 'I did try to call.'

'This better be important,' said May.

'I'll leave you to it,' said her father.

'What the hell, Jack?' said May, once he was gone.

'I told you. Check your phone. I've called ten times.'

Her phone was still upstairs. 'Okay. What is it?'

'There's been an incident. Possible suicide. You need to come to the scene.'

'Who?' said May.

Bradbury glanced at his shoes. 'Roger Haydon.'

Chapter 25

Bradbury was right. Her phone had been switched to silent, and there were ten missed calls from him. She dressed as quick as possible, glad she hadn't started the glass of wine her father had poured.

'I'll leave your dinner in the fridge,' said her father, as she went to leave.

'Sorry, Dad, it's an emergency.'

He kissed her on the cheek. 'There's no need to explain. You be careful.'

Bradbury was waiting in his car. 'Are you coming with me, ma'am?' Though the idea of spending thirty minutes or so in Bradbury's company did little to cheer her, it would be a good opportunity to get an update on what had happened. The inside of the car was immaculate as if he'd recently had it valeted. A disc hung from the rear-view mirror pouring out a noxious, citrus air freshener.

'Sorry again, ma'am,' said Bradbury, as he pulled away. 'I knew you'd want to know and as I said, I did call you.' It was a poorly concealed dig.

'That's fine, Jack, you made the right decision.'

They spent thirty minutes struggling out of Bristol, the traffic by the Portway gridlocked. 'What happened?' she said.

'The body was found at four p.m. this afternoon. There are

a couple of guys from Weston CID there now. Superintendent Rush has sent a team from our department.'

May rolled her eyes presuming Bradbury had told Rush he couldn't get hold of her. Bradbury went to speak on a couple of occasions during the journey. May kept her gaze straight on the road ahead and sensed him turning to her about to speak, his courage always failing at the last minute.

The SOCOs were already in place at the housing estate, as were Welling and others from her team. A man she didn't recognise sat outside the house, inside the police cordon.

'Thomas Langtree, ma'am. He was Mr Haydon's'...' Bradbury paused, 'housemate.' The young man didn't look up or acknowledge her as she walked by. A WPC, presumably from the Weston station, sat next to him. The woman raised her head, acknowledging May, and was duly ignored.

She was surprised to find that the SOCOs were already finished. The body had been taken down and photographed, the scene recorded from every angle. Roger Haydon's corpse lay on a gurney covered by a black sheet.

'Inspector May,' said a man in a thick West Country accent.

'Sergeant Hall,' said May shaking the man's hand. From Weston CID, Hall was of medium build. He had a curious face, narrow eyes and a jaw which jutted out at a sharp angle. She'd dealt with him on numerous occasions and they'd always worked well together.

'I called your department as soon as I knew his identity,' said Hall. 'According to his friend out there, Mr Langtree, the body was discovered at approximately four p.m.' Hall walked over to the gurney and pulled back the cover revealing Roger Haydon's corpse. His lifeless eyes stared back at her, thankfully still intact. A thick red mark, covered in lesions and welts, encircled his neck.

Hall replaced the cover. 'Silly bastard hung himself,' he said, his narrow eyes wide with animation.

Haydon had defecated himself and the room was still cloudy with the noxious fumes of the recently deceased. She didn't know if she was imagining it, but she swore she could smell the faint residue of the incense she'd smelt at Terrence Haydon's and Sandra Hopkins' flats. She told Bradbury to make sure SOCOs checked for any signs of incense.

Outside, Langtree was still shaking.

'WPC Fulham, ma'am,' said the young constable May had ignored on her way into the building. 'I haven't managed to get much sense out of him, I'm afraid.'

May sat down next to the man. Bradbury had said Langtree was Haydon's housemate. It wasn't in Bradbury's initial report, and had only come to light following Lambert's visit.

'Thomas, my name is Sarah May. Can you tell me what happened?' asked May, softening her voice.

The man's face crumpled with grief, making him look much younger than his bulk would suggest.

'Please, Thomas. It would really help me to know the circumstances.'

Langtree sighed. 'He'd been acting strangely the last few days. Obvious, I suppose, after what happened to Terry.'

'It must have been a huge shock,' said May.

Langtree blinked. 'He'd started drinking more, we both had. And to be fair he was never short of a drink or two in the first place.'

Bradbury's report stated that the living room had been

littered with empty two-litre bottles of White Lightning, and the occasional cheap whiskey bottle.

'But I never thought anything like this would happen,' continued Langtree.

'So you found him when you came home?'

'Yes. I went to him. I could tell it was too late. His eyes were bulging.'

'But you didn't cut him down?' asked May.

Langtree's eyes filled. 'I was too scared. I didn't even touch him.'

'I understand.'

Langtree continued. 'He was hanging there lifeless, something made me not want to touch him. I haven't been back in since.'

'It's okay, Thomas. You did the right thing. When was the last time you saw him before you came back?'

'This morning before I went to work.'

'How was he then?'

'Pissed.'

'Did he look particular unhappy? Say something out of character?'

'Not really. It was hard to tell at the moment. He'd been worse since that guy came around bringing up bad memories about that woman.'

'What woman?'

'His ex-wife.'

'Sandra Vernon?' said May.

'Yes.'

'Sorry, Thomas, you need to clarify this for me, who came around to speak to him?' said May, knowing the answer.

'One of your lot. Strong looking guy. He said he was at University with Terrence. He started asking Roger about why he'd abandoned Terrence as a child. I think that's what snapped him.'

'Do you remember the man's name?'

'Lambert,' said Langtree.

May shuddered at the thought of how this would impact on the case.

'There was one more thing,' said Langtree, pushing himself up from the floor. The man-boy was a formidable size. Beneath the jacket the WPC had given him he wore a vest, his torso thick with muscle. 'Roger said someone else had come to see him yesterday afternoon, after Lambert was here.'

'Oh yes?'

'He'd been a bit vague on the details. I'd popped out to a mate's. We were both pissed at the time and I don't remember everything he said.'

'Please try, Thomas, it could be very helpful.'

Langtree scrunched his face in thought. 'He might have said he was a policeman, I don't know. I'm getting things confused with the other guy, Lambert. Roger had sounded confused actually. The man had wanted to pay respects like Lambert had. When I'd come back from my mate's, Roger had been more gone than normal. He'd started on the whiskey before six, which was a rule he didn't normally break.'

'And he didn't say anything else about him? Anything about his appearance?'

'He didn't want to talk about it. I started on the whiskey soon after that too. I'm really sorry, I can't remember.'

'Okay, Thomas. You keep trying to remember. Let me know when you do.'

'I'm sure there was something. Something weird he said about him. Oh yes, that was it.' Langtree started laughing.

May suspected the man was in shock.

'Yes, he said the man gave off a funny smell. Smelt like a bordello I think was how he put it.'

'In what way? He was wearing aftershave?'

'I don't know. I remember him saying "bordello". It sounded like a funny word to me.'

'See we get this man fed and dressed properly,' said May to the WPC. She'd been sure she'd smelt the incense in the house. It was possible this was what Langtree was referring to. She stepped back into the house and told Hall her theory.

'So you think his son's killer paid Haydon senior a visit?'

'I think it's a possibility.'

'What, and then came back to finish him off?'

'Maybe it was something he said to him. Can you smell incense in here?' asked May.

'All I can smell is shit and blood but we can check for it.'

'We should,' said May. 'And we should treat this area as a crime scene for the time being.'

May walked outside. She knew Lambert had met Roger Haydon and Langtree. From the meeting, Lambert discovered that Terrence Haydon had visited the gay club but what Langtree had told her would cause a number of unwanted problems. Lambert was now one of the last people to have seen Roger Haydon alive. Aside from Lambert, only Bradbury from her team had met the man.

There was now the added complication of the second man who had visited Roger Haydon on the same day as Lambert. Would the killer really have visited Haydon? And if so, why? It was possible Haydon had known more than he'd been letting on and that the killer wanted him silenced. Why, then, the lack of his usual signature?

She called DCI Nielson and explained the situation to him.

'I'll bring Lambert in for questioning,' said Nielson, a little too eagerly.

'I agree. However, I think it's Simon Klatzky we really need to speak to.'

'We'll find him,' said Nielson.

Langtree was eating some food, still being looked after by the WPC. May feared she was searching for things that weren't there. The most likely solution was always the most obvious. Roger Haydon had been so distraught by his son's death that he'd taken his own life.

Chapter 26

The second man was only half as drunk as Klatzky but still stumbled as he stood up. 'Sorry about this, Michael,' he said. 'Simon said it would be okay.'

Lambert had seen Roddy Glover a handful of times since their graduation day nearly eighteen years ago. The years had been reasonably kind to him. His slight, thin frame had yet to be ravaged by middle-age spread and he still had a full head of hair, now decorated with the odd streak of grey.

'It's good to see you, Roddy,' said Lambert. Glover's handshake was weak, his eyes failing to hold Lambert's gaze.

Undeterred, Klatzky dropped the record needle onto a mint condition vinyl issue of Prefrab Sprout's Steve McQueen. 'I love these guys,' he said, now swigging from a pint glass brimming with red wine.

'Be careful with that,' warned Lambert. He went over and turned the volume down.

Roddy reclined on one of Lambert's armchairs, smiling at the exchange. 'I bought some beers,' he said, an inane grin spreading across his face.

'I gave Roddy a call and told him what had happened in Bristol,' said Klatzky, slurring.

Lambert took one of the cans of lager and sat in the chair opposite Roddy. 'What else has he told you?'

'Not much. Can hardly get any sense out of him as usual,' said Roddy, making Lambert smile. He'd seen Roddy Glover practically every day during his University years. They had been in halls in the first and third year and shared a house in the second year, along with Klatzky, Billy Nolan, and two others. Glover had been present the night Billy Nolan's body had been discovered.

With him in the room, it felt strange to Lambert that they hadn't kept in contact more. After graduating, Glover obtained a place on a graduate trainee programme with an international oil firm and had spent the subsequent years working abroad. But there had been many times when they'd both been in the same country, the same city. It wasn't their proximity that kept them apart, it was their shared memory. It was only Klatzky who had wanted to keep everyone together.

They spent the next hour reminiscing about their time at University. Lambert drank a couple more beers, his mood improving with each drink.

'Let's go out,' suggested Klatzky.

'Why not?' said Glover. 'The wife's at the mother-in-law's for the weekend. I haven't had a proper piss up in months.'

An old reflex made Lambert hesitate. He had to remind himself he was no longer working. The Souljacker investigation would progress without him. Perhaps this was exactly what he needed. He steered them clear of the pub at the end of his street. Klatzky was already making no sense and though Lambert was hardly a regular he didn't want to risk upsetting anyone he might know. They found a chain pub along the high street. The Goose was one of those discount places already bustling in the late afternoon. Lambert ordered a round of drinks and they found some seats next to an ancient-looking pool table.

'Of all things, I never thought you'd go into the police,' said Roddy, loading some pool balls onto the table.

'Why not?' asked Lambert.

'Well for one, all those laws you broke at Uni.'

'True, true,' said Lambert. 'But if they don't catch you, you don't have to declare it.'

Klatzky was close to falling asleep, his chin resting on his chest, his eyes slipping in and out of consciousness.

'But seriously,' said Roddy. 'I was still surprised when I heard. I didn't think you were that sort of person.'

'Do I want to hear this?' said Lambert.

'Hey, it's not a criticism, far from it. And what do I know anyway? It's, I don't know, I would have thought it took a certain type of person to work for the police. Especially for someone who reached the sort of level you did. Level you are. Sorry, I'm talking shit.'

'And you don't think I'm that type of person?'

'Not at Uni, Mike. As I said, it's not a criticism.'

'You think I'm too soft,' said Lambert, leaning toward Roddy in a mock threat.

'Well yeah, you were soft as shit, goes without saying, but no. I always thought you were, God I hate to say this, but I always thought you were a little bit too nice.'

Lambert finished his lager, thought about how his plans for the future had changed followed Billy Nolan's death. How he'd tried to make sense of his friend's death by becoming an officer. The childish aspirations he'd held to change the world, if only a little. 'I will try to take that as a compliment.'

'Another one?' said Roddy.

'Stay with us, Si,' said Lambert as Roddy went to the bar.

He'd remembered the beginning of their conversation last night, before Sophie had interrupted them. He'd thought at the time that Klatzky was going to share something with him. It would be pointless pushing it now. The man could hardly keep his eyes open. At least he'd showered. Lambert recognised the shirt he was wearing as one of his. 'Help yourself,' he mumbled to himself.

'So what happened?' said Roddy, returning from the bar with another round of drinks. He went to hand one to Klatzky who had finally given in and fallen asleep, a line of dribble falling from the left side of his mouth.

'Nothing in particular. I guess I had to grow up, and DI Hastings suggested I had a talent for it.'

'Hastings? What, that bastard who was there for the thing with Billy?'

Hastings hadn't been too popular with the students at the time, had treated each of them as a potential suspect. 'Yes, him. Hastings suggested I think about a career in the police. He's not that bad once you get to know him,' said Lambert, thinking that perhaps he didn't know as much about the man as he'd originally thought.

'And you thought it was a good idea? Even after seeing what happened to Billy?'

'Well, that's the thing. I was full of good intentions then. I wanted to catch people. The sort of people who were capable of doing the things, oh you know what I mean.'

'Did you make the right decision?'

Lambert took a large drink. 'I've seen some awful things but I've managed to catch some of those types of people. So who the hell knows?'

Lambert enjoyed himself more than he'd imagined. Being with Roddy and the sleeping Klatzky in the pub brought back memories of a simpler time. He couldn't count the amount of evenings he'd spent in a similar fashion whilst at University.

The alcohol helped. It desensitised him. His concerns over recent events – Haydon's death, the second Souljacker murder in London, and the supposedly unrelated murder of Burnham – faded as the evening progressed. Even his worry over Sophie and her dalliance with Jeremy Taylor stopped bothering him. All he cared about at that precise moment was where the next drink was coming from.

As if reading his mind Klatzky sprung back to consciousness. The transformation was remarkable and not a little funny. Lambert exchanged smiles with Roddy as, wide-eyed, Klatzky reacquainted himself with his location.

'What are you both drinking?' he said, stumbling to his feet. He strolled over to the bar before they had time to reply, walking with a comical limp.

'Do you ever think you'll go back?' asked Roddy.

'To work? I guess so. At some point I'll probably have to,' replied Lambert, thinking that in a way he'd already returned, albeit in an unpaid position. Klatzky had been gone for ten minutes before Lambert became worried.

Then he noticed DCI Nielson, flanked by two uniformed officers, talking to one of the barmen.

'I think Simon's gone,' he said.

Chapter 27

Nielson spotted Lambert and pointed him out to his colleagues.

'Friends of yours?' asked Roddy.

'Something like that.'

'You're a hard man to find, Mr Lambert,' said Nielson, his colleagues flanking him on either side. Each a little nervous, poised, ready for action as if Lambert would flee the scene.

'You should have phoned. Saved yourself the trouble,' said Lambert.

'I did. Straight to voicemail. You are?' Nielson turned to Roddy.

The alcohol had loosened his friend who beamed at the DCI. 'I'm Roddy, of course,' he said, sniggering.

'I need to speak to you,' continued Nielson, turning his attention back to Lambert.

'Can we do it another time? I'm busy.'

'I need you to come to the station.'

'Need? Like? Demand?'

'All three,' said Nielson.

'I think I need a reason,' said Lambert. He was being difficult, but Nielson's manner rubbed him up the wrong way. He'd decided early on he didn't like Nielson and nothing about the way the man was speaking to him now was changing his mind.

'Roger Haydon is dead,' said Nielson.

Lambert hid his surprise. He pulled himself straighter in his seat. 'How?' he asked.

'Suspected suicide. The body was discovered by a friend of his, Thomas Langtree.'

Lambert pictured the scene. For some reason, he imagined Haydon in a warm bath, blood pouring from sliced wrists. The young Thomas Langtree standing motionless beside him, gazing at the red water and his lifeless friend, a glass of cider in his hand. He shut his eyes. 'Poor guy,' he said.

'The thing is,' continued Nielson, 'you were one of the last people to see Mr Haydon alive.'

Lambert drank the black coffee and willed himself to sober up. He'd told Roddy to wait for him at the bar and accompanied Nielson back to the station. He sat in an interview room, the two uniformed officers hovering about him.

He'd enjoyed meeting Roger Haydon, despite the circumstances. Life had not treated the man well but the odd relationship he'd struck up with Thomas Langtree seemed to be working.

'I'm going to record this,' said Nielson, entering the room, followed by a young woman he introduced as DC Shah.

'Be my guest,' said Lambert.

Nielson went through the preliminaries, explaining Lambert's rights, announcing who was present. He even asked Lambert if he wanted a lawyer. It was a bit unusual. Lambert was still an officer despite his leave of absence. Technically, Nielson should have informed Tillman that he was questioning Lambert. Despite Lambert's urge to make life difficult for Nielson, he decided not to mention it for the time being.

'As you've been informed, Mr Lambert, Roger Haydon was found dead today in his home in Weston-super-Mare.'

'A bit outside your jurisdiction,' said Lambert, bristling at Nielson's manner.

'I'm assisting my colleague, Detective Inspector Sarah May from Bristol's MIT.'

'That's okay then.'

'According to Mr Haydon's housemate,' Nielson shuffled his notes, 'Thomas Langtree, you were one of the last people to see Roger Haydon alive.'

Lambert sighed. He had informed Sarah May about the meeting, which had led to one of the best lines of inquiry so far on the Souljacker case. Nielson would have to work harder if he wanted a direct answer from him.

Thick grooves appeared in the flesh of Nielson's forehead as he concentrated. 'What can you tell me about the last time you saw Mr Haydon?' he said eventually.

'We had a nice chat.'

'And what was the purpose of your visit?'

'I went to pay my condolences. I'm sure you're aware, I knew his son Terrence. We were at University together.'

'This is Terrence Haydon who was murdered two weeks ago?'

'The very same,' said Lambert.

'How did you find Mr Haydon? Roger Haydon that is.'

'It was the first time I'd met him so I can't tell if he was acting out of the ordinary, if that's what you're asking. Though I did take into account that his son had recently died and that it was early morning and he was already drunk. As was his friend.'

'Mr Langtree?'

'Yes, Thomas.'

'What did you talk about?'

'As I said, I wanted to pass on my condolences.'

'The thing is, Mr Lambert, this is not the picture Thomas Langtree has painted of your visit.'

'Oh no?'

'No. Mr Langtree has described it as somewhat of an interrogation.'

Lambert shrugged again.

'Mr Langtree said you questioned Mr Haydon over his past, his relationship with his son.'

'As I said, we talked about the past. I'm sure DI May informed you of the lead I discovered from talking to the man.'

Nielson shuffled in his seat. 'Let's forget for a moment that you're not working on the case. Langtree said you questioned Haydon about his relationship with his ex-wife as well?'

'I'd met Terrence's mother the day before.'

'To pay your condolences, I presume?'

'That's correct.'

'Mr Langtree also said he found you looking through his private belongings?'

'A misunderstanding.'

'Misunderstanding?' repeated Nielson.

'Yes. I went to use the bathroom and lost my way.'

'It seems the whole situation became a bit too much for Mr Haydon, according to Mr Langtree. Your visit...' Nielson shuffled his notes again. He scanned the document in front of him until he found the words. 'Upset Mr Haydon. He started drinking even more heavily after your visit.'

'I'm truly sorry if that happened,' said Lambert. 'And I'm

sorry for Mr Langtree's loss, but I don't have anything to add to the matter.'

'A man's dead, Lambert.'

Lambert presumed he was coming across as being cold and indifferent. There was no way he could be implicated in Haydon's suicide, and it had been pointless dragging him into the station. It was possible his conversation with Roger Haydon had triggered something in the old man. He was a chronic alcoholic, and his estranged son had recently been murdered. Perhaps it had been wrong of him to push him so much.

'I understand that,' he said, trying to soften his tone. 'As I said I'm truly sorry Mr Haydon took his life but I don't know what else I can offer you. I thought we had parted on reasonably amicable terms.'

Nielson turned over the sheets of papers in front of him as if he was about to say something confidential. The room went silent except for the low hum of the recorder. 'Who did you speak to about Roger Haydon after leaving his premises?'

Lambert looked at Shah, wondering if he was missing something. She looked back at him, nonplussed. 'Like I stated, DI Sarah May.'

'Anyone else?' asked Nielson, his tone less accusatory than before.

Lambert placed his hands on the table. 'What's this about?'

Nielson scratched his chest. 'Someone else paid Roger Haydon a visit later the same day you met him. As yet unidentified.'

Lambert noticed that Nielson and Shah had leant forward, as if he had some miraculous answer for them. He'd only told May about the incident, but he knew where this was going. 'I didn't tell Simon if that's what you think. You're heading down the wrong path if that's what you're thinking.'

Nielson leant back in his chair. 'Let us decide what's the right line of enquiry, Lambert. When did you last see Klatzky?'

Lambert thought about the way Lambert had disappeared when Nielson had appeared in the bar. He wasn't ready to give his friend in quite yet. 'Not since Bristol.'

Nielson lifted his hands into the air. 'So you came back to London without him?'

'That's correct.' Lambert understood the implication. That Klatzky could have stayed on, and paid Haydon a visit.

'This is a friendly warning,' said Nielson, his voice heavy. 'Whatever private investigation you're running into the murder of Terrence Haydon I need it to stop. You've seen what your meddling has caused. You're out of the game now. I will not accept any more interference. Have I made myself clear?'

Lambert considered telling the man where to go but held his tongue. 'Perfectly. May I go?'

'Show Mr Lambert out, Shah.'

Lambert was surprised to find Roddy still at the bar. It had been two hours since he'd left with Nielson. Roddy sat next to the pool table, slouched on a cushioned chair, a glass of red wine on the table in front of him. A group of three women stood by the pool table, occasionally glancing over at him.

'Mikey,' shouted Roddy on seeing Lambert, loud enough that the majority of the bar turned around.

'You waited,' said Lambert, sitting down next to his friend.

'What you having?'

'I've had enough. Think you have too. Does your wife know where you are?'

'She keeps texting me,' said Roddy in a slur. 'I've told her I'm out. It doesn't seem to be quite enough.'

'Come on, we'll get you a taxi.'

'Simon came back.'

'Did he now?' said Lambert.

'He had an extended stay in the toilets. I think he may have been avoiding the police,' said Roddy, laughing as if he'd said the most extraordinary joke. 'He's only gone and pulled though.'

'You're kidding?'

'No, one of that lot.' Roddy pointed at the group of women by the pool table who were less than pleased with the attention. 'He went home with her thirty minutes ago.'

'Jesus,' said Lambert. He walked over to the women. Each of them folded their arms as he approached. Were they upset by Klatzky leaving with one of their friends, or had Roddy in his inebriated state done something to offend them? 'Hi,' he said, to general silence. 'I know this is a bit weird but my friend Roddy over there said my other friend, Simon, has gone on with one of your friends.'

'With Cheryl,' said one of the three, a red-haired woman in her early forties.

'Cheryl, right. I don't suppose you know where they went?'

'Don't know, don't care,' said the woman, her pale face crinkling into a patchwork of lines as she spoke.

Lambert looked at the other two for some support but received only blank stares.

'Okay, thanks anyway.'

'And you can tell your friend, Roddy is it?' said the red-haired woman.

'Roddy, yes.'

'That he's lucky that I haven't called my boyfriend down here to teach him a lesson.'

'Right. Look, I'm sorry if either of them have been rude. They've both had a lot to drink. It's no excuse, I know, but they're decent guys normally.'

The red-haired woman's face softened a little. Lambert handed her a card with his number on it. 'Will you call me if you hear from your friend? I really need to speak to Simon.'

The woman took the card and placed it in her handbag.

'What have you been up to, Roddy?' asked Lambert outside the pub. He had his arm around the man's waist, straining to keep him steady so the taxis wouldn't keep driving by.

'Oh, I don't know. I was only messing around. I can't really remember anything now. It's been good to see you. Perhaps we can see each other in the next decade sometime. What did the police want?'

'Nothing much.'

'Offering you your job back?'

'Not exactly.'

Eventually a taxi pulled over. Lambert gave the driver forty pounds and managed to get a slurred address from Roddy. He called Klatzky as he walked home. The phone rang but Klatzky didn't answer.

Sophie was waiting for him by the front door, a suitcase by her side.

'What's that for?' asked Lambert.

'You've been drinking,' she said, softly.

'One or two. I had some bad news.' Lambert realised he still didn't know how Haydon had committed suicide. The picture of him in his bath, wrists opened by a rusty razor was so vivid in his mind's eye that he could swear it was a memory.

'I'm going away for a few days. This place is a mad house.'

'You don't need to go. I'll go,' said Lambert.

'No, it's fine.'

'Where are you going to be staying?' asked Lambert. Once again he was surprised by his jealousy. He didn't think she would tell him if she was staying with Taylor.

'A hotel. I'll text you.'

He couldn't tell if she was lying, didn't know if he wanted her to tell the truth.

'Tell me when he's gone,' she said, kissing him on the cheek, shutting the door.

Lambert realised he was more disorientated by the drinking than he'd thought. It took him a minute to understand what she'd meant.

He ran through the house. 'Simon?' he shouted. If he'd brought that woman home with him he'd drag them both outside, clothed or not, he thought, sprinting up the staircase, two steps at a time. He stopped as he entered the spare room and turned away. 'Jesus, that's enough to make me vomit,' he said.

Klatzky lay on the bed face down, stark naked. A branded bottle of vodka stood on the bedside table, a quarter of its contents missing. 'What happened to your date?'

Klatzky mumbled something inaudible.

'We're going to talk in the morning. Cover your hairy arse,' said Lambert. He took Klatzky's clothes to stop him making an early exit and switched off the light.

He tried to sleep but his mind was too active. He brewed a pot of coffee and recalled everything that had happened since the day Klatzky had first shown him the photos. He considered calling May but thought it best to steer clear of Nielson's radar for the time being. He wanted to find out the exact details of the suicide.

He packed his bags and booked a train for Bristol in the morning. He needed to speak to Klatzky before leaving. He logged onto The System and accessed the Burnham file. The notes were thorough, as he would have expected from his former colleague. He scanned the file, enduring the images of the crime scene. The corpse with its eyelids sealed shut, a fine black thread woven intricately into the thin flesh of the man's eyelids.

Once he'd read through the whole report, he began again. He concentrated on each line, each witness report, on the notes from his former colleague and his team. He clicked on Burnham's profile, scrolled through notes from his family, friends, work colleagues. And then he spotted a name he knew. He would need to make a detour before he went to Bristol.

He shut off the computer and collapsed on the bed, as his vision began to fade. Flashes of orange and violet formed behind his eyes, a familiar dizziness overwhelming him and sending him to sleep.

He snapped awake four hours later, fully refreshed. After showering and changing he packed a small holdall and walked into the spare room where Klatzky was sleeping.

Lambert opened the curtains and window, a gust of fresh air filtering into the musty room. 'Right, we're going to talk,' he told Klatzky, who had thankfully crawled beneath the covers since he'd last seen him.

Klatzky rubbed his eyes. 'Not now,' he groaned.

Lambert grabbed the man by the shoulders. 'Yes now. You asked for my help in the beginning and now you need to come up with some answers. There's some people who want to speak to you.'

Klatzky sat up in bed, pulling the duvet over his shoulders until only his face showed. The late nights were not doing him any favours. His face was drawn. Grey bags hung beneath his bloodshot eyes, his cheeks and chin were speckled with uneven stubble.

'Who wants to see me?' he said, his voice dry and brittle.

'Never mind that. You were going to tell me something the other night, before Sophie interrupted us.'

'I can't remember, Mikey, everything's a blur at the moment.'

'It was something about Billy and Terrence. What aren't you telling me?' Lambert saw the flicker of recognition in Klatzky's tired eyes. 'You're going to have to tell me sooner or later. Let's get it over with.'

'Billy told me not to tell anyone.'

Lambert rubbed his temples, tried to count to ten but stopped after reaching five.

'For Christ's sake, Simon, Billy's been dead nearly twenty years. I don't think he's going to mind much.'

Klatzky squirmed beneath the covers. 'Okay, okay,' he shouted. 'Billy told me something once. I'm not sure if he even remembered he'd told me. We were hammered. I thought he was joking to begin with but then the conversation got a little bit too real.'

'Go on.'

'I didn't know what to say to him. He started to go on about his dad. Things that happened in his childhood. It was fucking awful stuff, Mikey. He was crying by the end of it. I was only nineteen. I didn't know what to say or do.'

'No one's blaming you, Simon. Just tell me what he said.'

'I can't go into the details. Let's say his father was not a nice man.'

Lambert paused, confused and annoyed that Klatzky had hidden this from him.

'There's more isn't there? How does this link in with Terrence?'

'I didn't even think about it until the other day when we were in Bristol. Billy used to go to these counselling sessions. We never mentioned the conversation again but I knew when he'd been. He used to pretend he was going running. He'd always glance at me before he left as if asking me not to share his secret.'

'What sort of sessions were they? One person? A group?'

'Group sessions I think. But that night when he told me about it, when he was crying, he mentioned that he'd once seen Terrence Haydon at one of the meetings.'

'Jesus Christ, Simon, why didn't you tell me this before?'

'I told you, I forgot.'

'You forgot?' said Lambert, swaying on his feet. 'How stupid are you? In fact, how stupid do you take me to be, Si? You didn't forget.'

'I'm sorry, Mikey. I promise, man, I forgot.'

Lambert turned away. 'You're pathetic,' he said, leaving the room. He only hoped his friend's failure wouldn't cost him dearly. Lambert was now positive someone was trying to set Klatzky up.

Chapter 28

The snail-like traffic of the south circular came as a relief. Lance edged the car along, allowing other vehicles out at junctions and pedestrians to cross in front of him. He'd switched off his usual eighties station and sat in silence, only the hum of the engine and the peripheral sound of other car stereos keeping him company.

Since ditching his passenger yesterday, Lance had received two pieces of bad news.

The second piece of bad news came in the form of a summons that morning. Campbell had called, demanding his presence at a safe house in Surrey, hence his gratitude at the slow pace of the traffic.

He'd received the first piece of bad news last night.

After dumping the still drugged and sleeping Klatzky in a secluded area in Uxbridge, he'd dropped off the car and headed for The Bricklayer's Arms, in Wood Green. The Klatzky character had seen his face, and despite the man's lack of sobriety, and Campbell's assurances, this troubled Lance. Within an hour he'd drunk four pints of premium lager and the worry had faded in part. As he was ordering his fifth, a one-time acquaintance of his stumbled through the bar entrance.

Ollie Trench owned a small scaffolding firm which operated in the area. Trench was a legendary soak. Now in his fifties he spent most of the working day in various local pubs leaving the organisation of his business to his two sons.

'Drink, Ollie?' asked Lance.

'Why not?' said Ollie, hobbling over to Lance's position by the bar.

'Work injury?' asked Lance, pointing to Ollie's leg.

'Pissed,' said Ollie, slapping Lance across the back.

Lance sighed and ordered two drinks. 'Little dram with that,' said Ollie to the barmaid. 'What's new, boy?'

Lance had worked the odd job for Ollie over the years. He paid reasonably well and for Lance always made it cash in hand. However, once he knew Lance worked for Campbell the contracts stopped. 'This and that, you know. Business good?'

'Not bad, must give the boys credit they're driving things along. Another?'

'Why not, boy?' said Lance, mimicking the man.

Ollie ordered two more lagers, with a pair of whiskey chasers. 'You heard?'

'What's that, Ollie?'

'You heard about that thing?'

Lance downed his whiskey chaser and took a swig of the lager. 'I need something more to go on here, mate.'

'Your man, from over Essex way.'

Lance tried to recall who he knew from Essex, thinking it might be quicker than waiting for some sense from the man to his side. He couldn't think of anyone. 'Something more, a name perhaps?'

'What's the fella, Burnham.'

'Sam Burnham?'

'Yes.'

'He lives near Watford, but carry on.'

'He doesn't any longer.'

'Come on, Ollie, tell me what you have to tell me. This story is longer than The Bible.'

'I would take another sip of that first if I were you.'

Lance did as suggested.

'Dead. A few days back.'

Lance stood rigid and glared at Ollie. 'What the fuck, Ollie?'

'Savage it was. Body all messed up. Something fucking awful done to his eyes.'

Lance staggered over to the nearest seat and collapsed.

'Sorry, I thought you knew,' said Ollie.

Lance had known Sam Burnham about as well as he knew Ollie. With one major difference: Sam had been the contact who'd eventually led him to Campbell.

Lance carried on drinking until the early hours. At some point Ollie left. Various images of the remainder of the night flickered in his memory, mercifully out of reach. He couldn't remember leaving the bar or returning home. His girlfriend refused to speak to him as she dressed for work, Lance's aching body prone on their bed. Some time later, Campbell called.

And here he was now, heading towards a meeting with the man who'd probably butchered Samuel Burnham. He tried to call his ex-wife as the traffic thinned but she was not answering his calls.

He came off the south circular. The roads deteriorated as he headed into the countryside, until he was driving along a single lane road, little more than a dirt track. He'd arranged to meet at the same place he'd first met Campbell all those years before. On that occasion, two of Campbell's subordinates had picked him up from a parking lot in East Finchley, late at night. Without speaking, they'd blindfolded him and threw him in the back of a van. On that journey, Lance had feared for his life. But it had been an indistinct fear, something he could reason against. Campbell hadn't had a reason to want him dead then.

But now?

Now, he'd almost paid back the debt. Now, he'd seen things which could lead back to Campbell. Now, the thing with Lambert had gone wrong, Klatzky had seen his face and Sam Burnham was dead, his eyes sealed shut with wire.

As the turning for the safe house approached, Lance lowered the car into second gear. His pulse thumped in his neck and forehead, strong enough to hear. He considered not making the turn, continuing up the country lane until he was back in the real world, and then driving onwards as far away from Campbell as was possible.

But that was fantasy. Campbell had taken pictures of his ex-wife and child, had promised they would pay for any mistakes Lance made. He hadn't been the best husband or father, but he would be damned if he would sacrifice his family for his own safety. Even if it meant suffering like Sam Burnham.

He parked outside the safe house. The building was borderline derelict. Mounds of weeds splintered the concrete driveway. Half of the six front-facing windows were smashed, shards of glass jutting out from the window frames. Lance parked the car. His was the only vehicle outside the building. He prayed Campbell had forgotten their rendezvous.

With shaking hands, he knocked on the splintered wood of the front door. When there was no answer, he rapped three times on the one remaining window.

Still nothing.

He found the front door key in its prescribed position under the second of four rocks which bordered the concrete driveway. His back creaked as he lifted the boulder, the flesh on his right arm tearing on a jagged piece of rock as he picked up the keys. Sweat poured from his forehead. He wiped it from his eyes with his grime-layered hands and opened the door.

Cold air hung in layers within the house. Lance shivered, his skin breaking out in goosebumps. 'Mr Campbell?' he whispered, walking through a dust-covered rug into the house's main room.

Lance saw the body first. It was the man with the broken leg, the one he'd taken from the hospital in Bristol. What remained of the man, anyway. Lance bent down to look closer, only to see a second figure.

In the gloom of the safe house's front room, Lance witnessed something he would never have thought possible.

Campbell, who lurked in the shadows waiting for him, was scared.

Chapter 29

Campbell ordered him to take the body to the car. 'Put some gloves on, man, for pity's sake,' he said.

Lance switched on the light in the room, instantly regretting the action. The body must have already been moved once, as there was barely a trace of blood on the floor. The corpse was missing his left leg, the wound where it had been hacked off just below the knee had been cauterised. Lance froze, and stared at the corpse's face. The man's eyes were sealed shut by a line of crude stiches.

'Just do it, man,' said Campbell.

First Burnham and now this second victim. The nameless man who'd had his leg broken by Lambert. Lance retreated to his car and lined the boot with a sheet of polyethylene. He pulled on his gloves and returned to the body. The corpse was surprisingly light. He tried not to look at it, tried to ignore the questions in his head. He shut the boot, catching a glimpse of the corpse's sealed eyelids.

Campbell sat in the passenger seat.

'Where now?' asked Lance, sitting in the driver's seat, trying to control the tremors which ran through his body.

Campbell didn't answer. He punched a postcode into Lance's sat nav. Lance sighed and set off. They reached the destination an hour later, the forecourt of a disused petrol station.

'We're going to dump him here?' said Lance.

The fear Lance had seen, or thought he'd seen, back at the safe house had evaporated. Campbell glared at him, and he had to look away.

'He's going to be found if we leave him here,' said Lance.

'They need to find him,' said Campbell, signalling the end of the conversation. Lance did as he was told, dumping the body in full view.

It came as a relief when Campbell told him to drive to the train station. Lance pulled the car to the entry of the station, thankful to see other people.

Campbell took off his seatbelt. Lance froze as he reached into his inside jacket pocket, and let out a deep breath when Campbell handed him a brown manila envelope and a piece of white paper.

'Deliver these to the first address,' he said. 'Meet me at the second address by six p.m.'

Chapter 30

Lambert accessed The System, and searched for details of the counselling sessions Klatzky mentioned. Nothing appeared on the original police reports about Nolan attending such sessions. It was inconceivable that Hastings hadn't uncovered that aspect to Nolan's life. Lambert wasn't fully convinced Klatzky had told him everything. He decided not to push the man further for the time being. He left him at the house sleeping off his hangover, and caught the train into London.

It was after accessing the Burnham file, that Lambert had noticed a familiar name in the witness list. Myles Stoddard. Stoddard was one of Lambert's old informants. Stoddard worked as a mechanic at a small garage in Crouch End. He'd been an acquaintance of Burnham and, with a reasonably sized criminal record, had been questioned by DCI Bardsley about his whereabouts at the time of the murder.

Lambert found the garage on a leafy terraced street. The forecourt was only big enough for three cars. It was a quaint place, the result of two terraced houses being knocked together, the front garden used for servicing the cars. Distorted music screeched from two tiny speakers inside the Portakabin which served as the garage's front office.

A short, bald man dressed in blue overalls worked behind a battered shop counter. He ignored Lambert as he walked through the door. Lambert noted three shades of colour on the man's full beard. He folded his arms as the mechanic glanced down at something on his desk before eventually looking up.

'Help you?'

'I'm here to see Myles,' said Lambert.

'He's a bit busy at the moment, mate. We've got an important job on.'

'Tell him Lambert's here to see him.'

The man went to argue but a look at Lambert's body language changed his mind. Fifteen minutes later, Myles Stoddard walked through the front door of the Portakabin. He was dressed in identical overalls to the bearded man. It had been nearly five years since Lambert had seen him. He was the same beanpole figure. The lank hair which fell from his head was thinner, faded. His shoulders drooped on seeing Lambert.

'What do you want?'

'Good to see you too, Myles,' said Lambert.

The man straightened up. 'Don't think I haven't heard about you. You're no longer working.'

'Don't believe everything you hear, Myles. Take a seat.'

An old leather sofa took up half the space inside the Portakabin, next to an ancient drinks machine which offered instant coffee, tea and soup. Lambert sat down. 'Sit,' he instructed.

'I'll stand,' said Stoddard.

Lambert glared at the man. 'Sit.'

Stoddard rolled his eyes and sat next to Lambert, the sofa barely big enough for the pair of them. Lambert put his arm around the back of the sofa and glared at Stoddard. The man tried to recoil but there was no space for him to move. 'A colleague of mine came to see you recently, DCI Bardsley.'

'Jesus, not that again. Look, I'd nothing to do with that. I hardly ever see Burnham.'

'Well you won't be seeing him any time soon, will you?'

'No, but why are you guys hassling me? I was only his mechanic.'

Lambert laughed, an exaggerated humourless sound.

Stoddard rolled his eyes again.

'Look, I don't care whatever angle you were working with him, Myles.'

'I wasn't working any...'

Lambert raised his hand to stop the man's protests. 'Whatever it was, I don't care. I'm only interested in what happened to Burnham. Who was responsible?'

'Well, it wasn't me.'

'Well, of course it wasn't you, Myles. You're a two-bit criminal, you haven't the balls for murder. Not something like that anyway.'

Stoddard was deflated, as if not having the capacity for murder-mutilation was an insult.

'But I read your statement and there was something you didn't tell my colleague. You are holding some information back and I need to know what that is.'

'You don't know shit,' said Stoddard.

Lambert edged closer. Stoddard started blinking, a nervous habit Lambert remembered from before.

'Who was Burnham working with? There must have been someone. This wasn't a random thing.'

Stoddard rubbed his chin. His eyes darted to the ceiling. Lambert allowed him thirty seconds for his internal debate.

'You either tell me now,' said Lambert, 'or I'll get Bardsley back here with some uniformed police this time. And I'll start asking about you in local bars, get your name out there.'

Stoddard's thin body shrivelled more into the sofa.

'I don't work for you any more, Lambert. That was a long time ago.'

'Once you sign on with me, Myles, it's for life. Now what 'd'you have to tell me?'

'Oh Christ, I don't know. As I told your mate I only saw him once a year when he came in for a service and MOT. But I heard rumours.'

'Tell me.'

'Jesus, he had a few bad years apparently. Got into debt. I heard he was in big with some loan shark guy.'

'Name?'

'Oh come on, I can't tell you that.'

'Name,' repeated Lambert, and then softer, 'you're not going to be mentioned, Myles, and you won't see me again.'

'I don't know who the guy is. Never seen him. All I know is that he goes by the name of Campbell and if you ask the right people I guess he can be found.'

Lambert couldn't recall any mention of the name Campbell on the report. 'You must have more than that for me, Myles. A first name.'

'I swear, that's all I know. I'm not even sure this guy exists.'

'Don't get all existential on me, Myles.'

'What?'

Lambert sighed. 'What do you mean you're not sure he even exists?'

Stoddard's blinking intensified. 'I don't know. He's like an urban legend or something.'

'An urban legend?'

'Yeah. You go to Campbell if you need help, but no one ever sees him. I don't know, Mr Lambert. I have nothing to do with this nowadays. I hear rumours now and again, that's all.'

Lambert placed his hand on Myles' shoulder. 'Thanks, Myles. Pop back to work now.'

A name. Campbell. Lambert took the tube to Paddington. He called DCI Bardsley whilst he waited for his train to Bristol.

'You working on my case as well now?' asked Bardsley.

'I like to be of assistance,' said Lambert.

'Well, we could always use you here when you're ready to make a comeback.'

'I'll keep it in mind,' said Lambert. 'So what do you know about this Campbell?'

'I've heard the name before. I'll speak to the rest of the team and see what they know. I may need to pay Mr Stoddard a little visit.'

'I promised we'd stay away from his work.'

'Fair enough. I'll get back to you if we get more information.'

On the train to Bristol, Lambert began searching for Campbell on The System. It wouldn't have been much worse if he'd been called Smith. Stoddard didn't know the man's first name which made it near impossible. Lambert viewed the hundreds of hits which appeared on his screen and diverted his attention elsewhere.

The details of Roger Haydon's suicide now appeared on HOLMES as an entry on Terrence Haydon's murder. He'd managed to hang himself from a thick wooden beam in his spare room. The pathologist's report stated he'd snapped his neck so his death had thankfully been quick.

At Bristol Temple Meads station, Lambert caught a taxi to Whitchurch. May had warned him not to approach Sandra Vernon's house again, but she wasn't answering her calls so he couldn't ask her permission.

Sandra Vernon tried to shut the door on him but he managed to jam his left foot in between the door and frame. Her face contorted in rage. 'I'll call the police,' she hissed. 'They've told you not to come here any more.'

'We need to talk,' said Lambert.

'I've nothing to say to you.'

'This is about Roger.'

'Then I still have nothing to say to you.'

Lambert couldn't see any emotion for her ex-husband's death. All he saw was anger, fear, and hatred in her eyes.

'Miss Vernon, I need to talk to you about the counselling sessions your church used to run.'

Vernon stopped. Lambert knew his hunch, or at least part of it, had been a good one. 'May I come in to talk?'

'We can talk here.'

'What can you tell me about those sessions, Miss Vernon?'

'What sessions? The church has been running counselling sessions for twenty, thirty years. Many years before I joined the church. AA meetings, marriage guidance.'

'This was something a little different. More delicate. I think Billy Nolan used to come to your church for counselling.'

'Who?'

'Please, Miss Vernon. Billy was killed by the same killer who killed your son.'

Vernon feigned surprise as if the connection had just occurred to her. 'Oh him, yes well. What's that got to do with the counselling sessions?'

'As I said, I think he used to come here whilst he was at University.'

'Perhaps. Unlikely. Why would he use the church? I wouldn't know,' she said, as if trying to convince herself.

'Who used to run the sessions?'

'My God, it was twenty years ago. We had all sorts of people. Volunteers. People from the church. Professionals from the council. I'm only a volunteer myself.'

'Surely someone would have records from that time?'

Vernon folded her arms, pushing a line of flesh above the collar of her shirt.

'I don't know,' she insisted. 'I'm pretty sure we don't keep records of those things even now, let alone then. It was all supposed to be anonymous.'

'I can imagine. You would need to respect people's privacy,' said Lambert, trying to empathise with the woman. 'But could you perhaps ask around for me? It is important. Obviously I'm going to let DI May know about our meeting as well.'

Vernon unfolded her arms.

'There was one more thing, Miss Vernon. From what I understand, Billy attended these sessions with your son.'

'No, impossible,' said Vernon, shaking her head. 'Well, I suppose Billy may have seen him there but Terrence never attended any meetings. He used to volunteer, setting up chairs, serving tea and coffee, that sort of thing. But he didn't attend any meetings. He had no need.'

'No, of course not.'

The woman's voice rose in pitch. 'I would know if he did. And anyway, why would he? He had no reason to.'

Lambert decided not to question her about what Roger Haydon had told him. The way Vernon had turned her back on him, the malicious rumours she'd started.

'Okay, thank you for your time. In the meantime if you can think of anything, anyone else you think may have been at the meetings with Billy, will you let me know?'

'I will let DI May know. Good day, Mr Lambert,' said Vernon, slamming the door.

Sarah May called him back not long after, and they agreed to meet. He caught a taxi back into the city centre and was eating lunch in a small café by the riverside when she appeared. He'd been researching Sandra Vernon's old church, which had been based in a small village outside Neath in South Wales. The place had disbanded nineteen years ago, not long after Vernon had left for Bristol.

'You're alive then?' said Lambert, as she sat next to him.

'Very much so, Michael. I've just had a lovely chat with Sandra Vernon.'

'How is she?'

'She's devastated with the news about her husband. I did ask you not to speak to her again.'

'Oh come on, Sarah. Something came up and you weren't returning my calls. Let's not play these games any more. I'm involved, and I want to help.'

May remained non-committal. 'Why were you speaking to Sandra Vernon again?'

'What did she tell you?' asked Lambert.

'Nothing that made coherent sense. Something about you ramming your foot in her door. Bringing up bad memories.'

'Elements of truth in that,' said Lambert. He shared his information about the counselling session Billy Nolan had attended.

May rubbed her eyes. 'You should have come to me first with that,' she said, almost whispering.

'I tried,' said Lambert.

'Where did you get your information?'

'I can't disclose that. But Miss Vernon all but admitted it.'

'You can't disclose that?' said May, incredulous.

'Not at the moment.' He wanted to protect Klatzky for as long as possible. If she knew he'd been talking to him, then she would demand he give the man up.

May exhaled, deciding not to pursue it any further. 'So Vernon said Billy Nolan and her son used to go to counselling sessions at her church?'

'Not exactly. Haydon was just a volunteer. Her memory was fuzzy, but I think it's a promising lead. It links Nolan and Haydon,' said Lambert, thinking that it also implicated Klatzky.

'Well, thanks. I'll get the team straight onto it.'

'Tell me about the surgeon,' said Lambert.

'We've released him.'

'How come?'

'He was on call throughout the evening and early morning of Haydon's murder. We've pretty much ruled him out.'

'So what's next?' asked Lambert.

'I'm liaising with Nielson. We will work the cases concurrently.'

'So you're not coming back to London?' asked Lambert.

'Not yet. Why, would you like me to?' May ran her hand through her hair, holding his gaze. Lambert was again surprised by the hold the woman had started to have over him, especially considering their joint involvement in the case.

'I couldn't possibly comment,' he said.

She raised her eyebrows. 'I'll get onto the counselling sessions. I'll ask Nielson to check on Sandra Hopkins' past as well. If we can place her at any of the sessions we may have something to work on.'

Lambert changed the subject. 'I was sorry to hear about Roger Haydon,' he said.

'I heard Nielson brought you in for questioning.'

'It was more of an interrogation. You think it was a suicide?'

'Nothing to indicate otherwise, though I would like to find out who Haydon spoke to before he died.'

'Who do you think it was?' asked Lambert.

May shrugged.

'This wouldn't have anything to do with Nielson's desire to speak to Simon would it?'

'Put yourself in our position, Michael. Would you want to speak to Klatzky?'

'You're being distracted.'

'If that's true, get him to hand himself in. The sooner we can eliminate him the better.'

'Why didn't you bring him in when he was in Bristol?'

May scrunched her face, a look of unease on her face. 'We were going to. I had someone posted outside the hotel, then the Hopkins incident happened and everyone was needed back at the station.'

'Oh dear. You have time for lunch?'

'Twenty minutes.'

Lambert bought some sandwiches, and they moved outside. They sat side by side, looking out at the channelled path of the River Avon. Lambert felt the sun burning his skin as he lifted his arm to eat his sandwich. He wanted to share his theory with May that Klatzky was being set up, but that would bring with it too many complications. He stole the occasional glance at the woman, who sat facing the river enjoying the sunshine as if she was a tourist.

'I met someone interesting yesterday,' she said, not breaking her gaze away from the dirty brown water.

'Oh yes?'

'Another retired copper. Iain Hill.'

Lambert searched his memory for the name. 'He led the team on the Clive Hale case?'

'Yes, the first Souljacker killing. Hastings was his subordinate.'

'I can't imagine that old bastard being anyone's subordinate. What did you want with him?'

'Simply verifying my sources. Hastings' recollection was not the greatest. Either that, or he's not one of life's sharers.'

'That much is obvious. What did Hill tell you?'

'It was what he didn't tell me which is interesting. He reiterated what a good copper Hastings was, kept going on about him being a good leader.'

'So what didn't he tell you?'

'It's probably nothing, but there are some gaps in the investigations.'

'Gaps?' Lambert had read each Souljacker murder file numerous times and didn't know where this was leading.

'Nothing that would warrant a case review. Didn't you find the case histories on the victims to be lacking?' She turned to look at him, just as he was shovelling some baguette in his mouth.

He swallowed. 'I don't know,' he conceded. 'They're in line with the reports for that era. What do you think was missing?'

'As you know six of the victims had religious affiliates, even if they were to different organisations. I'm surprised Hastings didn't look into this more, especially as the bodies piled up.'

'Maybe he did. We should ask him.'

'I will. I'll be interested to see how this links in with the counselling sessions.'

Lambert paid for lunch and they walked back into the centre. 'Let me help,' he said, as they reached the turning for May's station.

'Can I stop you?' she said, touching him on the arm. 'Keep me informed.'

Lambert watched May's figure disappear around the corner, and hailed another taxi.

Chapter 31

'Where to, mate?'

'Weston.'

'Really? It'll cost you.'

'That's fine.'

Thirty minutes later, the taxi dropped him outside the estate where Roger Haydon had lived. Lambert paid the driver and held out an extra twenty pounds in front of him. 'Think you could wait for me? Hour at the most?' he said.

'I could do with some lunch,' said the driver, snatching the money from Lambert's grip.

Lambert took the short walk to Haydon's old residence and knocked on the door.

Langtree opened the door before he'd finished knocking. 'I saw you arrive in your taxi,' he said, swaying in the door frame.

'Can I come in, Thomas?'

'Do what you fucking like, you will anyway.' Langtree turned his back, and Lambert followed him into the house.

The place had transformed since the last time Lambert had visited. It had been a mess before. Now, it was a disaster. The place writhed with litter. Lambert waded through empty bottles and cans which coated the carpet of the living room. Discarded fast food packaging, cigarette butts, and piles of dirty laundry fought for every available space. Langtree sat on the same armchair Roger Haydon had sat in earlier in the week. He was dressed like the older man, in an oversized pair of boxer shorts and cotton vest. He picked up a tumbler filled to the brim with liquid, the colour of which suggested brandy or whiskey.

Lambert lifted a mound of soiled clothes from the sofa and sat down.

'So what do you what, Lambert?' said Langtree, slurring his words until they were almost unintelligible. 'Come to pay your condolences again?'

'I'm so sorry about Roger, Thomas. He seemed like a very nice guy.'

'Nice guy? Nice fucking guy. That's a good one.' Langtree took a gulp of his drink as if it was water, wiping his mouth with his forearm.

'DI May told me that someone else visited Roger before he...'

'Killed himself?' Langtree jumped to his feet, and fell back down onto his chair. He tried a second time, this time using the arm rest as a support. 'Drink?'

'Not for me.'

Langtree stumbled to the sideboard, a sixth sense helping him bypass the detritus surrounding the drinks cabinet. He pulled out a bottle of whiskey and refilled his tumbler. A quarter of the drink had spilt to the floor by the time he reached his seat.

'You'll do yourself a mischief,' said Lambert.

Langtree glared at him, his eyes struggling to maintain eye contact.

'So, this visitor, Thomas. What do you remember about him?'

Langtree sighed. He looked at his drink but didn't move the tumbler to his mouth. 'I didn't see him, I was at work.'

'Did Roger say anything about him? Give any clues about who he may have been?'

Langtree shrugged. 'If he did, he didn't let on.'

'So what happened?' Lambert guessed Langtree was about a drink away from collapse.

'By the time I was home, Roger had gone all quiet. He had a drink then he went out. Wouldn't let me come with.'

'Do you know where?'

'Pub, I guess, I don't fucking know.' Langtree raised his voice, the face contorting on the verge of tears or violence.

'Okay, Thomas, sorry. I'm only trying to help. Did you see Roger again after that?'

'No,' said Langtree, draining his glass, his eyes welling up. 'I had to go to work,' he said, between sobs. 'When I came back, he was...' Langtree was crying hard. 'I've told your colleagues everything I know.'

Lambert stood up and placed a hand on Langtree's shoulder. He was surprised when the man didn't flinch. 'Can I take a look?'

'Yes,' said Langtree, not looking up.

Police tape still cordoned the area but Lambert stepped under it. The SOCOs had finished their work so he couldn't damage the scene anyway. A few days ago, Langtree had caught him snooping around up here. Now it was the place where Roger Haydon had died. The room still smelt of bleach and cleaning materials. Lambert touched the wooden beam in the corner of the room, the grain rough and sticky. He pictured the thick rope wrapped around the beam, Haydon's lifeless body dangling beneath it.

He hadn't spent enough time with Haydon to tell if he'd been suicidal or not. He'd certainly been upset over his estranged son's death but hadn't given the impression of wanting to end his life. There was something about his relationship with Thomas which comforted him. It was possible that the man who'd visited him yesterday had been the catalyst, but until they found out who that was they were stumped.

Lambert returned downstairs to find Langtree asleep on the floor. After manoeuvring the man into the recovery position, he retrieved a duvet from upstairs and placed it over his sleeping body. Finally, he scrolled his name and mobile number onto a piece of paper and left it by his side.

Chapter 32

Lambert spent the night in Bristol, twice coming close to calling May. He read through the case files again, from Clive Hale to Sandra Hopkins, searching for the missing gaps suggested by May. He couldn't see anything of significance. There were always multiple avenues of approach to a murder, and Hastings had taken the normal route. Each victim's background had been investigated thoroughly enough, and after each fresh murder Hastings had crosschecked the new victim with the older cases.

Lambert knew the DS on the Billy Nolan case, Cormack Riley. Riley worked out of Greenwich when Lambert was in The Group and they'd exchanged resources on a couple of occasions. Billy Nolan was the only Souljacker case Riley had worked on, before joining the MET. Lambert took a note of his details and headed for the railway station.

Klatzky called as he was boarding the train at Temple Meads. He sounded panicked, his voice high, his speech pattern slurred. 'I've just been back to my place,' he said.

'And?'

'There was a package there, no stamp, delivered through the door same as before.'

'Have you opened it?' asked Lambert.

'Yes, and I wish I hadn't. There are more photos. Someone else this time.'

The train carriage was empty save for a lone businessman engrossed in his laptop. 'Same sort of thing as Haydon?' asked Lambert, not wanting to get into specifics over the phone.

'Not exactly,' said Klatzky.

Lambert could hear background noise on the other end of the line. 'Are you in a bar?'

'Where else?'

'Get to Paddington station. I'll be there in under two hours. Simon, don't speak to anyone.'

Klatzky was dressed in what Lambert imagined were last night's clothes. He'd aged a decade since Lambert had last seen him. His eyes were lifeless. Lambert spotted him as he left the train, walking trance-like outside the entry to the platforms, a brown envelope clutched to his chest.

'Let's get a coffee,' said Lambert.

'I need something stronger.'

Lambert lacked the strength to argue. They took an escalator to a bar which overlooked the station's concourse. Lambert ordered tea whilst Klatzky ordered a lager with a vodka chaser. With shaking hands, he gave Lambert the envelope.

It was only photos this time. Lambert knew immediately what he was looking at. It wasn't Samuel Burnham but it was an identical crime scene to the one DCI Bardsley had shown him. The victim was a black man, shaved head, late thirties. Like Burnham, his eyes had been sealed shut with lines of wire, his throat slit. The third picture showed a jagged line where his left leg had been severed; right at the point where Lambert had broken it.

'You didn't see who dropped this at your flat?' asked Lambert.

'No. It was there when I got back.'

'When had you last been back, prior to that?'

'The morning before we went to Bristol.'

Lambert examined the photos again. They were not police quality. The images were hazy, the resolution poor as if they'd been printed on a home printer. It was probable that the killer had taken them. It was unlikely he had left any prints, but Lambert held the photos with a napkin on the edge of the paper.

'Why is he sending them to me?' asked Klatzky, drinking the vodka in one gulp, his fingernails ratting against the hard wood of the table.

'I'm not sure. Did you ever tell anyone else about Billy's counselling sessions?'

'Not that I can remember.'

'Think carefully, Simon.'

'I didn't tell anyone at the time, I'm sure. Billy swore me to secrecy. I can't see any reason why I would have blurted it out since. I didn't even tell you until now.'

Klatzky now linked the Souljacker and the second killer and had received photos from both crime scenes which confirmed to Lambert that the Burnham killer was the Souljacker.

Things were closing in. The photos were important evidence but he planned to keep hold of them for the time being.

He realised now he'd been wrong. Klatzky wasn't being set up as he'd initially thought. The Souljacker was after him and was using Klatzky to draw him in.

'Okay, Si. You can stay at mine for the time being, until we've sorted this,' said Lambert.

'Thanks, Mikey. Can I get you a drink?'

'No. Listen, you should…'

His pleas fell on deaf ears. 'Look, sorry, man, but could you lend me some cash?'

Lambert emptied his wallet and gave the money to Klatzky. There was no way he would be able to talk him out of the bar. He tried anyway. 'I need to get back. You should come with me.'

'I'll think I'll stay here awhile. Stay out of trouble,' said Klatzky, pocketing the money and signalling the barman.

Lambert waited until he was home to look at the photos again. He caught the tube to London Bridge and the overground train home. He tried to steer his mind away from the case. Everything was a clutter, his mind a jumble of useless information. Experience told him that trying to think about other things often led to inspiration, to an insight that would otherwise elude him.

From Clockhouse train station he ambled back to the house, his limbs stiff, an ache building in his head. Reluctantly he opened his front door. Inside, he brewed a pot of coffee. Knowing Sophie was away made the house seem empty even though she was never usually at home during the day.

Coffee in hand he walked through each room of the house trying to think, avoiding looking again at the pictures. The ceilings felt higher than normal, the rooms less cluttered as if Sophie had taken half of the house's contents with her when she'd left. She'd be at work now. Lambert tried not to think about where she was spending her nights. She'd given him the name of a hotel but he'd yet to check if she was there. The possibility that she was spending her nights with Julian Taylor was too much for him to consider at the moment.

He sat on one of the armchairs in the living room where the other evening he'd shared the company of Klatzky and Roddy.

He opened the photo file which had been delivered to Klatzky. He'd seen hundreds of crime scene photos in his time but it never became any easier. Normally he could detach himself from the images but the pictures before him had a certain resonance. It wasn't the images themselves that troubled him, the naked middle-aged man, the puffy black skin splattered with patches of maroon, the neatness of the wire which sealed the man's eyes shut, the cleanness of the cut on the man's leg. It was the fact that he knew the victim, had fought with him only days before.

It was clear now. The pictures had been meant for him.

It wasn't Klatzky who linked the Souljacker and this second killer. It was him.

He walked back to the kitchen and filled his cup again with black coffee. On The System, he searched for details of the new victim but couldn't find anything. He ran a number of searches on Klatzky but nothing significant appeared beyond his existing arrest warrant. He cross-searched Klatzky's name with Campbell, then with Sandra Hopkins. He cross-searched Klatzky with Billy Nolan and Samuel Burnham. Running out of ideas he crosschecked Klatzky with all the previous victims, still nothing.

In the end, he called DCI Bardsley.

'I haven't seen you for ten years and now I can't bloody get rid of you,' said Bardsley, in his dour Black Country accent.

'Thought I'd check in,' said Lambert.

'Oh yes, why?'

'I was wondering if you had anything new to tell me.'

Bardsley didn't answer, only the faint sound of his breathing audible through the earpiece on Lambert's phone. Lambert wasn't about to break the silence.

Eventually Bardsley relented.

'Is there something you need to tell me, Mike?' he said.

'No, I'm only curious as to developments,' said Lambert.

Silence again.

'I guess you'd hear about it anyway,' said Bardsley. 'There's been a second victim. Kwasi Olumide. His body was discovered earlier today on the forecourt of a disused petrol station. Same MO as Samuel Burnham. Eyes sealed shut. The body had been moved. He'd been dead for at least forty-eight hours by the time we found him.'

'Any body part missing?' said Lambert, thinking about how the killer had removed Sam Burnham's lips.

'Leg,' said Bardsley. 'Something tells me you already know this, Mike.'

'Who is this character?'

'Ex-con. Minor stuff. Some house burglary. We grabbed your informant in, Myles Stoddard.'

'I bet that pleased him,' said Lambert.

'Caught him on his lunch break.'

'What did he have to say?'

'He knew him. Though it strikes me that he knows a lot of people.'

'And?'

'Seems Kwasi here was suffering some serious money worries. And according to Stoddard the rumours were that he'd been to a certain Mr Campbell for some advice.'

Chapter 33

May stood outside Gracelife church, Bristol, accompanied by Bradbury, and two uniformed constables. She had an appointment with the pastor, Neil Landsdale. In her hand she held a warrant to search the church's records.

A thin lady in a pale summer dress answered the door. The woman was nervous, her head jutting forward and back like a chicken. May introduced herself and showed her the warrant.

'I'm afraid the minister is very busy at the moment. Could you come back later?'

'I don't think you understand the nature of the warrant,' said Bradbury, barging past May.

May held her arm out to stop his progress. 'Miss?'

'Mrs Sally Davidson,' said the woman.

'Mrs Davidson, please read through the warrant again. You'll see that we have a legal right to enter and search the premises, whether or not the minister is ready.'

Bradbury mumbled to himself as the woman read the warrant. 'I really should check with the minister.'

'Okay, let's all go in together and we can ask him,' said May, moving past the woman, her patience fading.

The church was not like the churches she'd attended as a child. She was used to open spaces, with high ceilings and stained-glass windows. This was nothing more than a couple of houses knocked together. Dark brown walls added to the claustrophobic feel. The only light came from a pair of small, oval windows.

'Can I help you?' The shape of a lanky, grey-haired man came into view by a side door.

'Neil Landsdale?' asked May.

'Yes.'

'My name is Detective Inspector May. I believe you know my colleague, Detective Sergeant Bradbury. I have a warrant to search your premises.' May walked across the polished floor and handed him the document.

Davidson followed behind. 'I'm sorry, Neil. I did try to stop them.'

Landsdale ignored the woman and read through the file. 'That's fine, Sally,' he said, once he'd finished reading. 'What's this about, Inspector?'

'We're trying to find all documents relating to counselling sessions conducted here in the last twenty years. It would save us a lot of time if you could assist us.'

'Of course I'll assist you. Why all the drama?'

May applied for the warrant after talking to Lambert, and his revelation that Billy Nolan had once attended counselling sessions at the church during the period prior to his murder. She didn't want to take the risk of Landsdale destroying any potential evidence, however unlikely it was that such evidence existed.

Landsdale led her to the office. May instructed Bradbury and the others to check the rest of the church. 'Is that really necessary, Inspector?' said Landsdale.

'What do you have for me then?' asked May, ignoring the

minister's protestations. She told him the particular years she was interested in, when Billy Nolan had been a student.

'Do you have any details on the exact nature of the sessions? We run, and have run all manner of sessions over the years. From AA meetings to counselling for victims of abuse.'

'I need details on everything from those years. I take it you don't have the records computerised?' said May, glancing at an antiquated-looking PC on the man's desk.

'No. In fact, Inspector, we don't really keep any records. By their very nature, these gatherings are often anonymous. We would never make a list of attendees. The best I can do is to give you a list of what counselling sessions were taking place, and hopefully the name of the counsellor involved. Even that might be a longshot.'

'Were you the minister at this time?'

'Yes, it's my church.'

Landsdale exuded calmness. He had a gruff charisma, clearly practised. So far, he'd treated May as if she was the only person in the room. She imagined him using his charm on the parishioners, coaxing a small congregation into following his every word. 'Our filing system,' he said, unlocking a wooden door in the corner of the office.

The door led to a second room, little bigger than a broom cupboard. Shelves and bookcases lined the walls. Files and loose papers filled the shelves in no apparent order. May saw her day disappear in front of her.

Landsdale flicked a switch. A cloud of dust swirled around a naked bulb. The room was musty, a patch of damp darkening the left-hand corner of the ceiling. May watched as Landsdale worked through the mess, eventually handing her a small folder of papers. 'This is it?' she said.

'I'm afraid so. I told you we don't keep many records.'

'Aren't the people who come to these things vulnerable?'

'Sometimes. They come on a voluntary basis. Some of them want to be anonymous, some share their name but we don't take a record of it.'

Landsdale switched off the light and returned to his office. May followed him, and instructed one of the PCs to find Bradbury. 'May I use one of these desks?' she asked.

'Please, be my guest. Can I get you a drink?'

'I'm fine, thank you,' said May.

'Ma'am?' said Bradbury, sticking his head around the door into the office.

'In there,' said May, pointing to the other room. 'Box everything.'

Landsdale acted as if she'd struck him in the face. 'Is that really necessary?' he said.

'I appreciate your cooperation,' said May, opening the file before her.

May read intently, trying her best to ignore Landsdale who paced the room. 'This will take some time, Mr Landsdale,' she said.

'Take all the time you want.'

'What I mean is, you might want to get some fresh air.'

'I knew what you were implying, Inspector. This is my church, I want to be of any help I can.'

May finished reading the file and started again from the beginning, disappointed with the lack of information it contained. It was ten pages long. It contained a timetable, listing the days and times the hall was used, and a sheet for each of the sessions. They had used the main church area in much the same way large churches used their church halls. Monday to Wednesday, the church was for Brownies, Cubs, and Girl Scouts. The counselling sessions had taken place on a Thursday and Friday. Due to the nature of the sessions, and the lack of space, they had spread the sessions over different time periods. The last session had been nine to ten p.m. Only two of the sessions were titled. An Alcoholics Anonymous session on a Thursday at eight p.m., and a family bereavement session on a Friday at seven p.m.

'This is all rather vague,' said May.

'I did warn you.'

'Why aren't some of these sessions titled?'

'May I see?'

May handed him the file. Landsdale scanned the papers, a smile forming as he reminisced. 'The titled sessions were held by outside organisations. The other sessions were run by the church, and church counsellors.'

'Do you remember the specifics? Quite a lot of time is timetabled off. Surely you would have invoices, didn't the external organisations pay to hire the hall?'

'As I said, we ran and run a number of different courses. Some religious based, some focusing on the local community. I guess you might find some more detail through there, though I doubt it,' said Landsdale pointing to the cupboard.

May tried hard not to let her mistrust of religious leaders sway her judgment against Landsdale. 'But you must remember something?'

Landsdale sat down on one of the office chairs. He was composed, calm, borderline condescending. 'It was twenty years ago. Can you recall what you were doing twenty years ago?'

'To an extent, yes.'

'But to the extent you wish me to recall?'

May sighed. 'You do know why I am here. One of your parishioners was murdered less than a week ago. It is possible that the killer's previous victim used to attend some form of counselling session here. Even you must see there is a link?'

'Even me?' said Landsdale, chuckling. 'Inspector, I am not trying to withhold anything from you. If you really feel there is a link between the two murders then of course I will help as best I can. I want justice for Terrence as much as you do, but in the last twenty years, we've had hundreds, possibly thousands, of groups come and go. Also, I am not as young as I once was. My memory, as the local parlance would have it, is shot.'

May stifled a laugh. 'Could you access your shot memory, and see if you can recall any link the church may have had with the University at the time?'

Landsdale stared straight ahead. May thought he was ignoring her until she realised he was thinking. 'I believe we used to put up flyers at the University. In fact, I think Terrence used to help us with that when he started there. I have some vague recollection about us attending some sort of fayre at the place. A Freshers' Fayre, perhaps?'

'Okay. And who would have attended this?'

'We were a much bigger outfit back then, Inspector. Huge congregation.' He rubbed the loose skin on his face. 'Perhaps you can try Sally.'

'Sally?'

'Sally Davidson. I believe she'd started as one of our

counsellors back then. Come to think of it, it may have been her suggestion to approach the University. Something about the despair of being a student.'

'This being the same Sally Davidson who was here when we arrived?'

'The very same,' said Landsdale. 'I'll go and get her.'

Landsdale left the office. May wasn't sure if he was being deliberately obtuse or if his failure to identify Davidson as a counsellor at the time was an honest mistake. She recalled the nervous way Davidson had reacted to her arrival. How she'd tried to get them to come back another time.

Landsdale returned. 'Strange, she seems to have popped out,' he said.

Chapter 34

Landsdale wrote Sally Davidson's address on a piece of paper and handed it to May. 'It's only a mile from the church. She probably popped home for some lunch,' said the minister. 'It's not if she can do any work here.'

'Make sure he doesn't call anyone. He's not to leave your sight,' May instructed Bradbury. 'Wait until I get back before heading for the station.'

May passed a public house called The Cartwheel, and headed into a housing estate where Davidson lived. The sky had clouded over, the temperature plummeting. May kept alert, looking out on the off chance for the woman.

Sally Davidson lived in a terraced house on Jubilee Street. An overgrown hedgerow spread onto the pavement at the front of her house. As May opened the garden gate, flecks of black paint flaked off the rusted metal onto her hand.

Sally Davidson was waiting by the front door, the colour drained from her face. Her head bobbed forward involuntarily. 'Inspector May,' she said, her voice a whisper.

'Can I come in?'

'It's a bit difficult at the moment,' said Davidson.

'Don't start all that, Sally. Either I come in now or we take a visit to the police station.'

The woman stood aside and ushered her in, her face twitching as May walked past. Davidson led her to a cramped living room. The woman clearly had an eye for bright colours. The wallpaper was a floral design, heavy on shades of purple and maroon. A multi-coloured patchwork quilt was thrown over an ancient-looking sofa. 'Can I get you a drink?'

'Please, let's sit.'

Davidson sat on the sofa. May took a seat on the torn maroon leather armchair opposite. 'You understand from our earlier conversation why we attended the church today?'

'Yes, the warrant.'

'And you know what we're investigating?'

'Terrence,' said the woman, her head moving from side to side in an even cadence.

'Can you tell why you left the building in such a hurry?'

'You hadn't asked me to stay,' said Davidson, her face flushed with indignation.

'Nothing more than that?'

'I didn't appreciate you appearing and taking over like that. It is not fair on the minister, and it is not fair on the church.' Full of new-found confidence, Davidson held her head high. Her neck muscles were pulled tight, a gnarled vein snaking up the side looking fit to bust.

'Mr Landsdale informed me you have been with the church for a number of years.'

'That is correct.'

'He also mentioned that you were a counsellor during the time of Billy Nolan's death.'

Davidson slumped down into the plump cushions of the sofa, all pretence of confidence vanished.

'Did Billy Nolan attend counselling sessions with you, Mrs Davidson?'

Davidson tried to shake her head but her nerves had got the better of her. Her head moved of its own accord, a continued circular motion interspersed with the occasional spasm forwards. 'No,' she said.

'But he did attend the church?'

'I can't be sure but I believe so.'

'Were you questioned about Billy Nolan's death at the time?'

'No. No one ever contacted the church.'

The case files backed this up. 'And did you not volunteer the information?'

'I couldn't be sure, and anyway those boys were here anonymously.'

'Boys?'

'As I said, I'm not sure if it was Billy Nolan who attended. From the pictures I saw in the newspaper I think it was him. He always came with a friend. We ran two sessions at the same time. I ran one upstairs in the office, the other was held downstairs.'

'And Nolan went to the one downstairs.'

'It's possible. Yes, I believe so, yes.'

Davidson left her seat. 'Can I fetch something?' she asked. 'I kept some things which may be of help.' The woman returned a few minutes later holding a box-file. 'I kept this after the boy died. I realise I should have contacted someone earlier.'

Earlier, thought May. She was eighteen years late, could have prevented the death of Terrence Haydon. May opened the file and scanned the contents.

'Billy, if it was him, was in a group for victims of abuse. It was not an area I was comfortable in. The church brought in a specialist to run the session.'

'But it was still advertised as a church group?' asked May.

'I suppose so.'

'Do you remember the name of the person running the session? What organisation they were from?' May tried to hide her growing excitement.

Davidson handed her a piece of paper.

'This is it?' The piece of paper had a surname scribbled onto it in biro.

'I only knew him by his surname. This was before the days of CRBs and what have you. I didn't know anything about the man. I saw him once a week. He left at the end of the session. The minister might know something more.'

May sighed. 'And what about your group?'

'I ran a support group for carers. I nursed my old mum until her dying day. A lot of young people have to do the same. I wanted to help out in any way I could.'

'What about Billy Nolan's friend? What do you remember about him?'

'He was a lovely boy. Very handsome. He'd been looking after his mother as well. She'd died the year before he'd started at the University. He was such a modest young man. He claimed he shouldn't have been at the meetings as it had basically been a joy looking after her. The poor woman had been blinded after a particularly nasty cancer and his father had passed some time before.'

'Blinded?'

'Yes,' said Davidson.

'Do you remember the boy's name.'

'Of course. It was Simon Klatzky.'

May rushed back to the church and questioned Landsdale. Bradbury had finished packing the last of the boxes. She updated him on what Davidson had told her. 'Go through each document. We need to locate the counsellor in charge of Billy Nolan's sessions.'

'And you?'

'I need to go to London.'

She caught the first available train from Temple Meads. She called Superintendent Rush, informed him she was heading to London and told him to put out an urgent arrest warrant on Simon Klatzky.

She checked her email, in time to see a message from Sean. She sighed. It was becoming a pressing problem that she needed to solve. Their confrontation on The Triangle in Clifton had shaken her more than she'd realised at the time. Something about the way his face changed when she'd told him where to go, had given her cause to worry.

She didn't fear a direct confrontation. Sean didn't work that way. His attack would be covert. He'd suggested that he'd make the abortion public knowledge. Although she'd laughed it off, it would make things difficult for her. For one, she had never declared it on any medical form, or during any psych evaluation. That fact alone could put her in a heap of trouble.

She ignored the email, deciding she would meet the man when the case was completed, vowing she would then eliminate him from her life for good.

At Paddington station, she caught the tube to Holborn and took a short walk to the building of Barker and Price Solicitors. The foyer was as grandiose as a five-star hotel.

Two glass elevators stretched into the heavens. May waited in a short line to speak to one of the firm's receptionists. A young Asian man, dressed in a sharp pinstripe suit with a white turban wrapped around his head, asked how he could be of service.

'I would like to speak to Sophie Lambert,' said May.

'Do you have an appointment?'

May showed the man her warrant card. 'My name is DI May. Please inform Mrs Lambert that I would like to see her immediately.'

The receptionist didn't hesitate. 'Please take a seat,' he said, pointing to a row of plush leather armchairs.

Two minutes later, a woman approached her. 'DI May? My name is Matilda Sanford. I am Mrs Lambert's PA. If you would like to follow me, Mrs Lambert is waiting for you.'

They took the elevator to the thirty-sixth floor of the building. Sanford's perfume, a faint scent of rose, filled the interior of the elevator. The woman stood a respectful distance away from her, and didn't instigate any conversation.

The door pinged open, and Sanford walked her down a deserted corridor to a glass-panelled office. 'DI May to see you,' she said, to the woman sitting alone in the office.

'Thank you, Matilda. DI May? Sophie Lambert. How may I be of assistance?'

The woman's handshake was firm but not overly so. A petite woman, Sophie Lambert had large intense eyes. She exuded confidence. It was not the high-powered business suit and killer heels she wore. Sophie Lambert was one of the rare breed of people May sometimes encountered. She had an aura about her, a quality which was hard to define in specifics. May imagined the woman had a very loyal clientele. She was the sort of person people wanted to be around.

'Please excuse the unannounced visit. I'm here about your husband.'

A brief look of concern appeared on Sophie Lambert's face, and disappeared as if it had never been there. 'You better sit down then,' she said.

Chapter 35

Lambert considered what Bardsley had told him. 'So Stoddard's persisting with his Campbell theory?'

'Seems that way. Problem is, he doesn't know what Campbell looks like. Doesn't even have a first name. It's a pointless exercise searching for someone who may not exist,' replied Bardsley.

Tell me about it, thought Lambert. He decided not to tell Bardsley about the photos which had been sent to Klatzky. If the killer was trying to get his attention, then involving Bardsley might divert his attention. The Souljacker had been dormant for eighteen years. It was conceivable he could disappear again. He couldn't take the risk.

He asked Bardsley to keep him involved and hung up. He'd missed a call from Sophie. She hadn't left a message so he didn't call back. He sent a text message to Klatzky instructing him to return to the house as soon as possible.

He met Cormack Riley in the same coffee shop where Klatzky had shown him the photos. It was less than a week ago but felt like another age. 'Bit posh here,' said the man, holding out his hand. 'Sorry, I ordered ahead,' he added, nodding to his cup of coffee.

'No worries, thanks for coming all the way out here.'

Riley wore faded jeans, and an ancient cotton shirt with faded vertical lines. He had thin, wispy brown hair. His face was sun-burnt, the red skin pocketed with old acne scars. 'I was surprised when you called. Haven't heard about you for a time.'

'I've been off work for a couple of years now.'

Riley wiped a line of froth off his lip, nodding slightly. The officer would know about his leave of absence. 'So what's this all about?'

'As I mentioned on the phone, I'm working on the Souljacker case.'

Riley kept his gaze steady on Lambert. 'Before we continue, can I confirm your involvement is not official?'

'Is that a problem?'

'Not necessarily.'

'It's complicated,' said Lambert.

Riley wiped his hand across his mouth again. 'I imagine it is. Tell me what you want to know and we'll go from there.'

'You worked on the Billy Nolan case, back in Bristol?'

Riley swallowed. 'Yes, why do you think I work in vice now? I saw the next twenty years of my life visiting shit-smelling crime scenes, and worse-smelling autopsies, and thought I'd get out.'

'How's that panning out?'

Riley smirked. 'Now I visit shit-smelling crack dens and whorehouses. The dead bodies I see are normally a result of self-harm. It's a fucking picnic.'

'So the Nolan case,' said Lambert, getting back on track.

'Yeah, that was a wild one. You were a suspect as I remember?'

Lambert held up his hands. 'No charge.'

Riley didn't smile. 'It was all very fragmented, I remember that. The SIO had lost some of his team. I was called in along with some other new faces. The SIO, Hastings, wasn't happy. I don't think it was his choice. The Souljacker was getting a lot of press at that point, and we were nowhere near to catching him. He left us nothing. No discernible motive, no link between the victims...'

'No link between the victims?'

'No. Billy Nolan was a third year University student. The previous victim, David Welsh, was a twenty-eight-year-old divorced welder from Congresbury. The pressure was intense. There was talk of Hastings losing his position.'

Lambert had never realised Hastings had been under pressure, though it made complete sense. 'David Welsh was a member of a church, like some of the others.'

Riley shrugged, and folded his arms. 'Billy Nolan wasn't.'

'Did you look at the others?'

Riley's didn't respond immediately. 'What is this? Are you with IIU?'

Lambert couldn't tell if Riley was joking or not. The IIU were the force's internal investigation team. 'Don't be ridiculous. I'm looking for anything that may have been missed from the older cases, something that could relate to the two new murders. No one's under investigation, Cormack. I imagine I'd have to inform you if that was the case.' Lambert was surprised by Riley's defensiveness.

'I can tell you, there was nothing we missed. You forget, there were eight cases prior to Nolan. The victims' histories were explored thoroughly. Hastings was meticulous. Have you spoken to him?'

'Yes, of course. I'm trying to speak to everyone involved in all those all cases.'

258

Riley unfolded his arms. 'What's that old bastard up to now?'

'He's a writer.'

'Oh yeah, I heard about that.' Riley lifted his head, his tone softening. 'If I could read, I'd buy one of his books.'

'What was he like as SIO?' asked Lambert, pressing the officer whilst he was still in improved humour.

'No problems. Very level-headed, methodical. I only saw him lose his rag once.'

'Oh right?'

'One of the WPCs. She had some information about something or other. I can't remember what it was. He freaked out, real Jekyll and Hyde stuff. Made the poor girl cry. I've seen it hundreds of times, but it was a bit strange seeing it from him. I could tell then that the pressure was getting to him.'

Lambert struggled to picture Hastings losing his temper. 'It's a long shot, but do you remember the name Campbell ever being mentioned in the investigation?'

'A long shot? It was twenty years ago. You have anything more?'

'The name Campbell keeps cropping up. Nothing more at the moment.'

Riley sighed. 'Let me see what I can unearth. I've kept all my notebooks. If I can locate them, I'll take a look. See if I can find any mention of a Campbell.'

Lambert returned to his house via Croydon Rec. The playground area was busy, the local families enjoying the sunshine.

As he approached his front door, he was surprised to see Sarah May was outside waiting for him. She wore a tailored trouser suit, her hair tied back tightly in a ponytail.

'I thought you were in Bristol,' he said. 'Did you follow me back on the train?'

'You do have a high opinion of yourself sometimes, you know.' She was smiling, but not in the casual way he'd seen on previous occasions. There was a shift in her body language, a rigidity to the way she stood.

Lambert didn't know how to respond. He'd obviously pissed her off.

'Are you going to invite me in or not?'

'Sorry, please,' said Lambert holding the door open for her. She moved past him and waited in the hallway. He brushed past her. 'Coffee?'

'That would be heavenly,' she said, relaxing slightly.

'I take it this is business,' he said, grinding beans for the cafetiere.

'There are a couple of developments,' said May, taking a seat on a high-backed chair next to the breakfast counter. 'First of all I'd like to thank you for your assistance, however indirect it may have been.'

'How's that?' asked Lambert. He didn't like the formal way she talked to him, as if they hadn't spent any time alone together.

'It seems that, how shall we put it, your investigation into Sandra Vernon may have paid some dividends.'

Lambert poured hot water onto the ground coffee beans, the sharp aroma filling the room. 'That was quick. I've only just returned from Bristol myself.'

'We don't twiddle our thumbs in the West Country,' said May, accepting the cup of coffee from Lambert. 'We've a warrant for the church. One of the counsellors who still works there all but confirmed that Billy Nolan attended counselling session there when he was at University.'

'Name?'

'Sally Davidson.'

'She knew Nolan?'

'She remembered his murder. She didn't counsel him but is pretty sure he attended the church.'

'She didn't contact the police?'

'No.'

Lambert ran a hand through his hair. 'Christ. What were the sessions for?'

'The one she thinks Nolan attended were for victims of sexual abuse.'

Lambert remembered what Klatzky had told him. He still couldn't believe Billy had kept such a secret all that time. 'What did she remember?'

'She remembered Terrence Haydon was also there on those nights. She's known him since he was a boy. She verified his role as glorified coffee assistant. Nothing more. She used to run a second session at the same time Nolan attended his session. A help group for carers. Sick relatives, that sort of thing.'

'But she didn't deal with Nolan directly?'

'No, they brought it in a specialist. She claimed to be surprised that no one investigated the church following his murder.'

'But she didn't think to come forward? Jesus Christ. You should arrest her for obstruction. Terrence Haydon and Sandra Hopkins could be alive if it wasn't for her.'

May's face hardened. 'I share your anger, Michael, believe me.'

Lambert paced the kitchen, spilling coffee onto the laminated floor. 'Who oversaw Billy's meetings?' he said, forcing himself to calm.

May didn't answer directly. 'There's something else. There was someone in her group who was particularly friendly with Billy Nolan. Someone you know.'

Lambert rubbed the bridge of his nose, the answer dawning on him. 'Simon? You're kidding me?'

'Do you know where Klatzky is, Michael?'

Lambert deflected the question. 'Did she mention anyone else?'

'No. She couldn't confirm or deny that Sandra Hopkins attended sessions there. We showed her pictures of all the former victims but no luck. You're not answering me about Simon Klatzky?'

For the second time since asking for his help, Klatzky had hid something from him. He couldn't protect him any longer.

May told him about Klatzky's mother. In all the years he'd known Klatzky, he'd not once mentioned that his mother was blind. They'd all discussed their families at University. Lambert had met some of them during visits, but he realised he didn't know anything significant about any of his friends' parents or families. It was the way it was. They'd ask vague questions about one another, and settle for vague answers.

'Wait here,' he told May. He'd already scanned the photos from the two files Klatzky had been sent. He sought out the originals from his desk drawer and returned downstairs and handed them to May.

If she was surprised she hid it well.

'You must know about this victim?' said Lambert.

'Kwasi Olumide,' she said in agreement.

'Yes.'

'What the hell's going on, Michael? Why has Klatzky been sent these?' she demanded.

'Your guess is as good as mine at this point.

May sighed, unhappy by his ambiguous answer. 'When did Klatzky give you the photos?'

'He gave me the Haydon photos the day before I met you in Bristol. These newer ones were dropped at his house this morning.'

'Why didn't you inform us, Michael? You know you could get charged for this.'

'I'm sharing them now. I was working my own lines of investigation.'

May scanned the files once more. Lambert wondered if it was the withholding of information which was troubling her, or that they'd come close to spending the night together. 'Has it crossed your mind that Klatzky took them in the first place?'

'Don't be ridiculous,' said Lambert. He poured more coffee, gripped his cup tight. 'No, I'm not buying it.'

'I'm going to have to share this information with Nielson and Bardsley.'

'Be my guest.'

'So where is Klatzky now?'

'I saw him three or four hours ago at Paddington station when he showed me the photos. I left him in the bar drowning his sorrows.' He told her the name of the bar.

She immediately called it in. 'Is there anything else you're withholding from me?' she asked.

Lambert shrugged his shoulders. 'You were going to tell me who was running these counselling sessions?' he said.

'I'm not sure that's relevant now,' said May. She sat on one of the kitchen chairs. 'This is a right mess,' she said.

'Humour me, it might help.'

'Well, as I said, the woman I met was Sally Davidson. There was another counsellor, male, working on the same night. From an outside agency.'

'The one who took Billy Nolan's sessions?'

'Yes. She wasn't sure of his first name. She only knew him as Campbell.'

Chapter 36

'Campbell? You're sure?'

'Yes. Why? I thought you were going to spit your coffee all over me then.'

'You need to speak to DCI Bardsley immediately,' said Lambert. He explained about Campbell. How his source, Myles Stoddard, had linked a man named Campbell to the murders of Samuel Burnham and Kwasi Olumide.

'So Bardsley has an arrest warrant out on this guy?'

'Not quite. We only have the surname at the moment.'

'It could be a coincidence.'

'Could be. One hell of a coincidence if it is. Klatzky has been sent two sets of crime scene photos. One of a Souljacker victim, one of a second victim, this one with his eyes sealed shut. Two different forms of murder, both involving the eyes. Nolan and Haydon both attended counselling sessions. One was counselled by someone called Campbell. I think we can start considering the possibility they are linked, one way or another.'

'Why the different MO?'

'I think it's the victims he distinguishes. I don't fully understand why yet.'

'Right I'm going to call Bardsley now,' she said. 'I'll tell him, and Nielson, that you volunteered the information on Klatzky.'

'It's a bit late but you won't really be lying.'

She gripped his arm. 'You have to leave well alone now.'

'I'll tell you when Klatzky turns up,' said Lambert.

May loitered by the front door, as if she was waiting for something else from him. 'Perhaps we can talk further once this has all finished?'

'Okay, I'd like that,' he said, understanding how inadequate his words sounded. He sensed a distance between them, and feared it would only get bigger. As he opened the door to let her out, he saw Klatzky staggering down the street towards the house. The man meandered across the pavement, once walking into a parked car. He didn't look up until May walked onto the street.

Klatzky stopped. He swayed from side to side, at once pitiful and comical, his mouth wide open.

Lambert stepped out onto the street and waved to Klatzky who lifted his arm in acknowledgment. 'Simon,' he shouted. He beckoned him over trying to keep his body language neutral. May kept close, keen not to startle the man.

Klatzky continued staring at them blankly. He'd been drunk at the bar. He'd probably doubled his intake since then. Lambert could only imagine the unhinged thoughts going through his head. Klatzky inched forward like an errant puppy returning to its master.

He was five yards away when May made a move for him. Smiling as she grabbed his arm, she twisted it behind his back, cuffed him, and began reading him his rights.

Klatzky could barely talk. 'What's going on?' he mouthed to Lambert, his words horrendously slurred as if he had a speech impediment.

'I'll get you a solicitor,' said Lambert.

'There's some things you haven't been telling us, Mr Klatzky,' said May, calling for assistance.

Chapter 37

Sophie appeared as the riot van carted Klatzky away. May was getting into her car and Sophie nodded towards her as if they were acquaintances.

'What was that about?' asked Lambert, as May pulled away.

'What was that about? Are you kidding? You have noticed that a riot van has just turned up at our house and hauled away one of your friends.'

'Good point. But you're changing the subject. Did you know that woman?'

'Your pretty little friend?' asked Sophie, a hint of mischief in her voice.

'Sophie?'

'That's why I'm here. I wanted to tell you that you're under some form of surveillance.'

'She's questioned you?'

'Verifying some dates. Making sure you were safe and sound at home. Fortunately they matched up. What have you got yourself into, Mike?'

Lambert didn't know how to answer the question. He was convinced Klatzky was innocent and would have a suitable alibi for the killings. 'I'm not sure. I need a drink. Fancy going for something to eat?'

'Okay,' said Sophie, bemused.

Lambert called a solicitor as they walked to one of the restaurants on the high street. Lambert wasn't sure who he felt most betrayed by, Klatzky for his deception or May for investigating him behind his back. May was doing her job, and he supposed she didn't have to question Sophie herself, but still he couldn't get rid of the feeling that perhaps it had all been pretence. That she'd been toying with him ever since their first meeting.

Before they were married, they had visited the Italian restaurant at least once a month. The owner knew both of them by name. He greeted them with his usual cheer, and ushered them to a table by the window. Lambert ordered a bottle of wine.

'Not for me,' said Sophie.

The owner waited for a response. 'I'll get the bottle, anyway,' said Lambert.

'Sparkling water,' said Sophie, looking at him in the way only she could. Assessing him, working out his mood, deciding what would be best to ask him. When he refused to discuss the case, she updated him on her latest developments at work.

Lambert soon finished his second glass. 'You sure you don't want a glass?' he asked.

'I'm fine with water,' said Sophie.

'Come on, have a glass.'

'You can have some more, I won't tell,' she said, laughing.

Lambert poured another glass.

'You can't hold out all night,' said Sophie.

It was the second time in as many days he'd shared a meal with his wife. He wasn't naïve enough to give any significance to the fact. He decided to enjoy their time together whilst it lasted.

'Fine,' he said. He told her about everything. How Klatzky had first shown him the photos a few days ago, and the trips to Bristol. It was a relief to unburden everything.

'You don't really think Simon is the killer?' she asked.

Lambert went to protest, then thought about all the people he'd helped bring to justice over the years. So many times he'd encountered friends and families oblivious to the crimes of their loved ones. How much did he really know about Klatzky? He'd withheld so much from him: his blind mother, Billy's counselling sessions, his own counselling sessions at the church. Would he really be that surprised if Klatzky was revealed as the killer?

'Simon barely functions. He doesn't have the capacity for such things. Anyway, he was only seventeen or eighteen when Clive Hale was killed. I don't buy it.' Lambert took another drink, realising he sounded as if he was trying to convince himself.

'You're not going to let him back in the house are you?'

'No. If they do release him I'll help him get a hotel somewhere.' He sensed it was all coming to an end. Either Klatzky would be charged, or the killer would be after him.

'This means you're back at work now?' said Sophie.

'Tillman has suggested I could return.'

And?'

'I don't know. Maybe.'

Lambert declined the offer of a second bottle from the owner. They skipped dessert, Lambert ordering a double espresso before asking for the bill.

'What shall we do now?' he asked Sophie outside the restaurant. 'Are you coming home, or are you still at the hotel?'

'Let's go home for a bit,' she said. She linked her arm around his, a shiver running through him. His pulse thumped in his neck. He was excited to be so close to his wife once more, but scared as well. The matter with the solicitor had yet to be resolved. He had known Sophie for most of his adult life and could sense she was withholding something. He wasn't sure he wanted to know what.

As they reached their street Lambert slowed the pace. They'd walked in silence, enjoying each other's company, or perhaps preparing themselves for what lay ahead. Once through the door Lambert kissed her. Sophie stood with her arms by her sides not responding. They hadn't kissed properly in the two years since Chloe's death.

Lambert continued undeterred, placing his hands on her cheeks waiting for a response. Time had never moved so slowly. Eventually she lifted her hands to his chest and began kissing him back.

Lambert pulled her to her bedroom. 'Here, okay?' he said, embarrassed to have to ask permission to use her bedroom. She didn't answer, frantically tearing at his clothes. Within seconds they were undressed on the bed together. She kissed him with a fury he'd never encountered from her before. She began biting his lip, pulling at his hair, her desperate movements arousing, yet somehow disturbing, as if she was trying to convince herself she really wanted him.

'What is it?' he asked, holding her arms, pulling her face back from his.

She began to cry. 'I can't, Michael,' she said. 'I'm so sorry. I want to but I can't.'

Lambert dressed, his face reddening. He could feel his

temper rising, though it was not directed at Sophie. He could understand how she felt. Whatever she'd told him, whatever she'd said in the counselling meetings they'd attended, deep down she still blamed him for Chloe's death.

He couldn't blame her for that. It was his fault.

Sophie climbed beneath the duvet, wrapped herself in its protective cover. Her face peered out from the top, pleading for his forgiveness.

Fully-clothed, he sat next to her on the bed. 'It's not your fault,' he said.

She touched his face, smiling between the occasional sob. He'd always loved the way she looked after she'd been crying, her red cheeks and soft eyes.

'There's something else, Michael,' she said, the tears flowing again.

He may have loved the look of her after she'd been crying but crying itself was a different matter. It made him helpless. He wanted to put his arm around her, but after what had happened he didn't know the boundaries. All he could do was sit and watch. Her face crumpled in despair.

'What is it?' he mouthed.

She was unable to speak through the tears. It was over. He supposed he'd guessed as much at the restaurant. It was probably why he'd kissed her, because he hadn't wanted to hear the words. He tried to make it easier on her. 'You're leaving me,' he said, his words faltering.

She cried again, shaking her head. Not to deny the fact but to suggest there was something else. In the end, she blurted the words out in a high-pitched yelp interspersed with sobs.

'I'm pregnant,' she said.

He froze as a shiver of pain ran through him. He pushed himself from the bed, nauseous, a dull ache in his chest. He hadn't slept with Sophie since the accident. 'Who?' he asked.

'Does it matter?'

He turned from her, remembering her lift home the other evening with the solicitor. He pictured the man leaning towards her, Sophie rebuffing his advances. 'Jeremy Taylor,' he said, shaking his head.

'How the hell do you know that?' said Sophie.

Lambert stared at her, tried not to picture her fucking the man in their house.

'It was only the once. A couple of months back. An office party, I drank too much wine and he offered me a lift home. And…'

Lambert held his hands up. 'I don't need to know the details.'

'It was only the once, Michael. It's the first time, since…'

Lambert's skin prickled with heat. He had no right to be upset over the infidelity. He'd slept with two women in the last two years. Once with one of the nurses who'd helped him back to full fitness after the accident, once with a woman he'd met at the local gym. That affair had lasted for two months. He didn't know if Sophie had ever known but she'd never said anything.

'Have you told him?'

'Not yet.'

Lambert's eyes filled. 'You're going to keep it?' he said, softly.

'Boy or girl, it won't replace Chloe,' said Sophie. She untangled herself from the covers and moved towards him but Lambert turned his back.

'It's okay,' he said, and left the room.

He heard her leave the house ten minutes later. By which

time he was already on his second glass of red wine. She'd said goodbye to him as she'd left and he'd waved back unable to speak. He hoped she understood that he didn't blame her. It was none of his business who she slept with, and if she'd fallen pregnant so be it.

Yet it felt like a death, like Chloe dying all over again. He stumbled to the drinks cabinet and opened a bottle of vodka. He rarely touched spirits but he needed something to numb the pain. He poured a generous measure into a wine glass and sipped at the drink, wincing as the sharp liquid burned his throat.

He hadn't cried when Chloe had died. He only found out about it two days after the accident. Two days he'd spent unconscious. Sophie's mother had been the one to tell him, Sophie too wrapped up in her grief and, Lambert presumed, hatred for him to tell him herself.

He'd been unable to process the information at first. He knew all about the stages of grieving. He'd informed people before of the death of their loved ones. He'd always thought that maybe he'd react differently. Maybe he'd be able to handle it, or at least understand what he was being told.

'Utter bullshit,' he shouted into the empty air of the living room. How could his baby girl have died? Why was he still alive? Now with Sophie leaving and being pregnant everything came back to him. The trauma of the time, the bitterness of their lives, the rage he stored within him. He stood and threw the wine glass at the wall.

How could he have let things get to this? Chloe was dead. Sophie had left him. One of his old best friends was currently under arrest, and was possibly linked to the murder of another friend. Whilst Lambert, formally a Chief Inspector, was without a job, sitting in the dark in his living room feeling sorry for himself.

He attacked the drinks cabinet, smashing the bottles one by one against the wall. He screamed, a strange guttural sound he'd never heard escaping from his mouth. Then, as quickly as he'd begun, he stopped.

Stepping over the broken glass, and the merged rivers of whiskey and gin, he picked up the red wine bottle and began to gulp greedily from its neck. Once finished, he opened a second bottle and returned to the sofa. Using the remote he turned on the stereo and synced it with the music on his iPhone.

His last memory was of broken snippets from an ancient Joe Jackson song, and the noise of an empty bottle of wine rattling on the wooden floorboards.

Chapter 38

They decided to wait until morning to interview Klatzky. The man was in no state for questioning. He was unable to stand, his slurred speech incomprehensible.

May spent most of the evening at the Lewisham station, working with Nielson and his team. Nielson set up a conference call with Superintendent Rush and her team back in Bristol, and Bardsley's team in Watford. With the new information on Billy Nolan's counsellor, they began working on the hypothesis that the Souljacker was responsible for the death of Samuel Burnham and Kwasi Olumide.

There were two main suspects: Klatzky, drunk in the cells, and a man called Campbell, a man they knew nothing about.

'I think you should be the one to speak to Klatzky tomorrow,' said Nielson to May.

'Thank you, sir.'

Nielson's team were affable enough. May worked through a possible line of questioning with Nielson, and a young DC, Rebecca Shah. May tried to piece everything together in her head. The coincidence of Klatzky's blind mother, blind dead mother, had her preoccupied. Nothing concrete had yet appeared on the Campbell character. Everything was a little intangible, too in the air for May's liking. DCI Bardsley had stated during the conference call that his department was calling in all local informants, trying to get a handle on who this Campbell was but from what they'd uncovered, the man was something of an enigma, while they had a real, live suspect in the cells.

'Do you think Klatzky's our man?' said Shah.

'I wish he were sober enough so we could find out. We need to find out what he knows about the counselling sessions Nolan attended. See what he knows about Campbell.'

May had ordered Bradbury to pay Davidson and Landsdale another visit at the Gracelife church. It was a long shot but she wanted a physical description of Campbell, a facial composite if possible. Although, after twenty years she wasn't getting her hopes up.

'Just arrived for you,' said Nielson, handing her a file.

May opened the document, surprised to see the medical file of Martha Klatzky, Simon Klatzky's mother. 'That was quick.'

'I wouldn't get used to it,' said Nielson.

Martha Klatzky had been diagnosed with cancer when Klatzky was twelve, two years after his father had died. She lost her sight two years later. May didn't want to dwell on what that would do to a person. According to the file, the council appointed a carer to look after the woman at her home on a part-time basis whilst Simon Klatzky attended school. She died at a hospice the year before Klatzky started University with Lambert and Billy Nolan. The same year Clive Hale became the first Souljacker victim.

'We need to get someone over to the hospice. Get some background on the mother, on the young Simon Klatzky.'

'Agreed,' said Nielson. 'Let's see what we get from him in the morning and we can go from there. You should think about wrapping up now. Get some rest.'

'Sir,' said May.

May still had a locker from the last time she'd visited the station. She'd filled it with spare clothes for such an occasion. She took the bag she'd packed, and walked down the empty staircase to the front of the station. After saying goodnight to the duty sergeant, she walked out into the cold evening air of Lewisham.

It had been a long day. She rubbed her tense neck deciding to walk the two miles to her hotel in Blackheath. She considered calling Lambert, convincing herself that it would be polite to update him on the case. She needed some company but contacting him now would be unprofessional.

The town was alive with people, busy enjoying themselves oblivious to her troubles. She considered entering a bar for a quick drink. She had a need to be surrounded by people, by normality. She spotted a small bar, The Old Pier Tavern, on the main road out of Lewisham towards Blackheath. From the outside, it had the appearance of an old, traditional pub. The kind she imagined spending lazy Sunday afternoons in.

She was about to cross the street for a closer look when she saw him.

He stood in front of a shop window, staring at a display of flat screen televisions. Sean made a poor job of surveillance. May couldn't believe he'd followed her to London. And worse, that she'd not spotted him before. When she'd last seen him, she'd promised to arrest him if he came within five hundred metres of him. But now he was here, she lacked the energy. She still didn't consider him a threat. Physically, at least, she was more than a match for him.

She walked on, checking his following figure with her

periphery vision, occasionally losing him in the shadows. She turned left at the Lee Green crossroads, and began walking up the hill to Blackheath.

She upped her pace remembering the fall out after the abortion. It started when she'd first told him she planned to terminate the pregnancy. They'd arranged to meet at the local park. It was a summer evening and they took a spot behind an enclave of trees. A place they'd been together before. May had initially thought he'd understand. He was mature for his age. He'd never tried to rush her into sex the way some of the other boys in her class had, was always considerate of her feelings. She realised it would be painful for him, as it was for her, but she'd never expected his response.

'You can't,' he said, with a sense of finality which made her snort with laughter.

'Look, Sean, I know you are upset but you can't expect me to go through with this. I'm only seventeen.'

'You can't. God has given us this gift,' he said, and in that second she realised there would be no negotiating with him.

She'd explained everything. How they were both too young, how it would destroy their lives. She told him they couldn't afford a baby, that it wouldn't be fair to bring a child up in their situation.

He listened to every word, a strange pious look on his face. 'We're keeping it,' he said.

'It's my body,' she said, getting to her feet.

He'd made a grab for her arm and pulled himself up as she struggled to remain upright. She pushed him away, and they stood apart in a silent impasse which she broke by kicking him hard between the legs. He collapsed, as if the ground beneath him had been taken away.

She'd run all the way home, told her parents what had happened, and never saw him alone again until years later.

She stopped halfway up the hill, pretending to tie her shoe laces. He was a hundred metres away. He'd stopped when she had, and was looking at a menu on the outside of a restaurant. She considered walking back down the hill to confront him, to clear it all up once and for all, but was so riled up she feared what she would do to him.

She continued into Blackheath village. The hotel was on a back road, behind a small car park. Not an ideal location, although the hotel itself was of a high standard. She headed off the main road onto the side street. It was well lit and only a few hundred metres long. She refused to show any fear where Sean was concerned.

He called out for her as she rounded the corner. 'Sarah, Sarah, it's me,' he said. He ran towards her, oblivious to her look of distaste. 'I thought it was you. What are the chances?' he said, catching up on her.

May crossed her arms. 'The chances are very high. You're following me, Sean. I'm not an idiot.'

After the incident at the park, he'd ignored her for two weeks. Then the letters had started. Her parents had tried to protect her from them, but she'd insisted on reading every one. She now saw them for what they were, but back then they had come close to destroying her. If there was a cruel name, or insult, he hadn't used in those letters then she was yet to hear it. They arrived on a daily basis, poisonous missives accusing her of murder, condemning her to an afterlife of eternal damnation. She couldn't believe she'd been so blinded by him. He wasn't the person she thought he was, and that hurt almost as much as the vitriolic letters. In the end, her parents went to see his parents. They threatened to take the matter to the police and the letters stopped coming, for a time.

He still wrote to her, even now. Without fail, a letter appeared once a year on the anniversary of the day she had the abortion.

'I'm not following you. I live here,' said Sean.

'London's a big place, Sean. You followed me. I saw you a mile back on the high street pretending to look at television sets.'

Sean's eyes drooped, like a guilty child caught in a lie. 'I wanted to speak to you.'

'Have you followed me from Bristol?'

He didn't answer.

May was momentarily impressed. 'Have you lost your fucking mind? What's all this about?'

'I wanted to speak to you,' he repeated.

'About what? I don't know if you are harbouring some fantasy about us getting back together. But that's all it is, Sean. A fantasy.' She regretted losing her temper, Sean receiving the full blast of all the tension building in her from the case.

Sean was about to speak when two cars turned off the main road and headed towards them. The first car, a black cab continued driving to the hotel. The second car, a nondescript silver saloon stopped. May recognised the man who left the car. It was truly a night of coincidences.

'Is this person giving you any trouble?' said the man.

May was not sure how to feel. She wasn't some scared female needing protection. Sean was ready to run as the man approached and for that she was thankful. The man looked Sean up and down, his face full of distaste.

'Who are you?' said Sean, his voice softer than before.

In that second, it all clicked into place. May understood everything. Unfortunately, it was too late. The man was quick. Quicker than May would have ever imagined. Still looking at Sean, he punched May in her left temple with the side of his hand. May trained two or three times a week in martial arts. She'd received blows to the head numerous times, normally when she'd been wearing protective head gear. The impact from the man's punch was something else. It had been so unexpected, the force powerful and accurate. Her legs collapsed and she fell to the ground, her body nauseous. Through blurred vision she noticed a sliver of metal in the man's hand shining in the glow of the street lights. She tried to push herself up but her leg and arm muscles had liquefied.

Sean fell with a thud next to her. May had only a moment to note the vacant look in his eyes, the perfect slice of red across the flesh of his neck, before a second blow sent her into unconsciousness.

Chapter 39

Sunlight pierced the curtains, a shard of light momentarily blinding Lambert. His head thudded in time to the music which still played from the stereo. He switched off his iPhone but the thudding continued.

Somebody called his name from the front door.

'Mr Lambert,' they shouted, banging their fists, ringing the doorbell. He got to his feet, his legs buckling. He placed his left hand against the living room wall to steady himself. His stomach lurched. He groaned at the mess, remembered throwing the glass and bottles at the wall. He was surprised his neighbours hadn't called around earlier. He took some deep breaths and struggled towards the door, ready to apologise.

'Mr Lambert.' The sound was more insistent, louder. Through the glass panels of the front door Lambert made out three figures. He opened the door and shielded his eyes from the sunlight.

DCI Nielson stood before him, flanked by two plain-clothed officers. 'Sorry, did we wake you?' said Nielson.

Lambert checked his watch. It was one p.m. He hadn't slept in so late since he'd been at University.

'What do you want?' His voice came out as a growl, almost unrecognisable to his ears.

'You need to come with us, Lambert.'

'Like fuck,' said Lambert. He began pushing the door. Nielson stuck out his leg and kicked it open, splintering one of the panels.

'That was unnecessary.'

Nielson couldn't hide the look of disgust on his face. 'I'll give you ten minutes to shower and get ready,' said Nielson. 'DI Sarah May is missing.'

Nielson and his two accomplices shuffled around downstairs as he showered. Lambert's head still thumped, his mouth and throat dry. He stood beneath the shower attempting to reconcile what he'd been told.

DI May had last been seen leaving the Lewisham station at nine-thirty yesterday evening. She'd not returned to her hotel and hadn't been seen since. Her mobile phone went straight to answerphone and could not be traced by location services. A body had been found in an alleyway, two hundred yards from the hotel where May was staying. Sean Laws, Sarah May's ex-boyfriend. His throat had been sliced, a single surgical incision.

Lambert's hangover was of the type he'd started developing in his mid-twenties. He was anxious and on edge, remorseful for his behaviour the previous evening. He tried not to think about what Sophie had told him. Each time her words popped into his head he tried to blank them out. He knew she was lost to him now and he'd be damned if he was going to lose two women within twenty-four hours. He changed into one of his old work suits, a crisp white shirt which had returned from the dry cleaners two years ago and a navy blue tie.

Downstairs, Nielson paced the living room, his two colleagues sitting on an armchair each. 'Looks like you had quite a party last night,' he said, surveying the mess. The floor was littered with broken glass. One of the walls had a spreading damp patch from where the vodka bottle had hit it.

'I had some bad news,' said Lambert. He followed one of the officers outside, his legs still unsteady. The sound of thick blood pumping around his body reverberated in his ears. The journey to Lewisham was painful, the streets of south-east London gridlocked with traffic.

Lambert was flanked by Nielson's two colleagues as he entered the police station, Nielson walking in front. The four of them received curious glances as they walked through the station. Lambert spotted Cormack Riley who was about to say something when he noticed the strange formation of officers surrounding Lambert. Riley shot him a questioning look. 'Call,' mouthed Lambert under his breath.

In the incident room, the glances were reserved solely for Lambert.

The police officers didn't look at him as an ex-DCI any more. He was now a suspect in Sarah May's disappearance. He understood how they felt and didn't judge them for their presumptions.

'Come with me,' said Nielson, leading him to an interview room. The other two officers slipped away.

DCI Bardsley was waiting in the room. He stood as Nielson shut the door. 'Mike,' he said offering his hand.

Lambert rubbed his face, tried to focus.

'You need to tell us everything,' said Nielson.

'This is being taped?' asked Lambert.

'Just so we don't miss anything.'

Lambert repeated what he'd told May yesterday. From his first meeting in the coffee shop with Klatzky through to Sarah

May turning up at his house yesterday. He presumed May had already shared the information.

'Before we go any further, can you tell me your movements last night?' said Bardsley.

Lambert sighed. He was struggling to focus, the alcohol flooding his bloodstream.

'Sorry, Mike, let's just get it out of the way.'

'Fine. I was out with my wife, Sophie. We went to a restaurant then went home.'

'She'll verify this?' asked Nielson.

'No, she'll deny it. Of course, she'll fucking verify it.' Lambert thought back to Sophie's revelation, the near-empty drinks cabinet. 'However,' he said, lightening his tone. 'We had an argument and she left sometime around eleven. Hence, the state of the place when you called round.'

Bardsley exchanged looks with Nielson and they dropped it. 'You never thought of telling us about the photos?' asked Nielson.

'I did tell you,' said Lambert.

'You told DI May yesterday. Perhaps a few days late don't you think?' said Nielson.

'I was leading my own investigation. I shared the information when I felt it was pertinent.'

'Come on, Lambert, you're not actively working at the moment. You can't make those sorts of decisions. Put yourself in my place. When you were an active DCI, would you have let this sort of shit go down?'

Lambert thought about Tillman. It was possible that his former boss would back him up. It was conceivable he'd say he'd given him permission to work on the case and backed him up with resources. However, it was more likely that he would hang him out to dry. The thought occurred to him again that the Souljacker was setting him up. 'We're all on the same side, Nielson. I want this killer found as much as you do and I want Sarah May found even more.'

'You're quiet,' said Nielson, looking at Bardsley.

'I don't see what we're gaining from this,' said Bardsley in his Brummie drawl. 'Mike's not a suspect is he? Let's use his expertise. He's the one who found the link between the two sets of killings.'

Nielson's face fell, it was not the answer he expected from his colleague. 'You were protecting your friend, Lambert. There'll be an investigation into this afterwards,' he said.

'Where is Klatzky now?' said Lambert.

'In the cells. We questioned him earlier.'

'So he was in custody when May disappeared?'

'Yes.'

'And what do we have on Sarah's disappearance?'

'Fuck all,' said Bardsley. 'We have her on CCTV leaving the station, walking along Lewisham High Road. We have another picture of her passing a bank in Blackheath. It looks like the ex-boyfriend, Sean Laws, was following her as he appears a few minutes behind her each time. Unfortunately, the CCTV cameras at the hotel don't cover the ground where the body was found. We have a couple of number plates from cars passing the hotel at that time. Nothing of use yet.'

'No note or anything?' asked Lambert.

'No.'

'What do we know about this ex-boyfriend?' asked Lambert.

'Sean Laws, thirty-two. He was at school with DI May. We

interviewed his parents this morning. They told us about his relationship with DI May,' said Nielson.

May had already told him some details about the man. 'Was it serious?'

Bardsley exchanged a glance with Nielson. 'We're keeping this under wraps for the time being until we have confirmation. According to the parents, DI May was once pregnant with Sean Laws' child. She had an abortion. Laws has been obsessed with her ever since,' he said.

Lambert let the information sink in. He started to think like a policeman. 'You don't think Sarah had anything to do with Laws' death?'

'We can't rule that out. From what the parents said, Laws was properly obsessed. The dad sounded a little embarrassed. May had threatened Laws with a court order in the past.'

'And you think enough was enough, she sliced his neck two hundred yards from her hotel and fled the scene.'

Nielson grimaced, and ran his hand through his bouncer hair-cut. 'No, I don't think that but we would be foolish to rule it out.'

An image flashed into Lambert's head. Sarah May prone on a bed, a faceless killer guiding a scalpel towards her eyes. 'You need to scratch that idea. The Souljacker, Campbell, whoever the fuck he is. He's taken her. That's where we have to focus our energies.'

'Do you think this has something to do with you, Michael?' asked Bardsley, changing tack.

'It's crossed my mind, though I can't see how or why.'

'How well were you getting on with Sarah?' he asked.

'We were getting on fine. We went for drinks a couple of times.'

Nielson stopped pacing the room and sat down.

'So you were friends with Billy Nolan. You knew Terrence Haydon. Your friend Simon Klatzky was at counselling sessions the same time as Nolan. And you befriend a young DI and now she's gone missing.'

'Quick, lock me up,' said Lambert.

'Why do you think those photos were sent to Klatzky?' asked Bardsley, ignoring the bickering. 'Do you think the killer was trying to draw you into this?'

'If so, it's a very roundabout way of doing things,' said Lambert.

'Can you think of anyone who holds a grudge against you?'

'You're joking,' said Lambert thinking of the hundreds of criminals he'd helped put behind bars.

'Well, anyone specific related to Nolan, Haydon or Klatzky. Or even Sarah May.'

'No one I can think of.'

'Do you think you may have been the original target?'

'What? When Nolan was killed?'

'Just thinking aloud,' said Bardsley.

'I can't see it,' said Lambert. 'But then we don't have any real motive for Nolan's death, or Haydon's. Or any of them. Listen, I don't want to sound dumb here but is Simon still a suspect?'

Nielson sighed. 'We don't have enough to hold him. His whereabouts for the Haydon case has been confirmed. He was in rehab in Surrey. Was there for a month.'

Lambert couldn't help but laugh. 'That worked out well for him. Has he given you anything?'

'Not much initially. We'll be questioning him again. He confirmed what you told DI May about the photos and his

288

mysterious lift home from Bristol. Bristol CID are trying to track down the car.'

'What about the counselling sessions?' asked Lambert.

'He was less forthcoming on that but admits he did attend sessions there at the same time as Billy Nolan, though with a different counsellor. He remembered the Davidson woman. He didn't know much about Nolan's counsellor. He knew it was a man but couldn't recall ever seeing him.'

'Did you question him about his mother?'

'Yes. Everything he said checked out with the medical records.'

'Can I see him?'

'No. Despite what DCI Bardsley has said, I want no more interfering from you. I should charge you as it is.'

Lambert sighed. 'There's nothing else then?'

'Not for now,' said Nielson.

Lambert was about to inform Nielson that he wasn't asking for permission but decided he was too hungover for another confrontation. Bardsley walked him out of the station. 'Friend of yours then?' he said, when they reached outside.

'What, Nielson? Yeah we're best buddies.' The wind had picked up, the fresh air invigorating him. 'When will Klatzky be released?'

'Soon. His alibi covers him for the Samuel Burnham murder and obviously he has the best alibi of all for Sean Laws, and May disappearing.'

'So you're definitely treating Sam Burnham and Kwasi Olumide as Souljacker victims?'

'It's the working theory. What I don't understand is why Klatzky was sent the photos in the first place. I think you should be careful, Mike.'

'It's crossed my mind.'

Bardsley placed his arm on his back. 'It's possible you know the killer. Be careful.'

'That's also crossed my mind. Will you keep me updated?' asked Lambert.

'I'll do my best,' said Bardsley shaking his hand. 'You need to keep me updated as well. Where are you off to now?'

'I'm going to wait for Klatzky. Find out what the hell he's been playing at.'

The pub nearest the station was the obvious place to wait. It was mid-afternoon and the bar was already bustling. Lambert recognised a couple of faces from the police station but they paid him no attention. A young barmaid asked him what he wanted to drink. He'd been told the best cure for a hangover was to continue drinking but the thought of anything alcoholic passing his lips at that moment made him nauseous. 'Lemonade,' he said.

Lambert received a few looks from a group of off-duty policemen as he sat down, facing the door. It was probable his notoriety had spread.

He waited for three hours before Bardsley sent him a text message. 'Sorry, Mike, I've just heard. They released Klatzky twenty minutes ago.'

Lambert hung up and called Klatzky. The phone rang but Klatzky didn't answer. He sent him a text then called again. The phone was now switched off. He waited at the bar for a further twenty minutes, hoping that Klatzky would appear, then gave up and returned home. He called Klatzky again, then Sophie, receiving answerphone messages for both. At home, he made a bowl of soup but could only eat half of it.

Restless, he caught a taxi to Klatzky's flat in Plaistow, East London. The lights of the ground floor flat were switched off. He rang the doorbell to no avail. He shone his torch through the letterbox. A week's worth of post was piled high on the floor.

Trying to think like Klatzky, he went on a mini pub crawl of the bars in the area. The majority of the bar staff he met knew Klatzky and promised to call him if he appeared.

Leaving a grotty pub called The George, Lambert noticed a black Saab parked opposite. A man sat behind the steering wheel, blatantly avoiding Lambert's eye contact. Lambert remembered seeing the same car, and driver, outside Lewisham police station earlier that day.

He decided not to approach the driver yet. He wanted to make sure that he was actually being followed. His hunch was that Nielson had sent one of lackeys to monitor him. He walked along the main street to an Irish bar called McNulty's. It was like being inside a wooden box. Cheap wooden frames held pictures of football teams dressed in green, the ceiling was lined with old replica rugby and Gaelic football tops. The bar manager recognised the photo of Klatzky on Lambert's smartphone.

'I barred him two weeks ago,' said the man. 'What's he done now?'

Lambert gave the man his card. 'Will you call me if he returns?'

The man took the card with a shrug. 'He won't be coming back here again,' he said, 'unless he wants to leave the place in a wheelchair.'

'Humour me,' said Lambert. He left the bar and walked

back towards the main road. The Saab was two hundred metres down the road to his right.

He'd had enough of the games. He walked towards the car. When he was fifty yards away, it pulled out into traffic. It turned left into Lisbon Grove driving not much faster than walking pace. Lambert upped his own pace into a jog, his body not happy in its hungover state to be forced into such movement. He rounded the corner into a small street, lined with neglected office buildings and a trio of boarded-up shops.

The car had parked on the right-hand side of the road. The driver sat motionless behind the driving wheel. Lambert could see his eyes in the rear-view mirror. He stopped halfway across the street, the sound of screeching tyres freezing him in place.

'Fuck,' he mouthed to himself. It was a textbook ploy, the decoy driver in the Saab diverting his attention while a second vehicle tracked him. It happened in a matter of seconds. Not enough time for Lambert to adjust.

The van screeched to a halt in front of him, a side door sliding open. Lambert turned back to the pavement to see a man the size of a mountain bearing down on him. Six foot four of thundering muscle ran at him, driving him hard into the back of the van. The door was slammed shut, and the van sped away.

The manoeuvre had taken less than ten seconds.

Chapter 40

As Lambert tried to push himself up from the floor of the van, the rugby-tackling man knocked him back down. For good measure, he punched Lambert in the midriff causing him to bend double. Lambert clutched his stomach, trying to calm his heartbeat as he waited for his breath to return. As he gasped for air, the rugby player pulled him by his collar until he sat upright, his back against the padded wall of the van.

Two other men were in the van. One was another overgrown henchman like the rugby tackler. The man's eyes bored into Lambert's with unconcealed violence.

The other man Lambert recognised.

'Thanks for joining us,' said Tillman.

Lambert shuffled his body into a comfortable position. The rugby player goon still had his hands on Lambert's shoulders holding him in place.

'Tell this prick to get his hands off me,' said Lambert, looking directly at Tillman.

Tillman dipped his head and the man let him go and took a seat to Tillman's left.

Lambert considered striking out at him as he moved but decided against it. 'You could have called me,' he said.

Tillman laughed, his bloated face rippling with fake amusement. 'The last thing I'd want to do at this precise moment is let anyone know I'm associated with you in any way whatsoever. Would you like to tell me what the hell is going on?'

Lambert didn't recognise the two men with Tillman. He didn't think they were officially part of The Group. He imagined they were hired muscle, most likely ex-military. Lambert knew he was in a precarious position. The Group didn't officially exist. Although to some extent Tillman had to report to someone, Lambert was not sure who that someone was and how often that reporting took place. To put it simply, Lambert knew it was not beyond Tillman's power to have him disappear. Furthermore, Tillman knew Lambert understood this and would be happy to exploit the fact if necessary.

'I'm sure you are well aware of what's going on, sir.'

'What I'm aware of, Michael, is that you've been using The System to investigate a handful of murders which seem to be linked to you one way or another at every turn.'

'You sort of knew that when you assigned me to the case.'

'Don't fuck with me, Lambert. I didn't assign you to the case. You begged me for access to The System. Professional courtesy you called it. And my good will's about to run out. You need to explain everything to me now.'

Six years ago, Tillman had been kidnapped and tortured by two men who worked for an arms smuggling organisation. Lambert had tracked his boss to a house on the Isle of Dogs, and with time against him had entered the building alone. One of the men had escaped during the confrontation when he'd arrived. Tillman had killed the other man in cold blood, Lambert testifying that it had been in self-defence.

Despite this, Lambert knew the debt had now been repaid. He explained everything from investigating Haydon's and

Hopkins' murders to Klatzky's involvement, the murders of Samuel Burnham and Kwasi Olumide, and finally Sarah May's disappearance.

It was clear that he wasn't telling Tillman anything he didn't already know. 'So you're sure the same killer is responsible for both sets of murders?'

'Sure as can be.'

'Could the Burnham and Olumide murders be a copycat?'

'It's a poor copycat if it is,' said Lambert. 'One removes the eyes, the other seals them shut.'

'Where's Simon Klatzky now?' said Tillman.

'I happened to be trying to find that out, when your friend here rudely blindsided me.'

The rugby tackler smirked.

'Have you mentioned you've been using The System to anyone?' said Tillman.

Lambert shrugged. The question was redundant. Only a handful of people were aware of The System's existence. Public knowledge would result in a national outcry. Any disclosure of The System would be punished swiftly by Tillman, and Lambert was not foolish enough to see how far Tillman was willing to go.

'We've made a massive fucking footprint on this, Lambert. People have been asking after you. News has spread that you've been investigating on your own like some crazed vigilante. And now this bloody DI's missing it's become everyone's business. I didn't expect this shit when I gave you access again.'

'What can I say?'

'Tell me you'll find the fucking DI and the psychopath that's behind everything.'

'So am I officially working for you now?' asked Lambert.

Tillman knocked on the divider which separated the back of the van from the driver. The van pulled over.

'Are you fuck as like,' said Tillman. 'If you're involved in this in any way then you understand the consequences.'

A picture sprang into Lambert's mind. His house on fire, Lambert trapped within the burning shell. 'I'll find them,' he said.

'You won't see me again until then,' said Tillman. 'And then we need to make a decision on your future.' The statement was provocatively open-ended. Tillman's goon pulled the side door open and pointed to the pavement.

'I'm always open to a bit of career advice,' said Lambert, as he jumped out of the still moving van.

Once the van disappeared down the road, he continued the search of local bars for Klatzky. Tillman's last statement still rang in his ears. A decision on his future. Half threat, half opportunity. It was something he would have to consider soon.

He'd been trying his best not to think about Sophie. Just the thought of what she'd told him made him nauseous. He didn't care about her infidelity, apart from his wounded male pride. It was the thought of the baby growing within her which left him distraught.

There had been complications during Chloe's birth which had meant Lambert had held Chloe before Sophie. The midwives cleaned and wrapped the baby, and handed Chloe to him as Sophie was still being checked over by the emergency birthing team.

The memory was ingrained on him. Chloe had stopped crying as he held her in his arms, looking up at him and holding

296

his gaze. Even now, he could close his eyes and picture it in perfect clarity.

Lambert winced, taking in deep breaths. The new baby would be Chloe's sister, but would not be his child. He went into the next bar and ordered a double vodka. The liquid burnt his throat, and he ordered a second.

He would have to leave the house at some point. He owed it to Sophie to let her bring the baby up there, even if eventually she would share her life with someone else. He would need to return to work, whether that was in Tillman's department or not.

He didn't order a third drink, knowing one more would put him over the edge. The barman hadn't seen Klatzky and he received the same response in each of the subsequent bars he visited. He left his contact details at each place on the off chance that Klatzky would make an appearance. He stopped for a kebab at one of the endless supply of take away joints. As he took his first messy bite into a shish kebab, his phone rang.

'Lambert.'

A nervous voice stammered on the other end of the line. 'Um, Mr Lambert. It's Myles.'

'What can I do for you, Myles?'

'I have some information. Very important, but I want some money first.'

'Nothing for nothing,' said Lambert. 'What have you got for me?'

'Something you want. A possible link to Campbell.'

'How much?'

'A thousand.'

Lambert laughed. 'Don't be stupid, Myles.'

'It's worth it. When have I let you down before?'

'It will be the usual rate. I will double it if it leads to Campbell's arrest.'

'Oh come on. I've missed a whole day's work thanks to your buddy, Bardsley. Thanks for passing on my name by the way.'

'You're welcome,' said Lambert. 'It's take it or leave it, Myles. I'm not negotiating.'

Stoddard knew that with one call he would be arrested and would have to give the information without payment. 'Fine.'

'Where are you now?'

'Mile End,' said Stoddard.

'That's convenient. What brings you to the East End?'

'I met up with a mate.'

Lambert told him the name of a bar he knew in the area. 'I'll be there within half an hour,' he said.

Chapter 41

The bar was a five minute walk from Mile End tube station. Dimly lit, with faded carpets, the bar was badly in need of decoration. The smell of stale beer fought with the stench of urine which filtered into the room from the pub's toilets. Lambert had checked the exit points before entering. He tried to control the tension within him, knowing Stoddard couldn't be trusted. He examined each face in the bar for a clue. It was possible the Souljacker was in the room. It was possible, after May's disappearance, that he would be next.

Stoddard stood next to one of the fruit machines, nursing a pint of bitter. On seeing Lambert, his eyes darted around the room.

'Two more of those,' said Lambert to the unsmiling barman, pointing at Stoddard's drink. 'There you go, don't say I never get you anything,' he said, placing the two drinks on a table. 'Come sit, Myles.'

'Where's the money?' Stoddard sat, hugging himself as if he were cold. He couldn't keep eye contact with Lambert for more than a second.

'It's in my pocket, Myles. Now what do you have to tell me?'

Stoddard gulped down the remains of his first drink and started on his second. 'It's about that second killing,' he said, 'the one after Burnham.'

'You're talking about Kwasi Olumide,' said Lambert, leaning over the table conspiring with Stoddard in hushed tones.

'Yeah, Kwasi. Friend of a friend knew him.'

'Oh really.' He'd always been impressed by Stoddard's ability to gain information. He didn't seem to have much in the way of family and friends, at least not when he'd worked as an informant for Lambert. Yet the man had an uncanny ability to pick up news and snippets of information from the unlikeliest of sources. If things had worked out differently for him, he could have made a go of it in Lambert's profession.

'Yeah, he knew him quite well. Knows his widow even better if you know what I mean.'

'Have you told DCI Bardsley any of this?'

'Not yet. I thought I'd go to you first.'

'Good choice, Myles. Continue.'

'Anyway, this friend of a friend was talking to the widow after the funeral and whatnot. It seems Kwasi left something alongside his meagre will.'

'And what would that be?'

'I don't know exactly but it had the friend of a friend quite agitated. Something about some work Kwasi had been doing. It was one of those "if something should happen to me there's something you should know'" type of letter.'

'Who's the friend of a friend?' demanded Lambert.

'I don't know his name. But I know the widow was considering going to the police and from what he said she was too scared. She feared that whoever killed Kwasi would come for her next if she passed on the information.'

'And that's all you have?' asked Lambert.

'Hey, I think that's pretty good don't you? It's more information than Bardsley got from the widow.'

Lambert leant back in his chair and stared at Stoddard. The man crumpled further into himself, holding his jacket, making himself look as small as possible. One thing Lambert knew about Stoddard was that he didn't give bad information. He was too scared of the repercussions. Lambert took the money from his pocket and held it beneath the table. Stoddard snatched it like a toddler taking an offered sweet.

'You'll give me the rest?' asked Stoddard.

'I'll speak to the widow,' said Lambert. 'You can finish my drink,' he said getting to his feet.

He considered calling Bardsley to ask for permission to speak to Kwasi's widow but decided it would only complicate things. Better to face the consequences later. He already had her address on file. She lived in Stratford, one stop away on the Central line.

Again, he had the feeling that he was being directed. He wished he'd pushed Stoddard more. If he'd had more time, he may have discovered more about who had fed the information to him. It was too late now. The estate was two-storeys high. Each floor had a line of identical red bricked flats. The ex-Mrs Kwasi lived on the second floor, number forty-six. A white woman in her mid-forties opened the door to him. She wore a grey tracksuit. Her hair was dishevelled as if she'd recently left her bed, yet her face was caked in a layer of recently applied make-up.

'What?' she said to Lambert as a means of greeting.

'Mrs Olumide? My name is Michael Lambert, DCI Lambert. I'm sorry to bother you so late. May I come in? I have a few questions to ask you about what happened to your husband.'

'I've changed my name back to my maiden name,' said the woman. 'We've been separated for a year, though we were still technically married. Laney, Laney Richardson.'

'Miss Richardson, may I come in?'

'I just got off the phone to one of your lot,' said the woman, not answering his question. 'Something about one of your officers going missing?'

'Right, well this is linked. Can I come in?'

The woman hesitated by the door. Behind her a child screamed out for its mummy. Lambert was surprised the child was not in bed.

'Perfect,' said the woman. 'Come in then if you're going to.' She stormed down the hallway which was painted an overpowering shade of purple. It was a poor job, the walls pitted with holes and loose bits of plaster. In the kitchen, a toddler sat at a highchair wailing, his face covered with food. The child stopped on seeing Lambert, stared at him much like a wild animal ascertaining the threat level. Sensing no threat, he returned to his food.

'I take it you haven't any positive information for me?' said Richardson, her elbows propped on a spotted tablecloth covered with a week's worth of dirty dishes and moulding food.

'The investigation is progressing,' said Lambert. 'It's come to my attention,' he started and then hesitated. 'Look, can I be open with you, Miss Richardson?'

She shrugged her shoulders as if the idea of an honest police-man confused her. 'Whatever,' she said.

'The thing is I'm not officially attached to this case,' said Lambert. 'The missing inspector, the one you've just found out about, she's a close personal friend of mine.'

'So you're not in charge of the case?'

'No, I shouldn't really be here.'

'So what would happen if I phoned up your boss? The Brummie, what's his name?'

'DCI Bardsley?'

'Yes, him.'

'I don't know. Could be a rap on the knuckles, could be a suspension.' The lies dripped off his tongue as if he'd practised them many times before.

'Well, I haven't got all day,' she said. 'Ask me if you're going to ask me. Can I get you a tea?'

'If you're making one,' said Lambert.

The woman unfolded her arms and boiled the kettle. Mentioning Sarah May had obviously helped his case. Even the toddler smiled, tilting his head mimicking his mother.

'It's a bit awkward, Miss Richardson.'

'Laney.'

'Laney, but it's come to my attention that Kwasi left a note for you.'

The woman's back tensed as she poured the hot water into two chipped mugs. 'Who told you that? My solicitor? I didn't think they were allowed to tell you such things.'

'No, it wasn't your solicitor.'

The woman twisted her head to her shoulder as if Lambert was a magician who'd performed an unbelievable trick. 'I don't know how you know about it then. It scares me to death just to think about it.'

'Can I see it?'

She handed him his tea and left the kitchen. The toddler glanced over once more at Lambert and began to wail.

'Hold on, Kyle,' she shouted, returning with an opened envelope which she thrust into Lambert's hands. She swiped her child from the highchair and pulled the boy close, the child's sobbing fading into the tired fabric of her sweatshirt. Lambert took out the letter which was thirty or forty pages long, double-sided A4.

'Your husband was busy,' he said.

'I didn't even know he could write,' she replied, deadpan.

'Could you summarise it for me?'

'Sounds like some sort of fantasy story, though there are parts of it I can believe. Are you going to sit down?' she said, pointing to one of the kitchen chairs. 'It seems he got into some money trouble a few years back, which is no surprise. Though the lying bastard never told me how much debt he was in. We own this place believe it or not. Bought it years ago from the council. He remortgaged and remortgaged but we could still just about get by. But what he hadn't told me was that he'd started gambling again.'

Lambert nodded, keen not to interrupt.

Laney sat on one of the chairs, the toddler falling asleep in her arms. 'Yeah, but not the normal sort of gambling though. Not a few quid here and there on the horses. That would be too easy for him. It lists it all in there,' she said, pointing at the letter. 'He was doing private bets with someone or other. The sums got larger and larger. They kept giving him credit, and of course he kept taking their money until he'd reached some sort of limit.'

'Did he say who these people were?'

'No, not really. He said they weren't the sort of people you should owe money to. But that wasn't the real problem. They threatened to take the flat away you see so he became desperate. He said he'd heard about someone who helped in these sorts of situations. It all makes kind of sense now. He spent the last five years working nearly every day, sometimes day and night. We'd go weeks without seeing him. In the end it became too much and we split up.'

'So he went to this person for a loan?' asked Lambert.

'That he did. You'll read about it there. Kwasi was never the best with words but he sounded terrified. The man gave him the money and he's been working for him ever since.'

'Doing what?'

'Unimaginable things. Things I'm surprised he had the stomach for. He was scared of spiders you know, even the smallest one I had to rescue from him, tiny ones. He would scream down at me in the middle of the night when he was watching TV. "Laney," he'd shout, "there's a spider on the wall." He'd make me get out of bed in the middle of the night.' The woman laughed. 'Silly bastard,' she said, wiping her eyes with her free hand. 'Anyway,' she continued shaking her head as if trying to dislodge something from her hair. 'So he worked for this guy, Campbell, and then he starts getting scared.'

Lambert flicked through the pages, a mixture of blue and black biro on plain white paper, the handwriting barely legible. He skimmed through to the last couple of pages. The handwriting here was twice the size, scrawled in childish font as if written by someone else. The document made little sense.

'You see, he was scared. The man had summoned him and he'd just heard about a friend of his, Sam Burnham. He was murdered a few weeks back, I'm sure you know. It was the same...'

'I know,' said Lambert.

'Anyway, he thought he was in trouble. So he wrote that.'

'Why didn't you show it to the police?' asked Lambert.

'Read it. The Campbell guy sounds like a mad man. Well, he obviously is, isn't he? Look what he did to Kwasi and that other guy, Sam. I thought if I let you lot know and you didn't find him he'd come for me.'

'Is there something else, Laney? Something you're not showing me.' The woman placed the child down onto a small cloth sofa, and walked to the kitchen sideboard. She opened the top drawer and pulled out a second envelope.

'You know his name is Campbell,' said the woman.

'Yes,' said Lambert, trying to keep the growing excitement out of his voice.

'Well, this is where he lives,' she said, handing him the envelope.

Chapter 42

The man's outline blurred into view. May squinted through her one good eye, the other sealed shut from the initial attack.

'Some water?' said the man.

May attempted to speak, the words lost in her throat. A dry rasping sound escaped from her mouth. The man pulled her hair back and parted her lips. May maintained eye contact as the cold water trickled down her throat. She struggled, her wrists and ankles bound tight on a cast iron chair as she choked on the liquid.

The man released his grip. 'More?'

It had been at least twenty-four hours since she'd been taken. She couldn't remember anything about the journey from outside the hotel to her current location. She'd awoken in the darkness a few times, her limbs heavy, her body desperate for liquid. Each time she'd tried to stay awake only to fall back asleep within seconds. She wanted to accept more water, though feared the liquid was drugged.

'It's merely water,' said the man, reading her thoughts.

May nodded and he tipped more water down her throat. Her body was damp with sweat. She'd wet herself during the night, her underwear and trousers were damp and sticky. 'Can I have a shower?' she asked, her voice little more than a rasp. She knew the answer but wanted to start a dialogue.

'I'll bring you some food later,' he said.

May fought the drowsiness, the remnants of whatever drug he'd pumped into her still circling her bloodstream. 'What happened to Sean?' she asked, remembering the glint of silver. Her ex-boyfriend's vacant eyes, the slash of red on his neck.

'He won't be troubling you any more, Sarah.'

'And me. Am I going to be one of your victims?' She needed to keep him talking. Adrenalin flooded her system as she asked him the question. She tried not to think of his previous victims. What they'd endured before their death. Her mind was still sluggish as she tried to reconcile this new information. She remembered each of the victims, desperate to discover their connection to the man who stood before her. The man who was now walking to the door.

'I sincerely hope not,' said the man, switching off the light and closing the door.

Chapter 43

He had to hand it to her. Laney Richardson was one hell of an actress. She'd played her role to perfection: the grieving ex-wife. The reluctant and practised way she'd revealed the details of the letter Kwasi had left her.

It was all staged. Lambert was being further drawn in. What began with the photos sent to Klatzky was now reaching its conclusion. The killer was drawing him in, snaring him into a trap. Only, this time his potential victim was wise to the trick.

He studied the two documents on the journey home. With his smartphone he took pictures of each page and emailed them to his account. The more he read, the more he became accustomed to Kwasi's handwriting style. The words began to flow, though the language itself was often incoherent. The more he read, the more he admired Kwasi. It sounded as if everything he did was for his family, knowing that if he didn't do as Campbell asked then the man would come after his ex-wife and child.

The last entry came from his time at the hospital, following his altercation with Lambert. He must have posted the envelope to his ex-wife before escaping from police custody.

From the second envelope, Lambert took out a lone piece of paper, on which was printed Campbell's address. He couldn't call Bardsley, Nielson, or even Tillman for that matter. He had to consider Sarah May's safety.

The letter was a trap. If Campbell was the Souljacker, and the killer of Samuel Burnham and Kwasi Olumide, then it sounded unfeasible that he would have allowed such a slip up, that he would have so readily given away his address, unless he wanted Lambert to come to him alone. If Lambert told the police about the note they would never find Campbell at the house. He was one step ahead of them all.

In the document, Kwasi wrote about attacking Lambert in Bristol, how he'd been instructed to pick up Lambert alive. Then the style of the letter changed. The handwriting became wild, as if a child had scribbled it. 'The man Lambert surprised us,' he wrote. 'He broke my fucking leg.'

Back home, Lambert noticed one of the two locks on his front door was unlocked. Lambert distinctly remembered double locking before he'd left that morning. Despite his hangover, he recalled Nielson's glare as he bent down to the second lock. It was after midnight. He'd not given a spare set of keys to Klatzky and he presumed Sophie was still at the hotel. He peered through the windows and pressed his ear to the front door. He thought he could see a shadow moving within.

He put a key into the Yale lock and twisted it slowly, groaning inwardly as the door creaked.

He left the door ajar as he tiptoed down the hallway.

'Is that you, Michael?' said Sophie, as he reached the kitchen.

'Jesus, Soph, I thought we had burglars.'

'Burglars who shut the door after them?'

'What can you say, they're a polite lot around here,' said Lambert. The memory of last night's revelation rushed him. He gazed at Sophie's stomach where the alien body grew.

'I'm going to Mum and Dad's for a week or so. I've asked for some leave from work.'

'Have you told them about…you know,' said Lambert nodding his head towards her stomach.

'No not yet, it's too early for that.'

'Look, Soph, I'm the one who should move out. I've been thinking. You can have the house. We can sort something out financially.'

'Let's not rush into anything,' said Sophie. 'I know it must have been difficult for you to hear that last night. Let me go away for the week and we'll talk when I come back.'

'Okay,' said Lambert, though he couldn't see what else there was to discuss. 'Is it possible to borrow your car?' he asked.

'Yes. Are you sure you want to drive it?'

'Bit of an emergency,' he said.

'You want it now?'

'Yes please.'

She handed him the keys. 'I'll get a taxi. You know where I'll be,' she said, kissing him on the cheek.

'You're leaving now?'

'Yes.'

'Be safe,' he said, ten minutes later when the taxi arrived.

'And you.' She pulled him close, surprised him by kissing him hard on the lips. He watched her walk to the taxi and closed the door.

After she'd gone, he ran upstairs and logged onto The System. He sent a delayed, encrypted email to Tillman telling him where he was going. He timed it to be sent ten hours later which would give him enough time to cancel it if needed. He ran a search on the address Kwasi's widow had given him. The house was owned by a company called Oblong Industries. It was a holding company, the director's names were figureheads from a company formation firm. Lambert would need a warrant to find out the actual owner's name. By then it would be too late. He shut down The System. To the left of his desk was a walk-in wardrobe. Lambert pulled a row of hanging shirts to one side, revealing a wall safe. He punched in an eight-digit code and opened the safe door. He hesitated, then reached in for the gun.

He'd acquired the gun, a Glock 22, whilst working for The Group. It was a gun he'd used on secondment in the USA some years before. Tillman had issued him with an official firearm at the time but Lambert had decided he'd needed a backup weapon. It was easy enough to come by. He strapped on the harness and holster. The harness was so new the leather creaked as he strapped it around his body. He pulled on his jacket to cover the gun and practised accessing it with quick, rapid movements. An action he'd practised thousands of times before, in those initial months in Tillman's department. He clicked a magazine in place and placed the gun into the holster.

Outside, the streetlights glistened in the night air. Lambert hurried to Sophie's car which was parked opposite the house. If Nielson or any of his colleagues appeared now and discovered him carrying the weapon Lambert would face a custodial sentence. Even Tillman would struggle to help him.

Sophie's car was two years old. She'd purchased it with the insurance money from the crash. It was the first time Lambert had sat in it. It was a different make and model to her last one, but the fact that it came from the insurance money had been enough for Lambert to avoid it.

But there was no time to hire a car. Campbell wanted him there alone and if it was his best chance to save Sarah May then he was prepared to take that risk. He punched the address into the satnav on his phone, and followed a route around the south circular.

Memories of the accident threatened to engulf him at every turn. If he let it, he knew his mind would play tricks on him. It would create visions of Chloe in the passenger seat, seatbelt on, kicking her legs in excitement as Daddy drove her through the night to her grandparents' house. Lambert used a trick he'd learnt from the internet to keep the memories at bay. He took the images of that night and imagined placing them in a box, locking it tight with numerous unbreakable locks and chains. The psychologist he'd had to endure for the year following Chloe's death would no doubt have said it was an unhealthy form of repression but he needed it to work now.

He turned his thoughts to Sarah May. He was sure she was still alive and this fuelled his urgency. He weaved through the traffic, getting used to the light controls of Sophie's car. Soon he was in the backwaters of Surrey, his satnav guiding him through single-track lanes in the countryside. He passed the occasional house wondering how people could live in such solitude. He'd decided long ago he didn't need to speak to people all the time but he liked having them around.

The ETA on the satnav stated he was two minutes away. He slowed the car preparing himself for whatever lay ahead. 'You have reached your destination,' said the electronic female voice. Before him was the entrance to a muddied lane. Twisted vines grew over unkempt bushes. It didn't look as if there was enough space to manoeuvre the car through the narrow gap.

He wanted to go by foot, not announce himself to Campbell. He drove three hundred yards further along the road until he found a small layby. He parked Sophie's hatchback into the space, driving the left side of the car into thick brambles so there was enough space for other vehicles to drive by.

He switched off the car and thought about calling Tillman or Bardsley for backup. He considered the pros and cons, and decided Campbell would not tolerate such intrusion. It was only a hunch but it was all he had. The best chance of finding Sarah May alive depended on him going alone. It was pure instinct and instinct had served him well in the past.

He patted the gun in his inside jacket pocket and left the car. It was almost pitch black, no streetlights illuminating the night. Clouds blocked out the stars, and the odd drop of rain dripped onto Lambert's head. He stopped a hundred yards from the lane spotting a hole in the bushes which lined the dirt road. He clambered beneath hoping to find a less obvious route to the house.

His jacket caught on a loose vine. It pulled at the material ripping the skin beneath. Lambert muttered under his breath as a brief wave of pain ran up the left side of his body and vanished, leaving only a dull ache in its wake.

The house was visible from the other side of the bushes. It was a derelict building swamped by trees and unkempt bushes. As he edged closer he made out the front garden. Overgrown grass darted upwards from chipped patio slates. Lambert saw a solitary light burning in one of the downstairs rooms.

A lone car sat in the driveway. A silver Mercedes, the one which had followed him from Bristol. Lambert crept along the pathway, using the downstairs light of the house as a guide.

A gate separated the house from the woodland. The top of the gate was covered in a thick, slimy substance. Lambert pushed both hands down onto the gate and thrust himself over, landing with a squelch into a puddle of mud. He wiped the walking boots he'd bought for the journey on a grass verge, and pulled out the gun

He edged closer to the house, trying to keep to the shadows. The downstairs light was to his left. He waited for movement but nothing stirred. He pressed his body up against the house. The bricks were coated with lines of uneven stone which pulled at his jacket and skin. He moved towards the back of the house. A wood-panelled door led to a kitchen area.

Lambert pressed the handle and was surprised when the door opened. He edged into the kitchen and surveyed the room. He held the gun in front of him, cautious of any possible surprises. The kitchen lent weight to the argument that the house was uninhabitable. The air was ripe with the stench of mouldy food and something else, a bitter acrid smell.

He used his phone as a flashlight and scanned the kitchen. A puddle of vomit sat beneath the dining table. He edged closer and noticed a river of blood which flowed beneath the table surface, meandering towards the vomit.

Through the kitchen door he made out a beam of light which shone from a room at the end of the corridor. He listened but the house was silent save for the gentle hum of the light bulb. Lambert considered possible scenarios. If Campbell was in the room, he could be asleep, could be reading a book, or could be waiting for him. He tiptoed down the hallway towards the room and stopped a metre from the entrance.

He took a deep breath, and with a practised move swivelled his body into the room, his gun held out firm in front of him.

There had been a fourth possibility he hadn't considered.

A man was waiting for him but wasn't reading or sleeping. His broken body hung from a noose. A pool of excrement and urine dripped from his body onto the floor. With his gun still in front of him, Lambert walked around the body and peered up at the face. The man's eyes were sealed shut. It was almost an exact replica of the pictures Lambert had seen of the deceased Samuel Burnham and Kwasi Olumide. The only difference this time being that in addition to the eyes, the man's mouth was sealed shut as well.

Lambert was about to put his gun away, when a second figure entered the room carrying a sawn-off shotgun duly pointed in Lambert's direction.

Lambert pointed the Glock at the man. 'You are?' asked Lambert.

The man held the shotgun steady. This was obviously not a new situation for him. 'Why don't you put your gun down and I'll tell you?'

'That's not going to happen.'

They stood in silence for a time. 'You're Lambert,' said the man.

'And you are?'

The man didn't answer.

'What about him?' asked Lambert.

'That's Lance,' said the man.

Lambert kept his eyes focused on the man. He'd discharged a firearm on duty twice in his career. Once in America, and once when he'd rescued Tillman from his torturers. He had no issue in using it. He would have used it already. He was certain he could drop the man before he could use the shotgun, but he needed to know where Sarah May was being held.

The man retreated to the back wall. He took a seat on a frail-looking wooden chair, behind a small oval-shaped dining table. He kept the gun pointed at Lambert.

Lambert studied the man's face. He placed him in his late fifties, early sixties. He had a fine covering of grey hair on his head, his face sprinkled with shards of silver stubble. His eyes were alert, intelligent. 'Campbell?' asked Lambert.

A flicker of surprise appeared on the man's face, and disappeared in a flash.

'If you put your gun down, we can sort something out,' said Lambert.

'Right,' said the man, not moving a muscle. 'This has no happy ending.'

'Maybe, maybe not. Tell me where Sarah May is and I promise we can sort something out.'

The man laughed. 'I'm a bit long in the tooth for such horseshit, Mr Lambert.'

'Is she alive?'

'I believe so.'

'What the fuck does that mean? Where is she, what have you done to her?' Lambert gripped the gun tighter, willed himself not to use it.

'You're not in a position to negotiate, Mr Lambert.'

'Let me appeal to your decency then. You don't normally take females. I know many of your victims deserved to die.'

'You really think so?'

'Many were criminals. You went beyond what was necessary,

but I can understand the natural justice aspect. But why Sarah May? What has she done to you?'

'Nothing. I don't think you really understand what this is all about.'

'Why don't you clear up things for me?'

Campbell had called the dead man Lance. The name didn't register with Lambert. He hadn't come across it in the investigation so far. The corpse dangled to his left, the sound of the rope creaking in the close confines of the room. 'What about him?'

'Lance?'

'If you say so.'

'A loose end.'

'Why do you seal their eyes? Why Lance's mouth?'

'You need to look a bit harder,' said the man, placing the shotgun beneath his chin.

Lambert stepped forward, his voice urgent. 'What are you doing, Campbell? There's no need for that. Where's Sarah May, Campbell? Where the hell is she?'

For a split second, Campbell was confused, even a little scared.

'I don't know,' he said, pulling the trigger.

Chapter 44

The sound of the shotgun reverberated in the small confines of the room. The bullet travelled through the top of Campbell's head, tearing a hole in the roof, decorating the room with blood and matter.

Lambert froze on the spot, the sound of the gun still ringing in his ears. The sight of Campbell was enough to test the hardest of constitutions. Campbell's head simply no longer existed. It had been blown into a thousand tiny fragments. In its place, the stump of his neck vomited blood like a volcano leaking the occasional burst of lava.

Lambert realised he'd been holding his breath. He exhaled, falling to his knees. He took shallow breaths, told himself he had to continue. He checked the man's sodden clothing for any clue of Sarah May's location. His pockets were empty, as were the pockets of the man he'd called Lance.

He couldn't call it in yet, not with the gun on him. He made a frantic search of the house using a set of fragile aluminium step ladders to reach the attic. He covered every inch of the house then returned to his car and drove twenty miles to a hotel he'd passed on the journey there. He booked a room using a set of false ID he carried. Once in the room, he placed his gun and holster in the room's safe. He showered and changed into a set of fresh clothes and cancelled the delayed email he'd prepared for Tillman. Ten minutes later, he returned to the car and drove back towards the crime scene and called Bardsley.

'I think I've found Campbell,' he said.

It wasn't long before Campbell's house was alive with activity. A line of police cars snaked down the narrow lane which led to the house. The crime scene was cordoned off as the SOCOs arrived.

Lambert waited outside as Bardsley supervised the crime scene officers.

'This is foolhardy, even for you,' said Bardsley when he returned. His former colleague was more animated than Lambert could remember, the thick tendons of his neck springing to attention. 'What the hell were you thinking? You could have been killed.'

'It was only a hunch, I didn't want to bother you,' said Lambert.

Bardsley eye's opened wide to comical effect. 'You didn't want to bother me?' he said, mimicking Lambert's tone.

'I had a tip from an informant. If I came to you every time I had a thought we'd never be off the phone to one other.'

'Let me get this straight. You had a tip that this is where Campbell lives, Campbell being the only link we have between two mass murderers, and you thought you'd come alone with absolutely no backup. What were you expecting to find?'

'I was hoping to find Sarah,' said Lambert.

'You're lucky to be alive,' he repeated.

Lambert shrugged his shoulders.

'Fuck me. Why didn't Campbell shoot you?'

'Would that have made you happier?' said Lambert.

'Jesus Christ, Mike. I should arrest you, you know. Nielson warned you not to interfere. He's on his way over, by the way.'

'If I hadn't interfered, Josh, we'd never have found his body. Have you had any luck identifying either of them?'

'No. No forms of ID in the house as of yet. We've taken some photos of their faces but we don't hold many snapshots of people with their eyes and mouth sealed shut, or their faces obliterated by a shotgun.'

'I don't think Campbell is the killer,' said Lambert.

Bardsley paused. 'What makes you think that?'

'He was scared. I asked about Sarah May and he acted confused, and as you said, why didn't he shoot me and escape? He was resigned, as if he'd had enough. As if he was scared.'

'You came here unarmed?' asked Bardsley.

'Of course. May's not here, and time's running out, Josh.'

Bardsley sighed. 'Don't leave,' he said, moving to a group of officers who'd returned from the woodland to the side of the house.

DCI Nielson appeared, a number of colleagues in tow. The man glared at Lambert as if he was to blame for the atrocities he'd discovered in the house.

Lambert refused to speak to him. Bardsley took an official statement. 'You're the only one who's seen Campbell's face,' he said.

'You want me to scan the database?' asked Lambert.

'It would be helpful. Get to the station and we can get to work. We have a facial recognition expert.'

'Fancy.'

Bardsley let him leave four hours later. Nielson had insisted that his car was checked over before leaving, Lambert relieved to have taken the gun back to the hotel.

Lambert's vision began to blur as he drove the short distance to the hotel. He reached the place in time and collapsed asleep on the bed seconds after checking the safe for the weapon. He slept for three hours, his dreams peppered with images of Billy Nolan and Terrence Haydon, eyes missing, vague inscriptions on their bodies. The victim from earlier that evening, hanging from the rafters, his mouth sealed shut locked in an internal scream and Campbell, taking the shotgun to his mouth, a flicker of fear in his eyes.

Chapter 45

Lambert rushed through a breakfast of coffee and toast, and drove to Lewisham where a joint incident room had been set up. The night had clarified his thoughts. Campbell wasn't the Souljacker. At least not the only one. He was part of a team, and Lambert had an idea who led the cabal.

He parked a mile away and walked to the police station. The cold air bit at his skin as he called Klatzky, leaving a message warning him to go into hiding, and to call him as soon as possible.

Lambert couldn't remember seeing so many police officers in the same room at any one time. The open-plan office was divided into three sections. On one glass-backed noticeboard was the Souljacker investigation. Pictures of Terrence Haydon, Sandra Hopkins, and the older victims, Billy Nolan included, decorated the centre of the noticeboard. Other images were on the periphery, photos of those linked to the case, including one of Lambert and a much younger photo of Simon Klatzky.

A second noticeboard showed the victims of the second killer, Kwasi Olumide, Samuel Burnham, and last night's victim, known only as Lance. A blown-up picture of Lance glared down at him from the noticeboard. It showed in detail the rope marks on his neck, his bloated white cheeks, the line of thick thread through both his eyes and mouth. Next to him was a picture of Campbell's body, the only picture they had for him, taken from a distance, his face obliterated by the shotgun blast.

And finally a section of the room was dedicated to DI Sarah May. A picture of the missing police woman hung on a third noticeboard.

'Mike,' said DCI Josh Bardsley walking over to him. 'If there was ever a time to commit crime in Greater London it would be now,' he said, gesturing to the officers in the room. 'I'm afraid you're going to face questioning this morning. The Assistant Chief Constable's here. Shit is flowing in all directions.'

'That's fine with me,' said Lambert. 'Anything to help find Sarah.'

Bardsley walked him over to the middle section of the incident room. 'We've an ID on last night's hanging victim. Lance Crosby, forty-four. Served seven years for embezzlement in his twenties then went off the radar since his release. No known address. The man hasn't paid tax or national insurance since leaving prison.'

'The suicide? Campbell.'

'Haven't confirmed identification. However, we've matched his fingerprints. Present at the crime scenes of Haydon, Hopkins, Burnham, and Kwasi Olumide. His DNA was all over Lance Crosby as well.' He hesitated, lowered his voice. 'Look, we also found his DNA on Sean Laws.'

Lambert let the information settle. 'You think you've found him, don't you?'

'Don't you? Everything points to Campbell being the Souljacker and the second killer, yes,' said Bardsley. 'One thing still bothers me though.'

'Why didn't he shoot me?' said Lambert.

'Yes. Any thoughts yet?'

Lambert visualised the incident. He couldn't tell Bardsley he'd had a gun as well, and didn't think it made a difference. 'I think he was scared.'

'Scared? Of what?'

'I don't know. Being caught?'

'He could have shot you and fled the scene. It's not as if you had any backup.'

'Reprimand acknowledged. Listen, Josh, I can't offer any proof but I think Campbell was part of a team. If you think about all these recent killings, Haydon, Hopkins, Burnham, Olumide, and this Lance character, it sounds too far-fetched for me that one person is responsible,' said Lambert.

Bardsley sighed. 'You'll need to give us more than that. I realise it's a pointless question, as you'd tell if you wanted me to know, but are you holding anything back? Is there something you're not telling me?'

Lambert considered telling Bardsley the theory he'd been working over in his head since last night. It sounded too absurd to voice at the moment. He needed something concrete before he started making accusations. 'You're right. I'll tell you when I can.'

'Okay, Michael, have it your way. At the moment this is a missing person's case. Our focus is on where Campbell was hiding May.'

Nielson and Bardsley summoned the teams together. Nielson took the lead, explaining what everyone already knew about Campbell. 'DI May is our priority now,' he said. 'She's been missing for thirty-six hours so every minute counts.'

One of May's team, DS Bradbury, sat in the front row of officers. He wore a brown linen suit, his face downtrodden as if he hadn't slept in days.

'As you know this a joint operation across three departments. I'd expect nothing less than full cooperation from everyone.'

Lambert watched the officers leave, wondering if he would ever be part of their number again.

He exchanged looks with Nielson. 'What are you still doing here, Lambert?'

'I want to know if there is anything I can do to help. I can be of use to you.'

'I'm sure we'll get your help whether we like it or not,' said Nielson, his voice drained of animation.

Bardsley pulled Lambert to one side. 'Don't worry about him. He's under a lot of pressure at the moment. First thing, I need you to work with our face recognition expert. She'll be here in a moment. After that, the best thing you can do is to find Klatzky for us. We've officers checking his house again. When the bars are open we'll be checking there. But if you could think of anything else?'

'I'll get looking,' said Lambert.

'Thanks, Mike, and when you're ready to share...'

'You'll be first to know.' Lambert shook hands with Bardsley, knowing someone from his team was probably investigating him as well.

He spent the next hour with a sketch artist. Bardsley had worked with the woman before and insisted it was worth persevering with. Every time Lambert pictured Campbell it was with the gun beneath his chin, the mask of calmness evaporating. Bardsley was right, the sketch artist was exceptional.

Within the hour she'd mocked up a pencil sketch of the man which mirrored Lambert's memory from last night. Whether it would help identify the man was another matter. They would print the finished sketch and distribute it, and would use the measurements from the picture to compare it to images on their database.

'Mr Lambert?'

Lambert placed the finished sketch on the desk.

'DC Rebecca Shah, sir. I've been asked to go through the database with you.'

Lambert handed her the completed picture and thanked the sketch artist. 'Make copies of this first and get them distributed. We need to get the tech boys to see if they can find a match.'

Shah returned ten minutes later. 'I've sent the details to all teams. We'll get that bastard's picture to everybody,' she said.

Lambert didn't answer. He'd spent the last hour concentrating on Campbell's face, and now could think of nothing else. Those last minutes at the house still troubled him. Bardsley had mentioned it earlier. Campbell could have attempted to shoot him. He'd had nothing to lose. Something had stopped him, spooked him so much that he'd taken his own life rather than taking his chances with Lambert.

The young DC, Shah, worked through the software with him. Campbell's picture had been sent to a specialist department who were using photo recognition software to find a match on the database. Lambert was convinced they would be unsuccessful.

'Did you know her well?' asked Shah.

'I know her, yes,' said Lambert.

'No, sorry, I didn't mean to speak in the past tense. It's just, I was the last officer to see her before she left.'

'No one's blaming you, Shah. She was taken by the hotel.'

'I know. Anyway, I'll do anything to help find her.'

'Good, let's keep working.'

An hour later, Bradbury appeared. 'May I have a word, sir?'

Lambert still remembered the man's insolence at the station back in Bristol. He noted the respectful request and wondered if there was a catch.

'My team has been doing some more work on the church in Bristol. Gracelife?'

'I've had the pleasure of visiting that establishment, yes.'

'Following the information you uncovered about the counselling sessions, we contacted the churches linked to the other victims to see if they ran any counselling sessions. We've had a hit with one in Congresbury.'

Lambert recalled talking to Cormack Riley about the twenty-eight-year-old welder. The victim before Billy Nolan. 'David Welsh?' asked Lambert.

'Yes, sir. The parish priest is still there. He says Welsh went to counselling sessions, and a man called Campbell worked there as a counsellor in the early nineties.'

Lambert's heartbeat increased. 'Great. Have we sent the sketch of Campbell over yet?'

'I've emailed it. We're checking all the other churches now.'

Chapter 46

Lambert called Bardsley and told him about David Welsh. 'I think we need to revisit every Souljacker victim. See if we can make a link with counselling sessions.'

'Agreed. Either way, it all points to Campbell,' said Bardsley.

'I don't think he was acting alone, Josh. It doesn't add up.'

Bardsley ignored him. 'We've still had no luck on identifying him. Hopefully, your sketch will help. It's out nationwide, and we've arranged a press conference for this afternoon. We'll get it out on television.'

Lambert hung up. He tried not to blame himself but knew that if he'd managed to keep Campbell alive, then he could have led them to Sarah May. He gave his number to DC Shah. 'Call as soon as you hear from Bradbury or anyone else,' he told her.

He couldn't face going home. He returned to the car and checked the boot for the gun. Relieved it was still there, he sat behind the steering wheel trying to clear his thoughts. He tried Klatzky but as usual the phone went straight to answerphone. Everything about the previous night still bothered him. He'd been manipulated. The note Kwasi had left his widow had guided him to the house just in time to see Lance's body.

Campbell had committed suicide rather than shooting him. Despite Bardsley's protestations, he knew this was significant. Something had scared Campbell so much, that even death was a better alternative. Lambert was convinced that thing was the Souljacker.

He needed to see two people: Kwasi's widow, Laney Richardson, and Myles Stoddard, who had pointed him to Richardson in the first place. He decided to visit the latter first. Stoddard had hid something from him yesterday. He was an inexpert liar and Lambert chided himself for not pushing him further in the bar.

He was about to set off when someone knocked on the car's side window.

Cormack Riley stood on the pavement. Still wearing the same clothes as yesterday, Riley held a stack of papers in his hand.

Lambert wound down the window. 'Cormack.'

'Am I supposed to be speaking to you?' asked Riley.

'You tell me.'

Riley handed him the sheets of paper. 'You made me think the other day, and I don't like what I've discovered. Should I be going to Bardsley with this?'

Lambert scanned the papers which detailed some of the investigation in the Billy Nolan case. Nothing he read had appeared in the official records. It was all general stuff. Some more details of the students who'd been in the halls when Nolan's body had been discovered. Lambert read details on his own interview, which had been reported in the initial report. He then flicked through to the entry for Terrence Haydon, and saw something he couldn't quite believe. 'Can you leave this with me, Cormack?'

Cormack stared at him, his face passive. They didn't know each other well. Riley was scrutinising him, making a decision on whether he could be trusted. 'Why should I do that?'

'Look, I realise it's unusual, but I came to you with this. You've read the report. Who else are you going to trust?'

Cormack didn't move. He swayed on the spot as if stuck in place. 'I've made copies. I'll check back in twenty-four hours. I'm giving it to Bardsley if there's no progress.'

Lambert's body twitched as he drove to Crouch End. Each red light or badly driven vehicle provoked an outburst. All those months in therapy following Chloe's death had been wasted. Following her death, his life had been fuelled by an unquenchable rage. He'd vented it by starting fights with strangers, travelling to bars in areas where he wasn't welcome. Violence became a drug to him, a way of deadening, if only a little, the pain of losing his daughter. Now, after reading the files from Riley, that pain was returning.

The car in front slowed down and turned right without indicating. Lambert slammed on the brakes and pushed the car's horn. He started swearing at the driver, slamming his fist onto the dashboard and waving it wildly in front of him so the driver could see his displeasure in their rear-view mirror.

As the car turned, Lambert made out the form of an elderly woman, hunched over her steering wheel, oblivious to his pathetic complaints. He kept his temper intact for the rest of the journey, bottled it up ready to unleash it on Stoddard.

He gave no warning this time. He parked the car fifty yards from the garage where Stoddard worked, and jogged down the uneven path which led to the Portakabin and the garages.

He didn't bother with the Portakabin. He stormed through the first of the garages. An ancient hatchback was raised onto a plinth, two grease-covered mechanics studying the car's under carriage as if debating the intricacies of some vast puzzle.

To Lambert's right, a third figure disappeared out of a side entrance.

Lambert sighed then shouted at the figure. 'Wait, Myles.' Lambert stepped out of the garage to see Stoddard's figure disappearing up the stone pathway.

'Stop, Myles. I need to talk to you,' he said, trying to keep his tone neutral and calm, knowing his appearance betrayed him.

Stoddard chose not to listen. Lambert swore to himself, and took up the chase. Stoddard had headed off in the direction of Lambert's car. Lambert began at a steady pace, enough to keep Stoddard in his line of vision, and waited for the man to stop running. Stoddard knew Lambert would not leave it at this. That he would find him either at work or at home, so running away from him was pointless. But still he continued. Stoddard sprinted across the road into the entrance of a local park.

Lambert upped his run into a sprint and followed Stoddard as the man darted into a bank of trees. He was younger than Lambert but was not in the same shape as him. He stumbled through the undergrowth, his pace slowing.

'Stop, Myles, for Christ's sake. This isn't doing you any favours.'

The man glanced back at him, losing his footing. He tripped over a loose rock and tumbled head first into the trunk of an oak tree. Lambert sprinted forward, Stoddard scrambling on his hands and knees to get away.

Lambert kicked the man's left leg. Stoddard tried to get up again but Lambert was on him. He punched him twice in the stomach.

Stoddard curled into a ball. Lambert grabbed him by the collar of his overalls and yanked him to his feet. He punched him again in the stomach holding him upright so the man gasped for air. He fought the overwhelming urge to ram Stoddard's face into the nearest tree.

'Why did you run?' he said, trying to control his volume lest he attract attention.

Stoddard was unable to speak, his body desperate for oxygen.

Lambert pushed his forehead onto Stoddard's. 'Well?'

Stoddard tried to resist, his breath rank with onions and undigested meat. Lambert pushed him away, Stoddard's back crashing into the trunk of the tree. He slithered down the bark and sat on the ground, his head between his legs.

'I didn't know what you wanted, did I?' said Stoddard, gasping for air.

'So you ran? You never know what I want with you. It doesn't mean you run away.' Lambert hunched down so he was at the man's eye level. 'You set me up, Myles, and I need to know why. If you lie to me even once I'm going to haul you in and everything you've ever told me will come out. Do you understand what that means?'

Stoddard wiped his nose with the back of his hand. 'You're not even with the police any more,' he said, a look of victory on his face.

Lambert tensed his left hand and swung the back of it down so it hit Stoddard on his cheek. The man's face snapped to the side and a crooked line of blood trickled from his nose.

'You think that makes a difference? You know me, you know what I'll do. Now tell me why you set me up. It wasn't your idea. You haven't the brains. Someone put you up to it and I want to know who and how.'

The brief look of triumph on Stoddard's face vanished. Its replacement was part confusion, part terror. His body began to tremble but Lambert didn't think it was because he'd hit him. He'd never hit Stoddard before and it was something he despised having to do, but the man knew him well enough to know he wouldn't go any further. It was possible the threat of bringing him in had unnerved him.

'Listen, tell me what I need to know and you're free to go. You've been good to me over the years, Myles, and I don't want to destroy our working relationship.'

'I can't, Mr Lambert,' stammered the man.

'Can't what?'

'I can't tell you about the man.'

'Let's start somewhere else,' said Lambert. 'How did you manage to set me up? Was Kwasi's widow involved?'

'I've never even met the woman. I barely knew Kwasi.'

'But you knew about the note he left for her? The one which guided me to that house.'

'Yes.'

'How did you know about it?'

'He told me.'

'Who?'

'I can't,' said Stoddard.

'Was it him?' asked Lambert, showing Myles the sketch of Campbell on his smart phone.

Myles glanced at the phone, his face not changing. 'No, never seen that guy in my life.'

'Look closer, Myles.'

'I'm telling you, Mr Lambert. I've never seen that man before.'

Lambert put the phone away. 'So this other man, what did he tell you?'

'He said that Kwasi had left a note for his wife.'

'And how did he know that?'

'Oh God,' said Stoddard, shaking.

'Myles, I'm going to find out one way or another so tell me.'

'I don't know for sure. He sort of suggested he'd obtained the information from Kwasi, a kind of death bed thing.'

The images of Kwasi's corpse sprung into Lambert's mind. Had Kwasi given over the information before or after his eyes had been sealed shut?

'Who is he, Myles?'

'I don't know I swear.'

'Is it Campbell?'

'I don't think so.'

'You realise if I take you in now you're done for? You're an accessory to murder, minimum. And I will make sure everyone inside knows you're a grass.'

'I don't know, Mr Lambert. I swear if I knew who he was I'd tell you.'

'You'd never met him before?'

'Never.'

'Then, Myles, I have to ask you, why did you do what he asked?'

Stoddard scratched his chin searching for an answer. His body was in freefall now, every limb shaking, as if in beat to some distant sound.

'So help me God, Myles, if you don't tell me the truth I'll take you in right now. You know one of our DI's is missing?

335

Can you imagine what will happen to you at the station? And don't make it up. Tell me why you did what he said.'

'I wasn't going to make it up, Mr Lambert. He showed me some photos after he'd taken the knife away from my eyes. He said if I didn't do what he told me I'd be next.'

'Did he tell you his name?'

'Of course not.'

'What did he look like?'

'He was tall. Late forties, fifties perhaps. I didn't really look at him. He sprung out of nowhere. As I said he held a knife to my eyes and then once he'd let me go I was too scared to look at him. I was shitting myself, Mr Lambert. He threatened to tear my fucking eyes out and I believed he would do so.'

'Why didn't you go to the police?'

'Right, as if they'd be much use to me.'

'Hair? Eye colour?'

'I don't know. He was wearing one of those hats, beanies I think you call them. I don't know what colour eyes he had but he was strong.'

'And he gave you my name?'

'Yes. He said, "You know Michael Lambert?" Then he told me to tell you about Kwasi's widow. The note that Kwasi had left her.'

'Why didn't you tell me this the last time we met?'

'I told you, Mr Lambert, he said he'd kill me.'

Lambert took out his phone and ran a search, a face appearing on the screen. He gripped the phone tight, hoping Stoddard didn't see that his hand was shaking. He wasn't sure he wanted confirmation.

'Get up.'

Myles pushed himself up from the ground. 'Mr Lambert, you said you wouldn't take me in.'

'Do you have anywhere you can stay? Any friends?'

'My mum lives in Southend.'

Lambert showed him the photo on the screen. 'Is this him?' he asked, his body so full of adrenalin that he found it hard to stand still.

Stoddard let out a whimper. He slumped to his knees as if he'd been given life-defining news.

Lambert came close to joining him. He took all the cash he had from his wallet and gave it to Stoddard. 'Don't go back to work. Go straight to the train station and stay at your mum's until you hear back from me.'

Stoddard sprinted away before Lambert had time to change his mind.

Lambert was still having trouble with what he'd discovered, Stoddard's identification of the man matching the details he'd read in the file from Cormack Riley.

Klatzky called as he was walking back to the car.

'Simon, where are you?'

'Guess,' said Klatzky.

Lambert heard the sound of muted conversations in the background. 'Which pub?' he said.

'Not sure. The one on your high street. Where we went the other day.'

'Okay, you need to stay put. Surely that's an easy request.'

'I'm running short of funds, Mikey.'

'Stay put, Mikey. Do you hear me?' Lambert shouted into the phone.

'Okay,' said Klatzky, slurring.

Lambert lowered his tone. 'Simon, listen. Was there anyone else you told about Billy's counselling sessions? Think hard.' He wasn't sure why he was asking. He had all the information needed. Perhaps it was out of loyalty, or the hope that Stoddard was wrong.

The line was silent. 'Simon, you still there?'

'Yeah, sorry, Mikey. What were you saying?'

'Fucking hell, Simon, this is important. Billy's counselling session. Did you ever tell anyone else about them?'

'I told you, Mikey. No.'

'Think hard, Simon. A woman's life is on the line.'

Klatzky paused, and for a second he thought he'd hung up. 'Wait, there was that one time. When Billy died.'

Lambert felt the air leave him.

'I told that one person. Yeah, I forgot about that. That copper. What was his name again?'

'Hastings?' said Lambert, his voice sounding distant.

'Yeah, Hastings.'

Chapter 47

Lambert started driving, his mind working overtime in various directions. It made a certain kind of sense. The Souljacker being the SIO on the case, the one person whose name appeared on nearly every case report. The one person he'd never considered a suspect. From what Riley had said, it was probably why he'd stopped after Billy Nolan. He'd managed to hold out for nine killings, directing the investigation to hide his own sick desires, until it started affecting his career. He didn't want anyone else to take over the Souljacker case, so he'd stopped the killings. It was an unbelievable deception. He had enough to get everyone involved now. With the evidence he'd obtained, even Nielson would believe him.

But he couldn't call it in. Hastings had Sarah May and as soon as Lambert shared what he'd discovered her life would be over. Hastings had wanted him from the very start, from the day he sent the crime photos to Klatzky.

He sent a text to Klatzky telling him not to leave the bar. For once, it would be the safest place for him. He needed to get home, prepare himself for meeting Hastings.

He spent the next hour in traffic, trying to piece everything together. How had Hastings duped them all this time? What part did Campbell have to play?

He turned onto his street and immediately noticed his front door was ajar.

He ran from the car, praying Sophie hadn't returned, his gun held beneath his jacket as he tried the door. The lock was broken. He kicked the door down, the gun raised in front of him, hoping no one had seen him. Cold air blew through the hallway, tinged with the ripe smell of ammonia and something more perfumed. He shut the front door, securing it with a kitchen chair. He checked each room in turn securing his house until he reached the spare bedroom.

His mouth fell open at the scene before him. 'Oh, fucking hell, Simon, what have you done?' he howled.

Chapter 48

Lambert didn't check for a pulse. Klatzky was naked from the waist up, the Latin inscription In oculis animus habitat chiselled into his chest, his eyes two vacant holes.

'You silly bastard, why didn't you stay in the bar?' Lambert asked the corpse.

He found a pair of forensic gloves in the kitchen. It was far from perfect. He was contaminating the crime scene with every step and breath he took. He examined the body as much as possible without touching it. It was a perfect replica of every Souljacker murder. Klatzky's jacket had been dumped to his side. It languished in a pool of blood, sprinkled with specks of white which Lambert presumed was the pontifical incense, the smell of which brought back unwanted memories. Lambert tried to see what was in Klatzky's inside pocket but couldn't do so without touching the material.

He picked it up with his gloved left hand and used his right hand to fish out Klatzky's wallet. From the wallet he took out two credit cards, a five pound note and a piece of paper folded in two. The piece of paper was addressed to Lambert. He unfolded it.

'When you work it out, come alone or May dies.'

The note wasn't signed but he knew it was from Hastings. Lambert placed the note inside a plastic bag. He fixed the front door as best as he could and jammed the chair up against it once more. He retreated to his office. He wanted to stop everything, call in Bardsley and Nielson and mourn for his best friend, but he had to keep going.

Sarah May was alive, and the note had warned him to come alone.

Lambert closed his eyes as something clicked in his brain. 'It can't be,' he whispered to himself, a memory returning. He tripped over his feet leaving the office, and sprinted downstairs. He raced to the living room. 'Where is it?' he shouted, searching through the bookshelf. Books were stored on a purchase by purchase basis. Hundreds of them adorned his office, hundreds more spread out throughout the house. He scanned the spines looking for the surname he wanted. Eventually he located the title.

Kill Time.

His hands trembled as he opened the front cover. He checked the inscription. The handwriting was identical.

To Michael,

Best wishes,

Julian Hastings.

He collapsed onto his chair, his grip tight on the book. He opened the next page and everything became clear. The answer had been there all the time. He scrolled down to the second paragraph of the acknowledgements page. A simple note he'd read years before. Something which had lodged in his mind and had remained dormant for all this time.

Special thanks to Mr Campbell for all his help.

A sense of calm came over Lambert. Hastings lived in a little village near Orpington, Kent, less than thirty minutes away.

Come alone or May dies.

Nothing suggested Hastings didn't mean exactly what he said. To have carried out so many murders over such a number of years required intricate planning and discipline. It was not a chance Lambert could take. He sent another time-delayed email to Tillman telling him what he'd discovered and where he was going.

He changed, pulling on a thick black overcoat to conceal the Glock, and went downstairs. He opened the front door, surprised by the darkness of night, in time to see DCI Nielson stepping out of an unmarked police car, followed closely by two junior detectives. Lambert pulled the door shut and stood facing out to the road, his back against the door, hiding the damage to the lock. The Glock weighed heavy in its holster. Although concealed, it felt conspicuous as if it pointed out of his jacket.

'Going somewhere, Mr Lambert?' said Nielson.

'That's right.'

'Maybe we could go inside for a quick chat. You haven't been answering your phone.'

Thankfully his phone was in his trouser pocket so he didn't have to open his jacket. The screen displayed twelve missed calls. In the excitement of discovering Hastings was the killer, he hadn't noticed his phone was switched to silent.

'Oh, yes, sorry. On silent,' said Lambert.

'Have you made contact with Mr Klatzky?'

'Not yet. I'm going to try a few more bars now.'

'Let's go in and talk.'

'I told you, I'm heading out,' said Lambert, trying to control his breathing.

'You're not hiding Mr Klatzky in there are you? I know you two are close.'

'Don't be so ridiculous, Nielson.'

'Just put my mind at rest, Mr Lambert.'

'You can get a fucking warrant, Nielson, if you want to waste my time. Why would I lie to you?'

There'd be no explaining Klatzky's body, at least not immediately. And with the gun inside his jacket, he'd be arrested. He made a decision. If Nielson was going to pursue the matter he would have to use the gun. It was the only way to ensure Sarah May's safety.

Nielson clicked his tongue onto the roof of his mouth, swayed on the balls of his feet. He exchanged glances with his colleagues, who stared at Lambert as if they could possibly intimidate him.

'We're supposed to be working together on this,' said Nielson. He sounded like he didn't believe his own words.

'Well then, let me do my part of the job,' said Lambert. His back was still flat against the front door. He intended to stay there until the policemen left.

Nielson's facial muscles twitched as he decided his next move. 'DNA found at the crime scenes of Terrence Haydon, Sandra Hopkins, Sam Burnham, Kwasi Olumide and Lance Crosby all match that of Campbell,' he said, as if Lambert didn't already know.

'Result,' said Lambert. 'Do we know who he is yet?'

'Working on it. Two things outstanding. Our missing DI, and your missing friend.'

'You're the one who let him go.'

'We have some more questions for him.'

344

'I'll let you know if I hear from him, I promise,' said Lambert, the image of Klatzky's lifeless corpse springing into his mind. 'I want to find Sarah as much as you do.'

Nielson returned to his car. He opened the window and stared at Lambert. He went to say something else, and stopped, shaking his hand before the car pulled away.

Lambert waited ten minutes. From Sophie's car he called Tillman.

'What now?' said Tillman.

Lambert told him about Klatzky. 'I need the house secure,' he said.

'You need it secure. You mean you want it cleaned?' asked Tillman.

'No I don't want it clean, it's a crime scene. I want to keep it as such but I need some time. I don't want Nielson in there causing trouble.'

'What do you want me to do?'

'Send a couple of people around to protect the entrance. Make sure Nielson doesn't do anything stupid.'

'And in the meantime where are you going?'

'I can't tell you,' said Lambert, hanging up.

He took the SIM card from his phone and began driving towards Orpington. A couple of miles into the journey he threw the SIM card out of the window, a mile later the phone followed.

He knew the area well. He took an old shortcut through the woods until he was on the A20. He passed the hospital where he'd been born nearly forty years ago. His mind focused totally on Hastings and Sarah May. He took the turn into Farnham village and opened the driver side window, hoping a blast of fresh air would ease his exhaustion.

The satnav guided him through a labyrinth of lanes. The adrenalin which had fuelled him back at the house had dissipated. He'd managed one or two hours' sleep last night, and hadn't slept well for days. Hastings' house was less than half a mile away now. Lambert dropped a gear, the car accelerating through the night mist.

Without warning his vision blurred.

'Not again,' he said. He took his foot off the accelerator as his vision filled with a thousand shades of fiery colour, but was too late.

He was unconscious before the car hit the bank and span upside down into a ditch.

Chapter 49

Lambert slipped in and out of consciousness, his eyes unable to focus long enough on his predicament before he was dragged back under. The airbag had been deployed. His face was crushed up against it, his body pulled to his right as if the car had tilted over.

Unconscious, he was back in the car with Chloe. It was two years ago and he was driving her late at night to her grandparents, Sophie's parents. Like now, he hadn't slept properly for weeks. In his dream, Chloe sat next to him, nine years old and full of life, full of a future she would never see.

She was sulking. He'd wanted to wait until the morning to drive her but she'd insisted. It was that memory he'd never been able to shake. His beautiful, happy-go-lucky girl forever smiling, forever full of mischief and all he was left with was that one prominent memory. Of her sitting in the passenger seat, arms folded, her head turned away from him, a comical pout sketched onto her face.

He awoke with a shudder. Confused, he called out Chloe's name. His right leg ached, a sense of pressure building within him as if the weight of the whole car was pinning him down. He closed his eyes and fell asleep again.

They'd hardly talked on that journey. He'd made a few light-hearted attempts to get her back onside but she hadn't even cracked a smile.

The dream transformed him to the hospital bed where he'd lain in an enforced coma. His first words on waking had been, 'Chloe.' The look on Sophie's mother's face, sitting on the seat next to his bed, haunted him to this day. It was as if he'd stabbed her in the heart.

'What?' he mouthed, no sound leaving his throat.

She'd dropped a few chipped ice cubes into his mouth, the liquid coating his mouth and throat for a second. 'What?' he repeated.

She looked away and he understood.

The dream took him to the funeral, the day a morphine dream. Scores of well-meaning condolences. Sophie's parents unable to look him in the eye.

Then he was back in their living room, Sophie sitting on the sofa, crying as videos of Chloe played out on the TV screen before her. He pictured his dream self in the doorway, too cowardly to look at the pictures, too selfish to comfort his wife.

The memories continued.

He sat in conversation with Glenn Tillman, being told he was on forced absence of leave. Back at the house, Sophie suggesting spare bedrooms. Her body tensing as he moved to touch her.

Lambert knew he had to escape. He tried to open his eyes, to picture reality, but another image flashed before him.

He was back in the car with Chloe, on a narrow country lane. Dark, no street lights. As soon as the first flicker appeared in his vision he'd slammed on the brakes. He'd been going too fast. The car careered into an SUV travelling in the other direction.

The coroner's verdict was accidental death. Chloe had died

348

instantly. Her body crushed from the impact. He'd never had to identify her, had never seen her again. That sullen, comical pout the last thing he saw of her.

He awoke again with a shudder, reality returning like a blow to the head. The dreams of Chloe lingered. He had to subdue them before he continued, otherwise he wouldn't be able to continue.

It was Sarah May who needed him now.

His eyes struggled to acclimatise to the darkness. He sat in the driver's seat trying to get his bearings. The windshield was cracked but not broken. His body was being pulled to the right so he presumed the car had been spun onto its side. He held tight onto the steering wheel with one hand, the deployed airbag pushed against his chest. With his left hand he unclicked the seatbelt, fighting the pull of gravity as his body fell to the right. He was scrunched up on his side, his face pushed against the cold glass of the driver's door window. He tested all of his limbs in turn, everything in working order. It was going to take a while. He had no idea how long he'd been out, but knew rushing would be a false economy. Every part of him ached.

He grabbed hold of the steering wheel and tried to wrench his legs free from their position beneath the dashboard. A sharp pain cut through his left shoulder and vibrated upwards causing a dense ache in his head. He fell back into the car. His left shoulder was tender to touch. Lambert reached beneath his coat with his right hand and searched for a wound. He couldn't feel anything significant but his hand was laced with blood when he took it away. He placed his left hand beneath the driver's chair and reclined it as far as it would go. He hoisted first his right, then his left leg onto the chair so his knees were facing the driver's side door. Then he clenched his legs together with his hands and swivelled himself around so his back was against the door, his legs pointing upwards, the back of his knees resting on the gearbox.

It was a strain to hold the position. He inched backwards so he was more or less lying on his back. He lay there exhausted. It was possible he could stand up and try to open the passenger side door but it would be difficult to hoist his body upwards without the door slamming down on him. The other option was smashing the windscreen. It was cracked already so a few good kicks should destroy it completely.

He swivelled around again so he was in position. With his back against the driver's chair he kicked at the windscreen. It broke on first impact, cracking into safety glass which he cleared with a second kick.

With rapid breath, he cleared away as much glass as possible. He rested for a couple of minutes then clambered out into the night air, collapsing onto the ground next to the car. He reached into his jacket, thankful the gun was still in its holster.

He was about to get to his feet when he heard movement behind him, the sound of feet crunching on hard ground. As he withdrew the gun, someone attacked him from behind, pinning him to the ground.

It was a smart, economical move. Whoever held him had ferocious strength. Lambert tried to swing his elbow back but his arms were locked tight. From the shadows he heard the sound of a second person moving towards them. He jerked as something sharp stung his neck and the night, once more, went out of focus.

Chapter 50

A gunshot startled him awake.

He was inside the house, his hands and legs expertly tied to a heavy steel-framed chair. Lambert blinked. The room was in pitch darkness. If there were any windows, they were covered in blackout blinds.

He had no idea how long he'd been out. The delayed email was due to be sent to Tillman at nine a.m. It contained Hastings' address, though it was possible he'd since been moved. He'd lost track of time. His inner clock suggested it was somewhere between six and seven a.m. If he could stall Hastings for two hours or more then there might be a chance.

His left arm was covered in drying blood. Waves of pain swept over him as he moved his chin to prise open his jacket and see the extent of his wounds. Whatever Hastings had injected into his body was still present. The poison lingered in his blood, causing his muscles and joints to ache.

His thoughts turned to Sarah May.

'Hastings,' he shouted. His voice reverberated in the hollow confines of the room. He swallowed, moved his tongue around his mouth, trying to generate saliva.

'Hastings,' he shouted again, louder this time, more insistent. He tried to wriggle free but each movement sent horrendous slices of pain through his body. If anything it only tightened the hold of the grips which held him in place.

Lambert let out a wave of obscenities which concluded with the threat to kill his captor. He tried not to think about the gunshot he'd heard. He prayed it wasn't for Sarah May.

The door opened and light flooded the room. Hastings stood at the entrance, dressed immaculately in a three-piece suit, shirt and matching tie.

'You gave us quite a scare there, Michael. The car accident was not part of the story.'

'Even seeing you now, I can't quite believe it,' said Lambert.

Hastings smiled, something Lambert could barely recall him doing before. 'You've really let this thing drag on, haven't you, Michael?' he said.

'Where's Sarah?'

'She's fine.'

'The gunshot?'

'Oh no, that wasn't for her. That was someone else.' Hastings laughed, more animated than Lambert had ever seen him.

'The man who grabbed me outside?' asked Lambert.

'Correct.' Hastings sat on the floor, and pushed his back against the wall.

'Let me see Sarah,' said Lambert.

'In good time.'

Lambert pursed his lips, and stared at the man who had duped him for twenty years. He wanted answers but didn't want to give Hastings the satisfaction of telling his story. The how and the why weren't relevant at the moment. He needed to focus on May. She was all that was left now.

'You're desperate to know, aren't you?'

Lambert didn't respond. He needed to drag this out as long as possible, to give Tillman the chance to read his email. 'Not as desperate as you are to tell me.'

'Oh, I'm not too worried about that. You'll get to know my story soon, whether you want to or not. I'm in no rush to tell. I've kept it to myself all these years. I can tell it's eating you up. You want to know why I killed all those people. How I avoided detection. If I was in your position, I would be desperate to know the details.'

'But you're not in my position, are you?'

'No, and I'm thankful for that, but I can save you.' Hastings chuckled, the look on his face not changing. 'There's more though, isn't there, Michael? You want to know why I singled you out. You want to know where it started. You're doubting yourself. Wondering if this all began back at University with Billy Nolan. You think I might have planted the idea of you becoming a police officer into your head. That this was all one long-term plan to get to you. I can see you now, trawling your memory, that wonderful brain of yours, for an answer.'

'I think you're seeing things that aren't there.' Lambert had considered such things, but had quickly dismissed them. It was too elaborate, too coincidental. So many things had occurred outside Hastings' control. Lambert didn't doubt himself. It was possible that Hastings had wanted to get his attention with the Haydon killing but he refused to believe it was a twenty-year-old plan.

'Maybe,' said Hastings, getting up off the floor. He walked towards Lambert and pushed his face towards him until their foreheads touched. A sourness emanated from him. Hastings traced his finger around Lambert's eyes, Lambert trying hard not to show any sense of fear. 'Though perhaps, you're the one who is seeing things,' said Hastings, his voice a deep growl.

Hastings pushed Lambert's head backwards and walked back towards the door. 'Anyway,' he said, his tone lightening. 'I'll give you some time to consider the matter.'

He slammed the door shut, not looking back.

The hours passed. Lambert tried a number of times to break the binds around his ankles and wrists to no avail. His whole left side throbbed. Every time he tried to shake his left leg, a wave of pain flooded his body. It was possible he had broken it in the accident, or that Hastings had done something to him in the interim.

Tillman should have received his email by now. He tried to remain positive, focused on the task ahead. It would be too easy to dwell on the impossibility of the situation. He was locked in position, subject to Hastings' will, and history told him that people in his situation rarely lived to tell the tale. Despite his best efforts, images from the Souljacker crime scenes appeared in his head. He fooled himself that the pain could be managed. He'd undergone interrogation training when joining The Group, but knew nothing could fully prepare him for what lay in store.

His body cried out for sustenance. He'd had nothing to drink since the accident, and was severely dehydrated. He slipped in and out of dreamless sleep, startling himself awake every few minutes. In his lucid moments, he hypothesised that things were different this time. Hastings had two prisoners, not one. Although Tillman was not yet here, he would now know Hastings was the Souljacker. One way or another, it was the

354

end of the line for Hastings, and Hastings had allowed himself to be caught. This had to mean something.

His body tensed as the door opened and light filled the room. As his eyes adjusted, he noticed patches of dried blood on the floor and walls.

Hastings entered carrying a bottle of water. 'I have a little gift for you,' he said, as if they were the best of friends. 'But first you need to smarten up.'

Lambert's chest convulsed as Hastings tipped half of the ice-cold water over his head. He gulped for breath as the water trickled down his head, his dry tongue reaching out for loose droplets.

'I hate to see you this way. Here,' said Hastings, pulling Lambert's head back and trickling water into his mouth. Lambert kept still as the water coated his throat and mouth, knowing one false move could lead to Hastings choking him.

Hastings let go of Lambert's head and took the bottle away. 'Better?'

Lambert licked his lips, his body desperate for more water.

Hastings tipped the remainder of the bottle onto the floor. 'I almost forgot, your guest,' he said. He left the room and returned a minute later carrying a chair.

On the chair, bound and gagged, was something which resembled Sarah May.

Chapter 51

Hastings removed the gag from Sarah May's mouth and repeated his water trick, tipping a second bottle of water over the woman's head. May hardly moved.

'She's a bit depleted,' said Hastings. He lifted her head, and forced the bottle into her mouth. 'Drink now,' he said, like a caring parent nursing a sick child.

Lambert struggled in his chair, endured the pain in his leg in a desperate attempt to get free. 'What have you done to her, you sick fuck?'

'She's fine. She's here for your benefit, Michael.' He positioned Sarah so she faced Lambert and headed towards the door. 'I don't owe you this but I'll share this information with you anyway. If you're waiting for Glenn Tillman to come and rescue you, then you'll be waiting a long time.'

'Stop,' said Lambert, as Hastings began shutting the door.

'Do you really think I would keep DI May at my house? Come on, Michael. Give me some credit,' said Hastings, shutting the door.

So he'd moved him whilst he'd been unconscious. At least Tillman and the others would be on the trail. It was a hollow consolation but something to cling onto. 'Sarah,' he said. 'Sarah, it's Michael. Michael Lambert.'

They sat opposite each other, tied to the steel-framed chairs, their knees almost touching.

May lifted her head. In the gloom, Lambert made out the shape of her mouth curling into a smile. 'Is this your idea of a rescue?' she said, her voice faint.

Lambert laughed. She was wearing the same clothes she'd been wearing the night she'd disappeared. Her jeans, and cotton shirt were caked in filth as was her tangled hair, her face drawn like she hadn't eaten anything since Hastings had kidnapped her.

Lambert wanted to make a joke, about lulling Hastings into a false sense of security, but lacked the energy. 'What happened?'

At least the water had invigorated her. When Hastings had carried her into the room, Lambert feared she was dead.

'He took me outside the hotel. He must have been following me.' She stopped speaking as a memory returned. 'Sean?' she asked.

Lambert paused. 'Sorry,' he said.

'Didn't think so. I think I saw Hastings cut him. Can't be sure.'

'He left him at the scene. It was a clean cut. It would have been instantaneous.'

'Sean followed me from Bristol. He wanted us to get back together.'

'You don't have to explain anything,' said Lambert.

May locked eyes with him. 'I had an abortion. I was seventeen,' she said.

'I know.'

'He never got over it. If I'd only stopped to speak to him. I could have at least given him that courtesy.'

'Sarah, you know it's not your fault. You didn't owe Sean anything and how could you know about Hastings?'

May's neck drooped as if it was taking all her energy to keep it aloft. 'How did you know it was him?'

'I was as shocked as you. He had a team working for him. We found Campbell.'

'Really?'

'He killed himself in front of me, rather than tell me about Hastings. I uncovered some unreported notes on the Billy Nolan case. Information had come in about him attending the counselling session at Gracelife. Hastings had suppressed the information.' Lambert sighed. With his arms and legs tied, he felt absurdly vulnerable. 'He's killed Klatzky.'

'Oh, God, Michael, I'm so sorry.'

'He left a note, warned me to come alone. I sent a time-delayed email to my old boss, Tillman, but as you heard he must have moved me.'

'Did he drug you as well?'

'Must have.' Lambert hesitated. 'Has he done anything to you?' Lambert's pulse raced as he waited for her to answer.

'Nothing physical, well, nothing sexual at least. He's starved me, and subjected me to lengthy sermons about what he's done and why. Christ, this is absurd. I bet he's listening to every second of this.'

'Let him listen. Tell me everything he's told you.'

Chapter 52

May started to speak. 'He's thrown me snippets over the period I've been captive. It's hard to tell what is real and what I imagined. He's hardly fed me, and once or twice he's drugged me with God knows what.'

'Tell me what you remember,' said Lambert.

May sighed. 'He confessed to all the Souljacker murders except one.'

'Which one?'

'The first one, Clive Hale. He claims that was where he got the idea from. I'm not sure I shared this information with you, but I interviewed a handwriting expert the other day to examine the inscriptions on the body. The expert swore blind that the first one was different to the others. Hastings is right-handed and the first inscription was by a left-handed person.'

'Who was the first killer then?'

'Graham Jackett.'

Lambert let the information settle in. Jackett was the second Souljacker victim.

'Hastings worked out he was the killer, and eliminated his competition,' said May.

This didn't make immediate sense to Lambert. He'd presumed Hastings had some master plan. That the killings had a reason. 'So he's a copycat?'

'God, don't say that to him. I made that mistake. He went ape. Claimed it was his destiny and Jackett was sent to him as a guide.'

'A guide?'

May laughed. Lambert's eyes had adjusted to the gloom and he could make out her features more easily. She'd lost weight in her face, but despite everything there was still a light in her eyes. 'He believes he was sent to save twelve troubled souls.'

'He saves them by killing them? By removing their eyes?'

'Liberating their souls apparently.'

'Jesus. Did he let on how he chose his victims?' asked Lambert.

'I quizzed him about the church and he became a bit defensive.'

Lambert told her about the connections with the other churches, how they'd discovered Campbell was working as a counsellor in more than one church. 'Did you ask Hastings about Campbell?'

'A loyal friend, apparently. Helped him with his work.'

'How?'

'He specialised in victims of abuse. From what I could ascertain, Campbell found the victims and passed them on to Hastings.'

Lambert thought about the night at Campbell's house, the resigned look on the man's face when he turned the shotgun on himself. He still didn't know if it was guilt or fear which had made him take his own life. 'What about Sandra Hopkins?'

'She'd attended counselling sessions with Billy Nolan, had seen Terrence Haydon at the church, and knew Hastings. He called it a lovely symmetry.'

'Jesus. And the others? Burnham, Olumide, Crosby?'

'They worked for him and Campbell. He didn't go into great detail, except they didn't deserve to have their souls saved.'

'Let me guess, by sealing their eyes, he sealed in their souls?' said Lambert.

'Bingo.'

They sat in silence, each lost in their own thoughts. Lambert tried to piece together Hastings' motivation. He realised he didn't know that much about the man, save for his police career and latterly his books. He wished he'd done more research. He knew Hastings had been married, his wife passing three years ago. Had anything else happened in his childhood? Was there some clue he could latch onto which could help talk the man out of whatever he had planned? If what May told him was true, then he clearly had some religious motivation. If he knew more, then it was possible he could appeal to that side of him.

'Did he give a reason for his actions?' asked Lambert.

'Not beyond saving the twelve souls.'

'Why twelve?'

'He became evasive when I asked him. Then he became angry. He left the room and kept me in the darkness for hours.'

'What's your thinking?'

'I would like access to the internet,' said May, forcing a laugh. 'The only thing I could come up with was the twelve apostles. I have no idea what the relevance is though, and I went to Catholic school.'

'The number could have a personal significance.'

'Does it matter?' asked May.

'I don't know. If we can find out why he is doing this then we might be able to stop whatever he has planned.'

'You've done the maths?' asked May.

Lambert nodded. 'If you count Klatzky, and dismiss the first killing which Hastings claims he wasn't responsible for, then there have only been eleven Souljacker murders,' he said.

'He's only saved eleven souls,' agreed May.

'At least we know who the twelve is going to be,' said Lambert remembering what Hastings told him earlier. 'He told me he was going to save me.'

Chapter 53

Hastings abandoned them for hours. Lambert slipped in and out of sleep, his position in the chair making it impossible to stay asleep for longer than a few minutes. He wondered how Sarah had managed for all this time.

They both called out to Hastings on occasion, demanding food, more water. 'Do you think he's left us here?' said May.

In a way, abandonment was the worst thing that could happen to them. Lambert knew that Hastings was organised enough to imprison them in a place where they would never be found. The thought of a long drawn-out death was too much to consider. Even the alternative sounded better. At least Hastings had used anaesthetic on his victims in the past. Although they'd been alive when he'd removed their eyes, and carved the Latin into their chests, the pathologists agreed that the Souljacker victims had probably been too full of drugs to have suffered the worst of his actions.

'He hasn't left us,' said Lambert. 'He needs to finish his story.'

Sarah May was asleep when Hastings eventually returned. She'd been telling Lambert about her childhood, the Catholic school where she'd met Sean, when she'd drifted off. She was more used to sleeping in the chair, and had been asleep for what felt like thirty minutes when Hastings opened the door.

At first, he stood still in the entrance. A blurred silhouette surrounded by shades of darkness. Lambert was so dizzy with exhaustion, hunger and dehydration that it was almost a relief to see the man. He just wanted it over.

Lambert heard Hastings plug something into a socket in the hallway. 'Shield your eyes,' said Hastings, carrying a standing lamp into the room.

The light woke Sarah. Her eyes sprung open, her body struggling for a few seconds against the binds which tore into her flesh, before she settled in place, her eyes blinking and scanning the room. She scowled on seeing Hastings.

Illuminated, the room lost some of its claustrophobic power. It reminded Lambert of the nightclub he'd visited in Bristol a few days previous. How, without the darkness, the blinking lights and music, the place lost its power. It had become just an empty room, and so was their prison. He scanned the room for clues to their location, and possible means of escape which was ludicrous considering their predicament. Chipped plasterboard covered the once white walls. Splashes of red decorated the faded paint like an abstract painting.

'Sorry for the delay,' said Hastings. 'A few arrangements needed before the end.'

The brilliance of the light highlighted the wrinkles on Hastings' face, the laughter lines rarely used. Hastings left the room and returned with a third chair which he placed near the entrance.

Lambert watched, helpless, as Hastings dragged Sarah May's chair across the room. She managed to keep silent, her head swinging violently from side to side as he moved her. He placed her chair opposite his, a metre between the two seats.

'What are you doing, Hastings? You said I was your target,' said Lambert.

'Target? Don't be so dramatic,' said Hastings.

'Leave May out of this. You said you wanted to save me. So save me, and let her be.'

Hastings stood in the middle of the room, a tied prisoner to either side of him. He paused for psychological and dramatic effect. 'I don't think you realise how lucky you are.'

Lambert looked straight past the man towards May. The rope which bound her left ankle had come loose when Hastings dragged her across the room. She was trying to free it. Lambert knew he had to keep Hastings talking. 'Fine, I'll humour you. How am I lucky?'

Hastings hesitated, surprised by the response. 'Well, you forced me to change my story.'

Lambert was confused but continued asking questions. 'You sent Klatzky the pictures to get me involved?'

'Of course.'

'Why?'

Hastings shrugged. 'I wanted to save Klatzky and I wanted to involve you. I'd read about your problems. I knew you wouldn't be able to resist getting involved. Like I said to your colleague, there's a certain symmetry to the story. Revisiting Billy Nolan has been so delicious. Getting you and Simon involved, and our friend Sandra Hopkins.'

Lambert tried to not look at Sarah May who was still struggling with the rope. 'You'll need to clarify that.'

'I'm not sure how much you know about your friend Simon, but we had things in common.'

'Don't compare yourself to him,' said Lambert.

'There are things you don't know about him, about his mother.' Hastings grimaced, his face flushed with anger.

'What's that got to do with you?'

Hastings regained his composure. He played with the cuffs of his shirt. 'That's not relevant. Simon still struggled with his childhood, that much was obvious. He needed help and I helped him.'

'I think you'll find he was more troubled by Billy Nolan's death.'

'For someone who has a knack for seeing things others don't, you're surprisingly blind to the situation of those closest to you. Klatzky was a drunk, an addict, way before I rescued Billy Nolan. You didn't notice that he spent the whole three years at University escaping something.'

May was still struggling at the rope.

Lambert searched for an argument against what Hastings had told him. 'We were all like that,' he said.

'There are shades of dependency. Klatzky was a fuck-up then and he stayed one until the end. Anyway...'

'Why did you stop, Hastings?'

Hastings glared at him. 'Stop?'

'Why did you stop after Billy? And why did you start again?'

Hastings sat on the floor next to him, as if the three of them were having a friendly chat. 'I never stopped, Michael, you'll find that out soon enough. The Souljacker killings were drawing too much attention. It was becoming too hard to deflect interest, and it was affecting my career. I decided to go dark, as they say. There are a number of unmarked graves out there.'

It was difficult to relate the Hastings he thought he knew with the man before him. 'So why target me now?' said Lambert.

'Ah, you, Lambert. I know Miss May here has filled you in on some of the detail.' Hastings turned briefly, his hand pointing at Sarah. He stopped and took a deep breath. He was almost serene, the light of the standing lamp illuminating his face.

'God chose twelve apostles when his son was on Earth. There are twelve pearly gates. I am saving twelve lost souls.'

Hastings' speech sounded contrived, a little too prepared. Lambert was not convinced by the religious rhetoric. For one, the twelve apostles were all men, and Hastings had killed Sandra Hopkins. 'How am I lost?' he asked.

'Michael...' said Hastings, standing.

Lambert struggled in his position, as the man touched his hair and placed his palm onto his cheek.

'You lost your soul when you killed your daughter.'

Chapter 54

Lambert thrashed in his chair. He pushed at the rope which held his wrists fast, a pain spreading up his arms and into his chest. 'Don't you fucking talk about my daughter, you sadistic animal,' he screamed.

Hastings sounded genuinely shocked. 'I'm sorry, Michael, I didn't mean to upset you. By your own admission, you were responsible for your daughter's death. Officially it was an accident, and I'm sure it was, but you blame yourself don't you?'

Lambert eased his struggle. Saliva dripped from his mouth as his body cramped. 'Don't mention her,' he said, through gritted teeth.

Hastings left the room, leaving the door open. Lambert called over to May. 'Any use?' he asked, his mind still reeling from what Hastings had said.

Sarah May jiggled her left leg. 'It's coming loose slowly,' she said, her voice a whisper. 'Not that it will make any difference.'

'Keep working.'

Lambert shivered as the adrenalin in his body faded. He tried not to think about where Hastings had gone, but was unable to blank out his imagination. He pictured Hastings gathering his surgical set, the pontifical incense, and the anaesthetic. In his thoughts, Hastings smiled in anticipation of a new kill.

A wave of nausea hit Lambert. He tried to vomit, his throat contracting as he dry heaved, his stomach empty.

Hastings returned with a small wooden table which he placed next to Lambert. He left the room once more to retrieve two handguns which he placed side by side on the table. Lambert noticed one of the guns was his Glock.

'Okay, the end is near,' said Hastings. 'Let me explain what is going to happen.' He picked up one of the guns and held it in front of Lambert.

Lambert breathed deeply, tried to ease his raging heartbeat.

'I'm giving you one chance, and one chance only, to save your soul, Mr Lambert. You failed to save your daughter, little Chloe, and now I am going to give you the chance to redeem yourself.'

Hastings turned his palms face up, his arms held out wide waiting for a response.

Lambert's chest was bursting with pressure. 'Just tell us, you sick fuck.'

'I will be giving you the opportunity to save Sarah May's life,' said Hastings, who walked over and sat down in the chair opposite Sarah May. He unclicked the safety and lifted the gun so it pointed squarely at May's forehead.

'Don't,' said Lambert. 'It was me you were going to save,' said Lambert.

May closed her eyes, peaceful, save for the tremor in her chest. Lambert hoped she was lost somewhere in her thoughts, a fond memory taking her away from the stark reality.

'My life's work is over,' said Hastings, lowering the gun. 'I need a fitting end. A conclusion worthy to what I've achieved. A twelfth soul worth saving. Sarah May isn't part of my plans. Only you are, Michael.'

May opened her eyes. At first relieved that Hastings had lowered the gun, her face contorted into anger. If she hadn't been tied up at the moment, she would have torn Hastings to pieces with her bare hands.

'So fucking end it,' said Lambert.

'Fair enough,' said Hastings, getting to his feet. 'In a couple of minutes, Michael, I am going to untie you. I will leave the second gun where it is, on the table before you. As you can see, the gun is yours. I retrieved it from you after your accident. The magazine has one bullet left. After untying you, I will count to ten. If I finish counting to ten, then I will shoot Sarah May.'

Lambert fought against his ties, exchanged a look with Sarah. 'What's the catch?'

'No catch, but the shot needs to be a clean kill. If I am still alive then I will shoot the young detective here.'

'You expect me to believe that you're going to let me kill you?'

'Why not? I'm finished and gratefully so. I have already written the ending. Can you imagine it, the perfect way to save my twelfth soul. Giving you redemption for killing your daughter.'

Lambert ignored the mention of Chloe. It sounded too good to be true. 'The gun's loaded?'

'One bullet in the magazine. I warn you, it needs to be a clean kill.'

In Lambert's peripheral vision, May was still struggling with the loose rope on her leg. He couldn't see if she was succeeding.

'So do we have a deal, Mr Lambert?'

Lambert shrugged. 'I'm hardly in a position to negotiate.'

'Wonderful. I'll be back shortly.'

Lambert watched, horrified, as a man who had never previously betrayed any sense of emotion practically skipped out of the room.

'Do you think he means it?' said May.

Lambert didn't want to get too hopeful. 'It's possible. Also possible that he is toying with us. He could do this with all his victims for all we know.'

'If we ever get out of this, I think we need to get you to work on your motivational skills,' said May. 'Do you think you'll be able to do it?'

'What, shoot him? Are you kidding? Nothing would give me more pleasure.'

'I mean with your arms having been tied up for so long. They are going to be incredibly stiff.'

Lambert clenched his fists, tensed and released his arm muscles. 'Don't worry about me. I'd like to keep him alive so we can question him, but I'll make sure he goes down. What about your leg?'

'The rope is looser. I think I might be able to free it. I can't move anything else, though.'

'Keep trying, just in case.'

Hastings kept them waiting. Lambert took in the scene, tried to concentrate on what was to come. Sarah May was less than six metres away. Under normal circumstances, the shot would be easy. It was his gun, he'd practised with it on numerous occasions in various secluded woodland areas. He considered the variables in his current situation, concluding that the physical constraints were the least of his problems. He would have to turn his left shoulder to face Hastings. His legs would probably remain tied, but there would be enough freedom of movement to make the turn. His left leg still ached, and the remnants of whatever Hastings had drugged him with still travelled his system, but he would hold the gun steady enough to get off one shot. If there was an issue, it would be the psychological issue of knowing that if he missed he would be condemning Sarah May to death.

As if reading his mind, May said, 'whatever that bastard says, you know it wasn't your fault that Chloe died, and you have nothing to redeem yourself for. You do know that, don't you?'

'I'll probably still shoot him anyway,' he said.

May laughed, and Lambert thought it was probably the most beautiful thing he'd ever seen. 'Oh, good,' she said.

Another hour passed before Hastings returned. He'd kept the light on, the glow from the naked bulb so bright that Lambert was forced to keep his eyes shut. He managed to keep his arms moving as much as possible. He clenched his fists, tensing his biceps and chest muscles so that the shock of freedom, should it occur, would be manageable.

Hastings didn't talk, his demeanour more like the dour, humourless man Lambert had always known. He picked up Lambert's gun and unclipped the magazine. He checked it and clicked it back in place. In the glare of the standing lamp, Lambert noticed the mass of wrinkles on Hastings' face, a network of minuscule incisions on his leather-like skin.

'Ready?' asked Hastings, his voice a rasping growl.

During Hastings' absence, Lambert had deliberated as to how Hastings' little game would work.

A split second later he found out.

Chapter 55

It lasted longer than ten seconds.

The first impact came out of nowhere, Hastings' fist landing on Lambert's chin snapping his head back. Lambert twisted his head, a line of saliva coated in blood flying across the room. Hastings hit him again, three more times, once across each temple and a third in his mouth shattering a number of teeth until Lambert's head hung low on his chest. With no way to defend himself, the blows caused maximum damage. In his dizzied state, Lambert presumed Hastings had changed his mind. Supporting this new theory, Hastings punched him hard in the stomach. Again the blow was unexpected, Lambert not having time to offer even the merest resistance of clenching his stomach muscles. Lambert tried to breathe, a faint whistling sound escaping from his mouth. His chest muscles tightened and for a time and he feared he was going into cardiac arrest.

From somewhere in the room, he heard the distance voice of Sarah May, protesting at Hastings' actions. As his breath returned, he noticed his left hand was free. He made a feeble attempt to lift it and suffered another punch, this time to his throat.

The blow must have knocked him out, his body shocking itself back into consciousness as if waking from a nightmare. His eyes snapped open and took in everything. The brightly lit room. The sight of Sarah May tied to the chair, a gag rammed into her mouth. Hastings sitting in the chair opposite, his gun pointed directly at May's forehead.

Lambert noticed his hands were free, his Glock 22 within reach on the table before him.

'Ten seconds,' said Hastings.

Lambert tried not to hesitate. He watched his hand reach for the gun as if in slow motion. It reminded him of the dreams which at times had plagued his childhood, the nightmares where he'd tried to run from unknown assailants only for his legs to move as if stuck in treacle. The gun felt heavier than he remembered, a lead weight pulsating in his shaking hand. He thought he heard Hastings reach seven but couldn't be sure. His head throbbed, his throat constricted as if filled with a foreign object.

Lambert swivelled his body to face Hastings. He focused on the man, disturbed to see that Hastings' hand was shaking. His gun waved in front of Sarah May's face, who stared ahead dead eyed.

Lambert took aim. He tensed his arm to stop it shaking and aimed for Hastings' forehead.

Lambert closed his right eye and squeezed the trigger.

Later, he would have sworn that he saw the bullet leave his gun.

As Lambert went to squeeze the trigger, Hastings leant into May deciding his chosen finale was not for him. As he did so, May's left leg struggled free. She managed to dart her leg out just in time to kick Hastings backwards.

The bullet entered Hastings' neck. Lambert fired his gun again but Hastings had been telling the truth about the solitary bullet. Using his hands for leverage, Lambert swayed on the spot and managed to topple the chair. He landed on his hands, the impact almost breaking his wrists. He dragged his body across the floor to Hastings.

The strength had left Hastings. The gun by his side, his hands reached for his neck where a stream of blood flowed in thick gushes. Lambert didn't have time to say anything before Hastings closed his eyes for a final time.

Epilogue

They shook hands. It was an awkward exchange. It had been two months since they'd last seen each other.

'This is silly,' said May. 'Come here.' She kissed him on the cheek, wrapped her arms tight around him.

Lambert savoured the touch of her skin against his, the now familiar smell of vanilla on her skin. 'So you have it?'

'All here,' said May, waving the document in front of her.

They had successfully delayed publication of Hastings' book. An emergency hearing had upheld their argument that the book contained information sensitive to further investigations. This hadn't stopped thousands of people placing advanced orders online.

It hadn't stopped Hastings reaching out.

The day after his death, Hastings' book went viral online. It happened so fast, that it became impossible to take it down. It had appeared on Hastings' website first. Looking through older posts, he'd promised an online exclusive days before. A free download of his next, non-fiction title.

It only took a couple of downloads and soon it was national news. It was his life story and more. Lambert had since trawled through every word, countless times. It listed every Souljacker killing, plus the killings of Samuel Burnham, Kwasi Olumide, Lance Crosby, as well as a number of other murders which were currently under investigation. Hastings revealed that Campbell had paid Roger Haydon a visit on the day he'd committed suicide. He'd given him an ultimatum, his life or Thomas Langtree's. Haydon had made the ultimate sacrifice, and for Hastings it had merely been a diversionary tactic.

The latter chapters had been hastily put together. Thanks to these chapters, Lambert had become somewhat of a celebrity. Hastings had predicted the ending with an unnerving accuracy, though in his version things went much smoother. Lambert killed him with one bullet to the forehead. An instant kill, not the slower death he eventually endured.

The book was low on explanation. Hastings repeated what he'd told May and Lambert: that the first killer, and second Souljacker victim, Graham Jackett, had been sent as a guide. That his goal had been to save the soul of each victim whose eyes he'd removed.

Lambert spent the subsequent weeks researching Hastings' background. Both his parents had died years before. His mother had fallen down a flight of stairs when Hastings was twenty, his father a victim of hit and run when he was seventeen. Lambert tracked down some of Hastings' ex-school friends. He had been an awkward teenager, intelligent, but somewhat of a loner. There had been rumours of something odd occurring in the Hastings household, but nothing of significance had ever come to light.

Lambert's theory was that something had happened to Hastings when he was twelve which had changed the boy forever. Unfortunately, it was unlikely he would ever know.

They walked together across College Green, their hands by their sides never quite touching. He wanted to tell her he missed her, that it was possible they could be together.

'How's Sophie?' asked May.

'Large, grumpy.' He hesitated. 'I shouldn't say that really, should I?'

May's face crumpled into a smile. 'We can keep it between us. Is she working it out with whatshisname?'

'Taylor? No. I don't want to go into the sordid details but from what she's told me it was a fling. He's going to do the right thing financially, and he says he'll be there for the kid. So we'll see.'

The publisher's office was on the third floor of a large Victorian building. May buzzed up. 'DCI May and Michael Lambert to see Angela Sutton.'

'Please use the lift. Fifth floor,' replied a muffled voice on the other end of the line.

'DCI, huh?' said Lambert in the lift.

'You know it, buster.'

They had seen each other during the months following Hastings' death. It was strange that something so horrific could bring them together. Lambert rented a place in Bristol, but had spent nearly every evening at May's. It had been too much, too soon. Lambert told her he would return to London. That they could try again sometime in the future.

'DCI May, Mr Lambert,' said Angela Sutton, greeting them outside the lift. 'To what do I owe this pleasure?'

May in particular had spent time with the woman in the past few months. She was immaculately dressed, in a figure-hugging black skirt and cream blouse. Her face was heavily made up, and reminded Lambert of the women he occasion-ally saw at the make-up counters at Boots. What are you hiding, he thought.

May showed her the warrant. 'You could make it easy on us and you, by giving me the document.'

Sutton read the warrant, as if examining an ancient artefact in a long-extinguished language. She sighed. 'If you wait here, I can print up a copy.'

'Make that two copies, and we will need all electronic versions,' said May.

'It won't stop it getting out, you know that?' said Lambert, once Sutton had gone.

'I know but at least we can make a head start on things.'

May interlocked her hands and gazed at her shoes. 'So, is there anything keeping you in London?' she asked, eventually, not looking up.

'Tillman has asked me to return,' said Lambert.

'Oh?'

'I'm considering my options. Sophie's pregnancy has thrown me a bit.'

'Of course.'

'It's strange, a child growing inside her. You know, after Chloe and everything.'

'You don't have to explain, Mike.'

'But I do. We're not getting back together, it's just that I feel I should be there for her. She has this whole future ahead of her. Chloe would have been her sister. Oh, I didn't tell you, she's expecting a girl.'

May placed her hand on his.

'Anyway, this girl will be linked to Chloe forever, and Sophie will be linked to them both. But me, well...'

Angela Sutton returned with two documents, neatly tied in

a blue ribbon. She handed them to May along with a memory stick. 'This is everything,' she said.

'Do you know if he planned any surprise online launch?' asked Lambert.

'You've closed his website down.'

'So? If you know anything, Angela, you need to let us know,' said May. Lambert could tell she was going through the motions. There was no way the woman would share any information with her.

Lambert bought them drinks from the same coffee shop where they'd first met months ago. They walked to the green and sat on the lawn, reading the documents as if they were no different to the idling students who congregated in the area.

Hastings' book had concluded with a preview of a follow up. Lambert flicked through the pages, staggered by what he was reading, a list of missing people Hastings had claimed to have killed in the period since Billy Nolan's death.

'This can't be true, can it?' asked May.

Lambert thought about what Hastings had said to him about the unmarked graves. 'Nothing would surprise me now,' he said, frowning.

May stood, the hem of her dress tinged with smudges of grass. 'I need to get this back to the station.'

Lambert wanted to say so much but didn't know where to begin.

May pulled out something from her bag and dropped it onto his chest with a wink.

Lambert watched her walk away. He took the set of keys from his chest and placed them in his pocket.

Acknowledgements

I'd like to thank a number of people who have helped, directly or indirectly in the writing of this book:

The whole team at HQ Digital for their support and encouragement, with special thanks to Clio Cornish for signing me.

My wonderful editor, Charlotte Mursell, for her insightful comments and for pushing me to make this the best book it could be.

The Creative Writing team at Glasgow University. In particular, Zoe Strachan and Elizabeth Reeder for their great advice.

On a personal note, I'd like to thank my Mum and Dad, Carla and Joe, for their support and patience in waiting for my first book to be published.

Michael Brolly, for lending his first name.

My family and friends for being there over the years: Eileen Burnell, Claire and the Webbers, Mel and the Brollys, Ann and Jim Eardley, Beth and Warren Eardley, Alan, Ishy, Holly, Chris, Dan, Frank, Matt Lower, Ralph, Ryan, Simon, Alexia, Lizzie, Snuffy Walden, Elvis, Broll, Broll Junior, Dave the Dog, and many others who have made an impact on my life.

My children, Freya and Hamish, whose love is my greatest inspiration.

And Alison, my first reader and fiercest critic, for her unwavering belief and love.

Dear Reader,

Thank you so much for taking the time to read this book – we hope you enjoyed it! If you did, we'd be so appreciative if you left a review.

Here at HQ Digital we are dedicated to publishing fiction that will keep you turning the pages into the early hours. We publish a variety of genres, from heartwarming romance, to thrilling crime and sweeping historical fiction.

To find out more about our books, enter competitions and discover exclusive content, please join our community of readers by following us at:

🐦 @HQDigitalUK

📘 facebook.com/HQDigitalUK

Are you a budding writer? We're also looking for authors to join the HQ Digital family! Please submit your manuscript to:

HQDigital@harpercollins.co.uk.

Hope to hear from you soon!

If you loved *Dead Eyed* then turn the page for an exclusive extract from the second book in the DCI Michael Lambert series, *Dead Lucky*...

Matt BROLLY

Dead Lucky

A DCI Michael LAMBERT NOVEL

Chapter 1

He tried to stretch. His back was pushed tight against the wall, his covered head snagged between two coat hooks. Every other breath brought with it the stench of foot odour and moth bombs.

He'd been in the flat for three hours, the last two of which had been in the wardrobe. Preparation was important. The woman was predictable, she would return after work, the husband less so. His behaviour was erratic of late. He'd been spending more time at the bar than at work.

He stretched once more, savouring being alone, going over the plan again and again until it was so embedded in his mind that it was almost a memory.

The woman arrived on time. His pulse didn't alter as he listened to her move around the room, the strange noises she made, thinking she was alone.

Eventually she left the room. Realising he'd been holding his breath, he let it out in a rush, his lungs filling with the trapped, musty air of his hiding cell.

It was another two hours before the husband arrived. He heard the front door click open, the heavy steps as the husband walked into the living room, the muted voices as the couple exchanged pleasantries.

He was about to leave his confines when he heard the woman

enter the en-suite bathroom. He edged the wardrobe open. The bathroom door was ajar and he tiptoed across the bedroom floor in time to see the woman pulling up her garments.

As she left the room, he placed his right hand on her shoulder. She jumped, and rounded on him thinking he was her husband. She stared at him for a second, her mouth agape. A look of confusion crept across her face and for a heartbeat it was as if she'd been expecting his arrival. Then, realising what was happening was all too real, she went to scream.

With a practised move, he reached out and covered her mouth before she could give sound to her situation.

Chapter 2

Lambert sensed the decay as he entered the building.

He'd been here before.

Inside, the cloying stench of antiseptic and bleach did little to mask the subtle odours of illness and death which permeated from the walls of the hollow reception area.

He knew where he was going, he'd visited the same ward on numerous occasions many years ago. His body guided him along the route without him having to think, a homing instinct he'd thought long extinguished. He tried to ignore the people he passed. An elderly man, wisps of dry grey hair atop a wrinkled skull, wheeling a bag full of yellowing liquid which seeped into his veins. An obese teenage girl, pushed along in a wheelchair by two similar sized youths, her plastered leg protruding in the air like a weapon. And finally a man he'd hoped to avoid, leaving the lift as Lambert was about to enter.

The man, immaculate in a pinstriped suit and coiffured hair, froze. Lambert had to suppress a smile as the colour literally drained from the man's face. His healthy St Tropez tan faded into a ghost-like white.

'Michael,' said the man, holding out his hand.

Lambert ignored the outstretched limb, not yet ready to be fully grown up about the situation. He entered the lift and turned to watch Jeremy Taylor, partner of Price Barker Solicitors, shake himself as if from a daze and walk away.

'Michael Lambert,' he said, into the box outside the ward. 'I'm here to see Sophie Lambert.' He remembered a time twelve years ago when he'd said the very same thing into what looked like the very same box. Only then he'd been visiting on happier terms.

The screams started as soon as he was buzzed into the ward, the sound of tortured women, flesh being torn. The nurses' desk was empty. Lambert considered walking the corridors in search of Sophie but didn't want to risk intruding on the other patients. Eventually, a smiling nurse gave him directions to Sophie's room. The woman beamed at him as if this should be the greatest day of his life.

He ambled down the corridor, debating whether or not to turn and flee the scene, until he reached the entrance to Sophie's room.

Taking a deep breath, he stepped over the threshold. For a time he just stood there dumbstruck, forgetting to breathe. Sophie sat upright in bed, cheeks pinched red, a tiny figure clamped to her breast. Smiling, she beckoned him over.

It was too late to leave. He took a seat next to her bed. 'How did it go?' he asked, not knowing what else to say.

Lambert had been virtually estranged from his wife, Sophie, for the last three years following the death of their daughter, Chloe, though they had continued sharing a house together. During that time Sophie had had a brief affair with Jeremy Taylor, the solicitor Lambert had just encountered, who was the father of the child his wife was holding.

The child released itself from Sophie with a smacking sound

and looked in Lambert's direction. 'Do you want to hold her?' asked Sophie, as unsure about the situation as he was.

'No. Thank you. I'm okay.'

Tears welled in Sophie's eyes. 'This little thing is Chloe's sister,' she whispered, stroking the baby's head.

Lambert choked back his own tears. The baby was the closest thing there would ever be to Chloe but there was no avoiding the fact that she wasn't his. He poured a beaker of water, taking some time to think. 'Do you have a name for her?' he asked, his voice coming out as a squawk – like an adolescent boy's.

'I wanted to call her Jane.' Sophie hesitated, looked down at the baby for support. 'If you will give me permission, Jane Chloe.'

Lambert looked away, forcing back tears, picturing his little girl before the accident. Her curious smile and unending joy for the world, and how he had destroyed it all by losing control of his car. He didn't know if it was a good idea giving this new child Chloe's name. He didn't want her to be haunted by her dead sister, or for her to grow up feeling she was a replacement, but he knew Sophie would never ever let her feel that way. 'If you think that is best,' he said.

'What do you think, Michael?'

'I think it would be wonderful,' he said, darting his hand across his eyes, turning to face them. The child looked back at him as Chloe had done all those years before.

He left ten minutes later, refusing to be overwhelmed by his growing sense of loneliness. He'd left the family home three months earlier, informing Sophie that it wouldn't be appropriate for him to stay. He'd even discussed divorce proceedings with her but she'd wanted to get through the pregnancy before making any decisions. Although he was happy for her, he knew he should have been the father of that little girl back in the ward. As he took the lift, he envisaged a future without Sophie. He imagined her raising Jane without him.

His vision blurred as he entered the main lobby of the hospital. Fiery lights danced in front of his eyes. The dizzying colours – flickers of burning ember, a multitude of shades and sizes – signified the start of a hallucinatory episode. From research on the internet he'd self-diagnosed his condition as a form of hallucinatory narcolepsy. It was the same type of episode he'd suffered when driving Chloe.

The episodes had occurred more often in the last few months, ever since Sophie's pregnancy and the Souljacker case. The trigger was usually a lack of sleep, or stress. At the moment, he was suffering from both.

He sat down on a bench, the material cold and hard against his flesh, and closed his eyes. He told himself he was in a good place. The episodes normally occurred at home in bed, a smooth precursor to sleep. Knowing it was unwise to fight, he lay his head against the rough textured wall and fell asleep.

'Sir, sir.' The hand pulled at his shoulder, the accent foreign. 'I'm sorry, sir, I need to clean here.'

Lambert darted awake and took in his surroundings. He was still in the hospital. He checked his watch. He'd been asleep for three hours.

'Sorry, sir,' repeated the cleaner, switching on a floor polisher which whirred into life with a deafening drone.

Lambert stood and stretched. The place had thinned out

with normal visiting hours over. Lonely patients walked the floors like ghosts, occasionally passed by a hurrying doctor or nurse. The three hours had refreshed him and had evaporated, for a time, his worries over Sophie and the new child. It was eleven p.m. He considered calling Sarah, but decided it was too late. She would either be sleeping, or out working on the case. Either way, he wouldn't know what to tell her. He didn't fully understand how he felt about the situation at the moment, and was in no mood to analyse his feelings. Knowing he wouldn't get back to sleep that evening, there was little option but to return to work.

Lambert had resumed his position within the National Crime Agency two months previously, following his unofficial pursuit and capture of the notorious serial killer, dubbed the Souljacker. Since returning, he'd been working on an international drugs case. The case had proved challenging, and there was still months of work ahead.

Lambert was part of a small specialised team, his NCA team working with the Met's joint Organised Crime Partnership. So far they had arrested a number of small time dealers, and inroads were slowly being made into the main distributors.

Lambert caught the tube to Westminster and made the short walk to the NCA's headquarters, the June night air still thick with heat from the day.

His office was deserted. Lambert often survived on three to four hours' sleep a night so was often alone in the neon-lit open-plan office. He opened up The System, an unofficial amalgamated database of police computer systems, traffic systems, CCTV images, and social media back ends. The System had been created for the now defunct organisation called The

Group and was only available for select officers within the NCA. He was about to log in when the office doors exploded open.

'Just the person,' said the rotund bulldog-like man who had barged through the doors as if they were an unnecessary obstacle.

Chief Superintendent Glenn Tillman stood in front of him, hands on hips like some ageing superhero. Tillman had headed up The Group until it was disbanded six months ago and had recruited Lambert back into the NCA.

'Sir?'

'Sit,' said Tillman. 'Something important has come up.'

Lambert, who was already sitting, swivelled his chair around. 'I was just about to log in.'

Tillman pulled a second chair over. 'The drugs case? No, I want you to pass that over. Give your workload to Bryant. I need you on something else.'

He handed Lambert a piece of paper. Lambert turned it over and read an address in Dulwich.

'You know the journalist, Eustace Sackville?'

Lambert nodded. He'd met the man, a crime specialist on a national broadsheet, on a number of occasions.

'His wife's just been murdered and the case has been assigned to us. I want you to work with Kennedy. Get down there straight away and take the case over. The body was found three hours ago so you better be quick. An Inspector Wright is at the scene at the moment but knows it's passing to us.'

'That must have gone down well.'

Tillman shrugged.

'Why us?' asked Lambert, suspecting the truth.

'You know the sort of information Sackville has access to. We want the best on this and your name came up as someone suitable to lead the case.'

Lambert nodded.

'One more thing,' said Tillman, handing Lambert an iPad. 'Moira Sackville,' he said, pointing to a picture of sixty-year-old woman bound to a chair.

Lambert flicked through to a second image. The lifeless figure of Moira Sackville, drained of colour, slash marks on each wrist, a puddle of blood by her ankles.

Tillman rubbed his chin. Lambert had known Tillman for ten years. In that time, the only sign of insecurity he'd ever seen in the man was the odd propensity of rubbing his chin in times of stress.

'It took some time for Mrs Sackville to bleed out...' said Tillman, lowering the volume of his voice as Lambert continued scrolling through the images until he reached a picture of a second chair, empty save for two binds hanging loose from the armrests. '... and her husband was made to watch every minute of it.'

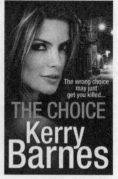

About the Publisher

Australia
HarperCollins Publishers (Australia) Pty. Ltd.
Level 13, 201 Elizabeth Street
Sydney, NSW 2000, Australia
http://www.harpercollins.com.au

Canada
HarperCollins Canada
2 Bloor Street East - 20th Floor
Toronto, ON, M4W, 1A8, Canada
http://www.harpercollins.ca
India

HarperCollins India
A 75, Sector 57
Noida, Uttar Pradesh 201 301, India
http://www.harpercollins.co.in

New Zealand
HarperCollins Publishers (New Zealand) Limited
P.O. Box 1
Auckland, New Zealand
http://www.harpercollins.co.nz

United Kingdom
HarperCollins Publishers Ltd.
1 London Bridge Street
London SE1 9GF
http://www.harpercollins.co.uk

United States
HarperCollins Publishers Inc.
195 Broadway
New York, NY 10007
http://www.harpercollins.com